A Mother's Heart

Carmel Harrington is from Co. Wexford, where she lives with her husband, her children and their rescue dog, George Bailey. A *USA Today* and *Irish Times* bestseller, and regular panellist on radio and TV, her warm and emotional storytelling has captured the hearts of readers worldwide.

Carmel's novels have been shortlisted for Irish Book Awards, and her debut, *Beyond Grace's Rainbow*, won Kindle Book of the Year. Her most recent book, *The Moon Over Kilmore Quay*, was an *Irish Times* bestseller.

To keep in touch with Carmel, follow her on social media or visit her website:

Twitter | Facebook | Instagram @HappyMrsH
www.carmelharrington.com

Carmel Harrington

A Mother's Heart

HarperCollins*Publishers*

HarperCollins*Publishers* Ltd
1 London Bridge Street,
London SE1 9GF
www.harpercollins.co.uk

HarperCollins*Publishers*
Macken House,
39/40 Mayor Street Upper,
Dublin 1
D01 C9W8
Ireland

First published by HarperCollins*Publishers* 2022
This edition published 2023
1

A catalogue record for this book is available from the British Library

ISBN: 978-0-00-841593-8

Set in Sabon LT Std by Palimpsest Book Production Ltd

Printed and bound in the UK using 100% Renewable Electricity
by CPI Group (UK) Ltd

For my agent, Rowan Lawton. Thank you for your professional guidance, all-round genius and gorgeous friendship.

P.S. I'll meet you at that rooftop bar one day very soon.

Author's Note

While writing *A Mother's Heart*, I had to imagine what the world might look like, both in Ireland and New Zealand, as it began to live with Covid-19, several years on. Since the story involves travel between the two countries, I had to assume that the predictions for opening up borders in New Zealand would happen as outlined at the time I wrote this. Please forgive any inaccuracies.

PART ONE

ONE

Rachel

Hawke's Bay, New Zealand

'Can you hear that?' Rachel called out to Olivia and Dylan, marvelling at how their matching blonde curls glistened in the afternoon sun.

'Cheep, cheep, cheep,' Dylan replied in a decent mimic of the sound that filled the air around them.

'Clever boy. That sound comes from the fantail. It's one of our native birds here. Funny, I've not thought about it since I left New Zealand, but hearing it now makes me realize how much I love it. Cheep, cheep, cheep!' Rachel did her own impersonation.

'You are silly,' Olivia said, smiling back at her.

Rachel clutched her waist and took several deep breaths. The ever-rising incline of the mountain was a stark reminder of how unfit she'd become. When she was a kid, she would have climbed all the way from the bottom up the most extended trek with her sister Claudia and her parents without even breaking a sweat.

Things had changed a lot since then. Now, as a single mom, some days she had to make a choice between eating, sleeping or showering. It was impossible to do all three and keep everything else going for the children and work, let alone anything additional.

As if on cue, Rachel felt a different stab of pain as she thought about her husband, Lorcan.

A little under two years ago, Rachel and the children's lives had changed forever when Lorcan's tyre blew out on the motorway. His car had spun out of control, colliding with a truck on the inside lane. Lorcan didn't stand a chance, the gardaí had said; he died before the paramedics even arrived.

Things had been easier when he was by her side. They shared the school run, he made the kids' lunches while she made breakfast, and then in the evenings, he helped her package purchases for her customers from her online clothing business, Rae's Closet. And while Rachel missed all of his practical help, she knew that she'd happily continue to do it all by herself if she could have just one more day with Lorcan. She missed his smile, his quiet calm, the warmth of his arms around her, making sure she knew that he was there.

Always by her side.

'I can smell lemons,' Olivia said, scrunching her nose up.

'Me too, sweetheart,' Rachel responded. 'That comes from the eucalyptus trees. They smell delicious, don't they? And now all of a sudden I want some of Grandma's lemon drizzle cake . . .'

Her stomach grumbled at the thought.

Memories of Claudia and herself eating cake still warm from the oven filled Rachel's mind. Her mom wearing her handmade, duck-egg blue apron, smiling indulgently at her girls.

Rachel felt a bittersweet ache flood her. But while there was comfort in remembering childhood moments with her family in New Zealand, they were tinged with sadness too – for all that she had lost when she'd made a new home thousands of miles away from them all.

Ahead, her dad, Joe, and Claudia paused for a moment to allow them to catch up.

'You're getting old, eh?' Claudia teased.

'I am old,' Rachel only half-joked.

'You'll pay for all this walking tomorrow,' Claudia said. 'Have a long soak in the tub when we get back to Mom and Dad's.'

'Whatever pain is coming my way, it's worth it,' Rachel said, gazing up at the blue skies.

She was home again.

New Zealand was one of the most gorgeous countries in the world, as far as Rachel was concerned. She had buried her love of her homeland deep inside her over the past five years. It was the only way she could live in Ireland, leaving her family and hometown behind.

'We're at the top of the world!' Olivia shouted, punching the air in delight when she realized they'd finally reached the top of the peak.

With the sun beating down on her face, Rachel could not fathom that she had been in Dublin with the children less than two days ago, juggling parenthood and work. By extending the kids' mid-term break, it meant they could spend the month of February here, which was New Zealand's summer.

Rachel sighed in pleasure as she took in the view. She loved this particular spot, because no matter which way a person looked, the vista changed. It was a true 360-degree spectacular. From the patchwork of green and grey hills, rippling their way upwards towards the sky, to the river, making its lazy way through the valley, it was a feast for her eyes.

As she took in the incredible views surrounding her, the warmth of the sun gave her comfort. How many times had she stood in this spot as a child, never genuinely appreciating its beauty?

'I've missed you. I'm so glad that while so much has changed, you haven't . . .' she whispered into the wind.

'Gramps Joe, can you tell us about the sleeping giant now?' Olivia asked, pulling his arm away from where he'd placed it on Rachel's shoulders.

'Me too! I want to know about the big old scary giant.' Dylan stood on his tiptoes, trying to make himself taller, then roaring as loudly as he could.

Joe pulled a similar pose, copying his grandson and eventually toppling over, which made them all laugh.

'Well,' he began, as he pulled himself upright again, 'the giant was so big it could make a T-Rex look small. But he wasn't the scary kind, Dylan. He was the epitome of a gentle giant. Do you remember me showing you both the shape of a body carved into the mountain when we were at the bottom of the peak, eh?'

The children nodded, bouncing up and down with excitement.

'Well, that was the giant, and this is his story. A love

story as it goes. Most of the best stories often are. Te Mata was the giant's name. He met his downfall when he fell in love with a beautiful tribeswoman called Hinerakau.'

'Those names are strange,' Olivia said, repeating them to herself.

'Yes, I suppose they must be to you both. But they are typical of the time and area. You'll get used to them,' Joe said. 'Now where was I? That's right, Te Mata the giant . . .'

As Joe continued his story, Claudia handed Rachel a bottle of water and she slugged back half the cold drink in one go.

'You really needed that,' Claudia said.

Rachel giggled, the word 'really' triggering a memory for her. 'You're really saying something,' she half sang in response, which had Claudia and her squealing with giggles.

'What's so funny?' Dylan asked.

'There was a girl band called Bananarama that your mother was obsessed with when she was a little older than you both are now. They had a song, "Really Saying Something", that was number one when she was born, so she decided it was *her* song. And that meant she sang it morning, noon and night. I swear she sang it in her sleep just to annoy me. I contemplated smothering her with a pillow to shut her up, but I reckoned she'd come back and haunt me forever – singing that song – so I desisted,' Claudia said.

'That's dark, even for you,' Rachel said, mock scolding her sister. 'Stop scaring my kids, you lunatic.'

It felt good to banter again with Claudia. Another thing she'd missed dreadfully over the past few years. She'd never found anything that came even close to the joy of an excellent sisterly back-and-forth.

Olivia stared up at the blue sky above, making sure everyone knew she was bored with their trip down memory lane. She wanted to get back to the giant. At eight years old, she was at that age where she changed her mind about what she liked and didn't like in life every five minutes. And Olivia wasn't afraid to let everyone know when something displeased her. Dylan, on the other hand, had a curious mind that never stopped asking questions.

Proving this point, he turned to Rachel. 'What song was number one when I was born?'

The small group fell silent and Rachel tried to find the right words to respond.

'She doesn't know, stupid,' Olivia said.

'Don't call your brother stupid. You know that's one of our non-negotiable rules,' Rachel chastised her.

'Sorry, Dylan,' Olivia mumbled, looking guilty.

'S'all right. But why doesn't Mom know what my song was when I was born?' Dylan asked, his little face still clouded with confusion.

Rachel's heart swelled with love for the two kids. And twisted in pain too. Because in answering Dylan, she would have to break his heart again. But she had learned over the years that there was only one way to deal with moments like these – and that was head-on.

'The reason I don't know which songs were number one when you and Olivia were born is that I didn't know you back then. Remember Daddy and I explained all of this to you before, sweetheart. When I met your daddy, you were both already born. Dylan, you were ten months old, and Olivia, you were four years old.'

Rachel watched their faces, making sure they understood what she was saying. It had always been important to Lorcan and her that there were no secrets in their family.

'I know all this,' Olivia said. 'You became our mom when you married Daddy.'

'I remember too. I forgot for a minute, that's all.' Dylan kicked a stone and dust danced in the sunshine around his feet. Then, in a whisper, he admitted, 'I don't remember my first mammy.'

Rachel crouched down low so that they were face to face. Pushing down a lump in her throat the size of a golf ball, she reached over to caress Dylan's face. 'I know. And that's not fair, is it? I wish I could find a way to fix that for you both, but I can't. But I bet if we ask Nanny Sheila when we get home what your mammy's favourite song was, she'd know. How does that sound?'

They both nodded, but their mood had shifted. Dylan had no memory of any mother other than Rachel, so he didn't feel the same loss for her as his sister, who could remember moments with her birth mother, and feelings of great love. She struggled with guilt, too, when she forgot Niamh, which was only natural. As a family, they had dealt with these moments as they arose over the years. For Rachel, this was just one more thing that felt a lot trickier without her husband. She reached over to clasp each of the children's hands.

'You know what I can tell you both straight away? When I met you both for the first time, the number one song was Ed Sheeran's "Perfect". I remember thinking that the word "perfect" summed up how I felt about you both. I had never seen cuter or cleverer children in my life.'

The small group held their breaths as they waited for the children to respond. They'd been through so much in their short lives. And moments like this exposed how raw the grief was lurking beneath the surface. The children threw themselves into Rachel's arms for a hug.

She looked over their shoulders towards her dad and mouthed the word 'giant' at him. Thankfully Joe understood that Rachel wanted him to get the mood back on track.

'Right, let's get back to my yarn about Te Mata, shall we?' he said. 'So, the giant's beloved Hinerakau told him that he must prove his devotion to her by doing a range of impossible tasks. And one of these was to bite his way through the hills between the coast and the plains.'

'That sounds very silly,' Olivia said at the exact moment Dylan declared it to be 'very cool'.

'Well, I think you are both right,' Joe agreed, tactfully. 'It was rather silly because Te Mata died as he ate his way through the hills. But it's also cool, because if you look over there,' he pointed to the cliffs to their right, 'that's the Pari Karangaranga, the gap he managed to eat.'

'I wish I could meet a giant,' Dylan said. 'I'd climb up his body and stand on his shoulder so I could touch the clouds.'

'I have met a giant, as it happens. When I was a kid in the olden days . . .' Joe said, a smile playing on his lips.

Rachel and Claudia groaned as Joe went on to tell the children the same yarn he'd told them when they were kids, about the time a giant came to visit him in his garden. As Rachel watched the kids listen enraptured by Joe's tale, she felt a glow of satisfaction. She'd been concerned that Olivia and Dylan wouldn't connect with her family on this trip, that too much distance and time had passed without a visit. But ever since they'd arrived in Bluff Hill two days previously, it had been clear to all that the kids loved their New Zealand family.

Leaving the children to question their grandpa further about giants and warring tribes, Rachel took a moment to take in the beautiful view from the mountain top, once again allowing her mind to wander.

Twelve years ago, she had stood on this exact spot with Lorcan himself. At eighteen years old, she'd known nothing about love or the world. Yes, she'd dated boys from home, but she'd always felt that there was something missing from those relationships. She wasn't sure what, until an Irish tourist had walked into the Italian deli where she worked part-time. A blackboard wall had displayed the brunch and lunch menu, with details of the daily specials. And to this day, when Rachel smelt good coffee, it took her back to that first job and the summer when she fell head over heels in love.

Rachel had noticed Lorcan as soon as he joined the queue for coffee. He had a presence, a self-assurance that made him stand out from any crowd. And as she took orders from the customers in front of him, she felt his eyes on her in return. When he finally reached the counter and placed his order, his soft Irish lilt made her insides melt. He was tall and lean, his hair cropped short. This was a stark contrast to the boys in Rachel's circle, who were more grungy than this clean-cut stranger. She took her time grinding the beans and heating the milk. When she handed him his drink, it was clear he wasn't in any rush to move on either. Their eyes lingered on each other until her supervisor reprimanded her for letting the queue build up.

As she watched him walk out the door she felt her heart sink in disappointment. Despite only spending mere moments in his company, Rachel had felt an instant connection. A knowing. And for the rest of her shift, she wished she was the type of girl who was brave enough to ask a man for his phone number.

But thankfully for Rachel, Lorcan was braver than she was. When she left the deli, she found him sitting on the wall outside, reading a book.

'What are you doing here?' Rachel asked, reaching up to pull her hair out of its ponytail. She felt a shiver of excitement that her mystery stranger had not walked out of her life after all.

He took a moment to answer, closing his book and placing it into the small backpack that lay at his feet. Then he looked at her and Rachel found herself walking towards him.

'I'm waiting for you, to ask if you would go out with me.' He spoke slowly, with intent.

'Yes.' Rachel didn't even hesitate before she answered; she felt only a need to start whatever *this* was.

The Irishman smiled at her, and that was it for Rachel. Whatever he wanted, she would give him.

And so a plan was made to spend the following day together, on Rachel's day off. She would show him the local sights, starting with a trek up to this very spot, on Te Mata Peak.

Now, as she stood there again, twelve years later, Rachel looked around her and whispered to a ghost, 'I wish you were here, Lorc.'

Claudia walked back over to stand next to her, linking

arms with her and bringing her back to the present. 'You okay, Sis? You look very serious,' she asked quietly.

'Yeah, nah, I was miles away. I brought Lorcan up here on our first date. And pretty much in this exact spot, he kissed me for the first time.'

'From my memory of that summer, you two never stopped kissing,' Claudia made a face, clearly trying to keep the mood light.

Rachel smiled in recognition. Their summer romance was intense. Their attraction to each other was instant, and only grew the more time they spent together.

'I remember tagging along with you both a few times on your dates and I know it drove you mad. But Lorcan was nice to me. He never made me feel like a third wheel,' Claudia said.

'He was a good man. He liked you back then, thought your sass was funny. Standing here without him, it's hard to believe that he'll never see this view again. It's . . .' Rachel trailed off, unable to finish the thought.

'It's shit. That's what it is,' Claudia said. 'But if I'm allowed to be selfish for a minute, despite everything, I'm glad you're here now.'

'Me too, Sis. When we went on our European travels, I never guessed that I'd end up living in Ireland permanently. You never know where life is going to take you, I suppose.' Rachel looked down at the Tukituki River twisting and turning below them.

'Mom, I'm hungry!' Dylan shouted suddenly.

Instinctively, Rachel moved to walk towards the children, pulling juice and crackers from her backpack.

Claudia put a hand out to stop her. 'We need you too, you know. Mom and Dad. Me.'

13

Rachel spun around, confused by the change in the conversation.

'And I think you might need us,' Claudia finished.

'Is there something I'm missing? Are you all okay?'

'Relax. Everyone is hale and hearty. I'm just saying that we miss you, Sis. And now that Lorcan is gone . . . well, I've been thinking. Why can't you and the kids move back home? You could come to live in Hawke's Bay with us all.'

Rachel laughed at the absurdity of Claudia's words. 'Don't be ridiculous. My home is in Ireland now, with the children, as well you know.'

'Why does it have to be? What's keeping you there? Your business is online. You could run Rae's Closet from here. New Zealanders need clothes too.'

Rachel shook her head, trying to shake off the ridiculous proposition her sister was making. As if she could ever move back home.

That was an impossible dream. *Wasn't it?*

TWO

Rachel

Hawke's Bay, New Zealand

They spent their days in New Zealand with trips to the local sights. They explored beauty spots, hiked, swam in the warm waters of Cape Kidnappers bay and wandered through pretty coastal towns. Rachel was determined for the children to follow in their daddy's footsteps, exploring the same routes that he had, all those years ago.

With every activity, she shared snippets with them about the summer she and Lorcan had spent together. They loved hearing stories about him, always hungry for details that might give them a new connection with their daddy.

Today, at the start of their second week, Rachel had surprised the kids with a whitewater raft ride down the Mohaka River. As they waited in line to board their raft,

Rachel checked their life jackets a second time. She caught the eye of a mother standing in front of them and they exchanged smiles of parenting solidarity.

'I hope you are both ready to get wet,' Rachel said, grinning at the kids.

'Will it be scary?' Olivia asked, looking out to the water a little doubtfully.

'Well, when I brought your daddy here he squealed every time there was a sudden drop!'

Like it was yesterday, Rachel remembered Lorcan's cries throughout the ride, and the look of relief on his face when they arrived back on solid ground.

'I'll make sure our next trip is a little less extreme,' she had reassured him, taking in his ashen face.

'Not at all, I enjoyed it,' Lorcan had lied in response, his voice weak.

'You are a terrible liar, but I appreciate the stoic attitude.' Rachel had stood up on her tiptoes to kiss him. 'We'll get you a coffee and you'll be right.'

'I wouldn't have agreed to go rafting with anyone else but you,' Lorcan had said. 'You've done something to me, Rachel.'

And they had kissed again, their passion for each other growing with every moment they spent together. Rachel's skin had flushed with desire and happiness, making her wish that she would never have to say goodbye to her Irish boyfriend.

Now, Olivia tugged at Rachel's arm to make her move forward in the line, pulling her away from her precious memory.

'If Daddy wasn't scared, I won't be either,' she said decisively.

Dylan stood a little taller as he boasted, 'I'm not scared of anything either.'

'So brave,' Rachel said, but her eyes were on Olivia, whose forehead was still scrunched into a frown.

'All okay?' Rachel asked, brushing a damp stray curl of her daughter's hair behind her ear, underneath the orange helmet they had all been given to wear. It always escaped no matter how many times they tied it back.

'Can I ask you a question?' Olivia said, continuing when Rachel nodded her consent. 'If Daddy met you here when you were eighteen, I don't understand why he married my mammy in heaven and not you.'

'Well, the thing was, your daddy was only here in New Zealand for a couple of months then. He returned home to Ireland to finish his degree, so we had to break up,' Rachel explained carefully.

'Were you sad to say goodbye to him? Did you cry?' Dylan asked, always ready for drama.

'It broke both of our hearts.' Rachel remembered clinging to Lorcan, sobbing her heart out that he had to go. It felt like an eternity ago, but also as if it happened yesterday. How was that possible?

'If Daddy had stayed here, what would have happened then?' Olivia persisted, the frown deepening on her forehead.

Rachel tried to find an answer that would help the children understand. It was impossible, because in truth, Rachel herself had pondered so many what-if scenarios.

What if Lorcan and Rachel had found a way to stay together back then?

What if Lorcan hadn't met Niamh and then married her, when he returned to Ireland?

17

What if the joy she'd experienced with Lorcan was so intense and perfect that it was *too* much, and the universe demanded a payback?

Rachel closed her eyes for a moment as she asked herself the most painful question of them all.

What if Lorcan hadn't died?

'Are you ready for the ride of your life? Jump in and hold on tight!' their guide shouted with perfect timing, saving Rachel from the one question she had never worked out how to answer. As they found their spot in the raft, the misty spray from the water cooling their faces, the kids squealed with excitement. And for now, all was forgotten.

Halfway through their vacation, Claudia arranged a surprise for Rachel, booking a local winery for lunch just for the two of them. Joe and Annie were more than happy to have an excuse to spoil their grandchildren without Rachel's watchful eye on their sugar intake. Rachel suspected a lot of ice cream would be involved.

Rachel watched her mom as she played cards with the children at the kitchen table, strands of her long brown hair escaping from their ponytail. And when Annie shouted 'Snap!' – laughing with delight at her win – the kids joined in too.

While Rachel got ready for her excursion, she hummed happily to herself, taking her time blow-drying her dark hair into soft waves and applying a full face of make-up. Her hair and make-up complete, she pulled a midi tea dress in emerald green over her head and smoothed it down into place. As she twirled, watching herself in the mirror, the dress's fabric moved around her legs and its printed gold butterflies seemed to dance.

'There you are,' Rachel whispered to her reflection in the mirror. 'It's been a while.' After one last happy look at her old self, she grabbed her crossbody bag and ran downstairs.

As they drove away from the house, Claudia turned the music up high so Taylor Swift beamed out from its pulsing speakers. They were both singing along, giddy with excitement at the taste of freedom and a return to their youth.

'I wouldn't swap the kids for anything, but I've missed this,' Rachel admitted. 'I can't wait to get there – my stomach is already grumbling at the thought of the gorgeous food.'

'Mine too. I haven't eaten all day in preparation,' Claudia giggled back. 'When was the last time you even had a night out?'

Rachel felt a flush of embarrassment at the question. The truth was that it had been years. She didn't feel ready to admit that to her sister though.

'A few months or so,' she lied instead. She knew she could blame her grief at Lorcan's death for her poor social life and Claudia wouldn't question it, but that would be untrue. Almost two years had passed since he died, but her excitement today at getting ready for her date with Claudia finally felt like substantial proof that she had moved on from the crippling pain of loss.

The real problem was that she didn't have any close friends in Dublin. Somehow, over the past few years, she'd not just lost her husband, but she'd lost herself too. The highlight of her social life was her regular walk along the Velvet Strand in Portmarnock, with only the seagulls for company.

'Note to self, we must discuss your non-existent social life over a glass of rosé. But before that, I have a little surprise for you.'

'Should I be worried?' Rachel asked, taking in Claudia's grin. She was definitely up to something. Growing up with Claudia, they had always had spontaneous and mischievous moments – Claudia had a knack for getting them into trouble. Now Claudia drove up France Road then on to the Hill, pulling up in front of a villa that Rachel knew well.

This was the route the girls used to cycle their bikes up on their way to and from school. And for reasons that Rachel never really understood, this property always stood out for her. She'd stop and stare at it every day while Claudia complained about her dawdling. It was as if the villa had a pulse that beckoned her towards it. It sat behind a quintessential white picket fence on an elevated site overlooking the picturesque Cape Kidnappers bay. Its timber frame was painted white with navy accents. Mature evergreen trees drooped and leaned towards the house as if bowing to their mistress.

'I haven't thought about this place in years,' Rachel said, staring at the house in awe, unable to take her eyes off it. 'The number of times I used to wish we lived here.'

'Every time I go by it, I think of you,' Claudia admitted. 'We still refer to it as Rachel's villa every time we pass it.'

'Oh Sis, you are getting sentimental in your old age,' Rachel teased, but she clasped her sister's hand across the gearbox in solidarity. In reality, she understood her sentiment and felt the exact same way. 'The garden looks a little overgrown now from how I remember it, but it's still so pretty. I always wondered what it was like inside. You don't get houses like this in Ireland – it's mostly bungalows or two-storey semi-detached houses like our own. That period fretwork on the portico-style entrance is so unique to New Zealand.'

'Well, how about we try to fire up your imagination even more? Shall we go in and have a look inside?'

'Yeah, right, I wish!' Rachel laughed. If her sister thought that she would break into a house just to see what colour the wallpaper was, she could think again.

But Claudia smiled mysteriously, waving a set of keys in front of Rachel's nose. They tinkled like sleigh bells on a snowy winter's night.

Rachel looked up to the villa's front door, back to the keys in Claudia's hand and then to the door again, before she managed to squeal, 'No way!'

'Yes. Way!' Claudia squealed back, revelling in her sister's excitement. 'You won't believe this. An unreal coincidence, but the villa is for sale and Howard is the realtor. When I spotted the paperwork on our dining room table, I was gobsmacked. I asked him for the keys to give you a sneak preview before it goes on the market next month. And of course, we all know that Howard cannot refuse me a single thing.'

'He's wrapped around your finger,' Rachel said, thinking about the previous evening visiting Claudia and her partner. He was clearly besotted and seemed happy to wait on her hand and foot. Tall and athletic, he was far quieter than her bubbly, outspoken sister.

'It's a truth I cannot deny,' Claudia said, looking like the cat who got the cream. 'Now come on. We are going in.'

Claudia jumped out of the car, with an open-mouthed Rachel scrabbling to follow her.

'Wait, what about the owners? We can't barge into their home unannounced.'

'It's empty. The owner died. I know, so sad. But hey ho, lucky for us!' Claudia ran up the cobblelock driveway without pausing to look back, and Rachel, laughing out loud, chased after her. Oh, how she'd missed the spontaneity of her sister.

As they walked up the steps, Rachel took a moment to admire the large wooden porch. There used to be a double swing seat sitting on the left where the owner would sit, reading a book. Rachel could almost hear the echoes of its creak as it moved backwards and forwards. Claudia unlocked the blue entrance door surrounded by beautiful stained glass, and as she pushed it open, the secrets of the house were revealed to the sisters for the first time.

Immediately, they found themselves in a large, sunny reception room, with high ceilings, sash bay windows, and a generous fireplace that made Rachel gasp. The villa was even more beautiful than she'd imagined it might be as a child.

'The furniture is a bit meh, but what can you expect with the previous owner being in her nineties. But it's included in the sale price,' Claudia explained.

'Oh, I quite like it actually,' Rachel replied. 'That's a plus point as far as I'm concerned. A wax polish and buff, it would soon get a new lease of life.' As she spoke, she ran her hands across an old Chesterfield leather armchair that was rippled with creases and cracks from years of offering comfort to its owners.

There was a second reception room used as a dining room, with the same high ceilings and period features, and after that a library which made Rachel want to cry it was so beautiful. It had floor-to-ceiling bookshelves on every wall and two large loveseats, perfect for curling up into.

'The kitchen is way too dated for my liking, but that's easily remedied,' Claudia was saying now, as they walked into a bright yellow kitchen. She opened and closed the white wooden cabinet doors one by one. 'And as for this lino floor, what on earth were the owners thinking?'

Rachel had to agree that the floor was an eyesore. But she'd also hazard a guess that underneath it was more of the natural timber floor that the rest of the house had. Unlike Claudia, the rest of the kitchen, even with its old cabinets, charmed her.

There were three good-sized bedrooms downstairs – all with a king-size bed in them and flooded with gorgeous sunshine from their large bay windows. Two had full bathrooms too, with pretty stained-glass windows.

Continuing through the house, they made their way upstairs, and Claudia could hardly contain her excitement as she explained to Rachel that a real gem awaited them. She wasn't exaggerating. A generous master suite took up the entire second floor, its floor-to-ceiling windows across two walls offering close to panoramic views of the bay.

'I feel a little overcome. It's stunning,' Rachel breathed, feeling surprisingly emotional as she took it all in. She had to take a seat on the edge of the mahogany bed.

'I know, it's magnificent,' Claudia agreed, barely concealing a look of smug satisfaction. 'Take your time. Have a good look at it all. Imagine waking up to that view every morning. And you haven't even seen the back yard yet. It's a dream for kids.'

Rachel looked at her suspiciously. What had she meant by that comment about the back yard being a dream for kids? Claudia gave her a pointed look before turning on her heels and making her way downstairs, leaving Rachel to follow her, feeling a little bemused.

The yard had a cobblelock patio, with a large outdoor pizza oven and a swimming pool. The pool was drained and needed a good clean, but Rachel knew it could be gorgeous with a little hard work and imagination.

'As soon as we get a hint of good weather in Ireland, the whole country buys a paddling pool,' Rachel explained to Claudia as she examined the garden. 'A nightmare to keep clean, and with my two, it never lasts more than a few weeks. If Olivia and Dylan saw this place, with its own pool, they'd never want to leave.'

'And it's got a gorgeous mature garden too,' Claudia said, in full realtor mode.

But Rachel was distracted by the fact that she had just spied an outdoor sunroom. It had yet more stained-glass windows to match the ones scattered inside the house, and more of the portico fretwork that gave the villa its distinct charm.

Rachel felt a little dazed by it all.

'I didn't think I could love it more than I did when I fantasized about it from outside,' she said, 'but it's even nicer than I could have envisioned.'

She pictured her nice but uninspiring semi-detached home in Ireland and had to shake the image away, feeling guilty for comparing the two houses.

'Well, you could live here, you know,' Claudia said. 'I'm putting that out there.'

'Don't be silly,' Rachel snapped, feeling angry at the flippant way Claudia had said that. As if she could uproot the kids and move here, just like that. She moved towards the whitewashed wall of the sunroom and leaned against it for support.

If Claudia noticed Rachel's discomfort, she chose to ignore it and instead pointed to her own arms, saying, 'I've got goosies just thinking about having you back home. It's where you belong.'

'You're making me dizzy, Claudia. It's too much. You've sprung all this on me so fast, I can't cope,' Rachel replied. She began to walk down the driveway towards the car.

'You feel like that because you know I'm right. You have to consider this. Please. I know this could be a wonderful home for you all. I know it,' Claudia called after her.

It took Claudia a few minutes to lock up the villa and Rachel was grateful for the time to compose herself. Why had she allowed Claudia's fantasy to get under her skin so much? When Claudia climbed back into the driver's seat, she carried on extolling the virtues of the villa. They picked up Howard and he joined in too, in what was a blatant well-rehearsed sales pitch. Even as they arrived at the Craggy Range Winery, Claudia continued to list the many – and, to be fair, valid – reasons why it made sense for Rachel and the kids to up sticks and move back home.

'Can we forget about the villa and just enjoy this incredible vineyard?' Rachel asked, as they pulled up in front of the entrance to the reception.

'Too much?' Claudia asked, frowning.

'Yes!' both Rachel and Howard replied together.

They said their goodbyes to Howard, who assured them he'd be ready to collect them whenever they wanted. And then, linking arms, they walked into the restaurant.

As they sat at their table, with a glass of wine in hand, Rachel sighed with pleasure as she took in the stunning views of the Te Mata Peak.

And now that Claudia had stopped trying to oversell the villa, Rachel found herself giving in to the dream too. She began to envision a different life for the children here, with all the opportunities that New Zealand offered.

What if a fresh start was exactly what they all needed? That was one question she hadn't thought of before.

'I could get used to this,' she said, raising her glass, filled with a Martinborough Pinot Noir, in a toast.

'You could have this every week if you wanted. You and me, having boozy lunches together. Not to mention the free babysitters you'd have with Mom and Dad. They are crying out to have kids around to spoil,' Claudia said.

'There will be no boozy lunches when you get pregnant!' Rachel countered.

'Ah, I disagree. If I get up the duff, then you have a ready-made designated driver. And then when I can drink too, Howard will drive us.' Claudia had an answer for everything; she'd clearly been planning this attack for a while.

Then her face changed, all joviality gone as she looked at Rachel intently. 'Can I ask you something? About the kids?'

'Course. You can ask me anything.'

Claudia gulped some wine, then said, 'You always said

you didn't want children. That you didn't have a maternal bone in your body. And yet here you are, a mother, all in. Has your opinion changed?'

Rachel needed some wine herself to deal with this question. It was a complicated one, there was no doubt about that.

'Before I met Olivia and Dylan, I could never imagine a life with babies, toddlers, children or teenagers. The image jarred,' she paused to consider it further. 'But things changed, I guess. I don't know when it happened, but one day I was changing Dylan's nappy and I realized that I was finally doing it without holding my nose, or in dread. And I'd begun to look forward to spending time, not just with Lorcan, but with the kids too. It kind of crept up on me.'

And in that thought of the kids, Rachel felt a pang for them. She mentally shook herself. It had only been a couple of hours since she'd seen them.

'I can't imagine you without kids now. I look at you and that's the kind of mother I want to be. And that's why I want you here. I need you to show me how to do all these things, like change a nappy,' Claudia said.

'You'll work it all out, with or without me. I've no doubt of that.'

They both picked up their wine glasses and sat in comfortable silence for a moment.

Rachel leaned in towards Claudia and said, 'You make it sound so simple, us moving everything back here. But it's far more complicated than that. The children have a good life in Ireland. School, friends, not to mention a family who would string me up if I took them away.'

'They are young enough to start again though,' Claudia

replied. 'In a few more years, it would be tricky to uproot them, I'll grant you that. But now . . .'

'Dylan doesn't start school until September. I suppose if we were to move, this year would be a good one,' Rachel admitted reluctantly.

The smile that spread across Claudia's face made Rachel's eyes fill with tears. It was clear how much her sister wanted her back home. And it felt nice to be wanted. Other than the children, she'd not felt that much since Lorcan died.

'Promise me you'll think about it. That's all I ask.'

THREE

Rachel

Napier, Hawke's Bay

Rachel had always believed that no good came from looking back. Because after all, that wasn't the direction you were going in. But ever since Claudia showed her the villa, she could think of little else. Her every thought was of her old life in Hawke's Bay, from her childhood to that one perfect summer with Lorcan.

And the more she looked back, the more she knew that she didn't want to return to Ireland. The acknowledgement was complicated; she felt guilt at the inferred slight to the children's birthplace and the home she and Lorcan had made there. Rachel felt a tension headache begin to make itself known. The thought of leaving Claudia and her parents was unbearable. But she also knew that she had to do it.

Rachel was determined not to ruin the last week of

their vacation by stressing about a silly dream that Claudia had cooked up. She poured herself a glass of her mom's homemade lemonade, taking in her parents' home as if for the first time. They'd redecorated their home many times over the decades they'd lived here, but always in the same colours. Her eyes greedily took in every detail in the kitchen, storing *everything* in her mind, for a time in the future when she needed them. A vase of yellow daffodils, bright and glorious, sat on the kitchen table. A pie was cooling down on a rack near the window, its scents of apple and caramel filling the room. Her mom had baked that same pie every Saturday afternoon her entire married life, a recipe handed down from her own mom. And, pride of place on the kitchen wall, two pieces of framed artwork made by Claudia and Rachel when they were kids. Rachel's mom had made the frames herself, with shells she'd picked up from the nearby bay.

When Rachel decided to settle in Ireland permanently almost four years ago, it had been an easy decision for her. She loved Lorcan and the children. That meant Rachel had to be where they were. Yes, of course she missed her family, but when Lorcan was with her, that loss felt less acute somehow. But, in truth, even before he died, she'd realized that while she loved Ireland, she still felt the tug of Hawke's Bay. This was her home, she supposed.

She'd never told her sister, but she had discussed relocating to New Zealand with Lorcan. He'd been quite keen on the idea. New Zealand had a lot going for it – in addition to the fact that Rachel's family lived there – and he'd never forgotten his time there. Its beauty rivalled the most stunning places in the world, and no matter where you lived, you were always close to outstandingly gorgeous beaches and lush national parks. More than that, it was a country that had managed to get the work/life balance right for its inhabitants. And as Rachel told him, it had a lot in common with Ireland, in that more often than not it offered a friendly and warm welcome.

Rachel couldn't help but wonder, if Lorcan hadn't died, would they have moved over here by now?

The back door flew open, and Olivia and Dylan raced towards their mom at full speed. They'd been out in the garden with their nanny and grandad, helping to weed the flower beds.

'I won,' Olivia gasped, grabbing her mom's hand seconds before Dylan did.

But you won't win for long. Rachel decided it was safer not to share that out loud. Dylan almost pipped his older sister to the post – he was fast – and although he was three years younger than eight-year-old Olivia, he was catching up with her in height and, it appeared, speed too.

Olivia gave her little brother a slight shove to his shoulder and Rachel gave her a warning look. Only yesterday, she'd been discussing the children's growing competitiveness with her mom, who'd pointed out that it was to be expected considering the children had lost so much; it was natural that they would want to keep Rachel close to them. Rachel would have to work harder to ensure that they both felt equal levels of love and attention from her. Her priority now was to make their worlds happy and secure.

For now, she gathered the children around her, making sure there was one on each side, so she could give them each a one-armed cuddle. She'd mastered this skill years before.

'You know, this kitchen hasn't changed much from when I was a little girl,' she told them, deciding distraction was a good tactic here, to avert a row.

'I like Nanny and Gramps' kitchen,' Olivia said, looking around her.

'Me too, sweetheart. I loved to do arts and crafts here with Claudia. Your Nanny Annie would sit us down at this table and we'd get creating.'

'What did you make?' Dylan asked.

'All sorts. Have you noticed the artwork over on that wall?' Rachel asked, nodding towards the other side of the kitchen. 'Claudia and I made those, fashioned from our handprints.'

'It's hearts!' Dylan said.

'Yes, it is. I can still remember showing my painting to Mom and Dad when we'd finished it. I was so proud of our efforts. Do you know what your Gramps Joe said to me?'

'That he loved it?' Olivia asked.

'Yes, he did love it. But as well as that, Grandad Joe told us both that the pictures we had created were true heartprints.'

'Do I hear my name being taken in vain?' Joe said, walking into the kitchen, with Annie following on behind him, with hand-cut flowers in her arms.

'What's a heartprint?' Dylan asked.

'A very good question, young man. For me, any handprint art that is made with love is a heartprint.' Joe walked over to the framed prints and ran his finger over them gently. 'Every line and nuance from the girls' handprints were filled with the girls' love at that time, and I can still feel it now when I touch it.'

Rachel felt tears in her eyes.

'That's so nice,' Olivia whispered.

'Yes, I rather think it is,' Rachel said. 'I can still remember your Nanny Annie hanging the art as if it had come from the most celebrated artist in a gallery.'

'That's because to us, they were and always will be priceless pieces of art,' Annie replied.

As Rachel looked at her parents and her children, a thought struck her. The love she felt for her children mirrored how her parents felt about her and Claudia. She'd never equated the two before, but now the realization filled her with awe. She walked over to her mom and moved into her embrace, breathing in her sugary lemon scent and holding her close.

'What's all this?' Annie said, returning the warm embrace. 'Not that I'm complaining . . .'

'I don't know how I'll say goodbye to you all,' Rachel whispered.

'Shush now . . . let's not think about that until we absolutely must,' Annie said. She nodded towards the children and the two women watched Olivia as she tried to place her own hand over the picture on the wall, to compare sizes.

'You kids should make heartprints of your own,' Annie suggested.

This was met with great enthusiasm, so Annie covered the table with a well-used oil tablecloth, multicoloured and scuffed from decades of arts and crafts. She grabbed six bottles of paint and some heavy white card that she always kept in the utility cupboard for art projects.

'I'll leave you to this. I'm going to get dinner started,' Annie said.

'And I've a date with the newspaper,' Joe said, retreating to the family room, leaving Rachel and the kids to start creating.

The children giggled as Rachel brushed the coloured paints on to each of their palms, saying the strokes tickled them. One by one, with Rachel's guidance, the kids each placed their prints on to the page, filling in the white space within the heart. Then Olivia sprinkled glitter on top so that it stuck to the gluey paint.

'It's the best heartprint I have ever seen,' Dylan said, before quickly adding, 'Oh, I'm sorry, Mom. I'm not saying yours wasn't as brilliant.'

Rachel smiled at her little boy, who was always quick to be fair. 'I agree with you, Dylan, because we all did this one together. Just think how much love there is in this one heart, with all our combined handprints. We're more powerful when we're together; always remember that.'

'Do you think Nanny Annie and Gramps would like to keep this?' Olivia whispered, looking towards Annie who was chopping vegetables at the kitchen island.

'What a lovely idea. But I have to admit I'd love to keep this one for ourselves so we can frame it like my mom did with mine. But if we do three more, we can not only give one to Nanny and Gramps here, we can give one to your other grandparents at home too.'

'I think we should sign them. All the best artists do that,' Olivia said.

'We could even write a little poem on them,' Rachel added.

'Can we post them to Ireland?' Olivia asked.

'I don't see why not. We've got another ten days left before we get home. We can race them to see what gets to Ireland first,' Rachel said, making the kids giggle at the thought.

They spent hours happily working on their heartprints. With every stamp of their palms, Rachel felt the children's love radiate on to the page in front of them. And she hoped that when the grandparents received their present, they felt that same love too.

FOUR

Rachel

Napier, Hawke's Bay

'I can't believe that today is your last full day,' Annie said sadly as she reached for another handful of flour, sprinkling it on to the dough in front of her. 'I'm not sure I'm ready to say goodbye tomorrow. Have you got any special plans, or do you want to hang around at the house?'

Rachel could hear the forced joviality in her mom's voice. She was struggling too. She wished she could just stay in this kitchen today, watching her mom bake fresh bread for their breakfast. It would be perfect. Her kids, however, would have something to say about that. They had big plans for their last day.

'I'm close to bursting into tears and we've not even had breakfast,' Rachel admitted.

'I'm as bad. I had a little cry already today with your

dad. I can't even think about saying goodbye without getting emotional.'

Rachel was afraid if she attempted to articulate how she felt, it would be her undoing. Her mom paused her kneading of the dough, and they looked at each other.

Mother and daughter, sharing so much in that held gaze.

A shared love.

And a shared sorrow too, that another goodbye was looming.

'I wish . . .' Rachel began, leaving the sentence hanging between them.

'I know, love. And I wish that too,' Annie said. 'But life doesn't give us our wishes in the way we want it to. You have to go back to Ireland. I'm clinging to the fact that you'll be back, or that we'll visit you over there. Either way, it's not goodbye forever; it's just goodbye for now.'

'I'll start saving for our next trip as soon as I get home,' Rachel promised. She looked upwards, surprised that the kids were still asleep. 'We've agreed that the kids can choose our itinerary this morning. If they ever get up, that is!'

The busy, high-energy days they'd packed into their vacation had tuckered the kids out.

'I like to think that they sleep so soundly here because they feel at home with us now.'

'They couldn't be more at home had they grown up in this house, as I did. They love it here with you and Dad. They are so lucky to have you both spoiling them rotten every day.'

'Nothing gives us greater pleasure than to treat them. And you, for that matter. I feel like the past four weeks have flown by, but we've all been so busy you and I have barely had a chance to chat properly. How are you really doing? And don't say fine. I want to know what's going on inside your head and your heart.'

'Most days, I'm okay. Honestly,' she added quickly, seeing disbelief on her mother's face. 'But then, something hits me when I least expect it and I fall down like a bowling pin.'

'I honestly don't know how you've coped so well. The worst bit for us was not being able to be with you at such a horrific time. It's counter-intuitive to a parent, not being able to be with their child when they need them most.'

'I know you would have come if it hadn't been for the travel restrictions. The Covid-19 virus held no prisoners when it came to personal tragedy, did it?'

'I'll never forget how horrendous it was to have to watch Lorcan's funeral online. My eyes never left you, not for a moment. All I could see was your back, your arms wrapped around each of the children, all of your heads bowed low.' Annie's voice wobbled with emotion.

There wasn't much Rachel could say in response to that. So she wrapped her arms around her mother's shoulders, and they took comfort from each other for a moment.

'It's going to be quiet tomorrow. The sound of the children's laughter in the house has been wonderful,' Annie said.

'That's my favourite sound. And I'm grateful to hear it again. For a while there, it felt like they'd never feel anything but sadness. I am in awe at their resilience, how they've come to terms with their losses at such a young age.'

'They are strong kids. They've coped and bounced back far more than anyone could have dared to hope.' Annie placed the bread dough into a lined tin and scored the top with a knife.

'They have more good days than bad ones now. I made

clips Lorcan had of Niamh on his phone into a video compilation for the kids and Olivia loves to watch it. Dylan doesn't bother so much, though. He prefers the more recent videos with only his dad and me in them.'

Rachel felt a twinge of sadness for Niamh. It wasn't fair, but as Lorcan always said to her when she worried, they had to let the children lead the way on this.

'Maybe when Dylan is a little older, he might get something more from them.'

'I suppose you're right. I think our complicated family confuses him. He's only five.'

'Show me a family that isn't complicated! Rachel, you are the only mother Dylan remembers. His only memories of a mother's love come from *you*.'

While Rachel recognized the truth in that statement, she couldn't help feeling saddened by it too. 'I just also want them to remember their first mammy. To know where they came from.'

'And I'm glad to hear you say that. It breaks my heart that the kids have learned at this young age how cruel life can be,' Annie replied.

At this, tears filled Rachel's eyes. She poured herself a glass of water and took a long sip to steady herself. No tears allowed. Not now, anyhow.

'I've being thinking a lot about your situation with Niamh's parents. Something you said when you arrived here keeps going around and around my head. The fact that they don't like you worries me. Talk to me, love. Tell me what's really going on,' Annie said.

Rachel felt a rush of love for her mom. She was always on her side, something Rachel dearly missed at home in Ireland. Because despite living close to the children's maternal grandparents, she was pretty sure they were not on Team Rachel.

'I know I've shared this with you before, but honestly, Sheila and Adrian can be tricky. I can't seem to find a way to bridge the gap that lies between us. I think to them, I'll always be the woman that Lorcan married far too soon after their daughter died.'

'But you can't help who you fall in love with,' Annie said. 'You've nothing to reproach yourself about.'

'I know that, and most people would agree. But it's different for them. I keep trying to find a way to connect with them, for the kids' sakes, who adore Sheila and Adrian. But it's as if we take two steps forward and three steps back, every single time.'

Annie frowned. 'What about their son Jack? You always speak about him with such warmth. I like to think you have one ally in that camp at least.'

Rachel thought about Niamh's younger brother, who was a firm favourite with the kids. And with her too. Yes, Jack was one of Rachel's only allies. When Sheila found fault with something Rachel was doing, which was a regular occurrence, Jack always defended her. And she felt that somewhere over the previous couple of years, they had formed a genuine friendship.

'Honestly, since Lorcan died, had Jack not been around, I'm not sure I could have coped,' she said.

'I'm glad you have him. But you would have coped no matter what, Rachel. Because you are strong. You are a natural mother. It's a joy to witness. And nobody can deny how much they adore you too. That's all that matters, not what the Butlers think about you.'

'Thanks, Mom. I would give up everything for them,' Rachel said.

'And some would say that you already have,' Annie said, patting her hand.

'Do you think that we have a preordained destiny, that comes true no matter what we do?' Rachel asked.

'Crikey, we might need coffee for this subject.' Annie poured coffee into two mugs, then added cream and sugar. 'There is much in our lives that we have no control over. But I believe that destiny is what we do with the fate we are dealt. Take your father, for instance. He was born to a dirt-poor family, and in the main, everyone in that family was uneducated. His fate. Getting to second grade was an achievement, never mind finishing high school. For your father, though, he wanted more for himself. That was his personal destiny.'

'He's pretty amazing, isn't he?' Rachel said. Growing up, she'd always known her parents were decent people, but the older she got, the more she appreciated how incredible they both were too.

'He's one of the good guys. I recognized that the moment I met him. Lorcan was too. And Howard.'

'Howard is a saint,' Rachel said and they both laughed for a moment. Claudia could be a handful.

'Niamh and Lorcan both died young, tragically. Was that their fate?' Rachel asked.

'Yes, I believe so, in the sense that it was inevitable for them both to die. They could not have done anything to avoid it.' Annie paused, watching her daughter. 'What's with all the questions, love?'

'I can't stop thinking that I was supposed to marry Lorcan

so that I could be there for the children. That somehow, they are the family I was destined to have,' Rachel said.

Annie nodded, understanding. 'That doesn't sound crazy to me at all. There were so many moments, big and small, that brought you to Olivia and Dylan. Choices you made,' Annie paused again, then whispered, 'Even Matthew.'

Hearing her ex-boyfriend's name felt strange for Rachel. She hadn't thought about him for years, yet at one time, he was a huge part of her life. Inevitably, as their relationship progressed, Rachel and Matthew had at some point begun to talk about a shared future. Matthew was a traditional guy and had always made it clear that he wanted to get married, buy a house and fill it with children.

But Rachel had no desire to have children, and any time Matthew spoke about family life, she felt like the walls were closing in on her. When Rachel decided to open up to him, he took her lack of maternal instinct as a personal rejection of him. He tried to change her mind and accused her of being selfish, but Rachel remained firm in her feelings. It was apparent that a future together would never work, with or without kids.

Finally, Rachel ran away, unable to bear the thought of being in Hawke's Bay, near him. She left New Zealand for a two-month tour of Europe, taking Claudia with her.

And it had been that tour, ultimately, that brought her back to Lorcan. Which in turn made her a mother, something she was so sure she never wanted to be.

Rachel remembered bumping into Lorcan on that European tour as if it had just happened. She and Claudia had finished a meal and were halfway down the cobbled lanes of Temple Bar when Rachel realized she'd left her purse behind, forcing them to run back to the booth they had vacated.

And the man now sitting there, holding her purse in his hand, sent such a jolt of recognition and yearning through her, she'd had to hold on to Claudia's arm for support.

Lorcan.

When they found their voices, he'd asked Rachel what she was doing in Dublin, to which Claudia helpfully answered that she was 'on the run' from an ex-boyfriend.

'Are you looking for a new relationship, then?' Lorcan had asked, in his teasing way.

'Well, as long as the guy comes with no baggage,' she'd replied flippantly.

Lorcan had calmly joked that that would rule him out, what with him being a widower with two babies at home. But in saying this, his words and his vulnerability had floored Rachel.

For the rest of their time in Dublin, she had felt a pull towards Lorcan that she couldn't move away from. The missing years fell away and they picked up where they'd left off that summer in New Zealand. And eventually, she made a conscious choice to stay in Dublin instead of continuing on to Scotland as she'd planned to do with Claudia. Rachel had been lucky her sister understood and was happy to finish their trip solo.

Within a few short months he'd asked her to marry him. He said he had learned through experience that life was too short not to grab happiness where you could.

But Rachel didn't just say yes to being his wife, she also said yes to becoming the children's stepmother. Now, as she thought about the sleeping kids upstairs, while she sat at the comforting kitchen table with her mother, she thought, not for the first time, that the 'baggage' she'd been so scared of, turned out to be the best thing that ever happened to her.

FIVE

Rachel

Maraetotara Waterfall, Napier

The aroma of caramel and vanilla wafted through the door as they made their way into the candy store for the first stop of their last day. The sweet smell was a nostalgic hit; every Saturday when Rachel and Claudia were children, their dad had brought them into this same store to spend their pocket money. Watching her own kids now, filling a bag each with treats, made Rachel's heart swell with joy as their hands hovered over spaceman candy sticks, jet planes, chocolate fish and pineapple rums.

In many ways, it was as if time had paused in Napier. Not much seemed to have changed since she left and that was a comfort to Rachel. It was as if the town had waited for her to have her adventure in Ireland but was now ready to welcome her back so they could all move on together.

They left the store and the sun beamed down on them

as they strolled through the coastal town. Olivia pointed out her favourites among the brightly coloured buildings. An earthquake had devastated Napier in the Twenties, and afterwards it had been completely rebuilt with Art Deco-inspired architecture. Olivia had declared that it looked like a movie set when she first saw it. The town was glamorous – a rare gem from another era. They all agreed that the prettiest building was the National Tobacco Company Building. The building's front held an elegant arch in the centre of a square, with wooden doors surrounded by sculpted roses and native bulrushes.

Seeing her hometown through the kids' eyes reawakened Rachel's love for her childhood neighbourhood too.

She could almost hear Claudia whispering in her ear, 'Go on, admit it. It's nicer than Malahide!'

She remembered her reaction to their home on the Yellow Walls Road in Malahide, the first time Lorcan brought her there. Rachel had thought the house and area were charming, and she'd grown to like it too, the more time she spent there. But lately, she had to admit, some of its charms had diminished.

Was it because there were now too many painful memories embedded into the fabric of the house?

Or maybe it was because Malahide wasn't home.

'I love it here, Mom,' Olivia said, not for the first time. 'I think it's the prettiest place in the whole world.'

'Yeah, it's cool and all that, but I'm bored. Remember I said I wanted to explore somewhere new that we've not been to yet?' Dylan asked.

'I've got the very spot in mind,' Rachel said.

They made their way back to her dad's car, and Rachel drove them to Maraetotara Falls.

'This was one of your daddy's favourite spots to visit. It's a short walk, but it's worth it, I promise.'

As soon as she parked the car, Dylan jumped out and bolted down the wooden stairs that led to the falls.

'Wait up, Dylan,' Rachel warned in her sternest don't-ignore-me tone of voice, following after him. At the foot of the stairs, they continued on their trek through lush greenery.

'What's that noise?' Olivia asked, pausing.

'Patience. Just you wait,' Rachel said, enjoying the children's obvious excitement.

The sound Olivia referred to was the rush of water and Rachel felt giddy when it reached her ears too. Together, the trio turned a corner, and then suddenly there it was in front of them – the Maraetotara Waterfall. The water cascaded down in a white blanket, framed by leafy greenery that seemed to bow to its majesty. And at the foot of the waterfall was a large pool of clear blue water. Even better, they seemed to have the beautiful spot to themselves.

'Wow! That's the biggest waterfall I've ever seen. It's so cool!' Dylan exclaimed. 'I wish we could jump right in there, Mom.'

'Don't be silly, Dylan, of course we can't,' Olivia said, giving her baby brother a withering look.

'Actually, sweetheart, we can. I've brought our costumes especially.' Rachel opened her small rucksack and pulled out their trunks and tankinis, plus a couple of bath sheets. 'Last one in is the loser!'

Ten minutes later, the three of them were in their costumes, splashing in the cold water, the early afternoon sun dancing its way through the canopies of trees and dark green foliage that surrounded them. And with every splash and squeal, Rachel felt more connected with the beauty of living. She was finally thriving, not just surviving. *She felt alive.*

'Uncle Jack would love it here,' Olivia said.

'I think if your Uncle Jack was here, he'd want me to do this,' Rachel said, suddenly lifting her hands through the water and splashing the kids. Olivia looked at Dylan, and he nodded in agreement.

'Let the battle commence!' Olivia screamed, scooping her own arms through the water in her mom's direction.

They lost all track of time swimming and playing at the foot of the waterfall. It was only Dylan's rumbling tummy that alerted them to the fact that they'd been in the water for over an hour. Rachel towelled the kids dry, telling them stories about the many times she and Claudia had lost track of time at the beach as kids and forgotten to go home.

'Your Gramps Joe would go looking for us, but more often than not when he found us in the ocean, instead of telling us off, he'd jump in too!'

Had her childhood been as idyllic as Rachel now remembered? Or had the years added rose-tinted glasses? She would have to ask Claudia later. Somehow, though, she didn't believe it was imagined. It had been that good. Her parents were decent, loving people whose only motivation in life was to make their children happy. And if Rachel could give a similar childhood to her two, she'd be doing okay. She looked at Olivia and Dylan's faces, bronzed from the New Zealand sun, freckles across their cheeks and noses, taking in their bright eyes, wide with excitement and happiness. She couldn't remember the last time they'd looked this happy.

And then another thought struck her.

Was she giving them their best childhood in Dublin?

Or were they treading water, not getting anywhere, because they were all drowning in sad memories?

Questions that she had no answers to fired around her head, over and over.

As they drove back to her parents' house, the kids were quiet and sleepy from their busy day so she let them nap in the back seat to renew their energy for the farewell party her parents had promised to throw them later on. As the children slept, Rachel found herself automatically heading back towards Bluff Hill. The magical pull of the villa she'd always felt as a child was at play again. She parked up outside the white picket fence and sighed.

'Who owns that house, Mom? It's so pretty,' Olivia said, waking up and sitting forward.

'Nobody owns it right now, sweetheart. It's for sale.'

'I bet it's really special to live in a house like that.'

Dylan joined Olivia at the window to look at the villa and Rachel turned around to face them. 'When I was a little girl, I believed that one day I would live in this house.'

'Really?' Olivia asked in wonder.

'Yes, really, sweetheart. There are four bedrooms with big bay windows, and the ceilings are so high you need a ladder to touch them. And you can see the ocean from the back of the villa.'

'I wish we lived in a house like that,' Dylan declared.

'Me too,' Olivia agreed.

'Well, the problem with that wish is that if we wanted to live in this house, we'd have to leave Ireland to do so,' Rachel said, unable to stop herself testing the waters.

'That wouldn't be nice. But I'd still like to live here,' Dylan said decisively.

For once, Olivia didn't disagree with him; instead, she nodded her agreement.

And finally, the dream that Rachel had let wander around her head since Claudia planted its seeds began to actually take root, so fast that she could barely catch her breath.

SIX

Belinda

Malone Park, Belfast

'You were quiet tonight at bridge club,' Oscar remarked to his wife as they drove the short distance home, down the tree-lined wide avenue of Malone Park.

'Was I?' Belinda was non-committal.

They had both been regular attendees of the Diamond Bridge Club for ten years, but since Oscar had sold his business two years previously, they rarely missed a club meeting. Usually, when she played bridge, Belinda forgot about everything else going on in the world, immersed only in the game in front of her and her next move. She was born with a competitive streak that she liked to flex most days in some way or other. No matter how much she tried, however, her head hadn't been in the game this evening. More often than not, Belinda found her mind falling on to a memory of Lorcan.

51

'Did you hear what I said? Do you want to?' An edge of annoyance had crept into Oscar's voice.

Belinda had let his voice fade out as they drove, and now felt guilty for the slight. 'Sorry, I was miles away. Forgive me.'

Oscar sighed, repeating his question, 'The Traynors want to know if we'll play doubles on Thursday morning. They have a court booked. We could go for a bite to eat afterwards. Make a day of it.' He frowned as he stole a glance at his wife. 'You've been in a funny mood all day.'

Belinda felt a flush of shame as she recognized the truth in his words. She rarely lost her composure. In social situations, she was known for her grace and exquisite manners. But once or twice this evening, she had been downright rude to their fellow club members. She would rather stick pins in her eyes than play tennis with the Traynors, but the traitorous thought was there for only a fleeting moment before sanity returned. She loved the tennis club. She couldn't deny that the Traynors were good company, and they played a decent game, evenly matched to both her and Oscar's skills.

'Belinda? Shall I say yes, then? I can book Deanes for lunch afterwards. We might as well treat ourselves. We've not been there for a little while.' Oscar was working hard to coax a positive response.

'We were there last week and the week before and the week before that,' Belinda replied, placing her hands on either side of her temple. The pain was back. A tension headache, her doctor had confirmed when she'd gone to see him the previous week.

'Were we? Yes, I suppose we were,' Oscar sounded

weary now. 'Is there somewhere else you'd prefer? We could try that new place down on the Quay if you'd like.'

Belinda saw only concern on her husband's face and felt a flash of guilt for being difficult. 'I'm sorry, I don't mean to be contrary. Doubles and then lunch sounds perfect. Please thank the Traynors for thinking of us.'

She was surprised to see that they were already outside their red-brick home. It had been one of those journeys that she had no recollection of making. Belinda typically would get a sense of pride when they arrived at the home that had been theirs for over thirty years. But what did any of it matter, when you really thought about it?

She took in the double-fronted, turn-of-the-century detached house with mature gardens. It was one of the most handsome houses on the road. Belinda herself had transformed it room by room until it was now a house worthy of the glossiest magazine. Her sisters would often remark that it was a world away from how Belinda was raised. And Belinda couldn't dispute the fact. She had been born on a farm in Antrim but had always had ambitions for a life far away from cows and dairy farming. As a young girl, as she helped move the animals from their field to the milking parlour, Belinda would daydream that a handsome prince would gallop towards her to save her from the mundane life she just about endured.

She'd watched her mother's face age quickly with lines caused by years spent outdoors in all the elements, and Belinda knew that she wanted more than that. Every night as she lay in bed, listening to the exhausted snores of her parents drifting down the hall corridor, she told herself she would do anything she could to achieve that goal.

Gradually, she thought up a plan of action, deciding that her best chance to escape would come courtesy of love.

Being pretty, Belinda had plenty of offers from locals, but she remained aloof, knowing there was something better for her. As soon as she was eighteen, she began to frequent the Belfast bars where professionals tended to socialize. She scoured the local newspapers and magazines for mentions of likely places where she might meet her handsome prince. It took less than three months for that to happen. When Oscar, the son of a wealthy packaging manufacturer, walked into her life, Belinda made a decision instantly that they would marry. Of course, Oscar had no idea that this was her plan, but he fell for her charms almost immediately. She pursued him with stealth and incredible skill, especially for an eighteen-year-old country girl. Her hard work paid off, and within a few months she wore a large two-carat diamond engagement ring.

Belinda insisted they book a date for their wedding immediately, ignoring advice from family members who warned her that she should take the time to enjoy their engagement. Allow time to get to know each other appropriately. But she was not going to take any chances that Oscar might slip through her fingers. She'd seen it before. Like a firework, the first flush of romance shone brightly but then burnt out, leaving nothing but a memory behind in the ashes.

Belinda need not have worried, though. Oscar was besotted with her then, and still was now, even all these years later. And to her surprise, Belinda had genuinely fallen in love with her husband. She'd always been a dutiful and loving wife. She also respected her husband's work ethic, proudly supporting Oscar as he took over his father's business on his thirtieth birthday. He went on to treble it in size in as many years, with her by his side. Nobody could deny that she'd played a part in its success, too, quietly guiding him from behind the scenes.

When a multinational corporation approached Oscar almost two years ago, they made him an offer he could not refuse. He had always hoped that his son Lorcan would one day take over the business, but Lorcan had been adamant in his refusal. He'd made a life for himself in Dublin with his young family and loved his career as a quantity surveyor. Oscar had been upset initially, but in the end, it didn't matter anyway.

Lorcan had never been destined to take over the firm.

Belinda flicked on the lights to their double-height great hall as they walked in. The house was the perfect place to entertain, and the Bradleys did so with style every year at their annual summer and Christmas parties. A baby grand piano sat in one corner, and a large chandelier danced lights on to its ebony surface.

'Oh look, we've got mail!' Oscar said, walking towards the hall table and holding up a brown cardboard tube. 'This looks interesting.'

Despite being out of the business, he still received fliers and posters advertising new machines or print techniques, but Belinda wasn't interested in whatever it was. Instead, she placed a pod into their coffee machine. These days she always needed caffeine or gin to give herself a jolt. She couldn't quite put her finger on the moment each day that she began to feel as if she was wading through sludgy water, but it always snuck up on her.

'Belinda, look at how sweet this is. It's a picture from

the children and Rachel,' Oscar said, following her into the kitchen.

She walked over to her husband's side, her heart beating faster with every step. Her eyes widened with delight as she took in the print.

Perhaps jolts came from other directions.

A verse was written on the top of the page by one of the children. Together they read it aloud.

Heartprints:
  While we may be apart, these prints come straight from our heart.
  We love you, Grandma Belinda and Grandpa Oscar.

Belinda felt quite overcome with emotion, surprising herself with the tears that fell. How long had it been since she felt anything, really, other than ambivalence for her life?

She felt her husband's eyes watching her. The subject of Rachel and the children had become a fraught one for them both. It was impossible to talk about them without talking about Lorcan. And that was something that Belinda refused to do.

There was a note from their daughter-in-law, Rachel, too. She sent love and once again extended an open invitation for them to visit Dublin as soon as she and the kids were home.

'Rachel is so good at staying in touch,' Oscar said.

Belinda watched him smooth his hand over the notepaper, back and forth. Receiving artwork like this was how she had imagined it would be for them as grandparents. Inclusive, loving, fun. It had been in the beginning with

Lorcan, Niamh and Olivia. And then it all went wrong, when Niamh was pregnant with Dylan. Belinda closed her eyes and pushed that thought from her mind.

'I'm so glad Lorcan had someone as lovely as Rachel, even if it was for such a short time,' she said. She gently took the notepaper from Oscar, but not before she gave him a reassuring squeeze.

'It's hard not to compare them, isn't it? Rachel and Niamh are so different,' Oscar said quietly.

They fell into a thoughtful silence and Belinda pondered her two daughters-in-law. She shivered. Did she regret not trying harder with Niamh? Yes, she supposed she did. Because the coldness between the two women had spread, like frostbite, to her relationship with Lorcan too. And no matter how hard she and Oscar tried after Niamh died, it had been impossible to thaw that frost.

Until Rachel came along, that was.

Their second daughter-in-law was like a ray of sunshine, who melted away their troubles. With a little more time, Belinda felt that Rachel might have given them all the second chance they needed to heal.

Until fate stepped in. Everything changed with one phone call, the words that no parent should ever receive.

At least once every day, Belinda relived Rachel's voice from the other end of the phone, barely able to get her words out, as she hysterically tried to explain that there had been an accident.

Belinda and Oscar had driven at breakneck speed to Beaumont Hospital in Dublin, neither saying a word during the journey, afraid that if they spoke, they would somehow invite heartbreak. A nurse brought them to a family room. And the implication of this gesture was not lost on Belinda. The family room was given for privacy, when the most horrific of news had to be delivered. Everyone kept saying how sorry they were, a heartfelt sentiment, but sorrow could not bring back the dead. Lorcan was gone, ripped from their lives before he'd had a chance to live.

Belinda and Oscar found their own separate ways to grieve. Oscar walked for miles every day. He would wake at dawn and disappear out the door, hoping that pounding the pavements would stop the pounding in his head and heart.

Meanwhile, Belinda felt the blood in her veins turn to ice and she welcomed the cold. She didn't want to feel anything ever again.

But now, as she ran her hand over her grandchildren's heartprints, she felt something give inside her.

And she welcomed it.

Maybe it was time for the thawing to begin.

SEVEN

Annie

Napier, Hawke's Bay

Joe stepped in closer to Annie's side and placed his hand gently under her elbow to give her some support as she walked up the slight incline towards their house. Her new hips were healing, but she still needed some help as she recovered from her operation. A fact that irritated her no end.

'Getting old is a privilege, but some days it's no fun,' Annie said, as she leaned on him gratefully.

'Ah, but getting old is lots of fun as long as we get to do it together,' Joe contradicted. 'And I don't think we do too bad for a pair of almost seventy-year-olds. We've a lot of life to live before we cark it.'

Annie paused and turned to kiss her husband. He was right; they were doing fine, painful joints notwithstanding. 'Once I totally get over this surgery, I'll feel like a young

59

woman of sixty again. You better rest up for that. Because there'll be no stopping me.'

'You'll always be thirty to me, Annie,' Joe said. As far as he was concerned, the only difference now to his then bride, was the colour of her hair. Her once dark brown tresses, always worn long, now had streaks of grey throughout.

'You old romantic. Don't ever change,' Annie said affectionately, words that she'd said to him many times in their marriage.

'They'll be on their way now,' Joe said, changing the subject and looking up to the sky.

'I can't bear it. The thought of waking up tomorrow morning, but not seeing Rachel or the kids . . .'

'I know, love. It's breaking my heart too. But we have to let her live her life, even if it's on the other side of the world.'

'The thing is, I'd accept her living over there if I thought she was happy. But I know my girl. She's lonely. And that's not right. She's only a young woman.'

'Rachel is strong. And while she might be lonely, she's not alone. She's a mother now, with two kids that she adores,' Joe said.

Annie put the key in their front door and together they made their way into the kitchen, where they spotted a long brown tube sitting on the kitchen table.

Intrigued, Joe picked it up as they sat down at their small Formica table. The same one that they'd eaten breakfast, lunch and dinner on since the Nineties. Joe used a small butter knife to aid the opening process and pulled out a rolled piece of cardboard paper.

'Hurry, here, give it to me,' Annie said, too impatient to wait for Joe to open the roll.

Later, Joe would go on to tell Rachel that Annie burst into tears when she saw the heartprints. Annie, however, would counter this and say that it was actually Joe who felt overcome with emotion. In reality, they both traced their hands over the multicoloured artwork, completely transfixed by it. Together they read the verse that Olivia had written so carefully on the top of the page.

Heartprints:
  While we have to now be apart, these prints come straight from our heart.
  We love you, Nanny Annie and Gramps Joe.

Annie grabbed her reading glasses and inspected the art more closely, 'Look, you can see that they've put their names in tiny writing on some of the prints too. This pink one here is signed by Dylan. And the green has Olivia's autograph.'

'He loves pink, our boy,' Joe said, his voice gruff with pride and emotion.

They looked up at the same time at the original heartprints that still hung in pride of place on their kitchen wall, all these years later.

'I'll have to make a frame for this heartprint now too.'

'Absolutely. And I guess I know where we'll go for our walk today – down to Cape Kidnappers bay to collect seashells for the frame.'

Joe knew what his wife was like. Annie wouldn't be happy until the frame was just right.

'Do you think she's going to be okay?' Annie asked.

It was a question that they'd all asked each other several

times over the past couple of years. And one that none of them had an answer to.

'She's come a long way since Lorcan's accident. I don't think she'll ever forget or ever get over losing him, but I think she has found a way to live without him. We have to be grateful that those children have been a blessing for her.'

'A blessing for all of us,' Annie agreed.

Joe reached over and clasped Annie's hands between his own. They sat like that for the longest time, quietly thinking about the heartbreaking goodbye they had made a few hours earlier, wishing that things could be different.

EIGHT

Sheila

Malahide, Dublin

'That'll be the post!' Adrian said to Sheila when the door-bell went. He got up from the kitchen table to answer the door, arriving back a few minutes later, a big grin on his face. 'It's Olivia's handwriting. Posted from New Zealand.'

'Oh, the little darlings. They could have brought it home with them as quick,' Sheila said.

Adrian flicked the cap of the tube off and pulled out the poster, then rolled the picture out flat on the table. They both reached for their glasses so they could have a good look and together, they read the words written by Olivia.

Heartprints:
  Sometimes you wipe our handprints away, but these heartprints are here to stay.
  We love you Nana and Grandad.

'What a lovely verse,' Adrian said. 'That's Olivia's print there. And this one is Dylan's. That must be Rachel's.'

Sheila couldn't answer because she was trying not to cry. She grabbed a nearby tea towel and began scrubbing the perfectly clean table with it.

'You big softie,' Adrian said.

Sheila turned the tea towel's attention to her tears, swiping them away quickly, 'Only tears of joy at such a beautiful gift. So colourful and one that we will both treasure forever.'

'Oh, we most surely will,' Adrian replied. 'Now, where will we put it?'

Sheila walked to the fridge to look for a spot in the already crowded 'art gallery' that had grown on the large American-style unit over the years. She began to rearrange the dozens of pictures the kids had drawn and gifted to them, held on to the grey door with magnets.

And then Sheila saw it.

Hidden behind a picture of an elephant drawn by Dylan was the first piece of 'grandparent artwork' she'd ever received, eight years ago. Sheila pulled it out. She could remember the day Niamh gave it to her like it was yesterday.

'Hey, Mam,' Niamh had called out as she walked into the kitchen, 'put the kettle on.'

'Not till I give this little one a cuddle,' Sheila said, carefully taking Olivia out from her car seat and cooing to her new granddaughter. She cradled her in her arms and rocked her gently. 'She gets more beautiful every day. And she's the living image of you, Niamh. It's like looking at you when you were that age.'

'It's gas, but Belinda insists she looks like Lorcan when he was a baby too.'

'She would!' Sheila said then sniffed loudly, just to make sure Niamh understood her annoyance at this tidbit of information.

'Olivia has a gift for you,' Niamh said and pulled a scroll from her changing bag.

Sheila unrolled it and gasped with delight when she saw Olivia's newborn baby hand and footprints stamped on to the page in bright yellow paint, as if they were sunbeams to a sun. And written underneath the prints, in her daughter's unmistakable, neat handwriting, were the words, 'You are always our sunshine. Happy Mother's Day, love Niamh and Olivia.'

That had been one of the happiest moments of Sheila's life. Seeing her daughter settled – married, in fact, and a mother herself – was a dream she'd hoped for, for many years. When Sheila had given birth to Niamh and her baby had been placed on her chest, the joy she'd felt was unlike anything she'd ever felt before. From that moment on, Sheila had never once stopped marvelling at the different stages of her daughter's life. And with each milestone Niamh passed, Sheila would think, *This is my favourite one*.

When Niamh became a mother herself, it had brought them even closer together, if that was possible. Niamh needed her mam again. She relied on Sheila to help with baby Olivia, to give advice and support as she got used to motherhood. Then when Niamh became pregnant with Dylan a few years later, she needed Sheila even more. This second pregnancy was harder for her daughter, and she was often melancholy.

Sheila worried that she wouldn't cope with two babies, and vowed that she would always be there to help Niamh. She would be a second mother to the children.

And then Dylan arrived. Walking into Niamh's hospital room, it was immediately clear that their daughter was happier than they'd seen her for a long time as she nursed her newborn son.

'I don't know what I was so worried about. I adore him as much as I do Olivia,' Niamh said.

'A gentleman's family,' Sheila replied with pride. 'A little boy and a girl. *Perfect.*'

When Lorcan went back to work a few days later, Niamh and the children spent their days at Sheila's. Three generations together. It was the happiest of times.

Until the universe decided it wanted payback for too much perfection.

Baby Dylan was only two months old when a pulmonary embolism stopped Niamh's heart. And she left them all behind, in broken fragments. They'd been trying ever since to glue themselves back together again.

As Sheila stared at the artwork the children had posted, her eyes began to play tricks on her. The heartprint split into two pieces.

Sheila felt panic rush at her, a familiar feeling these days. She would never understand how her family continued after Niamh died. She was convinced the pain of loss would surely stop all of their hearts. But life wasn't like that. They all placed one foot in front of the other. Her grandchildren needed her.

As did her son-in-law, Lorcan, who fell to pieces when Niamh died. Sheila's promise to be a second mother to the children was now more important than ever. Stepping into this role became her everything, her reason to continue living. It was her job to take care of Olivia and Dylan, for her daughter. And until she had no breath left in her body, she would continue putting one foot in front of the other for those kids.

They had been doing okay, getting through their heartbreak. Children were the great healers, smile-makers for them all.

But then Lorcan had to go ahead and ruin everything. Sheila sighed as she always did when she thought about Lorcan's betrayal of her daughter. At first, Sheila hoped his romance with the New Zealander would be a flash in the pan. She figured that no young woman wanted to take on two children, no matter how charming or good-looking their daddy was. And the girl was obviously close to her family, she spoke about them so lovingly, so surely she would want to go home eventually. But Rachel kept surprising them all. And much to Sheila's pain and frustration, the children fell in love with Lorcan's new girlfriend. Within moments of meeting her, all the children could talk about was Rachel.

Nothing could have prepared Sheila for the day Lorcan announced to them all that he had proposed and she'd said yes. Rachel flashed a large solitaire diamond with a smile as bright as the stone, and Olivia excitedly told them all that she was going to be a flower girl. But for Sheila, it felt like Lorcan and Rachel's happy news was tantamount to sticking a knife in her heart.

She wanted to be happy for them both, she really did. She always loved the hope and promise of weddings. But despite her best efforts, she felt resentment bubble its way up inside her. The final nail in the coffin on that difficult day came shortly after their announcement. As Rachel held Dylan in her arms, he called her 'Mama' for the first time.

Mama.

That word froze time and Sheila felt her heart shatter into tiny pieces. While everyone cooed and became emotional at Dylan's new word, Sheila cried for her daughter.

Niamh would never hear that word from her son.

Now, Sheila felt her heart harden as her eyes focused on the larger handprints on the page. Rachel was her . . . her what? What name do you give to the wife of your dead son-in-law? The stepmother of your grandchildren? There were no Hallmark cards for that. Sheila would never accept her as part of their family.

She placed the children's heartprints on the fridge, then, with a glance over her shoulder to make sure Adrian wasn't watching, she strategically placed Niamh's sunbeams right on top of Rachel's handprint.

NINE

Sheila

'The banner is up,' Adrian said, walking into the kitchen. 'Come have a look.'

Sheila could hear the excitement in his voice. They had both woken up giddy this morning, knowing that the children were coming home. It had been the longest month they'd ever endured. Sheila and Adrian had always held a spare key from the moment they'd helped Niamh and Lorcan move into their new home, only a few doors down from their own house. So today, they'd let themselves into Rachel's to get the place ready for the welcome home.

Sheila closed the fridge, now replenished with batch baked dinners, and turned to face her husband. She didn't expect or want any thanks for doing this; it was her pleasure to know that the children would have a square meal in their bellies every day. She'd spotted a lot of waffles and chicken goujons in the freezer. When her own two were kids, they had something like that once a month, as a special treat, but she knew for a fact that Niamh would never have allowed any frozen food near the kids. She'd insisted on making everything from scratch. Sheila recognized that not everyone could be a whizz in the kitchen, which is why she wanted to help Rachel.

She looked up at the large 'Welcome Home' banner now displayed above the fireplace in the family room. With its bright orange and green colours on a white background, it looked like a nod to Ireland's flag. But Sheila had chosen the colours specifically because they were the children's favourites.

'That looks perfect. Well done,' she said. She felt a rush of love for her husband and gave him a quick peck on the cheek.

'Shouldn't be too much longer now,' Adrian said, grabbing her into his arms and taking her for a quick waltz around the coffee table, making Sheila giggle as they spun about. 'Jack texted thirty minutes ago that they were in the car, ready for the off.'

'I know I should be used to him driving, but I still get jittery when he's out and about. I'll be glad when he arrives.'

'He's a thirty-year-old man and has been driving for years. We can't hold him back, and either way, he wouldn't let us,' Adrian said.

'I know I'm being irrational, but I'm worried he might turn around to the kids and get distracted . . .'

'Sheila, you worry too much. Jack is more than capable of telling them all to sit still.'

While Adrian might be right, knowing you shouldn't

worry about something and managing not to do it were two entirely different beasts.

Jack was partially deaf. He'd been born prematurely at twenty-eight weeks. Sheila and Adrian had prayed constantly as he fought for his life in those early weeks in the Special Care Unit of the Rotunda Hospital, but Jack had surprised everyone, getting stronger week by week. And now, between his speech therapy sessions and his hearing aid, coupled with his lip-reading skills, most people often were surprised to discover that he was partially deaf at all. It was a source of great pride for Sheila that Jack was unwilling to let anything stop him from living life on his own terms.

'I wonder if Rachel will be upset,' she said, changing the subject. 'It must have been hard for her to say goodbye to her mum and dad.'

Adrian nodded. 'They're a close lot, from all I've gathered. There's no doubt Rachel must be feeling it. We'll have to be extra kind to her.' He gave his wife a pointed look.

'Would you give over. I'm always kind to Rachel. She's overly sensitive, that's all. Always taking me up wrong, when any fool can see I'm trying to help.'

'I know, love. Your heart is in the right place; no one can doubt that. But you can be a little blunt,' Adrian said, ever the diplomat.

He loved his wife, but over forty years of marriage opened your eyes to all sides of a person – the good and the sometimes not so good.

A car pulled into the driveway and they both yelped with delight, running to the front door and opening it wide.

'Nana and Grandad!' Olivia and Dylan both cried, charging towards them.

Sheila wasn't one for public displays of affection, but just this once, she didn't give a damn who was rubber-necking and watching along the Yellow Walls Road.

'Look at how tall you are,' she said, measuring Olivia's head against her arm. 'Almost up to my shoulder now.'

'And both of you as brown as berries!' Adrian said. 'Rained every second day here.'

Rachel moved forward, reminding them of her presence. 'Hello, Sheila and Adrian. It's good to see you.'

'Sorry, love, got sidetracked by these two beauties. Hello, hello!' Adrian cried, giving her a warm hug.

Then Sheila leaned in to give Rachel one of their air hugs. They'd worked it to perfection – no part of their bodies actually touched. It was a perfunctory gesture, that was all.

'You've been baking,' Rachel said, sniffing the air. 'I hope you haven't gone to any trouble, Sheila.'

'It's no trouble to spoil my grandchildren,' Sheila said.

'Nor to spoil you either, of course, Rachel,' Adrian added.

Sheila turned away from what she assumed was another pointed look from her husband.

She did catch Jack winking conspiratorially at Rachel, though. There was a lot in that wink. Mostly, it said, 'Don't mind Mam.'

'You made good time,' Adrian said, as everyone bundled into the house.

'I'll put the kettle on. Let's have a cup of tea and hot chocolate for you two; then you can tell us all about your holiday. I've dinner made for later,' Sheila said.

'I'm sorry, I don't think we'll last till dinner, Sheila. We've been through several time zones and we're all hanging on by a thread! We need to catch up on some sleep soon,' Rachel said, smiling brightly.

'You'll regret it if you go to bed now. Mark my words. Stay up until at least eight p.m., and then you'll sleep all the way through,' Sheila said firmly.

'If we can manage to do that, it would be great. But I'm not sure we'll last that long,' Rachel said.

Sheila watched the kids stifle yawns as if to punctuate Rachel's point. The poor pets did look tired. But they had to be hungry too. They always were.

'I made lasagne, the kids' favourite. And baked my own garlic bread, from scratch.' Sheila knew that her voice now had a tinny edge. She could feel Adrian's eyes on her, berating her.

'They can have that tomorrow if they don't have it today,' Jack said diplomatically.

'Great idea. And I tell you what. I'd love that cup of tea you mentioned,' Rachel said.

'Can we give Nana Sheila, Grandad and Uncle Jack their presents?' Olivia asked.

'Of course we can,' Rachel said.

While Rachel opened a suitcase to retrieve the gifts, Sheila searched the cupboard for Niamh's old stainless-steel teapot. The pretty china pot that Rachel used looked great but was impractical in reality, and leaked every time you poured yourself a cup. She also sliced her famous chocolate fudge cake, putting a plate down in front of Dylan and Olivia. And, as if proving Sheila's point, when Dylan and Olivia tucked into a slice of the gooey cake, they found a second wind quick enough. Sheila and Adrian smiled indulgently at them as they bounced up and down, hyper with sugar and excitement.

'I chose this for you myself!' Olivia handed the first bag to Sheila.

Sheila opened the bag and pulled out a green necklace. She held it up and examined it, smiling at its beauty.

'It's a jade gemstone. And the symbol is a Maori twist,' Rachel explained.

'It means infinity. Not like in Marvel films. But like forever. The shopman said it was for someone special to show them that you have a forever relationship. Like we do, Nana,' Olivia added.

Tears sprang to Sheila's eyes. She pulled her grandchildren in to her for a big hug. They were such thoughtful children; she was fortunate to have them.

'Do you like it?' Dylan asked, looking worried at his grandmother's tears.

'I love it. The best present I've ever had,' Sheila declared.

'She always cries when she's happy, remember,' Olivia told him.

'Okay, now it's Grandad's turn!' Dylan said, handing a bag to him. 'We went to this huge aquarium.'

'It's called the National Aquarium of New Zealand,' Olivia butted in.

'Yeah, that,' Dylan said. 'And it had huge fish. The biggest fish in the world. They had the hugest sharks you've ever seen!'

'Like the aquarium I brought you both to a while back, the one in Bray,' Adrian said.

The children both shook their heads firmly.

'No, Grandad,' Dylan countered. 'That's really lame compared to this one. This one had real sharks. And there was an underwater tunnel that went on for miles.' He did his best imitation of a shark about to attack, using his arms as a mouth.

'Well, that sounds very exciting,' Adrian agreed, grabbing hold of Dylan around his waist and making him squeal with delight as he tickled him. 'Now did someone say something about a present?'

He opened the gift bag Dylan handed him and pulled out a black tee-shirt. It had a giant cartoon shark on it, with 'Grandad Shark, Doo, Doo, Doo', written underneath.

'Not this song again . . .' Adrian groaned, pretending to be outraged.

Dylan and Olivia began to sing the song and with every dramatic 'no!' their grandad screamed, they laughed harder. Amid the giggles, he pulled his jumper off and put the tee-shirt on over his blue checked shirt, declaring it to be a perfect fit.

When they calmed down, Olivia turned to Jack. 'You know your favourite movie?'

Jack answered without hesitation. 'Yeah, *Lord of the Rings.*'

Before Olivia had a chance to continue, Dylan shouted, 'We went there! We went to the Hobbits' village!'

'I'm telling the story. Tell him, Mom, I said I was doing Uncle Jack's gift.'

'Let Olivia talk,' Rachel said, with a weary tone.

'We went to the Shire,' Olivia said. 'Honestly, Uncle Jack, we really saw it. All of those tiny houses on the grassy hill. And we had a banquet there too.'

'They didn't have any nuggets and the sausages tasted funny,' Dylan complained.

'Wow! I'm so jealous that you've been to the Shire,' Jack said warmly to the kids.

'We thought of you all the time we were there, I promise you. I hope you like the gift,' Rachel joined in.

Jack opened his large gift bag, his eyes widening in surprise when it revealed a *Lord of the Rings* themed chess set.

'Lorcan told me once that you used to play chess with Niamh when you were kids. He said Niamh always loved playing with you, that there was no need for anyone to speak in a chess game, so you were both on the same page. I thought you might like to teach Olivia and Dylan. Maybe that way you can continue the tradition on with them? It might be nice that the thing that was Niamh's and yours could be theirs too?' A flush of colour stained Rachel's cheeks as everyone stared at her.

Sheila heard a strangled sound escape her before she could stop it. No matter how much time had passed, Niamh's death would always be a devastating subject for her family.

Olivia added, 'Mom said that our mammy in heaven was so good at playing chess that she always beat you.'

Sheila bit back a further sob and Adrian placed a hand of comfort on her knee.

'Don't you like it, Uncle Jack?' Dylan asked, noting that everyone had gone suspiciously quiet.

Jack's eyes filled with tears, but he blinked them away, smiling brightly at them all. He leaned over and clasped Rachel's hand for a moment. 'Thank you. This is very special. I will treasure it forever.' Then he turned to the children and said, 'Your mammy in heaven *did* beat me at chess. She was much better at chess than I ever was.

It was rare that I managed to win. And somehow, I bet both of you will be as good as her too. You have to promise me that you'll let your old uncle win the odd time.'

'Never!' Dylan screamed, jumping on top of him for an impromptu wrestling match, followed by Olivia too.

As Sheila watched them all, so easy in each other's company, she caught Rachel's eye.

Sheila smiled at her, but there was a sharpness behind it. If she'd been asked to articulate why, she couldn't have. But somehow Rachel had messed up once again.

TEN

Rachel

Balfe Street, Dublin

Rachel ran into Balfes brasserie and scanned the tables to see if Lorcan's cousin Ronan had arrived. He was their family lawyer, but he also kept in touch every month or so, checking in on her with a kind text. And every now and then they had a coffee. She hated to keep him waiting but she always seemed to be late these days. No matter how hard she tried to organize her day, there were never enough hours to complete her ever-growing to-do list. She heard a shout across the room and spied him waving at her.

'Good to see you, Rach. You're a sight for sore eyes. Looking great!' Ronan said, as she took her face mask off.

'Don't be using your lines on me, Ronan Bradley, you old charmer,' Rachel teased as she sat down. 'It's been a while; how have you been?'

'No lies, all truth. I've been crazy busy, you know yourself. But life is all good, I've no complaints. How was the holiday? You obviously had sunshine. I feel pasty beside you.'

'We were on the beach most days, it was glorious. Then we came home and have been freezing our asses off ever since. I can feel the tan fading every day.'

A waitress approached the table and they ordered coffees.

'It must have been great to see your parents and sister?' Ronan asked as she walked away.

'It was incredible. I didn't realize how much I'd missed them until I walked through the arrivals hall and saw them standing there together. Claudia had made this over-the-top big banner that she and her fella Howard were holding up. Mortified me. But it was also kind of lovely. And my parents spoiled the kids rotten; it's fair to say they are besotted with them. Which meant I got a marvellous rest too. The first one I've truly had since Lorcan died.'

'I thought your . . . sorry, what do I call the Butlers?' Ronan asked, shrugging.

'I usually refer to them as my in-laws, even though they were Lorcan's, not mine.'

'Maybe out-laws is a better name for them,' he joked.

Rachel spluttered her cappuccino all over the table in front of her. 'Yes!'

'I thought the out-laws were hands-on with the kids. Has that changed?'

Rachel made a face. 'Too hands-on. So much so that I never feel like I can relax. Sheila's always watching me, judging me. Adrian isn't as bad, I suppose.'

'Can you tell them to back off?'

'I suppose I could, but I haven't dared to. While we

79

were in New Zealand, she came in and rearranged my kitchen and the kids' closets. I can't find a bloody thing any more. But she did buy lots of new clothes for them, which is nice of her.'

'My mother always used to say that you should choose your battles. Maybe you're right to suck it up.'

'Your mother was a wise one. I'll remember that. Oh, I nearly forgot; I've got something for you too!' Rachel grabbed a small brown bag from her handbag. 'A souvenir I thought you'd like.'

As Ronan opened the bag, she explained, 'It's a stubbie holder.'

'That's class. Love it. Not sure what I'll do with it, mind you . . .' Ronan said, admiring the beer can holder with a picture of a sheep wearing sunglasses.

'The whole point of souvenirs is that they are unnecessary gifts that we don't really want,' Rachel replied, laughing.

They both took a sip of coffee, then Ronan leaned down to retrieve a folder from his briefcase.

'Hey, what's up? You look very serious all of a sudden,' Rachel said.

'When I called and asked to meet you for a coffee, it wasn't just for a catch-up. I'm here with my lawyer hat on too. There's something you need to see.' Ronan handed the folder to her, without saying a word. Rachel opened it up and gasped, cradling a certificate in her hands. Her stomach started to flip in nervous excitement.

'I'm not sure I trust my eyes that this is finally here,' she said quietly as she stared at the paper in disbelief.

Ronan reached over and pinched her arm lightly. 'Do you feel that?'

'Ow, yes!'

'Well, there's your answer. If you felt that pinch, this must be real.'

Rachel beamed a smile through tear-filled eyes. 'I wish Lorcan was here to see this,' she said eventually.

'Me too. He would be so happy right now.'

Rachel nodded, swallowing the lump in her throat. 'It's official then?'

'Yes, it's official. You are Olivia and Dylan's mother now.'

Rachel couldn't take her eyes off the piece of paper that weighed so little but meant so much. Her eyes blurred and she caught a sob before it escaped. But as fast as she wiped her cheeks, fresh tears arrived. She looked across the table to Ronan and apologized for her emotion.

He brushed it aside, handing her a napkin. 'You'll set me off in a minute. And that's a no-no for me. I've a reputation as a hardened lawyer to uphold!'

Rachel stared at her and Lorcan's signatures, side by side on the paperwork, feeling awe and wonder that this moment had finally come.

'You have been the kids' mom for years in every way that matters. This sets it in legal stone, that's all. And Rachel, I'm not into God and heaven and all that jazz, but if I did believe in something bigger than us here, I'd put my money on the fact that Lorcan is watching over you right now. This was one of the last things he did before he died. You know, I used to watch you both from the sidelines and I'd think: couple goals.'

Rachel raised an eyebrow. 'You have couple goals? And here I thought that you were a confirmed bachelor.'

'Guilty as charged. But that doesn't mean that I can't recognize true love when I see it.'

They clinked water glasses to toast the comment.

'I cannot wait to tell the kids about this. I need to find the right way to do it.'

'If Lorcan were here, what would he do?'

'He'd throw a party,' Rachel said confidently. She could see him now, plotting and planning one excitedly.

'Then that's your answer,' Ronan responded. 'You three deserve something good to celebrate. Tell you what, if you get some cake, I might even gatecrash.'

'I'd love that. It would be nice for the kids to have someone from their dad's side of the family there. I keep asking Belinda and Oscar to visit, but they never take me up on the offer. Do you think they might come if I ask them again?'

'Well, I'd like to see the kids again. I've not seen them since your wedding, which is my bad! As for Belinda and Oscar, it's worth a shot. I called in to see them a few weeks ago, actually, as I had a meeting up in Belfast. Uncle Oscar was his usual laid-back self, but Aunty Belinda was quiet. She's still grieving. But I do know one thing, they appreciate the kindness you've given them. They showed me the kids' artwork. It's been framed, professionally, with a small silver plaque with all your names and the date engraved on it.'

'Wow! Mom made a frame out of seashells for the one we sent them, Sheila and Adrian have theirs on their fridge, and our own one is framed in a Dealz one forty-nine-euro bargain. I'm happy that they enjoyed the gift, though. They sent a beautiful thank you note.'

'That print is priceless to them. They have a large collection of art in their home, you know, but I've never seen them showcase anything with as much enthusiasm as your gift. Ask them to the party. They might surprise you and come along.'

'Do you know what? I've never been to their house. They visited us a couple of times to see the children, but Lorcan always pushed against us going up to Belfast to visit them. I've always felt like I'm missing a piece of a puzzle with them all. He rarely spoke about Belinda and Oscar. I wish I understood more.' Rachel watched Ronan closely, but he seemed puzzled by the comment.

'Aunty Belinda and Uncle Oscar didn't get on with Niamh. I don't know all the ins and outs of it. Doesn't matter much now, anyhow.' He looked away awkwardly.

'No, I don't suppose it does,' Rachel said. 'It's just whenever we were in their company, they all seemed to walk around on eggshells. It was weird. But maybe them not getting on with Niamh was what I picked up on.'

'I probably got it wrong about that,' Ronan said. 'And as for Lorcan, don't lose sleep over his relationship with his parents either. He had it sweet when he was a kid. They doted on him. Whatever he wanted, he got. I'm still not over his fourteenth birthday when he got his own quad bike. He was never off that thing. Don't feel sorry for him, is all I'm saying. Lorcan was loved.'

'When he was in New Zealand for that summer during uni, he used to sit in the cafe I worked at, writing letters to them both. And back then he spoke with so much love about them. But I haven't imagined the fact that something changed between them by the time we reconnected.'

'I'm sorry I can't help more. Lorcan and I weren't exactly confidants. Typical blokes – when we met up at Christmas and such, we never talked about the important stuff. Just women, sport, booze.'

'When I asked him about it all, he always used to change the subject,' Rachel said. 'I feel it's a shame for everyone, because Belinda and Oscar clearly adore the children, sending gifts and writing cards to them. It's so bloody complicated.'

'Families usually are,' Ronan agreed. 'And it got all the more complicated for Lorcan after he married you. He took a lot of flak from the Butlers for that.'

'Lorcan always hoped that Sheila and Adrian would eventually come around and get used to his marriage to me.'

'He did nothing wrong,' Ronan said. 'His wife died and he met someone new. That's life for you. None of us can dictate who we fall in love with.' He made a face as his phone buzzed. 'Sorry, I have to take this call. Work.'

Rachel was happy to take a moment to gather her thoughts. This was a big moment for her. But Lorcan should be here to share it with her. She looked out on to the cobbled street as a young couple walked past the cafe, swinging a child between them. The sun bounced off the toddler's curly blonde locks and she squealed with delight as she flew into the air. Rachel felt a stab of pain as she watched them. Loss, jealousy, anger.

She had never felt the need to formally adopt the kids – until Lorcan brought the subject up, on a bright sunny day, just like today. And once he did, it felt like the most necessary thing in the world.

ELEVEN

Rachel

Balfe Street, Dublin

Rachel had never dreamed that she'd fall in love with a man who came with a ready-made family. It made her question everything about herself and the life she'd thought she was going to have. But life had a way of surprising you when you least expected it. She loved Lorcan so much, it felt only natural that she'd love his children too. Before they married, they'd had the baby talk, and Rachel had shared that she didn't want to have a baby of her own. Not immediately, and maybe not ever. Lorcan had understood and agreed that, either way, it was best to leave it for a while. Let the children get used to their new family dynamic before introducing another change.

Then with every passing day, Rachel forgot that Olivia and Dylan weren't hers from the beginning, and the need for a baby of her own became even less critical. In fact,

Lorcan stopped bringing it up. And Rachel assumed he'd changed his mind about extending the family.

Now, if she closed her eyes, she could almost feel the warmth of Lorcan's hand holding hers as they walked along the Malahide estuary the day he brought up the topic again. Olivia held Dylan's hand a few steps ahead of them, and they were both jumping in muddy puddles. The crazy thing was, when he'd broached the subject again, she'd felt a bubble of excitement spring up. With a shock, she'd realized that the idea of having a baby, a little brother or sister for Olivia and Dylan, made her happy, not scared.

'Let's have a baby,' Lorcan blurted out.

Rachel stopped in her tracks, startled by her husband's words. They had come from nowhere, or at least it felt that way to Rachel.

'I mean it, Rae. You are an incredible mother. Patient, kind, loving, fun . . . the children are so lucky to have you in their lives. It's a joy watching you parent them. You do it far better than I ever could.'

'That's not true. You are a wonderful father!'

'Well, let's agree that we're both amazing then. Which is why I think my idea to have a baby is genius.'

Rachel stared at him, genuinely shocked by his suggestion.

'What's brought this on?' she asked.

'I was in the attic the other day and spotted Dylan's old crib and pram, so I started to wonder if perhaps we should donate them to charity. But as soon as I posed the question to myself, I knew the answer. I want more children, Rae – with you.'

'I think I might want the same,' Rachel whispered.

Despite her previous uncertainty, they talked about little else for the rest of the day, both feeling excited and a little nervous for a possible new future.

Later that night, as they lay side by side on their bed holding hands, Rachel shared her worries about the impact a new baby might have on their happy family unit.

'I don't want them to feel that a baby would change how I feel about them. I want them to know that as far as I'm concerned, I'm not their stepmother – I'm their mom.'

'You show them that every day, Rachel,' Lorcan replied. 'I've never seen a mother more devoted to their children than you. As it happens, I've been thinking about something else for a little while now too. I think it's time you adopted the children. Make it official.'

Rachel's heart skipped several beats.

When she didn't respond immediately, Lorcan turned towards her, holding her hands between his own. 'That was clumsy. I can do better than that.' He paused, grinning. 'Rachel Bradley, will you adopt Olivia and Dylan?'

Rachel couldn't speak for a few moments. Then the tears came thick and fast.

'Rachel? Don't cry, darling.' Worry made Lorcan's forehead furrow.

Eventually, Rachel found her voice and screamed, 'Yes!'

'I don't think you were that enthusiastic when I proposed,' Lorcan joked, delightedly kissing his wife to seal the deal.

The smile left Rachel's face for a moment. 'Do you think Niamh would mind?' she asked sombrely.

Tears filled Lorcan's eyes as he thought about Niamh. He took a moment to respond, speaking softly, 'Niamh loved the kids. I'd like to think that she'd want the children to grow up with another mother's love as she's not here to give it them herself, and that she'd want them to feel safe *and secure. I cannot think of a better way to show them that. And I know that if something happened to me, I'd want the children to have someone else in their life to give them what I no longer could.'*

When he saw the look of worry that filled Rachel's face, he added, 'Nothing is ever going to happen to me though. I'm titanium.' He tapped his head with a wink.

'My hard man!' Rachel said, laughing.

The next day, they gathered the children on the sofa between them. Lorcan gently brought up the subject of their mammy in heaven. Rachel watched their faces as Lorcan spoke. Some days, they were more receptive to talking about Niamh than others. They'd grieved for her in different ways, trying to make sense of her death as much as was possible for young children.

'When I married Rachel, she didn't just become my wife, she became your mom too,' Lorcan explained.

Dylan snuggled in closer to Rachel at Lorcan's words, trying to understand.

'And it's been my greatest joy, becoming your mother,' Rachel added to them both. 'I hope you know that.'

'It's my greatest joy that you are my mother,' Dylan said, copying his mom's serious tone, making them all laugh.

'Mine too,' Olivia insisted, trying to elbow her way in between Dylan and Rachel.

'Do you know what adoption is, kids?' Lorcan asked, placing Dylan on his lap so Olivia could cuddle Rachel.

Olivia answered, 'It's for children who don't have a mammy and daddy. They get adopted by new parents. Remember that movie, Annie, that we saw at Nana and Grandad's last week, Dylan? Daddy Warbucks adopted Annie at the end of the movie.'

'*I don't remember it. Can we watch it again?*' Dylan asked.

'*In a minute, son, sure,*' Lorcan said. '*But before that, I've a question for you. How would you like it if Rachel adopted you both, so that she would officially be your mom?*'

'*But she is our mom already,*' Dylan said, looking at his father as if he were a complete idiot.

'*Yes, she is. But this way, she would be your mom in the eyes of the law too.*'

'*There is nothing in the world that would make me happier,*' Rachel added.

'*If you adopt us, does that mean you can never leave us?*' Olivia asked.

'*I would never leave you, Olivia, with or without a piece of paper that says I am your mother. But yes, if I adopt you, then I can never leave.*'

'*Then I want you to adopt us,*' Olivia said, snuggling herself deep into Rachel's arms.

'*Me too,*' Dylan said, moving from his daddy's lap into Rachel's too. Olivia made room for him, putting her arm around his shoulders.

'I'm sorry about that. Some calls I can't dodge,' Ronan said, making Rachel jump when he joined her again at their table.

'I was miles away, daydreaming,' she said.

'Thinking about Lorcan again, more like.'

When Rachel nodded, he continued, 'You always have a look on your face when you do. Has it got any easier?'

'It *has* gotten easier, actually. Getting through the first of all the big occasions – birthdays, Christmas, his anniversary –

was the hardest part. Now, we've gotten used to living with the pain of loss. And I'm grateful for all my memories. I like losing myself in them; it keeps him alive for me. My biggest fear is that one day I'll wake up and I'll have forgotten what he looked like.'

'That will never happen with Olivia around. She's so like her daddy.'

'True. But then I look at Dylan and he has the same infectious personality, full of fun. It takes my breath away.'

'You know that you have me in your corner any time you need me. Now that Lorcan is gone, I can't help but feel protective of you and the kids. You call me any time. Remember that.'

'You are a good friend, Ronan. One of the few I have here, so I appreciate your support.'

'Ah, you're good company. It's no hardship. If the out-laws get too rowdy, I'll sort them out for you.'

Rachel shivered, a feeling of foreboding creeping over her. 'I hope Sheila takes the adoption news well. A few weeks after Lorcan's funeral, she suggested that I should move back to New Zealand. Leave the children with her and Adrian. And she reassured me that nobody would think any less of me for doing so.'

'You are kidding me! That's shocking.'

'I know. Sheila doesn't seem to get that I'd never go anywhere without the kids. They are *my* children, with or without this piece of paper to confirm it,' Rachel said, waving the certificate in front of them both.

'Of course they are. But I feel happier that you have made it official now. Remember the hassle you had with the children's passports when planning your trip to New Zealand, because you weren't their official mother? All of that becomes standard family administration now that you have this document. It's a clarifier. So if you get a notion to emigrate, off you go!' he joked.

Rachel threw him a look of surprise. 'Have you been talking to my sister?' Her words came out in a high-pitched squeal. She cleared her throat, speaking in her normal voice again. 'It's just so odd that you mentioned emigrating. Claudia was banging on about me moving home to Hawke's Bay the whole time I was in New Zealand. This beautiful villa that I loved as a kid has gone on to the market. It's in a great neighbourhood, overlooking the bay, with excellent schools nearby. And it's only a short bike ride to my parents' house. If I were on my own, I'd buy it in the morning.'

Ronan seemed stunned into silence, his eyebrows raised in cartoon-like surprise. 'Wow, I had no idea you were actually thinking about moving. I'd miss you.'

'Don't worry, I'm not going anywhere,' Rachel explained hastily. 'Sure, while I was there it was impossible not to daydream of going back and I got carried away with the notion for a few days. But I'm back to reality now. And this is my home.'

'New Zealand's a great country. I'd say a lot of people would queue up to relocate there.'

Rachel nodded her agreement. 'Lorcan and I spoke about relocating there one day too, actually. A daydream that we thought we might make come true.'

'I never knew that. But it doesn't surprise me either. Lorcan always spoke about New Zealand in glowing terms. What's stopping you? The kids?'

'No, funnily enough, I think they'd be happy to go. Dylan is so young; he'd go anywhere I would. And Olivia is . . .

she's displaced, that's the best word I can think of. A change, a new beginning if you like, would be good for her.' Rachel paused, considering her thoughts. 'But when we got home, I saw how excited Sheila and Adrian were to see the kids. Any notions of emigrating evaporated. I couldn't take the children away from them, it would be cruel. And despite what some might think, I'm not an evil stepmother.'

They both laughed. It felt good to poke fun at herself and her situation with a friendly companion.

'I hope you're not just staying for the kids. You have friends here too, right?' Ronan asked.

Again, Rachel paused, wondering how much to confess. 'Not really. Lorc and I had such a whirlwind romance, getting married within a year of reconnecting again, that I didn't get a chance to really make my own friendships here in Ireland. And to be honest, I never felt lonely when Lorcan was alive. He wasn't just my husband, he was my best friend too. I don't think I can put into words how much I miss our life together. But lately, most of all, I've realized how much I miss his friendship.' She closed her eyes as she made her final admission, 'There are times I feel quite alone here.'

'I'm so sorry to hear this. I truly am,' Ronan looked as though he didn't know what else to say.

'Most of the other moms I see at the school gates were friends with Niamh, and they seem to distrust me. The wicked stepmother syndrome again. I'm telling you, Disney has a lot to answer to! I've tried to fit in, but I seem to be on the outside of the WhatsApp groups. I'll always be the new wife who dared to step into Niamh's shoes. Maybe if we didn't live so close to Niamh's family, it might be easier for me. They are literally down the street, a few minutes' walk away. And without Lorcan by my side, it can feel like I'm surrounded by a pack of wolves. Circling me, looking for a sign of weakness so that they can pounce on me and finish me off.' Rachel felt a blush rise from her neck upwards. She'd shared way more than she'd intended.

Ronan looked sympathetic. 'Here's something to ponder,' he said slowly. 'You could always put some distance between you and the out-laws without leaving the country. Dublin is a big place.'

Rachel had never considered that before. 'That's not a bad suggestion, actually,' she said, mulling the idea over in her mind.

'I have my moments,' Ronan said with a smile, some of the tension lifting from their conversation.

'You do, and I'm sorry to throw all of this at you. You are my lawyer, not my counsellor.'

'Well, we are friends too. And the kids are family, I should do more with them than I do. I know I was half-joking about gatecrashing your party, but I could come. I make a mean whiskey sour. I'll bring all the ingredients. That way, if the wolves come out, I'll help you ward them off.'

Rachel almost clapped her hands, she was so delighted to hear this.

'But for now, I do have to go. I've another client coming to see me at four and I need to look at the case file before then. Text me the details of the big party and I promise I'll be there. I'll talk to Belinda and Oscar too. See if I can persuade them to drive down.'

They stood up, and then Ronan muttered a 'to hell with it' and pulled her in for a hug. As he leaned in to her, he whispered into her hair, 'You're not alone, Rachel. I promise you.'

TWELVE

Sheila

Malahide, Dublin

Most people live for Fridays. Thank Crunchie and all that. But for Sheila, her favourite day of the week was everyone else's hump day, Wednesday. It was the day the kids were hers. And as they were still on school holidays, she had them all day, not just for a few hours in the afternoon.

Sheila used to have Dylan while Olivia was in school, too, but Rachel insisted that he start nursery when he was three years old. She said it was for socialization reasons. In Sheila's day, kids socialized at home and were all the better for it. Proof of point, as a consequence of Rachel's notions, Dylan had one bug after another. That's what socialization in a sandpit did for you.

Sheila had to concede though that little Dylan thrived in the environment there, making friends easily, as was

94

his way. He reminded her of Jack a lot. He had that ease about him that made everyone fall in love with him. It didn't matter one bit that Jack was partially deaf; he fitted in everywhere he went. A lot like Adrian too, when she thought about it.

Olivia was more like Niamh, pricklier and emotional, but with the softest, kindest, gentlest heart underneath.

As Sheila wiped the last of the breakfast dishes, her thoughts drifted to the children. Adrian had installed a dishwasher in their kitchen nearly ten years ago, but she never used it. It was handy at Christmas for storage, she supposed. Sheila would put tins of sweets and biscuits in there. Things that she didn't want the children to sniff out. Quite a clever spot to hide stuff as it happened. She never understood why more people didn't do the same.

Sheila heard the muffled footsteps of Adrian and Jack above her, getting ready to go into their hardware store to open up for the day. The past couple of years had been tough on the family business. Closed more than open, it felt like, with lockdowns every few months. Mind you, if it hadn't been for Jack and his quick thinking, they'd have gone bankrupt a long time ago. When Jack insisted on moving the business online, it had terrified Adrian and Sheila initially. What did they know about running a hardware store over the internet? They both knew that the secret to their family-run business was the personal touch. Customers knew that they could count on Adrian and Jack – and Sheila too – to answer their DIY questions.

If it hadn't been for Sheila, Boxer Murphy would have painted his whole house in a bathroom emulsion white paint. Sheila shuddered, thinking about the shine he'd have had to live with in the living room, without her tactful guidance. Instead she had guided him towards a lovely shade of dove grey, and now everyone who visited complimented him on his choice. And Sheila liked to think that his house makeover, plus the few little bits she'd persuaded him to add to each room, lampshades, light fittings, helped his new romance too. She didn't care what anyone said; a woman liked a man to keep a well-presented home. And his new girlfriend Mary was up at his house morning, noon and night, from what she'd heard. And good luck to them. Sheila loved a little bit of romance. There was someone for everyone if you kept your eyes and heart open. She truly believed that.

Then there was Mrs Donnelly. She came in looking for nails one day and would have gone home with a box of wall plugs if it hadn't been for Jack, taking the time to understand what she really needed. And bless him, Jack had gone over to her house himself. Her bookshelves, passed on from her father, had collapsed under the weight of books she'd collected. But he'd fixed the shelves up for her like they were new. Jack had saved more than a bit of wood that day.

While Sheila loved working in their hardware store, she would happily give it up if she could take care of the kids every day – as Niamh had wanted her to when she went back to work after her maternity leave. But that all changed when Niamh . . . Sheila shook her head to stop the thought from completing. When Niamh 'left' them. Sheila knew in her heart of hearts that Niamh still wanted her to have the children. More so now that she was gone.

It wasn't an exaggeration to say that taking care of her grandchildren had saved Sheila and Adrian's life, especially in the initial few months after Niamh's death. Olivia and

Dylan gave her a reason to get up every day and not throw herself into a grave beside her darling daughter. Sheila had even suggested to Lorcan that he sell up and move into their home. They lived five minutes' walk from each other anyhow. He'd considered it for a while, but when he began to come out the other side of his grief, any suggestion of him moving in disappeared.

The children adapted to their new normal with surprising ease. Olivia missed her mammy, of course she did, but baby Dylan never really knew Niamh. And that in itself caused Sheila so much pain. Dylan would never understand the love Niamh had for him, the plans and hopes she had for both her children. Listening to people refer to Niamh as the 'mammy in heaven' made her blood boil. Niamh was the children's mother, full stop! All Rachel would ever be was a stepmother. She wasn't their blood.

Every night, before Sheila went to sleep, she vowed that she would ensure the children never forgot Niamh.

Of course, Sheila wasn't naive. She'd seen the way a few of the single mothers had eyed Lorcan up at the Christmas tree lighting in the village a few years back. He became fair game. Adrian told her that they should be ready for the day that Lorcan moved on. He was young, they couldn't expect him to stay alone forever. But Sheila had felt great sadness at Adrian's observation. Sadness for her daughter and her happy family broken.

As it happened, Niamh was hardly cold in the ground when Lorcan met Rachel. She had loved her son-in-law, but now, every time she saw him look at Rachel adoringly, it felt like an insult to the memory of Niamh. Had he even loved Niamh in the first place? How could he forget her so quickly? And now, she was doubly angry with him.

Because not only had he married Rachel and brought her into all of their lives; he'd gone and died himself, leaving a hot mess behind him.

Sheila had to put down the pile of side plates she was carrying, her hands were shaking so much.

'You're muttering to yourself again, sure sign of madness,' Adrian said, walking back into the room.

'I was just thinking that we could bring up the subject of us taking the kids every day after school again. What do you think? We could drop them to school for Rachel, or collect them every afternoon,' Sheila said.

'It would give her more time for her online clothing malarkey, although she does always say that she can work around the kids' schedules,' Adrian said, considering his wife's suggestion. 'Whist, that's a car I hear pulling up. It must be Rachel arriving with the kids. Let's think about what we should say a little more. Say nothing for now. And maybe you should rearrange your face into a less mutinous one too.'

He kissed her cheek lightly, to soften the blow of his words, then walked out to open the door.

The kids bounced into the house as they always did, full of chatter and love and light. Within seconds of their arrival, any trace of Sheila's bad mood had melted away like snowflakes on a warm day. It was impossible to be annoyed about life when you felt the warm hugs of grand-children.

'Hi Sheila,' Rachel said, carrying two small rucksacks in her hands.

'What did I tell you about bringing over snacks . . .' Sheila said, a little snappier than she'd intended. She avoided the stare she felt coming her way from Adrian.

'Oh, it's only a few bits for Dylan. He doesn't seem to be doing well with gluten. I'm keeping an eye on it, but I think he might have an intolerance.'

'If you would give me a list of what he can eat, I'll buy it,' Sheila said. 'Although, I've not seen any issues. I don't believe a word about all these newfangled intolerances. In my day you ate what was put on the plate in front of you and were grateful for it.'

'I didn't want to put you to any trouble, Sheila. But thank you. That's very kind,' Rachel said calmly.

Sheila squinted her eyes to look at the woman better. The girl seemed sincere. That only made Sheila more annoyed.

'Where you off to today? Anywhere nice?' Adrian asked, jumping in quickly to try and avert a row.

'I've got meetings with my fashion wholesaler. I need to put my orders in for next season. And I cannot keep those printed rainbow tee-shirts in stock. I'm going to see if I can get some more. I've been thinking about branching out into footwear too. It's hard to tell if people will buy shoes online though.'

'I'm the wrong person to ask about that,' Adrian said. 'What do you think, love?' At this, he turned to his wife, bringing her into the conversation.

Sheila replied without missing a beat, 'I would never buy shoes online. I need to try them all on. But I don't suppose I'm your target customer.'

'Actually, a lot of my customers are your age, Sheila. I found customers like you loved shopping from home, as they cocooned. People buy more online now than they ever did before.'

'It's well for some,' Sheila said.

'Yes, I suppose it is. And I'm grateful for that one ray of light,' Rachel said, and to Sheila's horror, the girl's eyes filled up with tears. She glanced at Adrian to see if he'd noticed.

Damn it, he had. He made a face at Sheila and she had the grace to feel bad. She supposed she had been a bit tetchy with the girl, unnecessarily. Sheila softened her tone, 'Take your time today. If you want to grab dinner with a friend, I'm happy to hold on to the children as long as you need. You do work hard. And I always like to give credit where it's due.'

'My friends are all back home in Napier. If we were there, I'd take you up on that offer for sure.' Rachel walked into the kitchen, hugged and kissed the children goodbye, then she left.

There was something about the way Rachel spoke that made Sheila uncomfortable. She couldn't put her finger on it, but the hairs on her arms rose.

'Nana, Grandad, we have a present for you!' Dylan screamed at the top of his lungs, pulling her back from the worry. He waved a large seashell in his hands. 'We found it on the Velvet Strand yesterday.'

Adrian scooped the little boy up into his arms and swung him up high while Olivia snuggled into her Nanny Sheila's warm embrace.

She kissed the top of her granddaughter's head. 'You get taller every time I see you. You'll be at my shoulder in no time.'

'Well, you're a shortie, so that wouldn't be hard,' Adrian teased, making the kids laugh. Sheila pretended to get annoyed, but they all knew she didn't mind in the least. It was part of their double act, one they'd perfected over the years.

Rachel beeped the horn twice then waved out the driver's window as she drove off. As Sheila pulled the door closed she let her smile drop. Maybe it would be better for everyone if the girl dropped and ran, rather than coming in with the kids. It was becoming increasingly difficult to engage in any kind of small talk.

'Let's put the shell in the flower bed out in the garden,' Adrian said to the children.

Sheila smiled, genuinely now, as she watched the kids skip their way outside. It felt like only yesterday that Niamh and Jack had done the very same thing with him. There was something about a child skipping as they ran that uplifted you – their innocence and joy in life, within every hop.

With her heart swelling with love, Sheila wished that every day could be a Wednesday.

THIRTEEN

Sheila

Malahide, Dublin

Sheila put some force into her dusting to remove a stubborn piece of dried dirt above Lorcan's name on the black and grey granite headstone in front of her.

'The kids are in the car, Niamh, watching the new *Frozen* movie on their iPad,' Sheila said tenderly to the headstone. 'They'll be out in a bit to visit. You wait and see. I'll get you all tidied up first of all. That was quite a storm last night, wasn't it? But I'll have you spick and span in no time.' The wind caught the leaves on a nearby tree and as they rustled, Sheila smiled. Niamh always found a way to answer her.

When Lorcan died, everyone agreed that Rachel had been more than fair about the funeral arrangements. Sheila didn't need anyone to point out how hard the decision to bury him with Niamh must have been on

102

Rachel. If Rachel had dug her heels in and refused to allow Lorcan to be buried with his first wife, could anyone have blamed her? Rachel said that Lorcan's final resting place wasn't about her. It was about what was in the best interests of the children. And for their sake, having one grave for both their parents would be the easiest for their little heads to wrap themselves around. She felt it was what Lorcan would have wanted.

Lorcan's parents, Belinda and Oscar, had, as per usual, nothing of any use to say on the matter. They sent a blank cheque, their typical solution for everything. Throw some money at an issue or problem, then it was job done. Had they ever been to visit his grave other than on the day of the funeral? If they had, they'd done it quietly without telling anyone. She suspected Rachel might have mentioned if they had been around. And it couldn't be ignored that at the funeral, Belinda didn't even shed a tear. Like stone, she was, sitting at the top of the church. Oscar was red-eyed, but he looked like the kind of man who cried in private. But Sheila would never understand Belinda. It was as if she didn't give a jot that her only child was dead.

Five minutes later, the gravestone was back to its former glory, free from twigs, fallen leaves and dirt from the storm. Sheila unwrapped the plastic from the bunch of flowers she'd bought from the local supermarket and, pulling out the wilted, brown daisies from the heavy black vase at the top of the grave, she replaced them with the bright pink peonies she'd bought.

'When I saw these were in your favourite colour, I couldn't resist getting them. They give the grave a lift, such a lovely colour against the granite headstone. I'll see if I can buy the same next week too.'

Niamh had always loved fresh cut flowers; she'd found them terribly romantic. Her head had been in the clouds ever since she was a little girl and she loved happily-ever-after Disney stories. By the time she was a teen, she'd progressed from them to Mills and Boon books. Sheila smiled at the memory of finding her in her bedroom, head under her bedclothes, torch in hand, reading until late in the night. All she ever wanted was to fall in love with her very own Prince Charming.

And when Niamh had met Lorcan, that's precisely what she'd done. Niamh had fallen for him fast and hard. All Adrian and Sheila heard every day was *Lorcan this* and *Lorcan that*. They liked him too, Sheila was happy to admit. A nice, good, well-mannered young man who clearly doted on their daughter. And that's all a parent wanted – someone to love their child as much as they did. Lorcan proposed within a year of the meeting. They'd all been so happy for the young couple, who were evidently in love.

When Lorcan summoned the nerve up to tell them that he had proposed to Rachel, some years later, Sheila had said, before she could stop herself, 'It appears that proposing within a year of meeting a new woman is a classic Lorcan move.'

Sheila felt a flush of anger nip at her in the memory. Followed by guilt.

The leaves rustled again and Sheila fancied she could hear Niamh's voice reprimanding her, 'You do know he's lying right here beside me. You can't keep ignoring him.'

Sheila made a face. She hated it when Niamh was right. She gave in as gracefully as she could muster, saying begrudgingly, 'Hello, Lorcan.'

He would be looking down at her now from wherever he was, grinning, loving her discomfort. Lorcan was an awful messer, quick to tease and joke.

And the thing was, Sheila didn't enjoy feeling this way. Once upon a time he had been like another son to her.

There was a lot of water under that old bridge since then.

When Lorcan married Rachel, he as good as told the world that he'd moved on from Niamh. As far as Sheila was concerned – and she'd never be swayed from this fact – this was tantamount to cheating. She was sick to death of having to justify her feelings on this matter. Everyone else seemed hell-bent on giving Lorcan the benefit of the doubt. They'd say things like, 'Wasn't it great that he found some happiness?'

No, it bloody wasn't.

She leaned in closer to the headstone and whispered to Niamh, 'Are you happy that he's there beside you, darling?'

She'd lost sleep over this worry. Maybe Niamh didn't want to be reunited with him at all. It was possible that she was as cross with Lorcan as Sheila was about his second marriage. Maybe Rachel's kind gesture was another stab in the back for Niamh.

She spent a few more minutes rearranging the flowers until they sat just right in the vase, then took a step back to admire her handiwork, happy with the result. She turned to glance at her car, hoping the children might have lifted their heads from their iPad. Sheila couldn't put her finger on the change that had happened with her grandchildren over the past few months, but something had shifted.

Olivia and Dylan used to love visiting the grave; it was one of their traditions every Wednesday. Olivia would help her with the flowers and Dylan was surprisingly strong and adept at tearing out scraggly weeds. But lately, it was like pulling hens' teeth to get them enthused in the slightest.

When they did come, all Sheila could get out of them was a quick Amen. If Niamh and Lorcan were relying on whatever prayer the kids mumbled, well, God help them. Sheila knelt down on the cold marble surround and said a decade of the rosary to try and redress the balance.

When she had finished, Sheila whispered to Niamh, 'I have this terrible feeling that something bad is going to happen. I can't put my finger on what that might be, but I can feel it all the same.'

Sheila felt old as she stood up, her bones creaking and clicking in protest. Everyone said she was a young sixty years old. And most days, she didn't feel any older than she'd done twenty years ago. Age was a state of mind; she'd worked that out years ago. But there was nothing like a visit to the graveyard to make you acutely aware of your own age.

She sighed. Time to get the children and try to elicit some emotion from them.

Suddenly, she had an idea. Coaxing them out of the car, she called out to them, 'Follow me, kids!'

Sheila started to jog towards the back of the graveyard, pulling aside a low-hanging willow branch, to reveal a small wrought-iron gate. She pushed it open and, grabbing the kids' hands, brought them into a walled garden which was covered in clusters of bright yellow daffodils. Sheila smiled when she heard the kids' gasps of surprise.

'Are we allowed in here?' Olivia asked, looking around her in suspicion.

Technically this was private property. But she was confident that if Kathleen – or Kak, as she was known to all – found them here, she wouldn't mind.

'My friend Kak owns this house, and I happen to know that she has the best swing in the town. This way, quick.'

Pulling Olivia and Dylan along beside her, Sheila ran to a large treehouse that was built into a tall, broad oak tree. 'I used to play on this with Kak when I was a kid.' Sheila climbed up the wooden ladder to a platform about ten feet off the ground. She pulled a rope with a wooden plank attached to it in towards her. 'It's been a long time since I've done this, but I don't suppose the technique has changed much.' Sheila lowered her bum on to the wooden seat, wrapped her legs around the rope, then jumped, letting gravity swing her backwards and forwards. She screamed loudly as she flew through the air, and was gratified to hear the kids' squeals too.

'I want a go, Nana!' Dylan shouted.

Sheila swung herself back to the platform and stepped on to solid ground, a little shakily.

'You are so cool, Nana,' Olivia said with approval.

'Way cool,' Dylan agreed. 'Nanny Annie couldn't do that!'

'Not with her hips,' Olivia agreed.

Sheila had never been so pleased to hear anything in her life. She hid a smile of triumph as she helped the children on to the swing, one by one, and pulled her phone out to take photos of them as they had their turns flying through the air.

As they walked back to the graveyard, eyes shining bright with excitement, the kids held Sheila's hand tightly.

'I never know what to say at the grave,' Olivia said quietly.

Sheila could have kicked herself. She knew she had to learn to be more patient. To be more understanding. It was one of her worst faults, her tendency to judge too quickly. Maybe the reason the kids had been so wary to come and see the grave was because they felt uncomfortable, unsure around it, and Sheila had missed the signs. 'You don't have to say a thing. Just say a quick hello. Or you could tell Mammy and Daddy about school? I bet they will love to hear that.'

'I don't like school any more,' Olivia replied, her voice flat.

Sheila was surprised to hear that, but decided to switch to safer ground for now. 'Well, you've both talked about little else but your holiday in New Zealand – why don't you tell them both about that?'

No sooner was the suggestion made than Dylan was prattling on about the aquarium again, confidently telling Niamh and Lorcan how it was 'way cooler' than anything here in Ireland.

'If we move to New Zealand, I'm going to go see the sharks every single day,' Dylan said.

Suddenly, Sheila felt every muscle in her body tense up. What had the child just said? Had she imagined it?

Olivia peeped up at her grandmother through her fringe, her face pinched in worry. Then she shushed her brother.

'You're not moving to New Zealand, Dylan. What a strange thing to say to your mammy and daddy,' Sheila said, but her voice was unsteady, unsure.

Dylan shrugged. 'We might be. I heard Mom and Aunty Claudia talking about it. And Mom brought us to see her dream villa. It's even got a pool.'

'What exactly did Rachel say to Claudia?' Sheila tried to keep her voice even, but her tone was sharp, and the kids knew that they'd made a mistake. Olivia threw another look at Dylan and this time he got the message. They both shrugged and mumbled that they didn't know.

The good was gone from the day, then. Sheila led the kids back through the graveyard and car, and drove them straight home, barely talking, her heart racing.

FOURTEEN

Oscar

Malone Park, Belfast

Oscar had only been gone for a few hours. But when he returned home, it was to a very different house than the one he'd left. Their housekeeper, Bridie, was in the kitchen, drinking tea, shaking her head in despair.

'She's lost it. I can't get any good out of her.'

'What happened?' Oscar asked, a sinking feeling in his stomach.

'Herself is up in the attic and I can't get her down. It's as if she's finally tipped over the edge. She's possessed up there, going through boxes. You need to do something. I've tried, but she's having none of it.' At this, Bridie blessed herself for good measure.

Oscar ran upstairs to the end of the hallway, then continued up the small garret stairway to their attic. They rarely went up there. It was mostly used as storage for their extensive Christmas decoration collection.

'Belinda?' Oscar called out, slowing down as he walked into the attic. He wasn't sure he wanted to deal with whatever was in there.

Belinda looked up for a second, then turned her attention back to the large cardboard box in front of her that she was pulling items out of, one by one. Oscar looked around their attic in growing dismay. Every single box had been ripped open, their contents scattered like litter all over the wooden floor.

'I can't find it. I've looked everywhere, but it's not here,' Belinda said, her voice so full of sorrow that it brought a lump to Oscar's throat.

'We'll find it, whatever it is. I promise you,' he said, kneeling down beside her.

He took in her face smudged with dirt, her eyes red, from tears or dust, he didn't know, and a cobweb had attached itself to the back of her hair. In all the years of their life together, he'd never seen Belinda anything other than immaculately groomed. He reached over and gently removed the cobweb from her hair.

'Let me help, my darling. What are we looking for?'

'Lorcan's baby prints. Do you remember them? When he was a baby, we put his tiny feet and hand in blue paint and placed them on a piece of card. It was so darling. The cutest thing I'd ever seen. They were so tiny and yet so perfect. You must remember it. And I can't find them. Do you know where they are?' Belinda held her hands as if she was cradling Lorcan's tiny feet.

'Of course I remember,' he lied.

Oscar felt ashamed that he couldn't remember the prints, especially when it was so important to his wife.

'It was when I saw the children's heartprints, that it reminded me of Lorcan's baby prints. And since then, I can't stop thinking about them. When I try to sleep, that's all I can think about. Every waking minute. I've looked everywhere, but I can't find them.'

'Did you try the drawer?' Oscar asked, referring to the large, deep drawer in their kitchen which was home to important paperwork that they needed close by.

'That was the first place I tried. And today, I thought, I'll go through everything up here one more time. Just in case we left the print in a box by mistake. It was in that large white frame. We used to have it on his nursery wall.'

Oscar thought he vaguely remembered now. But it was such a long time ago, he wasn't sure he could trust the memory.

'I thought if I found them, we could show Olivia and Dylan. I think they'd like to see their daddy's baby prints. Do you think they would?'

'That's a lovely idea. I think the children would love that.'

'We could visit them. Rachel asked us to visit, didn't she? Do you think she meant it, or was she being polite?' Belinda asked, tears now running down her face, leaving dirt tracks in their path.

'She meant it. You know, we haven't seen the children since Lorcan's funeral. We've locked ourselves away for too long. And darling,' he added tentatively, 'we don't need to find Lorcan's baby prints as an excuse to see the children. We can go anytime you like. Why don't we go downstairs and have a nice cup of tea? Or maybe we could be naughty and have something stronger. What do you say? It's five o'clock somewhere. Let's leave this for now. I'll come back and search for Lorcan's prints and if they are here, I'll find them. I give you my word.'

He stood up and pulled Belinda to her feet beside him.

'I can't bear it if we threw them out. Lorcan deserves better, Oscar. We've let him down. We should have done more.'

Belinda began to sob and Oscar joined in too, crying for the missing baby mementos and for so much more.

FIFTEEN

Rachel

Malahide, Dublin

Rachel and Olivia looked around the open-plan kitchen, dining and family room, pleased with how well the room looked. Rachel had splashed out on several bunches of flowers from their local retailer. Olivia then placed them in jam jars they'd collected and tied brightly coloured ribbons around their middle. The kids knew they were having a party, but they didn't know why. The only person who was in on the secret was Ronan.

The doorbell rang. As if this thought had conjured him up, there Ronan was. And he held a large brown box in his arms.

'I've got all the ingredients for whiskey sours, as promised, and French 75s for the gin lovers,' he said with a grin, barely giving Rachel time to say hello. 'And you look beautiful, by the way.'

Rachel peered into the box. 'Crikey, you've thought of everything. Thank you for that and the compliment.' She gave a little curtsey. 'Dylan said I looked like a Barbie doll earlier. I wasn't sure how to take that. Beautiful is a little more reassuring!' She peered at Ronan. 'And speaking of looking well, right back at you. I like this casual look on you.'

'I promise you, jeans are my wardrobe of choice. And who is this gorgeous princess hiding behind you? Because it can't be little Olivia, so grown up!'

Olivia peeped out from behind Rachel, smiling shyly. She'd met Ronan a few times before, but that was when she was much younger.

'I like your top, nice slogan,' Ronan said to her, as he read the 'Be Kind' script emblazoned across the blue tunic.

'I don't do dresses,' Olivia said with a shrug, then she moved a little closer to him.

'Me either; I've never had the legs for them,' Ronan said, making the little girl giggle in delight. Rachel could sense a friendship blooming there.

'Could you go and check on Dylan for me, Olivia? Make sure he's gotten changed from his PJs into his clothes?'

'Sure,' Olivia agreed with a smile, then she skipped off.

'It's good to see her looking so happy,' Ronan said, watching the little girl disappear through the door.

'It is,' Rachel agreed. 'Isn't it a pity we ever grow out of skipping?'

'Speak for yourself. I enjoy a good skip at least once every day.'

To prove his point, Ronan skipped in front of her down the hall towards the kitchen. And before she had a moment to think about it, Rachel did the same, suddenly laughing as she went. She hadn't been silly for a very long time.

'Right, other than your out-laws, who else is coming? Did you get a firm yes from my aunt and uncle?' Ronan asked.

Rachel slapped him lightly on his arm. 'Behave! And yes, Belinda and Oscar have confirmed, which I'm so happy about.'

'I'm delighted to hear that. They are good people, you'll love them when you get to know them properly. I remember when I graduated, they both turned up to congratulate me. Meant a great deal at the time.'

'That's lovely to hear,' Rachel replied, taking the box from him and starting to unpack the drinks.

'What do you think everyone will make of the adoption news?' Ronan lowered his voice, so the children couldn't hear.

'I've no idea what any of them will say. But it's good news, which I think we all have been in short supply of recently. So I'm hopeful they will all be pleased for the children and me.'

'It will be grand. But I'm making popcorn for when the Butlers and Bradleys meet again. It's always gas watching them politely throw daggers at each other. I remember Lorcan and Niamh's wedding; Belinda and Sheila were hilarious. Both giving shade to each other.'

'I'm all there for anyone who can give Sheila shade. I'll take notes!' Rachel whispered back.

'Between your too hands-on out-laws and your too hands-off in-laws, it should be quite the party.'

'What on earth was I thinking?' Rachel said. She was beginning to regret inviting everyone already. Today more than ever, she wished her parents and Claudia were in her corner, and she meant that physically, not just on the end of a video call. She offered up a silent prayer of thanks that at least she had Ronan.

'Are you sure you are okay getting a taxi home, Ronan? We don't have a spare room, but the couch is yours if you need it.'

Ronan lived in an apartment near Stephen's Green in Dublin city centre.

'Quite sure. I always prefer to wake up in my own bed, unless it's for a very good reason,' Ronan winked.

Incorrigible as Ronan was, he had a knack for making Rachel feel less stressed. Despite her better judgement, she found herself giggling at his comment.

'Are you dating?' she asked, curious. She realized she didn't know much about the man's private life at all. Lorcan always said he was a 'terror for the women'.

Ronan shook his head. 'My dad always said to me that I should be a lawyer when I grew up because I could talk my way out of anything. Well, it appears he's right. Because I seem to have particularly good skills at talking myself out of relationships too!'

'There's nobody special in your life right now?'

'I wouldn't say that. I've been seeing someone on and off for the past year or so. Things are going all right at the minute, but as soon as I hear rumblings from her that she needs me to make space in my boxer drawer for her knickers, I'm out of there.'

'Or rather, she's out of there,' Rachel joked, this time her turn to make Ronan laugh. 'You're such a stereotype, Ronan. Classic commitment-phobe.'

Ronan clutched his chest in mock outrage. 'Never! I'm

happy to do everything that normal couples do. Except commit, of course.'

'I predict that one day you'll meet the right woman and you'll fall hard. And I'll laugh and remind you of this conversation.'

'I'm ready,' Dylan said, walking into the room and disrupting their conversation.

'You look very handsome,' Rachel said, turning her attention to her son. 'Nice brooch,' she added, referring to the gold brooch he'd pinned on to his shirt.

Dylan said, formally, 'Thank you. I borrowed it from your jewellery box.'

'An eye for the expensive stuff. Yep, you're a Bradley all right,' Ronan laughed.

'Who are you?' Dylan asked, giving Ronan the stink eye.

'We have met before, but as you were only a toddler the last time I saw you, I'll let you away with forgetting me. I'm your dad's cousin, Ronan. And a friend of your mom's. Plus, I'm the guy who has these.' Ronan grabbed two large bars of Oreo chocolate from the inside pocket of his blazer jacket and handed them over to the kids. 'Only eat them when your mom says it's okay.'

'Nice to meet you. Again,' Dylan said, licking his lips as he eyed up the treats.

'You too, mate,' Ronan said.

Rachel retrieved the chocolate and put it away for now.

As she did, the doorbell went. Rachel checked her watch. There were ten minutes to go before the official kick-off time for the party, which meant it could only be Sheila and Adrian.

SIXTEEN

Rachel

Malahide, Dublin

Sure enough, Sheila, Adrian and Jack stood on her doorstep, each armed with a tray of food.

'I made a Victoria sponge and a chocolate fudge cake,' Sheila said, then added, 'It's the children's favourite.'

As if Rachel wouldn't know what the children's favourite cake was.

But Sheila had one more sting in her tail, 'I wasn't sure what you would have for us all this afternoon, so I thought I'd better make several options.'

'I'm pretty sure I did say specifically that all you should bring was yourself, Sheila.' Rachel caught the tone in her voice, afraid she was sounding a little too snippy, then continued, 'But I think we can all agree that there can never be too much cake for a tea party. Come on inside.'

'I did tell her there was no need to bake, but you know

what Mam is like. She is a law unto herself,' Jack said apologetically.

'It's fine,' Rachel replied, leading the way into the kitchen. She pushed offence out of her head for the moment. Right now, she had introductions to make. 'You all remember Lorcan's cousin?'

Adrian moved forward to shake his hand, apologizing that he was a terror for remembering people's names.

'Never mind my husband. Of course we remember you, Ronan,' Sheila said as she also shook his hand. 'We met at Lorcan's wedding. His first wedding to Niamh, I mean of course – not the one to Rachel.' She smiled sweetly as she spoke.

Ronan nodded politely then, as Sheila went towards the sink, whispered to Rachel, 'Oh, she's good.'

Which, of course, made Rachel snigger. Despite her best efforts to cover it up, she saw Sheila's eyes narrow, taking it all in. Ronan would get her in trouble before the day was out if he kept making her laugh at inappropriate times.

'Who else is coming? I thought it was only family?' Sheila queried. 'No offence meant,' she added, nodding towards Ronan.

'I always say that when somebody mutters the words, "No offence", their intention is pretty clear. But you're okay, Sheila. I've a neck like a jockey's bollox, or so I've been told, so I can take it,' he grinned as he spoke, ever the charmer. 'Plus,' he added, almost cheekily, 'I like to think that I *am* family, as Lorcan's cousin.'

Rachel had to run out of the kitchen at this. Sheila, meanwhile, looked like she was going to have a stroke.

Waiting for her on the other side of the front door were a tense-looking Belinda and Oscar. They stood poker straight, their faces fixed with a smile that couldn't hide the furrows of worry on their foreheads. Rachel's heart went out to them both. She hated that anybody would feel so unsure or awkward about visiting her home.

Everything Lorcan had said about his parents was the opposite of what she saw now. He described them as poster adults for self-assurance, but Rachel knew that this had to be a tough day for them. She had issued several invitations to them to visit since Lorcan had died. All politely declined. She wondered what the change of heart was now.

Rachel leaned in for a set of air kisses from Oscar, then turned to do the same to Belinda. But to her surprise, Belinda pulled her in for a hug. It lasted for but a moment, yet there was no doubt that it was laced with warmth.

'Thank you for that, Belinda. I can't tell you how much I needed a hug! And you are both very welcome. I'm glad you could come.' Rachel opened the door wide to let them in. 'Your timing is perfect.'

Oscar smiled at his wife before he said, 'Belinda has a cast-iron rule for all social commitments. Never arrive early; from personal experience we know all too well that it can throw a host's plans into disarray.'

'Don't give all our secrets away,' Belinda said.

'I think that's a great rule to follow,' Rachel said quickly. 'For me, equally unmentionable is to arrive late. I mean, that could play havoc on the timings of a scallop starter right through to a soufflé dessert. Not that we're having either of those today.'

'Five minutes late, no less, no more, is our magic number. It's served us well for decades,' Oscar said.

'I shall rob that,' Rachel said warmly, leading them inside to the other guests.

Sheila's face was priceless when she caught sight of who the other guests were. She opened her mouth, let it gape for a second, then closed it with a splutter.

Rachel ignored her and called out to the kids, 'Come over to say hello to your Grandma Belinda and Grandpa Oscar.'

Olivia and Dylan ran towards them, then stopped short just in front of them, both feeling a little shy and unsure. Other than a couple of polite phone calls to say thank you for gifts, they didn't really know each other. Not to mention that the last time they'd been in their grandparents' company in person had been at their father's funeral. Rachel was about to step in to help make the re-introductions easier, but Belinda leaned down, taking the matter into her own hands. 'Would you mind terribly if I gave you a hug? I should very much love one.'

Dylan was first to answer, 'Sure, Grandma!' He moved forward and gave them each a hug, followed by Olivia.

Rachel saw Belinda's eyes fill with tears as she held them both. Then Oscar spotted Ronan and as they both warmly said their hellos to each other, Rachel finally began to relax.

Maybe they wouldn't need that popcorn after all.

It was only then that she realized neither the Butlers nor the Bradleys were making a move towards each other. They stood on opposite sides of the kitchen and eyed each other up, like gladiators in an arena.

'You remember Belinda and Oscar?' Rachel asked eventually, looking from one couple to the next. 'And you must remember Niamh's parents, Sheila and Adrian, and their son Jack?'

They all nodded in unison but remained mute. The air was thick with the unsaid. Rachel looked desperately over to Ronan for help, but thankfully everyone's manners kicked in, and there was a rush of, 'how lovely to see you,' from the four of them, followed by an awkward pumping of hands.

Turning to Jack, Oscar began to shout, so loudly it made everyone jump in shock, 'It's. Good. To. See. You. Again. Jack.'

Rachel saw annoyance flash on Sheila's face.

'Jack is partially deaf and yelling at him is pointless. It won't return his hearing.' Sheila clearly wasn't bothering to keep the irritation from her voice.

Oscar flushed, appearing genuinely embarrassed and sorry for his mistake. 'I'm an oaf. My apologies, I meant no disrespect, I assure you.' Then, seemingly worried he'd said that too loudly as well, he repeated it, several tones lower.

A silence fell over the room, the tension reaching a breaking point.

Rachel watched Ronan move closer to his aunt and uncle on their side of the kitchen, which left Sheila, Adrian and Jack huddled together on the other. The kids joined Rachel, and the three of them found themselves standing in an awkward middle ground between the two sides.

Rachel looked at Jack, silently pleading with him to say something to save the day.

He got the message and stepped up.

'Please don't worry, Oscar. I know you meant well. As Mam said, I can hear pretty well. But if you could look in my direction when you talk, that would be a great help. Sometimes when lots of people talk at once, it can be tricky.'

'I will remember that. Thank you for being so gracious,' Oscar responded. Then he turned to Sheila and said again, 'I really am sorry.'

Rachel's heart went out to him, and Belinda too, who looked equally stricken by Oscar's faux pas. She said to the quiet children, 'Olivia and Dylan, will you take everyone's jackets? Then I'll get some drinks organized. Why don't we all take a seat around the dining table?'

'I'll help with drinks,' Jack said, but as he reached the fridge, Ronan stepped in front of him, ensuring he was facing Jack as he spoke. 'It's okay, take a load off. I'm going to make some cocktails for us all. Dylan is going to be my helper, aren't you, mate?'

'Yes!' Dylan said, his smile showing his delight with the job.

Once everyone had taken their seats, Rachel relaxed a little more. A chorus of approval made its way around the room at the pretty table decorations, making Olivia beam with pride, as she had handwritten table names for them all.

Rachel brought out the pre-prepared stands of food while Ronan mixed whiskey sours and French 75s with a speed that suggested it wasn't his first gig as a barman. Polite chit-chat about the traffic and weather was made until everyone had a drink of choice.

'There's sandwiches, scones, clotted cream and jam, plus petit fours. And if that's not enough, we also have some beautiful cakes that Sheila brought over too. I hope you're all hungry,' Rachel said. 'Please, tuck in.'

Adrian licked his lips. 'This looks gorgeous. You've excelled yourselves.'

'Very nice,' Sheila agreed begrudgingly. 'Although I'm not a fan of smoked salmon, and eggs always repeat on me. But the ham looks delicious. Where did you buy the petits fours and scones from?'

Rachel bristled at Sheila's question, the implication being that of course she couldn't have made them.

Olivia jumped in and Rachel's heart soared at the small win. 'We made the scones together this morning, Nana.'

'I helped too,' Dylan said. 'I stirred in those black things.'

'They are called raisins, remember?' Rachel interrupted.

'No wonder Mam thought they were shop bought – everything looks so professional,' Jack said diplomatically.

Rachel smiled her thanks at him again. He never let her down. 'Full disclosure, Jack, I did buy the petits fours from one of the school mams who has her own bakery business. I'm afraid I'm not quite the same whiz in the kitchen as you are, Sheila.'

Another awkward silence filled the small room. Rachel worried that the assembled group was getting too good at them.

Then Belinda finally spoke, 'You know, Oscar and I have a tradition that we have afternoon tea whenever we visit a new city. And we've had wonderful trays of delicacies in the best hotels, from all over the world. But I don't think I've ever had one as special as this one. And as for not making the petits fours, well, I always say the same thing when someone asks me what I like to make. My favourite thing to make is reservations.'

'And I can concur that she's rather excellent at that,' Oscar said, biting into a scone piled high with jam and cream.

Everyone laughed, genuinely. Rachel felt a swell of relief as she watched them all tuck into the food with gusto. The children began to entertain the room, chattering about stories from school and playschool. Rachel decided that she worried too much. It was time to enjoy the afternoon.

SEVENTEEN

Rachel

Malahide, Dublin

'I didn't know that you and Rachel were still in touch,' Jack said to Ronan, who sat to his right.

'Lorcan and I used to go for lunch every now and then, and Rachel came along once or twice, so we got to know each other that way. We had lunch not long before he died. I'm grateful for that. I keep in touch with Rachel from time to time. I'm sorry that I've not done more, actually.'

'You've done enough,' Rachel said, joining their conversation. 'And Ronan is our family solicitor too.' She felt Sheila's eyes on them as they spoke. That woman missed nothing.

Dylan tugged on Rachel's arm, pulling her away from the conversation. 'Why was Nana Sheila cross with Grandpa Oscar?'

'A misunderstanding, that's all. They're friends really,' Rachel reassured him.

'What's a misunderstanding?' Dylan asked, a little bit louder. They were all listening now. Rachel looked over to Sheila and raised an eyebrow in question. *Your move.*

Sheila nodded and turned to talk to Oscar and Belinda. 'How is life treating you both in Belfast?' she asked.

Rachel was gratified that Sheila was making an effort to reassure the children that there was no row. Good for her. But she couldn't help noticing that Sheila's voice had changed, an unmistakably genteel tone edging into her voice. A distinct whiff of the Queen's speech about it. Adrian obviously copped it too, because his face was a picture as he watched his wife in action, glued to Belinda's words.

'Very well, thank you. We've had some work done in our garden, adding a pergola to the gable end of our house. It's a nice area to sit and drink a coffee, when the weather allows. And we have travelled quite a bit this year,' Belinda said.

Hearing the word 'travel', Dylan couldn't resist jumping in. 'When we were in New Zealand, we saw a shark,' he announced.

'Good grief, not this again,' Sheila mumbled.

Belinda threw a shocked look in Sheila's direction, then said, 'Oh my goodness, that sounds terribly scary.'

'I'm a big boy now, Grandma Belinda, I wasn't scared at all,' Dylan said.

'Of course you weren't,' Belinda agreed, beaming at the boy.

'And we saw a sleeping giant,' Olivia added.

'Now that I'd like to hear about,' Oscar said.

Between Dylan and Olivia, they told the adults all about the giant Te Mata.

'That sounds like a lot of fun. I think I'd like to visit Te Mata Peak one day,' Oscar said.

'Gramps Joe is really clever. He knows lots and lots about giants and sharks. He'll bring you up there if you want to go,' Dylan said.

'I'll remember that, thank you, Dylan,' Oscar said.

'And Nanny Annie taught me how to crochet. I'm making a blanket for her as a surprise. Mom will post it to her for her birthday in November,' Olivia added.

'What a thoughtful little girl you are,' Belinda said.

'I can make you one too, if you'd like?'

'I'd love that. Thank you!'

'I have some beautiful items that the children have made me over the years,' Sheila joined in, refusing to be outdone by 'Grandma Belinda'.

Rachel caught Ronan's eye and he pretended to shove imaginary popcorn into his mouth. She quickly put her napkin to her face, to hide her grin.

'It sounds like you had a lot of fun with your New Zealand grandparents,' Oscar said, bringing the conversation back round.

Sheila sighed loudly. Was it Rachel's imagination, or had Sheila been getting increasingly fed up with New Zealand vacation stories over the previous few weeks? Before she had a chance to analyse that thought further, Sheila made a comment that left her in no doubt of her true feelings.

'You mean to say their step-grandparents,' she corrected coldly.

The eyes of the room turned towards her.

'Sheila!' Adrian exclaimed, turning to his wife in shock.

Two dots of bright red stained Sheila's cheeks, and she looked stricken as she went on to explain, 'Technically speaking, that's all. I mean, they aren't the children's grand-parents like we are, or like Belinda and Oscar are for that matter.'

Rachel watched Sheila look to the Bradleys for support. And she felt relief that they were looking at Sheila in horror. It wasn't just her, then.

A flush of red flooded Sheila's face. If Rachel wasn't so angry and hurt by her comment, she would have felt sorry for her.

'What does Nana mean by step-grandparents?' Dylan asked Rachel.

'Your nana didn't mean anything by that,' Adrian jumped in.

'I can speak for myself,' Sheila said.

Rachel noted that her voice was back to its normal Dublin twang again. No more Queen's speech.

'I'd like to hear what you can say that explains that comment, because it was made in terrible taste from where I'm sitting,' Ronan said, but this time his voice was clipped and accusing, all signs of his previous teasing gone.

Rachel held her hands up, trying to stop everyone from digging any more holes for themselves. She could see the day beginning to unravel in front of them already, and they hadn't even got to the big announcement.

'There's no need to explain. I'd prefer if we leave it for now, please,' she said, with authority. 'I actually have an announcement to make.' She flicked open her iPad. 'As it happens, I'd like the children's *grandparents* in New Zealand to hear this too.'

Rachel made a point of looking at Sheila as she empha-sized the word. Sheila defiantly returned her stare, obviously unwilling to let Rachel shame her.

'What's the announcement?' Olivia asked.

'Are we having a baby? Can it be a boy if we are?' Dylan asked, which made everyone laugh, breaking the tension slightly.

'Not that, but something just as wonderful, you'll see,' Rachel said, gently caressing his cheek. She couldn't wait to share the news with them. She would not let Sheila and her snide comments taint this moment in any way. She closed her eyes and thought of Lorcan, imagining that he was by her side, as he should have been. And as had happened on occasion before, for a moment, she felt the warmth of her husband's touch. It was as if he were holding her hand to give her strength.

Rachel looked around the room. Everyone watched her, waiting for her announcement. Almost everyone showed only kindness on their face, but there was something about the steel in Sheila's eyes that made her feel uneasy.

Rachel crossed her fingers that technology was on her side, then hit the FaceTime icon on her dad's phone number. He answered immediately, as arranged. Rachel hadn't told them what her announcement was, but they did at least know that she'd started the procedure for adoption, so it would be less of a surprise for them than for everyone else. Seeing their faces fill the screen on her phone made her wish she could transport herself into the warmth of her parents' kitchen. Her family weren't perfect, but at least Rachel always knew they were on her side. Here, she didn't know who was an ally and who was a foe.

'Hello, love,' Annie said warmly. 'And hello to everyone in Dublin!'

'Hello, Mom and Dad, hey Claudia.'

A chorus of hellos from the room were made back and forth.

'Let me say hello.' Dylan stood on his chair to ensure he was seen properly by the New Zealand gang.

'There's my best boy,' Annie said.

'I'm here too, Nanny Annie,' Olivia cried, climbing on top of Rachel so that she had a better vantage point too.

Rachel had rehearsed what she wanted to say for days, but now that the time had come to share her news, she felt her stomach flip with nerves. Ronan gave her a reassuring wink.

There was no point delaying things any further; it was now or never.

'Well, I've asked you all here today because I have some special news to share with the children. And I wanted you all to be here too, to witness this moment.'

'This is all very dramatic,' Sheila said, her face scrunched up in a frown.

'Do you remember Daddy asking you both a very important question a few months before he died?' Rachel asked the children, ignoring Sheila altogether.

Dylan shook his head. 'Was it about the dinosaurs? I remember him asking me which was my favourite. And I didn't know on that day. But I do now. It's the Stegosaurus. They don't eat people, just leaves and things.'

Everyone smiled and the tension in the room was dissipated a little by Dylan's childhood innocence.

'I think the Stegosaurus was Daddy's favourite dinosaur too. But it's not the question I was thinking about. It was Daddy's question asking if you would like me to adopt you both,' Rachel said. Her heart had started to beat so fast she was sure the room could hear it.

'I remember,' Olivia said, her voice a little over a whisper. 'He said that if we wanted, we could make it official in the eyes of the law so that everyone knew that you were our mom.'

'That's right,' Rachel said, feeling emotion race to overcome her. She swallowed a golf ball lump down, determined to get through the moment without going to the ugly cry.

'Oh yeah, now I remember. I thought it was silly because you are our mom already,' Dylan said simply.

'You are such a clever boy. But Daddy was super excited to make this adoption happen because he never liked the title stepmom. Do you remember that?'

'Me either,' Olivia said. 'It's stupid.'

'Me too!' Dylan said.

'Well, that makes me very happy. Because I have some special news to tell you. Last week, all of our wishes came true. Because the court issued our adoption papers. It's happened. I'm now – officially – your mom!'

Rachel wasn't aware of anything for a moment, other than the feel of her children's arms as they threw themselves at her.

'So nobody can take you away from us?' Olivia said.

'Never, ever, I promise,' Rachel said.

She heard her dad's voice whoop from the video screen, and then everyone else joined in. But there was one voice that remained distinctly silent – Sheila's.

'Does this mean Gramps Joe and Nanny Annie are really our grandparents too?' Olivia asked. 'Not step-grandparents as Nana said they were?'

'Who said we weren't real grandparents?' Joe asked in response, unaware that this question was rubbing salt in a wound around the table. 'I didn't need a piece of paper for that to be true, no more than your mom did. But I don't mind telling you that this is the happiest day of my life. I only wish you were all here so I could cuddle you.'

'Mom, are you okay?' Rachel asked, seeing Annie holding her hands over her face.

'She'll be good soon enough, Sis,' Claudia jumped in. 'I think we might need to get the medicinal brandy out. She's happy. We all are. I'm super proud of you. I told Mom and Dad you wouldn't get us out of our beds at the crack of dawn unless it was for a really good reason! I'll miss my beauty sleep for news like this, any day of the week.'

'Thanks, Claudia. I'll let you get back to bed or have a cuppa – and call you all later, okay?'

'We'll look forward to it,' Joe said. They all said their goodbyes before hitting the end to the call.

The room fell silent as the video call ended. And it wasn't one of those comfortable silences.

'I'm so glad you could all be here for this,' Rachel began to babble. 'I was so nervous, but really wanted everyone here to see this. If there's something we've learned over the past couple of years, it's that we need our family, right? And the kids need you all, each and every one of you; you are so important to them. So thank you for all you do for them, and for me too. And thank you for being here today . . .' Her voice drifted off on the last word.

'So happy for you all,' Ronan said, jumping in and smiling brightly, clapping his hands together in a round of applause that nobody joined in with.

'I'm honoured that you asked us to be here for this tremendous moment,' Belinda said, stepping in with her impeccable manners. 'Thank you for including us.'

Rachel felt a rush of gratitude for Belinda. She had been

a little nervous about seeing her in-laws again, but there had been no need. They'd only been in each other's company a short time, but Rachel felt bolstered by Belinda and Oscar's support. She glanced at Sheila and wished that she could say the same for her out-laws.

'You made a beautiful speech there, Rachel. I'm not sure we deserved your thanks, but it's appreciated nonetheless,' Oscar said now, nodding at her.

'He can say that again,' Sheila hissed to Adrian.

'Not now,' Adrian replied in a warning tone.

'I suppose it was you who handled the adoption?' Sheila continued, pointing a finger at Ronan, ignoring her husband.

'Yes, I did,' Ronan answered, professionally. 'Lorcan called me a few months before he died, to put this all in place. It's taken till now for the papers to come through. It can be a slow process.'

'I wish he was here to see it finally happen,' Belinda whispered.

'Me too,' Rachel said, clasping the woman's hand for a moment.

'Well, I'm a little confused that Rachel could still adopt the children, even though Lorcan is dead,' Sheila said, her voice rising with every word. 'And I'm dumbfounded that we have not been included in a decision as big as this. You didn't have our permission. As the children's grandparents, we have rights, you know.'

Ronan put a hand on Rachel's arm, answering Sheila's question in a calm voice. 'It's a simple enough procedure. The step-parent must have lived with the children for a minimum of two years. Rachel has. Lorcan, as the biological parent, gave permission for the adoption before he died. As there were no other non-parental guardians in the mix, there was no need to consult anyone. The state bases their decisions on what's in the best interests of the children. In this case, it was a no-brainer, I'm sure you will all agree.'

Sheila remained tight-lipped.

'We could not be happier with the news. I'm not sure I believe in heaven, but if there is one and our son Lorcan is there, he'll be so happy knowing his children are in the safe and loving hands of you, Rachel,' Oscar said, changing the mood. 'I'd like everyone to raise their glasses and toast this lovely family.'

'Well said,' Adrian concurred, raising his mug of tea. Rachel noted that he avoided Sheila's eyes as he did so.

Then Jack tapped the side of his glass with a teaspoon to get everyone's attention. There was a faint blush on his cheeks as he spoke, 'I wanted to say how happy I am with this news. I've never seen a more loving family than Rachel and the children.'

'And now we have three sets of grandparents!' Olivia said. 'None of my friends have that many.'

'That's three sets of presents for birthdays and Christmas too,' Ronan said, teasingly.

On this happy note, Rachel suggested the kids go watch a movie, which they happily skipped off to do. They seemed to be okay and relatively unaffected by the underlying drama, or maybe it had just gone over their heads.

No sooner had the children left than Sheila turned to Rachel. 'Now that it's us adults, have you any further shocking announcements to make?'

Rachel shook her head, surprised by the question. 'I think we've had quite enough excitement for one day. I'm sorry you thought it was shocking, though. I had hoped you would see it as good news.'

Sheila's face hardened in response. Rachel sighed and tried to work out her next move. Should she ask Sheila what was bugging her, or leave it alone for another day? Before Rachel had a chance to dwell on that conundrum any further, Sheila stood up. She looked around the table. 'While everyone else seems happy to celebrate this news, I'm afraid I'm in a different space. Because unlike everyone else, I can see straight through your little adoption scheme.'

'Mam, would you relax. There's no scheme!' Jack said, clearly appalled by his mother's behaviour.

'Oh, but there is. Tell everyone the real reason you're here,' Sheila turned her attention to Ronan.

'I came for the cakes,' Ronan said, not missing a beat. At any other moment, Rachel might have laughed.

'What has gotten into you? Would you sit down?' Adrian asked, pulling the sleeve of Sheila's blouse. She shook him off like she was batting a fly away.

'I'll tell you what has gotten into me. This . . . this *madam* here . . . has been plotting all along to take the children away from us. From you two as well,' she said to Belinda and Oscar, desperately trying to pull them on to her side. 'Not that you'd notice much because you're never here anyhow.'

'I beg your pardon?' Belinda said.

'There's no need to be so rude and inflammatory with your remarks,' Oscar joined in.

'Sheila, please don't ruin today for the children and me,' Rachel pleaded, looking through the door to the other room where Olivia and Dylan were sitting cross-legged in front of the TV, thankfully oblivious.

'I'm sorry, Rachel,' Jack said, his face now tinged pink. 'I think we should go.'

'Tell them,' Sheila said, her voice low but with steel laced through every word.

Rachel was baffled. She looked around the room in puzzlement, trying to work out what exactly she'd done to cause so much anger.

'I can assure you that I have no plan or scheme to do anything but love my children, Sheila. Honestly, all I wanted was to share this special moment with you all. Because you are all the children's family.'

Sheila had worked herself up to a frenzy and there was no stopping her. 'When were you going to tell everyone that you plan to take the children to live in New Zealand?'

The room fell silent for a moment. Then, suddenly, it exploded into a chorus of surprised, and *hurt*, whats and whys.

Rachel felt two spots of colour jump on to her cheeks. She was astonished by Sheila's comments. How had she gotten wind of that?

'I don't know where you've gotten that information from, but I can promise you, it's incorrect.'

'Oh, pull the other one. It's as clear as crystal now. Stage one, you adopt the kids. Stage two, you announce it to all of us, but only when it is a done deal, so we have no chance to stop it. Very sneaky of you, Rachel, that was very sneaky indeed. Then stage three, let me guess, you pack your bags and we never see the children again, as they go and live with Gramps Joe and Nanny Annie and all the fecking sharks!'

It was as if every word that Sheila spoke was filled with electricity.

Rachel felt her stomach churn. She wiped a line of sweat from her upper lip, feeling the eyes of the room on her, as they waited for her to respond to Sheila's accusations. 'Hold on a moment, Sheila. Why would you want to stop the adoption? I am the children's mother. I have been for three years now. And no matter how much you try to undermine me or change that fact, you can't. As for me scheming, have you not listened to anything I've said? Lorcan suggested the adoption, not me. But I'm so glad he did because it's the right thing for the kids and me, to make it official. We need this.'

'A likely story. Very convenient of you all to say that when he's not here to answer for himself,' Sheila retorted.

'Are you calling me a liar too?' Ronan said coolly. 'I've been Lorcan's solicitor for years, and he spoke to me about the adoption even before he mentioned it to Rachel. He wanted to find out what was involved before he got her hopes up. So I can assure you that this was far from any scheme from Rachel.'

'You would say that,' Sheila said, but her voice had lost its assurance now.

'Why would I say that? I've nothing to gain by saying that.'

'For all we know you are both in cahoots together. You look very friendly from what I've seen,' Sheila said.

'Now I'm dating Ronan?' Rachel asked, stunned beyond all belief. She clenched her hands into tight fists on her lap. 'Listen to yourself, Sheila! I haven't looked at another man since Lorcan died.'.

Adrian and Jack were now both on their feet, clasping Sheila's arms on either side of her. 'There's no need to pull me anywhere, because I'm going. Gladly. But Rachel, you listen here; you'll be hearing from our solicitor. If you think you're going to take Niamh's children from me, you have another think coming. We are going to fight for custody and I will not stop until those children are back where they belong, with their blood family.'

'What?' Rachel said, falling back into her seat. 'Why would you say that? It's monstrous.'

Adrian hadn't said very much, but he spoke up now, 'Those children are our life, Rachel. You can't take them from us.'

'I'm not taking them anywhere, Adrian,' Rachel said.

'So you didn't look at a house when you were over there? Do you deny it?' Sheila said as she moved towards the door. 'The lies keep tripping from your mouth.'

Rachel felt tears prick her eyes. She could not believe that the day had dissolved into such a mess in the space of a few moments.

'Stop it,' Jack said. 'This is getting out of hand. Rachel, you're not moving to New Zealand, are you?' His tone was light, but there was no mistaking the plea in his words.

Before Rachel had a chance to respond, Belinda stood up, then moved behind Rachel's chair. She placed her hands on her shoulders. 'I've heard enough. You cannot bully this young woman for one more moment. I will not allow it. If you fight Rachel for custody of the children, then I shall be standing firmly in her corner. And we'll fight you in every court to make sure that the children stay with their mother. Isn't that right, Oscar?'

'Yes, of course, it is. Frankly, I'm astounded by you, Sheila and Adrian. It really is the most appalling way to behave,' Oscar said.

Unnoticed, the children had slipped back into the room.

'What's wrong, Mom?' Olivia asked, her little face scrunched up in worry.

'For the love of God, that is not your mother,' Sheila scolded.

The room fell into a shocked silence, so thick it coated every part of them all.

Nobody moved, each lost in their own horror at Sheila's words.

The silence only broke when Dylan started to cry loud, racking sobs.

Rachel picked him up in her arms and held him close as Olivia moved to her side and snuggled under her arm, her tears joining her baby brother's.

'I don't understand. What does Nana Sheila mean?' Olivia said.

'Nothing, sweetheart. Your nana meant nothing at all. She's just joking.' Rachel couldn't look at Sheila. Or Adrian, for that matter.

'I think it's time you left,' Ronan said, moving towards the Butlers.

'This has nothing to do with you. You cannot tell us to leave,' Jack said, pointing at Ronan with so much force, it looked like he was boxing the air between the men.

When no one moved, Rachel turned to plead, 'Jack, please, I need you to take your parents home. If not for me, then do it for the children. You can see how upset they are.'

'I'm sorry,' Jack said. He touched the children's backs, but they didn't look up.

'It's not you who should be sorry,' Belinda corrected. By now, Sheila had lost all her fight, watching the children cry.

She let Adrian and Jack lead her from the house and as they left, Rachel allowed the tears that had been hovering all day to finally fall.

EIGHTEEN

Sheila

Malahide, Dublin

It took Adrian and Jack over an hour to calm Sheila down once they got back home. It frightened both of them to their core to see her so upset. She cried and keened, holding her head between her hands, rocking backwards and forwards. Adrian made tea because that's what you were supposed to do when someone got into such a state, but Sheila wouldn't even look at the cup he placed in front of her. Jack wrapped a velvet throw around her shoulders, a gift from the children the previous Christmas. Sheila loved it and always said it gave her comfort and warmth. But she shrugged it off her shoulders in annoyance and carried on her lament. Then, finally, after what felt like an eternity, she was spent. She stopped as suddenly as she had started. The silence, however, became as unnerving as the keening.

141

Adrian watched her, then looked to his son for help, unsure about what to do next. It took another forty-five minutes for Sheila to speak.

'How could I have said that in front of the children?' she said finally, her voice quiet and hollow. Her face crumpled with pain. 'I am a wicked woman. Truly wicked. To make Dylan cry like that. And Olivia looked so cross with me. I'll never forgive myself.'

Adrian looked again to Jack for guidance on what to reply. This was not what he'd been expecting Sheila to say. And he didn't know how to respond, because he couldn't deny that he, too, was shocked to his core by Sheila's behaviour. He was afraid that if he responded, he might say something that everyone regretted later on. And there had been enough of that today already.

'Say something, please,' Sheila railed at them, unwilling to let them remain a silent witness to her shame.

'You didn't mean it,' Adrian jumped in loyally. 'You need to just apologize and tell Rachel and the children that you made a mistake. That you were upset and were not yourself. You can make them understand.'

But before he could congratulate himself on the perfect response, Sheila took the wind out of his sails. 'But the thing is, I did mean it.'

'What part did you mean?' Jack asked.

'All of it,' Sheila replied, with barely a hesitation.

'Sheila, you can't say stuff like that; it's not right. Whether you like it or not, Rachel is the children's mother now. She has been for years.'

'Why can't I say what I'm feeling? Who are you worried about me offending? The woman who is about to take the only part of Niamh we have left away from us?'

Adrian slumped down into a chair opposite Sheila. Was Rachel really going to take the children to New Zealand?

'What about the children and how this affects them?' Jack said.

Sheila clutched her stomach, feeling queasy all of a sudden.

'I'd cut my arm off rather than upset them both. But they'll understand when they are older that I'm fighting for them. And sometimes, in a fight, you have to get your hands dirty.'

Jack banged the kitchen table, the sound reverberating through the room. 'The children love Rachel. She is a good mother to them.'

'She's not their mother,' Sheila said firmly. 'Don't you dare say that to me again. Niamh is and always will be.'

Adrian realized that they would not get anything sensible from Sheila on this subject while she was so upset.

'Well, Rachel insisted she isn't taking the kids to New Zealand,' Jack said now, changing tack.

'Well, she would say that! The kids told me about the plans she hatched with her sister while they were on holiday,' Sheila practically spat out. There was a silence at this, neither of the men wanting to think about what this could mean, but then Jack came to his senses.

'What if you are wrong and the kids made a mistake? What if you've caused a huge row for nothing?' Jack's words were tumbling out now, fast and furious. 'You should have asked Rachel quietly, rather than shouting the odds in front of everyone.'

'Well, of course, that's what I *should* have done. And I planned to do so next Wednesday when she called with the kids. But then she sidelined us with the surprise adoption party and I could see what she was up to, clear as day. I had to say something. For *Niamh*! And not just for her, for *all* of us. Do you want to lose the children? Are you ready to sit back and watch them get on an aeroplane? Because if that happens, they'll forget all about us and we'll never see them again.'

'Rachel would never do that,' Jack said, but he looked less sure now.

Sheila felt another explosion of rage ripple its way through her. She felt anger clip every word she spoke. 'Wake up, Jack. Of course she will. And I, for one, will not allow that girl to take the children from us. Are you with me or against me? It's as simple as that.'

Sheila watched a flash of anger on her son's face, and it took her by surprise. Jack rarely lost his cool; he was one of life's easy goers. Adrian held up his arms between mother and son, to placate them both. 'There are no sides. Would you listen to yourselves! The only side we are on is the children's, surely? And I won't sleep tonight because I for one cannot get the image of Olivia and Dylan's face from my head. That's on . . .' He paused for a moment, then changed his words just in time, 'Their pain, well that's on all of us.'

'I regret saying anything in front of them. I'm sorry I did. But you have to understand, Adrian, if she goes to New Zealand, that's it. It won't be the same if they go. Look what happened on their holiday. The sharks are bigger over there, the mountains have giants carved in them, the waterfalls are more spectacular. We can't compete with any of that.'

'They would never forget us. Olivia and Dylan love us as much as we love them.'

Sheila looked at her husband and whispered, 'They loved Niamh, but they forgot her all the same, didn't they?'

NINETEEN

Belinda

Malahide, Dublin

Belinda and Oscar sat in their car down the road from Rachel's house for almost ten minutes in stunned silence. They had said their goodbyes to Rachel and the children but found that they needed a moment to decompress before they began their journey home. More than once, they began to speak, only to find themselves dumbstruck. What could they possibly say about the last thirty minutes?

'I could do with a drink,' Oscar was the first to break the silence.

'I don't think we should go home tonight,' Belinda replied, staring straight ahead. 'How would you feel about finding a hotel round here and getting that drink sooner rather than later?'

Oscar nodded slowly. 'I think that's a splendid idea, darling. Let me take a look on my phone, see what's nearby.'

Within moments, a hotel was located, a phone call made and a reservation confirmed. Only when they had checked into the Grand Hotel in Malahide village, begging the receptionist for toothbrushes and toothpaste to see them through until morning, and were sitting in the bar, each with an amaretto on ice in front of them, did they allow themselves to discuss the afternoon.

'I'll start, will I?' Oscar said. 'That Sheila Butler . . . she's got quite a mouth on her. She seems to really have it in for young Rachel, doesn't she?'

'Rachel never stood a chance with her. From the moment Lorcan brought her home, she was on to a losing battle with the Butlers.' Belinda took a slow sip of her liqueur, allowing it to warm her throat. She pulled her scarf a little tighter around her.

'Why do you say that?'

'Unfortunately for Rachel, she's got one big flaw – she's not Niamh. And while I don't like how Sheila behaved, as one mother to another, I understand her. Grief can make us all act in unusual ways.'

'You're right, of course,' Oscar agreed. 'But I don't mind telling you, Sheila scares me all the same.'

'Oh, me too. I suppose I can't help feeling sorry for her as well,' Belinda said, surprising herself as she spoke. She hadn't realized she felt that way until the very minute the words were uttered.

'You're a kinder person than me.'

'You know that I've not felt myself since Lorcan died. If Sheila feels even a fraction of that, she deserves only our sympathy.'

Oscar leaned across and kissed his wife on her cheek, and they took a pause for a moment. The barman asked them if they wanted another drink and Oscar nodded his consent. It was the first time Belinda had opened up to him in months. He didn't want to lose her again, to whatever fog she'd lived in for the past couple of years, and he was desperate to cling on to the moment while it lasted.

'What about this business with New Zealand? Do you think Rachel was lying, like Sheila kept saying?' Oscar asked, as he tapped his debit card to pay for their next drinks.

'No, actually, I don't,' his wife answered assertively. 'Rachel seemed sincere when she said that she had no plans to relocate and I'm choosing to believe her. She's given us no reason not to. It sounds as if it's been a case of Chinese whispers. The kids have repeated something they overheard and it's gained legs.'

'How would you feel if she *was* moving back to New Zealand?'

They looked at each other and from their matching frowns, knew without speaking that both were thinking about a possible future without Olivia and Dylan in their lives, taken from them before they had a chance to get to know them again.

'I just can't imagine the children being that far away,' Belinda replied in a small voice. 'I thought my heart was going to burst out of my chest when they hugged us earlier. I was quite overcome.' She felt a faint ache in her stomach and guessed that until she held the children in her arms again, that wasn't going anywhere.

'Let's not think about them moving. Not until we speak to Rachel properly about it and find out what's really going on. Did you notice how articulate they've become? Clever children. I'd say far cleverer than I ever was at that age,' Oscar said with pride. His face had a reddish tint, courtesy of the drinks, and his smile broadened as he spoke.

'Rachel and Lorcan have done a wonderful job raising them.'

'And Rachel's had to do a lot of it all on her own.'

He sipped his drink and shook his head, seemingly unable to articulate his thoughts properly.

'I know,' Belinda said reassuringly. 'We should have done more to help.'

She could read her husband's mind. She knew him well. That was one of the joys of spending a near lifetime with someone.

They sat in silence for a moment as the barman swapped their empty tumblers for more fresh drinks, both contemplating why they *hadn't* done more.

Eventually, Belinda broke the silence again. 'I'm sorry I didn't discuss it with you first before I jumped in to say we'd support Rachel. But I was so incensed on her behalf,' she said.

'You got there before me, that's all.' Oscar reached out and rested a comforting hand on his wife's. 'My heart broke seeing how worried Rachel looked as Sheila threw the accusations at her.'

'It's the children's faces I can't stop thinking about. An unforgivable thing to say in their presence – that Rachel wasn't their mother. That must have been so confusing for them.'

'And when Dylan started to sob, it was the darnedest thing. It reminded me of something that happened with Lorcan years ago. Do you remember the day his pet rabbit died? He was about Dylan's age, I reckon.'

'How could I forget? That dog that broke into the garden – it was like a Tarantino movie.'

'That's a good description for it. Lorcan sobbed his heart out then. It's funny how a sound can take you back. Dylan looked so like his father then. I hadn't thought he looked like him at all until that moment . . .'

Belinda took another sip of her drink and closed her eyes for a moment, her mind latched on to an image of Lorcan morphing into Dylan.

'Do you think there's anything we can do to help Rachel? Lorcan would want us to.'

'We haven't earned the right to be her confidants yet. We don't deserve her trust. And she must have felt like a sacrificial lamb today, as everyone fought around her. Maybe she doesn't want our help?'

Shaking his head, Oscar replied, 'I'm not sure I agree with that. I don't believe Rachel is fragile at all. She's stronger than she may even realize herself. She would never have gotten through the past two years if not. I do think we could do something to at least show our support, though. Send her flowers, maybe?'

'Well, as we're still in Malahide, why don't we call to see them all again tomorrow. That way, we can hand-deliver a gift for each of them. It might give them a lift after all the upset. And we want to do something for them to celebrate their new official family status,' Belinda said determinedly.

'Splendid idea. We better call first, though. Don't want to ambush the girl.'

'We'll message in the morning, and if it doesn't suit her to see us, we can leave gifts on her doorstep quietly.'

With a plan made, they both felt something they'd not had in their lives for some time – hope.

And yet, that hope could well be on the verge of shattering. As they both climbed into their unfamiliar hotel bed that night, they lay in silence holding hands. And the last thing Belinda thought, before sleep overcame her, was, *What if Rachel does decide to leave?*

TWENTY

Annie

Napier, Hawke's Bay

It was low tide as Annie, Joe and Claudia walked along the beach. They passed the dramatic rock beds, the towering cliffs giving shelter to the evening wind. They walked in silence, each thinking about their earlier chat with Rachel, until they took a seat at a benched area, on a hill overlooking the bay. When Rachel had phoned them in tears earlier, after her party ended in disaster, they were horrified to hear the things Sheila had said.

'I feel so bloody useless,' Annie said. 'I'm her mother. But what use am I to her? No good whatsoever when I'm here and she's over there. I can't bear to think of her on her own with that awful family.'

'I feel guilty. It was me who put the idea of them moving back here into the kids' heads in the first place. Poor Rachel is copping the blame!' Claudia said, then added in a whisper, 'Do you think she might actually come home?'

The hope and ache in Claudia's voice made Annie want to weep, because she felt exactly the same way. But she couldn't allow herself to go there.

'Stop feeling guilty,' she said, 'you've done nothing wrong. But I think we shouldn't run ahead of ourselves. And from what I can gather, there has been a lot of things unsaid from the Butler family – this isn't just about the possibility of New Zealand.'

'Thanks, Mom. I'm still a little in shock at how the afternoon turned out for Rachel.'

'Things fester when you let them build up inside of you. They'd all do well to go see a grief counsellor if you ask me.'

'Exactly,' Joe agreed. 'Why didn't Sheila ask Rachel about New Zealand when the kids mentioned it, rather than wait until the party to say it and ruin a special day for everyone?'

'I can understand why the idea of losing the kids would make them so upset. They love them. We can't fault them for that,' Annie acknowledged carefully. When she'd seen Rachel's tears on their earlier video call, it had broken her heart. And she'd felt a piercing pain because, thousands of miles away, there was absolutely nothing she could do to help her daughter. But then again, at least her daughter was alive.

'Fair enough, Mom. But it still doesn't excuse those awful things she said,' Claudia reminded her. 'It was spiteful. And calling you two step-grandparents. I hate that term.'

'I couldn't love those children any more than I already

do,' Annie said sadly. 'I've never thought of myself as a step-grandparent. Ever.'

'I know, love. I'm the same,' Joe said. 'But it appears that Sheila and Adrian have ideas about the hierarchy of us all in the family. It's obvious that they feel they are the number one grandparents.'

'And what are we? Number three, I suppose, by their reckoning.' Annie kicked a pebble beneath her as she spoke, sending it flying across the path.

'And now she's threatening to take her to court for custody? That's on another level. The old bitch,' Claudia said bitterly.

'I think we should do something to make sure they know we don't care about blood, or step this or step that,' Joe said. 'We just want what's best for the kids, and so should they.'

'All we can do is continue doing what we've always done,' Annie replied, ever the level-headed one. 'And that's love those children. That's all any grandparent can do. Love, unconditionally.'

'You're right,' Joe said, his eyes soft with emotion.

'I know what I'm going to do,' Claudia said. 'I've got some vacation time banked. I'm going to go to Ireland.'

'That's not a bad idea, actually. Maybe we should wait a few months, though, and plan to go for Christmas? We can all go,' Joe said.

'I love that. Christmas as a family together would be amazing. And I think it's exactly what Rachel needs right now,' Annie agreed. Up to this point, she had always prided herself on being supportive to Rachel about living in Ireland. And not once had she ever put pressure on her to return home, no matter how much she wanted to.

But as she spoke with Joe and Claudia about Rachel's situation in Dublin, Annie had to admit that she felt a trace of excitement too. What if, when they visited Rachel in Dublin, they could convince her to return to her homeland with them when they came back?

'I'll talk to Howard, see if he can swing a few weeks off in December. I'm warning you though, Mom and Dad, if the Butlers want a fight, well, they can bloody well have one. But they better know that if they take on one Anderson, they take on the lot of us!'

TWENTY-ONE

Rachel

Malahide, Dublin

When Rachel awoke the following day, she felt disorientated. Her mouth was dry and the start of a headache made itself known. Had she dreamt the whole sorry affair at her adoption party? Her phone confirmed not, with several text messages. The first was from Ronan.

Hope you get some sleep. Don't let the out-laws get you down. You have done nothing wrong.

Then from Claudia:

I've put a hex on the Butlers. The next time you see them, they will all have little piggy tails.

This came with a GIF of three little pigs running around a farmyard.

And from Jack:

I'm worried about you. Are you okay?

And perhaps most surprising of all, from Belinda:

Good morning, Rachel. We decided to stay overnight in the Grand Hotel. If you felt up to it, we would love to call in to say hello before returning to Belfast. You have been in our thoughts ever since we left yesterday. And we've been so worried about you.

She hadn't heard from her in-laws in ages and now twice in two days. She let her head drop back on to the pillow. It was typical. In all honesty, right now she would have liked a day off from all of Lorcan's family. Both the in-laws and the out-laws. She hauled herself out of bed, dry-swallowed two Nurofen from her bathroom cabinet, then offered up a silent prayer that they do their job quickly.

She'd hoped that the only plans for this Sunday were those that included staying in pyjamas for the day and eating large tubs of ice cream with the kids. But Belinda and Oscar had shown her solidarity the afternoon before, so she felt she couldn't say no.

The kids moaned at having to wear clothes when a PJ day had been promised, but when they saw Grandma Belinda and Grandpa Oscar arrive, armed with presents, they soon brightened up. They looked impeccable as usual, despite wearing yesterday's clothes. Not a wrinkle or stain in sight.

'You brought them gifts yesterday,' Rachel protested. She felt a little unnerved by their generosity. She remembered how cross Lorcan got whenever large parcels arrived for the kids from his parents. He thought that they bought affection as opposed to earning it. And she could see where he was coming from, looking at the extravagance in front of her.

'It's just a few bits we found in the cutest little toy shop we passed in Malahide village. We went for an early walk and it called to us as we walked by,' Oscar explained. His eyes, so like Lorcan's, were pleading with her not to disapprove.

'It's very generous, but really, too much. It's enough for the children to spend time with you. That's the real gift,' Rachel said.

'I think it's just the right amount, Mom,' Dylan said, in a serious tone, which made them all laugh, breaking the uneasiness.

Rachel knew she was fighting a losing battle. The kids had already ripped open the gift bags and there was a pile of rainbow-coloured tissue paper strewn at their feet. And somehow, she knew instinctively that Belinda and Oscar were not only offering gifts this time, but something far more important – themselves.

'We worried about the children all evening, after yesterday's . . . drama. We couldn't help ourselves. We wanted to spoil them a little,' Oscar said apologetically, and it made Rachel's heart go out to him.

'You are quite right, Rachel, of course you are. It shouldn't be all about gifts. But please let us spoil them this one time. We promise we'll rein it in again in future,' Belinda said.

Rachel was mollified by Belinda's words and the anxiety she could see on the woman's face, and besides, what could she do now the children had already opened their gifts?

'It's a train set!' Dylan screamed.

'I had one like it when I was a boy. I can help you set it up if you like,' Oscar said.

Dylan looked at Rachel, unsure, and she nodded encouragingly.

'Okay, Grandpa,' Dylan said, making space so that Oscar could sit beside him.

'Oh, Grandma and Grandpa, I really like this pen set,' Olivia said, having opened hers too now. 'Mom, what's that fancy word for writing?'

'Calligraphy,' Rachel replied.

'Your handwriting was so beautiful on the heartprint you sent us; we hoped you might enjoy it,' Belinda said.

Olivia beamed at the compliment. 'I'm going to write something straight away. What should I write?'

'Why don't you find one of the Dr Seuss poems you like from your book and then copy one of those?' Rachel suggested. Olivia ran off immediately to get started.

'Coffee?' Rachel asked, turning to Belinda and Oscar with a polite smile. Without waiting for a response, she began to get the machine ready, filling the water tank and placing a cartridge in the pod slot. Her head still banging, she was in desperate need of the coffee herself. Oscar nodded enthusiastically before taking Dylan and the train set off to the family room, leaving Rachel and Belinda alone in the kitchen.

'How are you feeling today? That was quite an afternoon,' Belinda said, her quiet, cultured voice making it

difficult for Rachel to know how her mother-in-law really
felt. She didn't want to start crying again, but even the
mention of the disaster the tea party had become nearly
set her off. But despite barely knowing Belinda, there
was something about being asked how she was, by an
adult, that made Rachel want to spill all her thoughts,
and she found herself opening up to Belinda almost
straight away.

'I didn't think Sheila could shock me any more,' Rachel
admitted cautiously. 'She's had her moments over the
years. But she outdid herself yesterday.'

'I've been witness to her moments once or twice, so I
hear you.' Belinda paused for a moment, then said, 'Can
I ask you something? You don't have to answer if you
don't want to.'

'You want to know if I'm planning on moving home
to New Zealand?'

Belinda nodded, as Rachel handed a latte to her.

'One moment, I'll just take this drink to Oscar,' Rachel
said, sneaking a glance at her mother-in-law. Her face
was impassive as it often was, and she couldn't work out
what Belinda was thinking. Was she here for a row too?
Rachel had only felt support from her over the past
twenty-four hours. And up to yesterday, she would have
thought that her in-laws really didn't care what she or
the children did. But now she wasn't sure of anything.
Belinda followed her out of the kitchen and they took a
seat at the dining room table, talking quietly while the
kids played with Oscar in the family room.

'As I tried to say yesterday, I have no secret plans to
leave Ireland. Sheila got her wires crossed. I can only
assume that the children mentioned something to her about

our recent vacation back home. Yes, it's true that while we were in Napier, my sister Claudia showed me a house that had recently gone on to the market. It's a beautiful villa and it has sentimental attachments for me. As a child, I'd always dreamt of living in it. For a few short hours, while I was with my family, I fantasized about selling up and taking the children over there. I dreamt about a new beginning for us all. And after the past couple of years, that was a tempting dream.'

'I can understand why that might be something you'd consider. I've often thought that you must miss your family terribly. And how hard it must be for your parents to not have you and the children close by.' Belinda took a delicate sip of her coffee as she spoke, sighing with pleasure.

'It's difficult, and that's why I get why the children's grandparents here would find it so hard if we were to go.'

The two women shared a look at the parallels between both scenarios.

'It's hard to explain how good it felt to be home again over summer. To see my parents and my sister in person and not at the end of an iPad screen.' Rachel paused for a moment, her voice cracking as she remembered that first hug from her parents after so long.

Belinda opened her handbag and silently passed Rachel a white linen handkerchief.

Rachel gathered herself, then continued, 'It hurts to live on the other side of the world to a large part of my family. When we arrived home at Napier, I immediately felt enveloped by their support and love, two things I just don't have here in Ireland. I didn't know how much I needed to feel that, until . . .'

Rachel stopped as she realized she was being too emotionally vulnerable with someone she didn't know that well. But Belinda looked sympathetic, not uncomfortable, at her display of emotion.

'That's always the way, isn't it? You don't know how much you miss someone until they are taken from you.' And this time it was Belinda's voice filled with sorrow. Unused to seeing emotion from her normally composed mother-in-law, Rachel was startled.

For a second, she thought Belinda was going to lose her usual self-control as a shadow passed over her face. But it passed as quickly as it arrived. Rachel surmised that if Belinda hadn't lost it at her only son's funeral, she wasn't going to do so here, now, in a suburban kitchen.

'So you're no longer tempted?' Belinda asked.

'I've booked three one-way tickets. We're leaving in an hour,' Rachel said, deadpan, then quickly added, 'Joke!' when she saw Belinda's shocked face. 'No, is the actual answer. In all honesty, as soon as I came back to Ireland, I forgot all about emigrating. I couldn't take the children from any of you.'

Belinda seemed to visibly breathe a sigh of relief. She had clearly been waiting for a confirmed answer to that question ever since yesterday afternoon.

'What a silly woman Sheila is. She could have clarified the issue, rather than refusing to ask for the whole story and causing such an upsetting scene for everyone.'

'My mother reckons that Sheila has been angry for some time, that it's not just about New Zealand. I suppose it came to an unfortunate head yesterday. Jack texted me earlier, actually; he wants to come over for a chat. I feel sorry for him. He's stuck in the middle of it all.'

Belinda nodded supportively, then seemed to want to take Rachel's mind on to happy things. 'So, tell me about this house in New Zealand. Why is it so special for you?'

Rachel smiled; she couldn't help it. Whenever she thought about that villa, it made her happy.

'It's a traditional villa, laced with white portico trim. With a front porch and shutters on the windows. And it's nestled at the top of Bluff Hill, overlooking the most spectacular views of Cape Kidnappers bay. It sounds fanciful, but as I walked through it, I could almost hear the house whispering to me, sharing its secrets.' Rachel blushed, picking up her coffee, worried what Belinda would think of her waxing lyrically about a house.

'I think that sounds wonderful,' Belinda said, not looking in the least bit shocked by Rachel's description.

'When I was a kid, I'd dream about living there with at least half a dozen rescue dogs,' Rachel laughed as she recalled this outrageous dream of hers.

'Ah, the hopes and dreams of young girls should never be undermined. We all had them one way or the other. I also dreamt of living in a big house on a fancy tree-lined avenue when I was younger.'

'And you've done that,' Rachel smiled.

'Yes, I have. And I love our house, but I suppose I've realized now that it's not bricks and mortar that make a home. It's the love inside the four walls. You may not have the rescue dogs, but you have a home filled with love here, Rachel. I felt it the second I walked through the front door.' Belinda looked around the kitchen and dining room with approval as she took in the children's artwork and toys that sat among the warm, comfortable decor.

'That's nice to hear. It *is* a house filled with love. Always has been. But if I'm honest, I don't feel an emotional connection to it. As you know, this house was Lorcan and Niamh's originally, and in some ways it's always felt like theirs, not ours.'

Rachel's eyes scanned the room, landing on the light oak laminated floors, which she'd never cared for, preferring darker tones.

'Anyway, the villa in Hawke's Bay is architecturally beautiful, of course. But it's also so much more than just the aesthetics. It's the feeling I get when I'm there. And the children felt it too. I know it sounds silly and romantic . . .'

'Nothing wrong with romantic notions,' Belinda put her coffee cup down and reached over to touch Rachel's hand. 'It sounds to me like you haven't firmly closed the door on the villa. And while Oscar and I would be upset to see you and the children leave, we also would never stand in your way. I want you to know that.'

Rachel could barely believe the words Belinda was saying. She'd assumed that taking the children out of Ireland would have made her more enemies than just Sheila. Now, she realized how much having Belinda's support meant to her. She wished Lorcan were here to witness it.

'That's kind of you. It really is. For now, I'm just thinking of alternatives. Ronan pointed out that Dublin is a big place. Maybe I just need to think about moving from this house, this road, so close to the Butlers. This clearly isn't working.'

'I'd love to help you look, if you ever decide to go house-hunting.' A flush stained Belinda's perfectly made-up face. 'Of course, I would never impose. It's just . . . it would be good to have a task to focus on.'

'I'd love your help, Belinda, if and when the time comes. Maybe I can find an Irish villa. That's a nice thought.'

As she spoke, the doorbell rang. Dashing to the hallway from the dining room, Rachel pulled open the door and was surprised to see Ronan standing on the doorstep. He gave her a rueful grin.

'Sorry for dropping by unannounced. I wanted to call in to see how you are.'

'Join the club,' Rachel said, nodding behind her, where Belinda and Oscar were poking their heads round. 'Your aunt and uncle are here too.'

Leaving the children to their new toys and a fresh stash of Oreo chocolate courtesy of Ronan, the adults all sat at the dining room table with fresh coffee. Rachel brought out a plate of cakes left over from the party the day before. Strangely enough, no one had eaten much with everything else going on.

'You look very fancy for a Sunday morning,' Rachel noted, as she placed a steaming mug of coffee on the table in front of Ronan, taking in his navy jacket and white shirt. 'Where are you off to?'

'I'm meeting a friend for brunch. Apparently, it's the new thing to do at the weekend. I hope they serve roast beef. I've a real goo on me for one with all the trimmings,' Ronan said.

'It will be all egg white omelettes and fruit, my boy,' Oscar said with a shiver as if the mere mention made him ill.

Ronan's face made them all laugh.

'It must be a special friend,' Rachel teased gently,

delighted when she saw the hint of a blush on Ronan's face. 'I knew it. Does this mean you're currently "on" with your girlfriend?'

'Is there someone special in your life?' Belinda asked. 'I hadn't heard. But then again, your father never tells us anything.'

Ronan put his hands up. 'Woah there, you two! Women, you're all the same. Always looking for a chance to wear a hat.' He looked sheepish and paused before continuing. 'Okay, I'll admit it. This is a date, but there's no need for anyone to get excited,' he added quickly, watching delight and intrigue flash across everyone's faces.

Olivia and Dylan ran over to see what all the laughter was about.

'Ronan here is in love,' Rachel told them, to which the children both squealed 'Ewww' loudly in unison.

'Your mother is mistaken. My heart is firmly secure right here. It will take a very fair maiden to seduce it,' Ronan pointed to his chest.

'What does seduce mean?' Dylan asked, which made the grown-ups laugh some more.

'I bet you wish you *were* moving now, to get away from all of this drama,' Ronan said, once they'd disappeared.

'She has one-way tickets booked, actually,' Belinda said, as deadpan as Rachel had been earlier. It was the first time Rachel had seen a part of Lorcan shine through in his mother. It was nice to see where he had got his sense of humour from.

'Well, if Sheila does insist on going forward with the idiocy of looking for custody, give me a call.' He looked at Rachel, serious now.

'And you can send any legal bills to me,' Oscar jumped in. 'I'll be taking care of them.'

Rachel blinked. This was all moving too fast for her. Yesterday, she was happy to celebrate the children's adoption. And in less than twenty-four hours, she was talking about getting legal representation for a custody battle.

'The Butlers couldn't take the children from me, could they?' she asked. Saying this out loud made her feel shivery, and a cold sweat broke out above her upper lip and on her palms.

Belinda and Oscar began reassuring Rachel that of course the children were going nowhere, but Ronan remained quiet.

'Can they take the children from me?' she repeated.

He paused before answering. 'They can try,' he eventually replied, all merriment gone from his voice now.

'And what will happen if they do try?' Rachel whispered.

'Well, what I can tell you for sure is that the grandparents would need a strong case to succeed in taking custody of a grandchild. First of all, they would have to show that their age, health and financial situation allows them to take care of Olivia and Dylan.'

'They are as fit as I am. And are financially doing okay. They own their own house, business . . .' Rachel's voice trailed off.

'Well, it's a good job that's not all, then. They also have to show that the parent is unfit. If there was a history of child abuse or neglect, then naturally, that's a different story.'

'Rachel is an exemplary mother,' Oscar said defensively.

'I know that. Remember, the courts will always award custody based on the best interest of the children. And unless something is going on here that I'm not aware of, there isn't a court that would take the children from Rachel. But once again, let's not get ahead of ourselves and worry about something that might not happen. If, and only if, the Butlers go ahead with their plan to fight for custody, *then* we can get into what our strategy should be.'

'Strategy?' Rachel asked, her voice coming out in a squeak now. She was falling more out of her depth with each passing moment.

'Unfortunately, strategy is necessary for any custody battle. But honestly, let's park that. Sheila will realize that she's not got a hope in hell of winning and will back down with a bit of luck. If she came to me, that's what I'd tell her at least. Courts will always prefer to keep the children with the parent.'

'Surely the adoption helps too?' Oscar asked.

'Yes. Look, while this is a complex case, we've got lots going in our favour, not least of which, the children have been in your care for several years. There's no need to panic just yet; we'll take care of this if it comes.'

'Is there anything Rachel should be doing in the meantime?' Oscar asked. 'You know, getting our ducks in a row, so to speak?'

Belinda opened her handbag and pulled a small leather notebook and pen from it, handing it to Oscar, who began to take notes. Rachel was beginning to get a handle on these two. They were a strong double act and, she suspected, a force to be reckoned with.

'Perception is everything, Rachel,' Ronan explained. 'One of the first things you'll have to get your head around is that it doesn't matter if the things being said about you are true; what matters is whether the court believes them.

Keep being a loving, committed, involved and competent parent to Olivia and Dylan. If the Butlers do come gunning for you, let's make sure you have not left them out any ammunition for free.'

'I can't believe they will actually go ahead with this. Try not to worry,' Belinda said, placing a protective arm over Rachel's. But her face didn't look as convincing as her words sounded.

'It's not just me who will suffer if they go through with this. It's the children,' Rachel answered, looking over at the two of them, who were giggling as they pushed Dylan's new train around its track. 'Regardless of custody suits, I'm going to have to sort this issue out with the Butlers. This morning, Olivia shared that Sheila had corrected them on several occasions when they referred to Niamh as their mammy in heaven. Dylan had a nightmare last night for the first time in months, and I don't believe that was not connected. I can't have Sheila saying things like that to the children again. It's not fair.'

'I think you have no choice but to confront this head-on,' Ronan agreed. He looked at his watch and made a face. 'I'm gonna have to go. Sorry.'

And then the doorbell went for the third time.

'It hasn't been this busy on a Sunday morning in years,' Rachel muttered, rushing once again to answer it.

This time it was Jack. As he followed Rachel into the kitchen, a round of subdued good mornings were exchanged. Oscar made a point to speak in a quieter than usual tone, whilst looking Jack squarely in the eye.

'No offence, mate, but I was just leaving,' Ronan said, pushing his chair back and standing up.

'Don't hang around on my behalf. Mate,' Jack replied.

Rachel couldn't miss the sharpness to both their tones, and ushered Ronan to the door before any further blood was shed in her house.

He leaned in close to her as she opened the door for him to leave, 'Just be careful with Jack. I know he's a friend, but he's also Sheila and Adrian's son. Blood is thicker than water and all that . . .'

When Rachel made a face, he said, 'What?'

'You're saying that to the adopted mother, remember?'

'Oh shit. Yeah. Poor choice of words. Look, we all know that blood doesn't make a family. Love does. But you know what I meant all the same. I'm just not sure I'd trust Jack to side with you over his parents, that's all.'

Rachel batted away his concern. 'Jack, more than anyone else, has seen first-hand how close I am to the children. We won't have to worry about him. Honestly.'

'I wouldn't be doing my job if I didn't at least mention it,' Ronan responded.

Rachel thanked him, wishing him luck on his date, and then returned to the dining room, where she found an awkward trio sitting in silence. Oscar and Belinda stood up and made their excuses, saying they wanted to get a head start on traffic. Olivia and Dylan hugged them tightly and Rachel was happy to witness that the distance of the past couple of years hadn't affected the love between them all.

'Can we see you next weekend?' Dylan asked.

'I'm not sure about that, as Grandma and Grandpa live a little bit away from us,' Rachel answered, worried that the children had put them on the spot.

'We'll see you again very soon, though,' Belinda said, as she squeezed Dylan.

'I want to go for a sleepover,' Olivia said.

Belinda and Oscar looked at each other for the briefest of moments, then nodded with big grins. 'We'd love that,' Belinda said, quickly looking to Rachel to make sure she'd not overstepped the mark.

'That sounds like a great plan,' Rachel answered warmly.

The three of them waved Oscar and Belinda off at the door, waiting until their car disappeared from sight before they returned inside.

TWENTY-TWO

Rachel

Malahide, Dublin

'Why don't you both see how tall you can make a Lego tower?' Rachel suggested to Dylan and Olivia, hoping they'd find something to distract themselves so she could chat privately to Jack. Once they were knee-deep in coloured blocks, she turned her attention to Jack. They looked at each other in silence, each trying to work out what to say.

And then Rachel felt a bubble of laughter creep into her throat. Before she could stop it, she was laughing out loud. She clasped a hand over her mouth, but not before Jack began to laugh too. And once they both started, neither could stop. They laughed until tears were spilling from their eyes. And as soon as they stopped, one of them would say, 'But not a real grandparent . . .' and then they were off again.

When they eventually calmed down, Rachel felt like lead weights had fallen from her shoulders.

'I needed that.'

'Me too,' Jack agreed, finally regaining his composure. 'I have been so stressed about seeing you. I was worried you'd slam the door in my face.'

Rachel made another round of coffees and tried not to think about the caffeine she'd had. It wasn't even lunchtime yet. She'd cut down tomorrow.

'Before we go any further, we need to clarify something. I have no plans to move to New Zealand. There's no big scheme going on behind all of your backs.'

'At the moment or ever?' Jack asked.

Rachel shook her head. 'I don't know what the future holds, any more than you do. But right now is all that matters.' She said this definitively, not wanting a counter argument back from Jack.

He nodded.

Rachel moved to the fridge and pulled out the Victoria sponge Sheila had brought with her yesterday, as yet untouched. She cut two large slices, then placed one in front of each of them. It felt like they needed it.

'Say what you like about your mam,' she said, lifting a slice to her mouth, 'there's nobody who has as light a touch as her.' She bit into the soft, airy sponge, filled with sweet cream and raspberry jam.

Jack grabbed a napkin and reached over to wipe a dusting of icing sugar that now coated Rachel's nose. 'I really am sorry, Rachel.'

'You've done nothing wrong, Jack. But it's going to take me some time to forgive your mother. She upset me. But more importantly, she upset the children. Not to mention my parents and Claudia too.'

Jack nodded, unable to disagree. 'She'll calm down. She just needs a little time.'

Suddenly, Rachel was angry. This wasn't just a case of *calming down*. 'No,' she spoke clearly. 'Sheila interferes, she criticizes, she undermines. I take it all on the chin, for the sake of the children and out of respect for Niamh. But now, enough is enough.'

She stood up and paced around the room for a moment, trying to gather her thoughts. She needed to regain some control in her life. She couldn't go on feeling like she was spiralling down a hole. 'Would you do something for me?'

'If I can, of course. I'd do anything for you. And the kids . . .'

'I want the spare key back to my home. Sheila has been letting herself in and out of here for years. I cannot let that happen any more.'

'She'll go crazy,' Jack said, recoiling at the thought.

'As opposed to the rational way she behaves now? I have to know that I can wake up and not find someone in my kitchen, ironing the kids' clothes, and making a snide remark at me for not being dressed at ten a.m. on a Sunday morning with "so much to be done".'

'She never . . .' Jack's voice faltered.

'She did. A few weeks after we got back from our vacation, that's exactly what I found when I came downstairs, clutching my hairdryer as a weapon because I heard a noise. I thought we were being burgled. She's lucky I didn't do her head in.'

'Or give her a blow dry,' Jack said, and then they were off again, laughing hysterically.

When they calmed down, Rachel said, 'If you'd rather not get in the middle, it's okay. I'll ask Sheila myself.'

'No, no, leave it with me. The least I can do,' Jack replied, although he didn't look confident. Instead, he changed the topic. 'So what brought Ronan here today?'

'He called to see how I was, just like you,' Rachel said, confused why Jack would ask.

Jack made a face. It was clear that he didn't like the Bradleys, old or young.

'You should be careful with that fella Ronan.'

Rachel couldn't believe her ears. Less than an hour ago, Ronan had said much the same thing about Jack. What was going on with those two?

'He's only ever been kind to me,' she answered, feeling the need to speak up for Ronan, in the same way as she'd done for Jack earlier.

'All I know is that Niamh always said he was a bad influence on Lorcan. That when they got together, there was always trouble.'

'Well, that's news to me. Lorcan only spoke highly of him.'

Jack didn't look convinced.

'I saw the way he looked at you,' he shook his head. 'Niamh said he was a womanizer. Different women on the go all the time.'

'Well, I don't suppose that's changed. Ronan was on his way to meet a new girlfriend when he left here. But I'd warrant a guess that the last thing Ronan Bradley wants is a widow with two small children. Relax.' Rachel spoke briskly, tired of feeling that her entire life was everyone's business. She wanted the conversation to be over, and Jack took the hint.

Instead, they played Lego with the kids for an hour, and Jack ended up staying for Sunday lunch. Rachel didn't have the energy to make a traditional roast, so she opted for a quick quiche Lorraine, with a side of homemade chips. It was one of her tried and tested, quick and easy meals that they all loved.

After a pleasant couple of hours, they settled down to watch some TV, Jack helping Rachel put the kids to bed after a late-night supper of ham and cheese sandwiches. Somewhere along the way, Rachel realized that not only had Jack been with them the whole day, but her tension headache had finally left her for the first time in twenty-four hours.

'I'm glad you called over,' she turned to look at him, sitting next to her on the sofa.

'I love spending time with you all,' he replied simply.

As he spoke, he looked at Rachel with such sincerity she felt a rush of warmth for her brother-out-law. Ronan clearly didn't know what he was talking about.

'And we love you being here too. The children adore you, and I have to admit that having a second pair of hands to wrestle the children into their PJs and bed is most welcome.'

'I can come over any night to help.'

'Don't say that too often or I might take you up on the offer!' Rachel joked.

'Would you like a glass of wine to finish the night off?' Jack asked. 'I can go out to the off-licence if you don't have anything in the house.'

'Nice idea, but do you mind if we call it quits now? I'm such a lightweight, and if I'm honest, I'm exhausted after the drama of yesterday. I want to flop into bed, maybe read for an hour.'

Jack nodded. As he left, he said confidently, 'I'll get that key from Mam, I promise.'

'You're a good friend,' Rachel told him. She thought for a moment he was going to say something else, but he thought better of whatever it was and disappeared into the dark blue night, with just a wave of his hand.

TWENTY-THREE

Rachel

Malahide, Dublin

Days passed and the spring made its goodbyes, making way for the summer. Jack continued to be a regular visitor, and as promised, he returned the spare key. Rachel didn't ask any questions about how Sheila had taken it. He had become like a buffer, too, when the children visited their grandparents, collecting and dropping them off so that Sheila and Rachel had no reason to meet. Rachel was grateful for his support and knew she couldn't have managed without him. There was no further mention of custody battles. Rachel hoped that they had held off that storm.

But right now, Rachel's only concern was her son's first day of school. While he wouldn't officially start until September, tradition was that all the new children went into school for one day in May, to get used to their classrooms and meet their teacher. A big moment for everyone.

On the day, Dylan chose what they would eat for breakfast (pancakes), and what time they would leave home so there would be no issues with last-minute traffic. How long Rachel would stay with Dylan when he arrived at school was still up for negotiation. She'd prepared both his and Olivia's lunches with great care, and cut sandwiches into four triangles, just as her mom had done for her as a child. Opening their lunchboxes, she placed the sandwich, a yoghurt and some chopped melon into each one. Then she added a folded note she'd prepared the previous night. The note had a drawing of a melon slice, next to which she'd written, 'You are one in a MELON.'

Dylan would have to ask his teacher to help him read it, but that might be a good thing, she figured.

As they arrived at the school gates, they sat in the car for a moment to gather themselves, giving them an overview of the other families as they arrived. Dylan grew quieter by the second, and when Rachel suggested they make a move, his mood switched from excited nervousness to full-on stressed-out child. It was as if someone had flipped a switch.

'I'm not going and you can't make me,' he said, bottom lip wobbling in defiance.

A look passed between them, so many layers hidden within that short glance.

Helplessness.

Stubbornness.

Fear.

And more than anything else, sorrow. One so deep that there were no words that could adequately describe the feeling.

'I know you're scared . . .' Rachel began.

'I'm not scared,' Dylan insisted, 'I just don't want to go.'

'You have to go. Plus, I don't want to be late,' Olivia said, in a voice that reminded Rachel so much of herself. Olivia was anxious to go in. She wanted to show off her French braids to her best friends Jane and Annemarie, a hairstyle that Rachel had spent hours watching YouTube tutorials in order to perfect.

'We've got plenty of time, don't worry,' Rachel said to her, desperate to placate both children, then turned her attention back to Dylan, trying to think of ways to entice him out of the car. 'Don't you want your classmates to see your new lunchbox and water bottle?'

'Does it have my special treats in it?' Dylan asked.

'Yes, it does. And a little surprise for you too.' She made an effort to keep her voice bright and then continued, 'Remember that it's only for a few hours. I'll be back to collect you before you've had a chance to even miss me.'

'Why can't I stay home? I'll be so good and won't make any noise. See.' He pulled an imaginary zip closed across his little mouth.

'Can I tell you a secret?' Rachel asked. 'If I had my way, you'd stay home with me – both of you would. And you could make as much noise as you wanted. But it's not my way. And that's a good thing. Because you are both going to have so much fun today in school, you'll learn lots and make friends . . .'

'I have to go in now, Dylan,' Olivia interrupted her mother's words. 'Miss is changing our seats today and I want to make sure she lets me sit beside Jane and Annemarie.'

Rachel looked at her daughter and marvelled at how grown up she looked.

Olivia softened. 'I had the best time on my first day,' she said now, stepping into the big sister role and speaking with a kindness Rachel didn't know she had mastered. 'You will too, Dylan, I promise.'

But Dylan had started to cry, a low, quiet whimper, with fat tears splashing down his cheeks.

'Oh, sweetheart . . .' Rachel leaned through the seats and tried to pull him into her arms. But he wiggled away and pushed himself against the side of the car. He didn't want any comfort from her at that moment.

'Talk to me, tell me what's wrong,' Rachel pleaded.

Dylan refused to speak.

Then Olivia said in a voice far too old for her eight years, 'He misses Daddy. He saw those families go by and they all had a mam and dad holding their hands. Dylan wants Daddy.'

Relief flooded Dylan's face as she spoke.

Rachel kicked herself that she hadn't worked this out, but felt joy that the two of them could understand each other in a way that only siblings could.

'Well, I miss your daddy too,' she said now. 'Last night I dreamt of him and when I woke up, for a moment, I thought he was still with us.'

It was always the same for Rachel; before any big moment, she dreamt of Lorcan. He was always with her somehow.

For a moment, she wished she could run back to their bedroom, climb into bed and weep for her husband. She would close her eyes and find her favourite memories of her darling man and savour them slowly, one by one, pretending she didn't live in a world where he no longer was.

But of course, she couldn't do that.

She had responsibilities. And today, whether Dylan liked it or not, was the first day of a new adventure for him. Big school, something he'd spoken about in excited anticipation ever since he'd watched Olivia walk through the gates four years previously. Rachel willed herself to get it together. To find a way to say the right words to her children, to help them through this day.

'I know today isn't the day that either of you wants. That the world we live in now isn't the one that we wish with all our might that we lived in. But it's the only one we have, and at least we have each other. And while your daddy isn't here to hold your hand today, Dylan, he is still with us. He's always with you both because he's in your hearts.' Rachel clasped each of their hands between her own. 'He would be so proud of you both. And especially proud of his big boy about to start school. So, let's wipe our tears away and together, we'll walk into your classroom and get you settled. Then when you finish at noon, which is only a few hours away, after all, I'll be at the gates waiting for you. And there's something you probably don't know, but as it's your first day of school, that means you get a treat this afternoon.'

Dylan looked up with interest.

'There's going to be sundaes. The biggest ice-cream sundae I can fit into our bowls.'

'With a chocolate flake?' Dylan asked.

'Oh yes. Maybe even *two* flakes,' Rachel said, feeling not one bit guilty for using ice cream to bribe him.

'But we're not allowed treats during the week,' Olivia said, shocked.

'Quite right, sweetheart. But today is a special day, so you each get an exemption.'

The bribery did the trick and, finally, they made their way towards the school gate.

Rachel paused in front of the entrance, where a large placard announced its welcome to the school. Rachel took out her phone and swiped open the camera.

'Let's take some photos quickly before we go in.'

Olivia and Dylan held hands, standing close beside each other as Rachel clicked half a dozen shots off. They would never look at those photographs without feeling a huge lump in their throats; the faces that looked back at the camera were mirrors to each of their silent grief. They walked in through the double glass doors in silence, lost in their thoughts.

They dropped Olivia at her class first, then walked a little further down the corridor to the Junior Infants class. Mr Sheehan walked over to greet them, 'Oh, you must be Dylan, the last of our newbies.'

Rachel felt the eyes of the room on them all. Standing beside each of the new schoolgoers were their parents. Young, bright, shiny-faced couples, all aglow with pride as they joined their child for their first day of school. And for a moment, Rachel hated them all; for being alive and together, a united proud front for their child.

Mr Sheehan gestured towards a table of four at the back of the room and pulled out the last remaining seat, telling Dylan to leave his bag on the floor beside him. 'There are crayons and paper; why don't you do a picture for us. Anything at all that you want to draw.'

'I don't want to draw,' Dylan whispered.

'That's okay. We'll find something else for you to do instead; I've got some blocks over here that you can build?'

Mr Sheehan placed the blocks in front of him, then began stacking them, one by one, to encourage Dylan to do the same.

'I want to go home, Mom,' Dylan said, tears threatening to reappear.

Rachel furtively whispered to the teacher that Dylan was especially sad about his daddy today and Mr Sheehan promised he would keep a close eye on Dylan, that she shouldn't worry. He moved away to talk to another parent who caught his attention.

Rachel knelt beside Dylan and together they built the Lego blocks up to a tall tower. Eventually, Mr Sheehan coughed to get all their attention. 'Right, children,' he spoke calmly and warmly, 'it's time to say goodbye to your mammies and daddies . . .'

But as soon as he spoke, he caught Rachel's eye, realizing too late he had said exactly the wrong thing.

Dylan raised his hand and swiped it across the newly built blocks, scattering them in every direction.

TWENTY-FOUR

Rachel

Malahide, Dublin

Rachel drove home numb, her mind full of memories of Olivia's first day of school, when Lorcan was still alive. Her pinafore was so sweet on her and her smile, so proud and happy. It made Lorcan and Rachel both burst with pride and happiness too. They had both taken the day off work and as Dylan was in the creche, they had the day to themselves. They'd eaten a late leisurely breakfast in Avoca at Malahide Castle, swapping supplements in the daily newspaper they shared, then gone home and watched a movie, snuggling together on the couch.

Today, Rachel arrived home on her own, feeling the weight of loneliness pressing her down, her heart sore from walking away from a grief-stricken Dylan. She made a cup of coffee, the hiss of her coffee machine fracturing the silence. She wrapped her hands around the coffee, trying to warm herself; despite the sun shining outside, she felt ice-cold.

She would have loved to take the day off, but she couldn't afford to. She had half a dozen returns to sort out and credits to issue. Not to mention her regular daily Rae's Closet Facebook Live. Her customers had become accustomed to having their morning coffee while watching her share the latest range of clothes she had in stock. Maybe she could forget Dylan's tear-stained face as she left the classroom if she threw herself into work for a couple of hours.

She began looking through the items she wanted to focus on and hung them up on the clothes rail, ready to share.

It was hard not to replay on loop Dylan's face as he scattered his blocks every which way, but as always when Rachel began to think about work, she managed to forget about almost everything else for a short time.

By eleven-thirty, when she waved goodbye to her online customers, she felt like she'd run a marathon. And if her customers could see the carnage that was off camera, they'd be shocked. Clothes were piled up on the sofa in a heap, waiting to be folded or re-hung on the velvet hangers. She took a quick peek at her inbox and was delighted to see over a hundred messages. Some would be asking for information on fit and function, but there were plenty of orders, too. Rachel would have a busy afternoon getting the orders processed, packed and ready for the courier, who arrived at five p.m. every day.

For now, though, they'd have to wait. She needed to get back to the school gates to collect Dylan after his half-day.

Just as she was about to leave, her phone buzzed. It was Claudia on video call.

'Hey, Sis!' Rachel said, delighted with the surprise, then stopped in shock. Claudia was crying. 'What's wrong?'

'These are happy tears!' Claudia squealed.

'What for?'

'You know how much I love being an aunty to Olivia and Dylan . . .'

'Yeah . . .' Rachel was impatient, knowing she couldn't be late for Dylan.

'Well, in another eight months or so, you will get to be an aunty too!' Claudia tried to wipe away tears as fast as they arrived, but they kept streaming down her face.

It took Rachel a moment to catch on to what her sister meant. When the penny finally dropped she began to run around the house, phone in hand, squealing and laughing and whooping.

'You're making me dizzy; slow down. I have a baby to think about now, you know!' But Claudia was laughing and squealing herself, doing a dance on the spot so vigorously the video frame was bouncing up and down as if it too was dancing.

'When did you find out?' Rachel asked when they finally calmed down enough to talk. 'Tell me everything! But quickly. I've got exactly three minutes until I have to collect Dylan.'

'Just now. I haven't even told Howard yet. He's fast asleep. I know you'll think I'm mad, but I couldn't sleep this evening; I just had this *urge* to do a test. I want to say it to him when he's wide awake in the morning, but I had to tell you straight away. You can't say anything to Mom or Dad, though.'

'Mom's the word!' Rachel cried, making Claudia laugh through her happy tears. 'Oh Sis, I am so happy. I wish I were there with you to give you the biggest hug. You are going to be the best mother. What a lucky, lucky baby this will be.'

'Honestly, I've never felt happier than I do right in this moment. I thought it was never going to happen for us.'

'It's the best news. But I have to go! I'll ring you tomorrow; then you can tell me how Howard reacted. He's going to faint, isn't he?'

'Totally. He'll hit the deck before I've finished telling him,' Claudia giggled. 'Go get your boy. Please give him a big hug from his Aunty Claudia.'

As Rachel stood alongside the other parents, her mind kept drifting back to her sister's news. She was excited for Claudia, but amongst the excitement she also, if she was honest, felt a twinge of sadness. Because she would miss out on so much of this baby so far away here in Ireland.

'It's nerve-racking, isn't it?' a woman said to Rachel, stepping a few inches closer to her.

Rachel didn't know her, but she warmed to her big, bright smile instantly. They had a quick chat about their kids and who had the worst first-day nerves, the children or the parents.

'I'm Lucinda. We've just moved to the area, so I don't know anybody. I suppose this is a first day for all of us really.'

Rachel smiled and replied, 'Well, you know one person now. I'm Rachel. Malahide is a beautiful town, I think you'll enjoy it here.'

Then she spotted Mr Sheehan walking out, so all the parents moved forward, craning their necks for a first glimpse of their kids. The children followed him, looking so sweet as they walked in twos, holding hands. Rachel searched the group looking for Dylan and was jubilant when she saw him chatting happily with a little girl with blonde pigtails. Whatever Dylan was saying, the little girl was giggling away.

Once the children saw their parents, all pretence at an orderly walk to the gate disappeared and they ran at full speed, crying out in delight. Dylan leapt into Rachel's arms and she lifted him into a warm embrace, burying her face in his hair.

'I drew a picture for you!' Dylan said, beaming with delight as he shoved the art at her.

'That's the coolest monster I've ever seen!' she replied in wonder, staring at the creation in front of her.

'It's a tree, Mom,' Dylan said, then added, 'But if you want, it can be a tree monster.'

Rachel laughed, and they walked back to the car, hand in hand.

And that's when Rachel spotted them. Hovering at their car, a few feet away, stood Sheila and Adrian. Rachel supposed she could have bundled Dylan into the car and he wouldn't have even noticed they were there, but, knowing Dylan would want to see his grandparents, she pointed at them, 'Look, Dylan. It's your nana and grandad.'

As soon as he spotted them, Dylan broke free, delight spreading across his face. And seeing the reciprocal smile on Sheila and Adrian's faces as they all embraced made Rachel's heart constrict. Their love for the kids was undisputed. And the kids adored them right back. She couldn't come between that, no matter how much Sheila drove her scatty.

'We couldn't resist coming to see you in your uniform,' Sheila said.

'You're a big lad now. No doubt about it. Very smart indeed. And one of the tallest in the class too,' Adrian added, with obvious pride.

Dylan shuffled his feet, a little embarrassed by all the focused attention.

'So what did you do today?' Sheila pressed him.

'We played in the yard and I drew a picture for Mom,' Dylan answered.

Rachel held up the picture and Sheila and Adrian both made the appropriate noises of appreciation.

'Next time, I'll make you both one if you like,' Dylan assured them.

'That would be wonderful,' Sheila said warmly.

Rachel noted that Sheila was making a concerted effort to avoid eye contact with her.

Adrian, however, jumped right in with attempts to mend bridges.

'How are you, Rachel?' he asked pleasantly. 'We hope you don't mind us turning up. We couldn't help ourselves; we've been thinking of this big boy all morning.'

'We've every right to be here,' Sheila said defensively, before Rachel even had a chance to reassure him that it was fine.

Rachel bit back a sigh, aware that Dylan was watching their interaction a little too closely. Kids were clever; they picked up on things far quicker than adults might think.

She turned her frown into a bright smile and replied, 'Of course I don't mind you being here. I took photographs this morning and I plan to send *all* of the grandparents a copy.'

She couldn't help herself emphasizing the word 'all'.

'That's kind of you, Rachel. I'll look forward to seeing them,' Adrian replied politely.

'We're having a special treat when Olivia comes home from school. An ice-cream sundae with two flakes!' Dylan added.

'Well, I made you a treat, too,' Sheila said, handing Dylan a Tupperware box. 'It's a batch of my special brownies. With extra chocolate chips, just for you.'

'Oh wow, that's so cool. Thanks, Nana!' Dylan exclaimed, thrilled with the thought of yet more treats. 'Am I allowed them too, Mom?'

As Sheila rolled her eyes, Rachel couldn't help but feel a little smug that Dylan had checked with her first. 'Of course you can. It's a special day, and that means treats are allowed.'

Sheila cleared her throat as if she planned to say something, but she clearly thought better of it and instead gave Adrian's arm a dig. Rachel thought it would be amusing if it weren't so annoying; Sheila clearly had something she wanted to say but needed Adrian to say it for her.

'We were wondering if the children could come to us for a sleepover on Saturday?' he said, a little awkwardly. 'It's been a while since they've stayed overnight and it would be . . .'

Rachel put her hand up to stop him mid-flow in his prepared speech. It was maddening that they continued to think so little of her that they believed she was petty enough to keep the children from them.

'They love staying with you both. That's not going to change just because you . . .' She stopped and let the unfinished sentence hang in the air between them.

'Thank you, thank you,' Adrian said hurriedly, clearly slightly embarrassed that he'd even had to broach the subject, and throwing in a third thank you for good measure. 'Will you give our love to Olivia?'

'Why don't you do it yourself?' Dylan asked.

An awkward silence followed this question. Again, Rachel watched her youngest look between the grown-ups, a puzzled and slightly worried look on his little face. She was going to have to be the bigger person here. It didn't look like Sheila was ever going to apologize for her behaviour, but one of them was going to have to make a gesture of conciliation, for the children's sake. And today was as good a day as any.

'Here's an idea. Why don't you all come over this afternoon and join us for our celebratory back-to-school ice-cream sundaes? Say, three-thirty? Once Dylan and I are back from the school run?'

Sheila and Adrian glanced at each other and Rachel couldn't miss the look of relief on both their faces.

'That would be very nice,' Sheila said stiffly.

Dylan whooped and gave them both a hug, then pulled Rachel away, talking about the colossal fort he wanted to build with his Lego pieces.

Rachel couldn't help but think she'd done some impressive building herself – the bridge between them all was a little sturdier.

TWENTY-FIVE

Rachel

Malone Park, Belfast

As Rachel turned into Malone Park, where Belinda and Oscar lived, her thoughts turned to Niamh and how she too must have driven along this same road. It was one of those moments that were inevitable for a second wife. And in Rachel's case, she followed in the footsteps of a ghost.

She glanced in the rear-view mirror. The children's faces matched hers. They stared at the road in wonder, soaking up every detail. Olivia couldn't remember being here as a young child, but like Rachel, this was Dylan's first visit.

Not for the first time, Rachel wished she knew more about Lorcan's life before she'd met him. They hadn't done much talking about their families during their hot summer romance. At eighteen, her only thought had been the present, soaking up every moment with her sexy Irish boyfriend. But when he did speak about his parents it was with unmistakable warmth, and she knew she hadn't imagined the closeness between them all, especially as Lorcan was an only son. Somewhere between his marriage to Niamh, and his reconnection with Rachel, something must have gone wrong, to the point that he had become estranged from them.

Looking back now, Rachel kicked herself that she hadn't pushed him more about the rift. Her only excuse was that she'd thought they had a lifetime to learn more about each other, and to mend it.

'Grandma and Grandpa live on a fancy road,' Dylan observed as he stared out the car window.

'I know. The houses are pretty, aren't they?' Rachel said, as she passed an ivy-clad Victorian house.

'Not as fancy as the villa in Hawke's Bay,' Olivia said flatly.

Rachel was worried about Olivia. She'd become increasingly withdrawn over the past couple of weeks. She refused to talk about whatever was bothering her, but Rachel suspected that there was something up with her friendship with Annemarie and Jane. Rachel hoped that having a break away from home at her grandparents' house might cheer her up a little. They'd all been looking forward to it since the date was set a few weeks earlier.

'Keep your eye out for Grandma and Grandpa's house. I think it must be coming up soon on the right-hand side.'

'There it is!' Olivia squealed, and sure enough, they had arrived at Willow Lodge. Rachel pulled into the gravelled driveway, surrounded by meticulously manicured gardens with beautiful mature trees and shrubs. The house was just as impressive as the grounds, the red brick a splash of bright colour peeking through the layers of green ivy creeping up the house's facade.

'Can you believe that Daddy used to play in these gardens when he was a little boy?' Rachel asked, turning back to look at the children, whose faces were pictures of excitement.

'Wow,' Dylan exhaled. 'Can I play in them too?'

'I don't see why not. We'll ask Grandma and Grandpa when we get in. It's a nice day for a game of outside hide and seek, I think!'

Belinda and Oscar stood at the front door, waiting for them and smiling warmly, arms open wide as the kids jumped out of the car and ran towards them. They now had regular video calls with each other and the bond between grandparents and grandchildren had grown stronger with each chat.

'Was the drive okay?' Oscar asked, taking the suitcase from Rachel's hand and kissing her cheek. Rachel nodded as Belinda ushered them into the hall.

Rachel couldn't help herself, she gasped out loud when they walked inside. It felt like she had fallen into the pages of a glossy interior design magazine. She tried to imagine Lorcan here, as a kid, a gangly teenager and the tall, broad man he became. It was disconcerting.

'We're so happy you could come. We've been counting down the days and hours until your visit,' Belinda said, holding each of the children's hands in hers.

And Rachel felt that here, she *was* welcome. It was in stark contrast to how she felt when she walked into the Butlers' house, where there was always a degree of awkwardness. Then a scary thought struck her as she looked around and took in the pristine cream decor.

'Kids, let's all take our shoes off,' she ordered.

'Don't you dare!' Belinda said. 'You must all make yourselves at home. Treat it as you would your own house.'

'Well, we'd take our shoes off at home if we had cream tiles, I promise you,' Rachel said, kicking her trainers off quickly and giving the kids a look that told them under no circumstances were they to walk inside in anything but stockinged feet.

Dylan was way ahead of them, skidding along the polished tiled floor in his socks, delighted with the speed he could get without his trainers.

'Lorcan used to do that all the time as a kid too . . .' Oscar began, but before he could finish the sentence, Dylan came to a crashing stop at the long hall table, knocking a porcelain mask to the ground.

Rachel watched it fall as if in slow motion, but her feet wouldn't move fast enough. Despite reaching out, she saw the object whizz by her fingertips, landing on the floor with a thud. The sound of a crack pierced any hope that it might have survived its fall.

'I'm so sorry. I'll pay for it, of course.' She couldn't believe that she was apologizing for breakages three minutes into their visit. That was a new record.

To her surprise, Belinda and Oscar laughed. 'We never liked that damn thing,' Oscar chuckled. 'It was a gift from friends of ours, bought on their travels in Mozambique. They insisted we place it in the hall, and it's irritated us for years. I wanted to throw it out, but Belinda wouldn't let me. So thank you, Dylan. You've saved us from the torment of that thing and its evil eye!'

'You're welcome, Grandpa Oscar,' Dylan said formally, as if he'd given them the most significant gift of their life.

'You worry too much,' Belinda chastised Rachel, but affectionately. 'Come on, let me show you your bedrooms.' They followed her and Oscar upstairs.

'This is your room, Rachel. I hope you'll be comfortable here.'

Rachel looked at the king-size bed, which was piled high with at least a dozen pillows and cushions in rich jewel tones and had a large velvet burgundy throw at the foot. Once again, she felt overwhelmed by the perfection of the room. She looked down to her skinny blue jeans and stockinged feet and felt too grubby for it.

'Let me know if you need any more blankets or pillows,' Belinda continued obliviously, picking up a fluffy topaz cushion, plumping it, then returning it to the bed once again.

'Erm, I think I'm set. I feel like I've jumped into an Instagram photograph. This bed is gorgeous.' Rachel tried to commit the way it was dressed to memory, so she could recreate it in the morning. Had she even made her bed this morning before she left Dublin?

'I'm thrilled to see our guest room get some use. It's been empty for far too long. We've had the room aired, and all the linen is new,' Belinda explained. 'And next door is the children's room, which has had a little make-over this week. I'm excited to show it to you both,' she turned to Olivia and Dylan as she said this last bit.

Rachel wasn't sure if she or the children gasped the loudest when the door opened to the kids' room. Twin beds sat on either side of a large, sunny room, which was painted in vertical navy and white strips and had two large letters, O & D, in pride of place above each of the beds. The nautical theme continued with navy starred bedlinen, and there were more soft cushions and pillows than they had in their whole house in Dublin.

Olivia almost swooned as she took it all in.

'We used an interior designer to help us,' Belinda continued. 'We wanted to get it right for you.'

'But Belinda chose all of the books for the library area herself,' Oscar said proudly, walking over to a floor-to-ceiling bookshelf stacked with brightly coloured books.

The children ran over to inspect, picking up books from all their favourite authors.

'We weren't sure what games you like, so we bought a selection,' Oscar pointed to a shelf that was overflowing with every game imaginable, from Monopoly to Snakes and Ladders.

Belinda walked over to a side door and, when she opened it, revealed that it was directly connected to Rachel's room. 'Oscar came up with the idea to do this. He had a builder put the door in when we redecorated. We thought that the children can still run in to you for those early-morning snuggles we hear so much about.'

'You've done all of this just for us?' Olivia asked. She seemed as overwhelmed by it all as Rachel was.

Dylan, however, threw himself on to his bed with a satisfied sigh, cushions cascading on either side of him.

'Of course we did it for you all. We want you to be comfortable here and hopefully come back to see us again and again,' Belinda said.

'You didn't need to go to all this trouble,' Rachel said. She felt a confusing rush of emotions wind her. Sadness that the children had missed out on the obvious love their grandparents had for them. And regret that Lorcan had not reconciled properly with them earlier in the children's lives. How she wished he was here with her, to share the children's giddiness at their new bedroom. But Rachel had to admit, she also felt excited. It was nice to have someone fuss and spoil her, to look after her.

'It truly was not any trouble. We've loved working on this, knowing that you were coming to visit,' Oscar said.

'We'll leave you to get settled. You can have a proper look at everything. And I have some refreshments ready for us downstairs, so come down when you're ready and you can meet Bridie, our housekeeper,' Belinda said.

Housekeeper. Crikey, Rachel thought.

'And we can play with these toys if we want?' Olivia asked, still incredulous.

'They are yours to do as you wish,' Belinda confirmed. And with that, she and Oscar walked out, leaving a somewhat bemused Rachel behind.

'Mom,' Olivia whispered loudly, 'I think Grandma Belinda and Grandpa Oscar are very rich. Like the Queen of England.'

'I think you might be right,' Rachel stage-whispered back to her wide-eyed daughter. 'Come on, let's have a nosy at everything!'

Belinda and Oscar had thought of everything. In each of their sizes, dressing gowns and slippers hung on the inside of their shared bathroom. Toiletries from toothpaste to shampoo sat in a pretty basket. And when she felt the thick and fluffy towels, Rachel knew that she'd have to have a bath this evening before she fell into the soft bed.

They went downstairs, where the refreshments that Belinda referred to turned out to be a full-on feast. Bridie walked over and greeted them as if they were family, hugging the children close and exclaiming at how big they were.

'You must be famished,' Bridie said, leading them to the food. Homemade sausage rolls and Scotch eggs, sandwiches and wraps, yoghurts, fresh fruit and cupcakes made Rachel's mouth water.

'Bridie has been busy all morning baking in preparation for your arrival. She wouldn't let me touch a thing until you got here,' Oscar said, reaching over for a sausage roll and stuffing it into his mouth. Flakes of pastry fell like confetti to the floor. Rachel waited for a reaction from Belinda, but she didn't seem to mind.

'The last time I saw you, Olivia, you were just a wee thing,' Bridie said.

Rachel had never met anyone who had a housekeeper before. It had always seemed like an unnecessary luxury, from a different era. But she liked the woman; she was warm and friendly. And it was obvious she cared for her employers, from the ease with which they all spoke to each other.

By the time they'd all eaten far too much, they'd settled into their new environment as if they'd been visiting for years. Oscar brought the kids outside to play hide and seek, happily showing them where their dad used to hide when he was their age.

Belinda stood side by side with her housekeeper. Watching the two older women, Rachel thought they looked almost like sisters, rather than employer and housekeeper. A stab of loneliness for her sister hit Rachel. She wished she were with her right now to share this new world she found herself in. They'd snuggle into the big bed upstairs together and dissect everything, from the presence of a housekeeper to the matching velvety, rose-smelling hand lotions in all the bathrooms. Rachel hoped

Claudia's early morning sickness was easing up. Last time they had spoken on video call, she'd looked so pale.

'It's good to hear the sound of a child laughing in the house again, Bridie,' Belinda said now.

'Aye, and it's good to see you smiling again too. You've had a face as long as a Lurgan spade for years,' Bridie replied, in her thick Northern Irish accent.

Belinda turned to Rachel and explained, 'Bridie has been telling me to catch myself on, for quite some time now.'

'I've been up to high doh, worried for you, I don't mind telling you,' Bridie said.

'I'm sorry to hear you've been so low, Belinda,' Rachel said, just about deciphering what the housekeeper was saying.

'No mother should ever bury her child,' Bridie said.

'Nor a wife bury a husband,' Belinda said, reaching out to hold Rachel's hand for a moment.

A loud cry from Dylan, complaining he couldn't find Olivia or Grandpa Oscar, floated in through the open door. As Rachel made a move to go outside, Belinda said, 'No, let me go. You finish your drink. We want you to have some time to yourself this weekend. I can only imagine how tiring it is for you, doing everything on your own. If you are happy for us to do so, of course, we don't want to interfere.'

Rachel felt quite emotional hearing the sincerity in Belinda's offer.

'Thank you. And I'll remember that.'

Belinda ran outside, telling Dylan she was on her way to help him find the others.

'Promise me you won't break her heart again. I don't

think she could take any more heartache,' Bridie said, suddenly appearing beside Rachel.

Rachel looked at the housekeeper in surprise. Was she implying that she'd done something to upset Belinda in the past?

'I can assure you that I've never meant to upset either Belinda or Oscar. I'm sorry if I have in the past?'

'Wind your neck in, I'm not talking about you. Yer wan, Niamh. She was a terror and made Belinda's life a living hell.'

This piqued Rachel's interest. Saint Niamh, being referred to as something other than perfect. She couldn't help herself from probing a little further. 'What did Niamh do?'

Bridie shook her head, ever the loyal employee. 'You'll need to talk to Belinda about that. I'm not one for gossip. But I can tell you that Niamh made it her business to drive a wedge between Lorcan and his parents. She kept Olivia from them, which broke everyone's hearts. And then, when they had that big row, Lorcan had to make a choice. And the buck eejit made the wrong one, of course.'

Big row?

'I guessed that there was some bad blood between everyone,' Rachel responded carefully, 'but I didn't realize there had been a big row?'

'Oh, it was big, all right,' Bridie nodded vigorously. 'Niamh insisted that Lorcan throw Oscar and Belinda out of their house in Dublin – your house now, I suppose. Niamh sent them packing. They were supposed to visit for a couple of days but came home late on the first night.'

'I'm shocked,' Rachel admitted.

'People rarely shock me any more. I've seen it all over the years. But this mess needs to end now. Lorcan was so stubborn. He wouldn't apologize, and he didn't lick that from the stones . . .'

Rachel thought about the obstinate look that Lorcan always had whenever she asked him about his parents.

'If you knew how excited they've been these past few months, having you all back in their lives again. It's done my heart good, I don't mind telling you. That's the second time they've done those rooms up. They did the same for Lorcan and Niamh. But she didn't come here often; Lorcan visited on his own most of the time. He'd make an excuse up about why Niamh wasn't with him. She was pregnant, she was tired, the baby was gurning. But back then, at least he visited. Until the row, that is.'

Rachel looked uncomfortably out the window at Belinda and Oscar as they ran around the garden with the kids. What had happened between Niamh and her in-laws? And what would Belinda and Oscar say, if they knew what she was hearing?

TWENTY-SIX

Rachel

Malone Park, Belfast

The following morning, Oscar and the kids went riding at a nearby stables. While they were off on that adventure, Belinda had surprised Rachel with a trip to a local spa, where she'd booked a series of treatments for Rachel to enjoy before they had lunch together. By the time Rachel had her last treatment, a hot stone massage, she was so relaxed she fell asleep, only awaking when her masseuse gently shook her shoulder. She found Belinda in the quiet room, reading a magazine, and took a seat beside her, sighing in contentment as she sipped a cranberry juice.

'That was divine. I've never had a warm stone massage before. It released so much tension from my neck. I feel looser!'

'Glad to hear it. And your skin looks radiant from the facial. Oh, to be young,' Belinda added wistfully.

'If I look half as good as you when I'm your age, I'll be happy!' Rachel replied. Then she realized she hadn't got a clue what age Belinda was.

'Sixty-two next birthday,' Belinda answered, reading the question in Rachel's face.

'Well, you don't look a day more than fifty,' Rachel said, and meant it.

'Thank you. I take care of my skin. Always have done. Do you cleanse, tone and moisturize every day, dear?'

'Sure,' Rachel flushed as she thought about the pack of facial wipes that constituted her skincare regime.

'We have a lunch reservation in twenty minutes. And the great part is that we can eat in our bathrobes.'

'I never want to leave!' Rachel sighed ecstatically. 'My sister Claudia would love it here.'

'We can bring her the next time she visits, if you'd like?' Belinda said.

'Thanks, Belinda. I'll remember that kind offer. I'd love to show them another part of Ireland when they next visit,' Rachel said. 'Do you have any sisters yourself?'

'Yes, I do, but we're not that close. We see each other for family occasions – weddings and funerals and the like – but once my parents died there was little to connect us.'

'That's sad,' Rachel said. 'I can't imagine not being close to Claudia. She's my best friend.'

'Everyone needs one of those,' Belinda nodded wisely.

'Well, when you and Bridie were chatting yesterday, it really reminded me of how Claudia is with me.'

'I'm closer to Bridie than I am to anyone in my family. Or Oscar's, for that matter. She's been with me through a lot, from miscarriages to when I finally held Lorcan in my arms, to . . . after he died.'

Belinda's eyes glassed over for a moment, but then she seemed to pull herself together, smiling once more.

'I can't imagine how difficult it must have been to have a miscarriage,' Rachel said, shivering suddenly as she thought about Claudia at home. 'My sister is pregnant and if something were to happen, I'm not sure she'd cope.'

'You'd be surprised with what you can endure, when you have no choice,' Belinda said quietly. 'It was a long time ago and for many years, broke both our hearts. We'd always thought we'd fill our house with lots of children. But that wasn't to be . . . I wonder if Oscar managed to stay upright on the horse this morning,' she said suddenly, abruptly changing the subject.

'He's very good to take them. The kids won't want to go home.' Rachel stretched her legs out, sinking into the cushioned lounge chair.

'I know we are a little over the top. It's all a blatant attempt to ensure that you want to come back again.'

Rachel laughed, appreciating her mother-in-law's deadpan humour again. 'I think I can safely guarantee we'll be back. But we don't need any of this. Just your company. I hope you and Oscar will come down to Dublin regularly too. You don't need a special reason to come; there's an open invitation to visit. I mean that.'

'I know you do, and that means a great deal to us. More than you'll ever know.'

There was a pause, and then Rachel found herself broaching the question she'd been longing to ask since Belinda and Oscar had come back into her life. 'What happened between you, Lorcan and Niamh?' The question popped out of her mouth before she even really had a chance to think if it was a good idea or not to ask it.

Belinda sipped her juice, then lay back on her lounger, closing her eyes. Did that mean the subject was closed?

'What did Lorcan tell you?'

'Nothing of any consequence. He didn't like to talk about Niamh much, or you and Oscar if I'm honest. He got visibly upset if I pushed him for any information, so I learned to leave it.'

'As a boy, he never liked to talk about his problems either. And I think that Oscar and I need to take responsibility for our parts in that. We had very different childhoods, but we shared one thing in common. We both felt invisible growing up. We were part of the generation where children were to be seen but not heard.'

Rachel nodded but said nothing, sensing there was more Belinda wanted to say.

'I used to feel that nobody *saw* me. Until I met Oscar, that is. He was and still is my mirror in many ways. We all need one of those. Remember that, Rachel. You'll need your own mirror again one day too.'

'I don't think I understand,' Rachel said curiously.

'We all need to be seen by someone. And if you are lucky and meet the right person, they will be your mirror. I see Oscar, and he sees me.'

'Lorcan was that for me,' Rachel whispered. 'But I only got him only for the shortest time.'

'I recognized that the moment he introduced you to us, after your engagement. And if I'm completely honest, I don't believe that he and Niamh were mirrors for each other.'

This, again, was a shock to Rachel. 'I thought they were soulmates?'

'I think at first they might have thought they were . . .'

Belinda paused, sat up straight, and took another sip of her juice. 'Don't mind me. I'm fanciful. Ignore me.'

And with that, she was on her feet and walking towards the door.

Rachel followed her in frustration, her mind full of questions that she had no answers to. Whatever had gone on between the Bradleys and Niamh, nobody wanted to talk about it.

TWENTY-SEVEN

Sheila

Malahide, Dublin

For the first time in her almost sixty years, Sheila understood what the phrase 'fit to be tied' meant. She was so furious with Rachel, she needed somebody to put a rope around her before she did damage to the girl. She put her foot down, accelerating further, as she drove towards the local shopping centre in Swords.

What on earth was Rachel thinking of, taking off to see Belinda and Oscar when she'd invited her and the kids for a roast on Sunday? Sheila knew that she had made mistakes with Rachel. She had truly never meant to upset her, but somehow or other, she always seemed to be on the wrong foot when she was around her. So she'd come up with a plan. She'd do a special meal for them all, use her good delph and cutlery and make a fuss of Rachel, in the best way she knew how – with good food.

When Rachel declined it felt like a slap in her face – she was sure it was a deliberate snub.

'Maybe she's still upset over the row,' Adrian had suggested, after Sheila put down the phone to Rachel.

Well, that wasn't one bit helpful. Sheila had been charm personified ever since then, biting her tongue. When they called round for the ice-cream sundaes on the kids' first day of school, she'd made an enormous effort with Rachel. When the door to the living room flew open and she saw clothes strewn from one side to the other, she'd said nothing. Someone else might have asked how anyone could run a business from such chaos.

Sheila reversed into a parking spot at the centre. The more she thought about it, the more she was sure that this trip to Belfast was another step in Rachel's grand plan to oust her and Adrian. She couldn't forget Belinda standing behind Rachel at the adoption party, declaring allegiance and pledging to fight on their behalf. They were most likely plotting up there now. Next thing she'd hear, the Bradleys would be buying a villa in New Zealand too and they'd all go off into the sunset and live happily ever after without her.

To Sheila, it felt like Rachel was continually finding new ways to keep the children from her and Adrian. All in an effort to weaken their bond, so that the children had no ties in Ireland.

She walked aimlessly in and out of boutiques, not really paying attention to anything she picked up. Her heart wasn't in shopping. She had only come out because she couldn't bear to be at home with Adrian right now, with his constant suggestions and pep talks on how they could make things right with Rachel.

Sheila stopped suddenly, causing someone to almost crash into her. She was outside *the* boutique. Niamh's favourite boutique. Sheila's heart began to race and she had to move closer to the wall so that she could lean into it for support.

A few weeks before Niamh died, they had both been window shopping, laughing as they navigated the bulky double buggy they now needed. Niamh had fallen in love with a brown leather jacket from this boutique. It felt as soft as butter and was the colour of rich caramel. Niamh couldn't justify buying it and, as she still had her baby tummy, she didn't even want to try it on. But Sheila could see how much Niamh had fallen in love with it, and also knew it would look gorgeous on Niamh. So she'd snuck back in the following day and put a deposit on the coat, paying a little off each week.

She'd never gone back to pick up the coat. Niamh never got to wear it and feel a million dollars.

Sheila couldn't stop the tears. They came thick and fast.

'Are you okay?' a young boy stopped to ask. People often gave out about the youth of today, but Sheila thought that was nonsense. They were as good and decent as any generation. This was proof of it.

She took a steadying breath, wiped her eyes and thanked the boy for his kindness. One day she would have to go into that boutique and do something about that coat. They'd said at the time that they could hold on to it as long as she needed, but she'd never returned. Maybe she would donate it to charity. Just not today.

As she walked back towards the car park, still empty-handed and feeling empty and lost, she prayed for a sign, anything at all to give her strength and guidance to carry on.

And then she saw it. A digital screen changed, showing an advert for a family law firm.

She'd had conversations in her head for weeks, debating whether she should seek professional help. She'd even chosen a lawyer, a woman called Maria Johnson, recommended by a friend. It was finally time to make the call.

TWENTY-EIGHT

Rachel

Malahide, Dublin

Rachel continued to be worried about Olivia, who was quiet. *Too quiet*. Whenever Rachel asked her if anything was wrong, she shrugged and said everything was fine, although it clearly wasn't. This morning, Olivia claimed she had a tummy ache and couldn't go to school. Rachel was pretty sure that Olivia was feeling okay, physically at least. But she decided to let her stay home all the same, suggesting that Olivia come with her to visit her fashion wholesaler in Dublin. She wanted to look at a new range of winter loungewear she was considering for Rae's Closet. Dylan was at playschool and Jack had agreed to collect him for her, so they were in no rush to get home.

Usually, Rachel played audiobooks in the car for longer journeys, something they all loved. But she'd learned early on as a stepmom that the children seemed to open up more while they drove. Rachel wasn't sure if it was the confined space or the fact that they were looking at the road in front of them, rather than each other. Either way, it seemed to work a charm. A car confessional.

'Not long until the summer holidays. I bet you'll miss your friends when you finish up?' she asked, as casually as she could.

'Yes,' Olivia said neutrally.

Rachel resisted the urge to speak; she knew from experience that often it was better to tread softly with her daughter than continually push.

'Annemarie and Jane are still sitting beside each other.'

Whatever was wrong with Olivia, it was evident to Rachel that these two were at the heart of the story. The poor thing's voice tremored when she mentioned their names.

'Could you all take turns to sit beside each other?'

Another quiet moment that felt like it dragged on for an eternity. And then Olivia said the words that every parent hates their child to utter.

'Annemarie and Jane said that they don't want to be my friends any more.'

Her little voice was filled with such sorrow, it made Rachel want to turn the car around and drive at full speed to the girls' houses to demand an answer as to why they would hurt her daughter like this.

Instead, she made a considerable effort to keep her voice calm as she probed a little more. 'Oh sweetheart, I'm so sorry. Did they say that in those words to you? Or does it seem like that because of their actions?'

'They said it. We always used to walk around the yard

213

together in our breaks. But Jane said that she and Annemarie were best friends now, and that I should find another best friend of my own.'

Rachel was speechless. She wasn't that old that she didn't remember playground antics in her childhood, too. But this seemed particularly cruel.

'I'm so sorry. That must have been such a hard thing to hear. No wonder you have been so sad.'

'Why don't they like me any more?' Olivia asked, and as she did, the tears began, falling fast and furious – a release of what must be months of torment for the little girl. Rachel spied a petrol station ahead so she pulled into its forecourt, finding a spot to park up. She stopped the car, then un-clicked her seatbelt, doing the same for Olivia's. Rachel pulled the little girl over the gearbox on to her lap. She crooned her daughter into her embrace, as she used to when she was small and couldn't sleep, and held her until Olivia's tears stopped. Her own, too, because it was impossible not to be moved by Olivia's pain. She pulled a pack of tissues from the glove compartment, and they both blew their noses.

'It's been a rough time for you recently, hasn't it?'

'It feels like it's been rough for a long time, Mom.'

'I bet it does.'

'Annemarie has been my best friend since we were in playschool. I thought we would be best friends forever. But she prefers Jane now.'

In Rachel's experience, three-way friendships were problematic. One person usually felt left out. Olivia always said she and Annemarie were best friends forever, a phrase that she never seemed to tire of repeating. And if you looked at the scrapbook wall in her room, which had dozens of photos of the two girls, arm in arm, you'd think their bond was unbreakable.

But nothing lasted forever. Rachel knew that better than anyone.

As she cradled Olivia, she tried to find the right words to say that might make things easier. She couldn't solve the issue for Olivia, but she wanted to help her come to terms with the changes.

'You know, something like this happened to me in high school. I became friends with Louise on my first day. And for two weeks it was perfect. Then, one Monday morning, when I walked into my classroom, Louise was with another girl called Grace. They had their heads together and were giggling in a way that suggested they were really close. And when Louise glanced up and saw me, she looked really guilty.'

'What for?' Olivia asked.

'Well, at the time, I didn't recognize the look as guilt, but now that I'm older and wiser, I can see that's what it was. Louise felt guilty because she knew she had dumped me for Grace. She just hadn't gotten around to telling me that fact yet.'

'Did she tell you she didn't want to be your friend too?'

'Not quite, but when the bell rang each day after class, she walked out of the room with Grace. And she never looked behind her to see where I was.'

'Did you cry too?' Olivia was searching for some reassurance that she wasn't alone.

'Oh absolutely,' Rachel confirmed. 'I was sad for a bit. But then I made a new best friend – Margaret. And she turned out to be lovely. I now think how sad it would have been if I had missed out on being Margaret's friend because

I was friends with Louise. She lives in Australia now with her wife, Lisa. One day I hope we can visit her, or maybe she'll visit us all here. I think you'd like her a lot.'

Olivia listened intently, mulling over Rachel's words. 'There isn't anyone else in my class left for me. Everyone already has a best friend.'

'I can't believe that out of twenty girls in your class, there isn't a single person you can be friends with. You never know, maybe someone else in the class feels like you do now. Or maybe another group would love to have you join them. Who says that there can't be more than one best friend for a person? You are such a fun and caring person. Anyone would be lucky to have you on their side.'

'You have to say that because you're my mom.'

'I have to say that because it's true,' Rachel said assertively. 'In the meantime, what can we do that will make it better for you right now?'

Olivia scrunched her nose up and pondered the question, then a slight grin appeared, making Rachel's heart lift. 'Could I have a hot chocolate?'

'I think we can arrange that! Let's see what they have in the deli here.'

Twenty minutes later, with a sugar hit that managed to restore their good spirits, they continued on their way to the wholesaler.

Rachel loved this part of her job. She could spend hours happily looking through rails of clothes, trying things on, trying to predict if a colour, fabric, print, cut would work well for her loyal customers. She gave Olivia the title, 'Chief Photographer', and her little girl took her role seriously. She snapped photographs of Rachel as she tried items on and proved to have a keen eye, picking things from rails that were quirky and a little different. It was a productive two hours and they left happy and satisfied with a job well done – orders placed for the next season. A leisurely lunch with a large cream bun for dessert finished off a gorgeous day for them, both substantially happier than they'd been when they took off.

Jack and Dylan were already in the kitchen when they arrived home. They'd made pizza dough and were busy decorating their creations with chopped ham and cheese. Dylan rushed towards his mom, his face covered in flour, delighted with himself. 'Look! I'm a chef!'

'A better one than me as well,' Jack said.

'All okay?' Rachel asked, turning to Jack as she pulled Dylan in for another hug. Why was it that when she was with them twenty-four-seven, she often felt overwhelmed with her need for some alone time, but as soon as she did manage time away from one or both of them, she missed them like crazy?

'All good here,' Jack confirmed. 'We've had a lot of fun, haven't we, kiddo?' He ruffled Dylan's hair as he spoke. 'Did you get everything you wanted?'

'Yes, and more! Huge success. Thanks again for taking care of this munchkin until we got back. Any plans this evening?' Rachel asked Jack as he placed the pizzas into the warm oven. Olivia and Dylan happily settled themselves in front of the TV.

'I'm meeting a friend later on. Remember Lydia? You met her at the annual Christmas fundraiser a few times. We're going to the cinema. They have an open-caption edition of *The Godfather* on.'

'Is that when they display dialogue and scene-setting information too on the screen?

'Yeah. Subtitles are great, but this is better.'

'You've seen quite a lot of Lydia recently. Is there anything you want to tell me?' Rachel asked, raising her eyebrows, and only half teasing.

'Just because we both have a hearing loss and we enjoy going to events together doesn't mean we have to date each other,' Jack said, a little colder than Rachel had been expecting.

'Hey, I know that. I thought I sensed a vibe between you both, that's all,' she responded, stung by the rebuke.

'Sorry,' Jack replied, 'that was a bit snappy. I've had that assumption made a lot, so it annoys me. This stupid idea that as we are both deaf, we will understand each other better than a non-deaf person. That if you have special needs, you should stick to your kind. It bothers me.'

'I can see how that would irritate, I'm sorry,' Rachel replied, nodding in understanding.

'I mean, you and I can communicate well enough, and you aren't deaf!' Jack's shoulders visibly relaxed as he spoke. Whatever annoyance he'd felt had clearly disappeared. He was one of the most even-tempered people Rachel knew, so she hated seeing him upset.

'But don't think I don't know your game, Jack Butler! You wanted to dodge a difficult question, but no can do siree. I'm going back to my original question. Are you sure nothing's going on with Lydia?'

'Lydia is great. And I like her a lot. But . . .' he paused, leaving the sentence unfinished.

Rachel wasn't letting him off that easily. 'Go on,' she pushed him, 'but what?'

'Well, there's someone else if you must know,' he finished, and Rachel laughed when she saw a blush on his cheeks.

'Now things are getting interesting! Who is the lucky lady? Do I know her?'

'Ah, that would be telling,' Jack said coyly.

'Whoever she is, she'll be a lucky lady to get you,' Rachel said.

The oven timer beeped, putting an end to their discussion. The pizza was ready. Rachel left them to eat and got to work on the laundry.

'You know, I swear the neighbours are sneaking their dirty clothes into our baskets while we sleep. Because based on the amount of laundry I do every week, there's no way it's for the four . . . three of us . . .' she muttered to herself.

Rachel wondered when she'd get to the stage where she stopped automatically including Lorcan in all she did. And as soon as she had the thought, she regretted it. She didn't want to get to that stage. She wanted to remember everything about her husband every day for the rest of her life.

TWENTY-NINE

Rachel

Malahide, Dublin

Rachel stood at her kitchen island, peering at the recipe on her iPad screen. Time to fold raisins into a gooey oatmeal mixture. Satisfied that they were evenly dispersed, she pressed the dough into a tray and popped them into the oven. The heat of the oven blasted her as she opened it, so she moved outside into the back garden to cool off. The weather had changed this week and they were beginning to see signs of a sunny summer. The kids only had two more weeks of school and playschool until they broke up for two months' holidays.

Rachel checked her watch, making a mental note to take her flapjacks out in twenty-five minutes. She was following a supposed foolproof recipe given to her by Lucinda. They'd swapped numbers at the school gate and met for coffee one morning. Despite Lucinda's words of encouragement, however, Rachel wasn't so sure it was proof enough for this fool.

She'd have to just buy some if they tasted horrible.

Her phone buzzed, and Rachel felt a burst of happiness when she saw it was her mom. Wiping her hands, she hit the green button to accept the call. But as soon as she saw her mom's grave face, she knew that bad news was coming her way.

Annie began to share how Claudia had been feeling unwell, complaining about a piercing niggle in her side. A few hours later, she had collapsed at home and, as he was luckily at home, Howard had called for an ambulance straight away.

'We met them at the hospital entrance,' Annie explained, her voice shaking with emotion.

'Oh Mom,' Rachel whispered.

'I've never seen anything like it. Howard was hysterical, and as soon as they took Claudia out on the stretcher, we could see why. She was fitting and convulsing.'

Rachel felt hysteria bubble its way up inside herself too as she listened to her mom continue her story. Pretty quickly, the doctors had confirmed that Claudia had suffered an ectopic pregnancy. When she'd become pregnant, the fertilized egg had implanted into one of her fallopian tubes rather than her womb. And as it had been undetected thus far, it had ruptured. Claudia was in surgery, and they were told to prepare themselves – the internal bleeding had reached a critical point, undetected as it was.

Rachel felt herself grow numb as her mother tearfully explained the situation, as though she was having an out-of-body experience. She watched herself press end on the call as if from afar, not as though she was actually experiencing it herself.

And worst of all, she felt utterly useless. She was on the other side of the world and she could do absolutely nothing to support her family right when they needed her most. Rachel's heart broke for Claudia and Howard. It was a cruel twist of fate, and goodness knew their family had suffered enough at her fickle hands.

Rachel turned on Doctor Google and searched for information on ectopic pregnancies. She had to do something; she couldn't sit at her dining room table and do nothing. Knowledge was power, she told herself.

But with every click and page opening, she became more scared – her poor baby sister.

Her phone beeped, an alarm to remind her that she was due to start her Facebook Live in fifteen minutes. There was no way she could do it. She didn't have it in her, not right now. She shared a message saying that the live video would be postponed for one day due to a family emergency. Meanwhile, the minutes crawled by as she waited for further updates from her mom. She couldn't sit still, so took to pacing the floor of her kitchen, walking around the small island with her phone in her hand, willing it to ring again with the promised update from her mom.

When her mom did eventually call, the phone didn't even get a chance to ring once, Rachel answered it so quickly.

'She's okay, she's okay,' was all her mom could say as she sobbed down the phone. Eventually she managed, 'She's out of surgery. Howard is with her; we've not been in yet.'

'And the baby?' Rachel asked, even though she knew

it was stupid. There was no baby. Doctor Google had outlined the hard facts, clear and simple.

Her mother's answering sigh washed over Rachel, from her head to her toes, like a cloud of fog.

'They had to do abdominal surgery – a laparotomy, they called it. And they also had to take out the ruptured fallopian tube.'

Rachel's heart broke. She knew this would mean her sister's fertility would be compromised further.

'Is she awake yet?'

'Not yet. Howard said he'll call us when she comes round. He wants to be the one to tell her about the surgery and the baby. He's been a superstar, to be honest. Claudia's surgeon told him that his job was to be strong for her now. And he's clinging to that like a life raft.'

'Thank God for Howard,' Rachel said, feeling a rush of affection for her sister's partner. 'And how are you and Dad coping?'

'We've had better days, love. We're devastated for Claudia. But we are also relieved that she's okay. We thought we might lose her for a while.'

'I wish I was there with you all,' Rachel whispered, as though if she said it quietly it would make her feel less guilty.

'We know. It's exactly how we felt when Lorcan died. We understand that you can't be here, Rachel. And Claudia will too. As soon as she's able to chat, we'll let you know. I promise. Now try not to worry.'

But that was impossible. Rachel felt panicky, on edge, and once again found herself pacing the kitchen. Until she smelt something burning, the acidic, heavy aroma filling the air.

The bloody flapjacks. She opened the oven and a haze of dark smoke hit, stinging her eyes. It was the final straw. Using a tea towel, she flung the hot mess into the sink then buried her face in her hands in sheer desperation.

When her phone buzzed again, she hoped it might have been Claudia, but it was Belinda.

'Is everything okay? I noticed you cancelled your Rae's Closet live video. We were concerned about you over here.'

Maybe it was the flapjacks, maybe it was the kindness in Belinda's voice, but the tears she'd not shed all day suddenly spilled through her like a devastating tsunami. Belinda listened without interruption, somehow managing to make sense of Rachel's words and offer some comfort and advice. It went unsaid, but she clearly shared Rachel's terror of losing someone else.

When Rachel had sobbed her heart out and stopped hiccupping, there was a pause before Belinda said,

'You must go to New Zealand. You need to, and your sister will need you.'

'But how can I?' Rachel asked. She'd been thinking of little else all day, but just couldn't find a way to make it work. 'The kids have school. Not to mention my job. I have several large shipments due in this week.'

'All of those problems can be easily solved. Oscar and I can come down to take care of the kids. That would be our pleasure. As for work, well, the beauty of being one's boss is that you can take time off if you need to.'

Rachel felt a rush of gratitude at the offer, and somewhat stunned. 'You make it sound so easy.'

'I always think that as we live in such a complicated world, it makes sense not to complicate the simple things in life. You mentioned you were expecting new stock to arrive. Well, Oscar wasn't just the boss of a manufacturing business, he also worked in every division, including the warehouse, so he can handle that for you with ease, I'm sure. And I know how much your fans love to see you every day for the Facebook Lives. How about you pre-film some videos, then schedule them for posting each day you are away?'

Rachel was surprised to hear that Belinda knew that much about her work, and even more surprised at how well she'd thought everything through. 'I suppose I could do that.' Then she added nervously, 'You watch me on Facebook?'

'Of course, and I have told all of my friends at the tennis club about your business. I didn't bother mentioning it to the bridge club; they are not your target audience, dear.' For the first time since she'd heard the news about Claudia, Rachel managed a small laugh. She supposed Belinda was probably right, there.

'You know what, I've had a few orders recently from Belfast. I wondered where they came from.'

'Oh yes, that would be my ladies. You are quite the hit with them. I think it made me quite hip in the younger women's eyes, having you as my daughter-in-law. While the children are in school, Oscar and I could take care of any orders you receive. I promise you, we both work well under instruction. It would be fun!'

In less than five minutes, Belinda had managed to circumnavigate every possible roadblock. Rachel would need to speak to the children, see what they thought, but this *could* work. She promised to call Belinda back once she'd had a chance to think through the kind offer, but the more she did think about it, the more viable it seemed.

Once again, Rachel was struck by how easy she felt when talking to Belinda. She reminded her a little of her mom, which was strange because they were so different. But they were both calming and whenever she spoke to them, they always made her feel supported.

When Olivia got home from school and pre-school, the kids were upset to hear that Aunty Claudia was ill and wanted to go to New Zealand themselves. Rachel explained that she couldn't afford to buy tickets for them all, plus they couldn't miss school. Olivia had missed a couple of weeks on their recent vacation, so Rachel could not justify keeping her out now. They were both pretty excited at the thought of having Belinda and Oscar come to stay with them, though, and soon came round to the idea of not joining Rachel in New Zealand.

Still not entirely convinced, Rachel decided to at least look up flights, and discovered that there was availability in forty-eight hours.

She rang her parents and tentatively told them her plans. And their relief and gratitude were the final nudge she needed to make the decision and just get on the plane.

She knew she should call the Butlers too, to let them know about her trip, but she couldn't face another difficult conversation today. She was too fragile and knew that the slightest thing could set her off again. She'd tell Jack the next time they spoke and he could relay the information. It felt a little cowardly, but she needed all her strength for Claudia right now.

Belinda decided they should arrive the evening before Rachel left so that they had time to go through the children's schedules and the business requirements. Rachel planned to be away for one week. It was a long way to go for such a short trip, but she was grateful that she could make it work, all the same.

'Are you sure you don't mind handling the orders for me too?' she asked one last time.

'I'm sure that we can make sure your stock keeps moving. But I draw the line at a Facebook Live,' Belinda said.

'You know what, Belinda, I think if you decided to do my Facebook Lives, you'd do it with style and panache. I just can't believe that you are willing to do this as well as taking care of the kids. Who can be a handful, I don't mind telling you. It's not too late to back out,' Rachel said, half joking, but desperately praying Belinda didn't take her up on that offer.

'Oh, shh. Both Oscar and I are excited to spend time with the children. If anything, you're doing *us* a favour. And you can pre-warn them that we plan to spoil them rotten.'

'Of that, I've no doubt. I'll see you both tomorrow evening?'

'Yes, you will. But don't cook for us, we'll stop somewhere on the way down. We'll aim to get to you by six p.m.' And with that, the two women hung up, Rachel feeling a surprising new warmth for her mother-in-law. Why had she spent so many years thinking this woman was a terror?

Rachel began to make a list of everything she needed to do to prepare for house guests, not to mention her trip away. She realized that she would have little time to fret about Claudia, which was a small mercy. The house needed a good clean, for one thing, and she'd also nip into Dunnes to buy new bed linen for her bed. She didn't have a guest room for Belinda and Oscar and couldn't even begin to compete with Willow Lodge in Belfast, but she could at least make sure her room was comfortable and clean. She added towels to her list. Some of the ones in her hot press had seen better days and would offer the user an added exfoliation whether they wanted one or not.

By the time Rachel crawled into bed at midnight, she had managed to tick off most items from her list of things to do. She fell into a deep sleep.

For the first time since Lorcan died, Rachel's village had grown a little bigger.

THIRTY

Rachel

Napier, Hawke's Bay

When Howard opened his front door, Rachel got a shock. His face was grey and lined, as if he'd aged years in the past couple of days.

'Can I hug you?' she asked, and he nodded, opening his arms for the embrace. 'I'm so sorry, so very sorry.'

Annie and Joe stood behind Rachel, giving her a moment with Howard, before moving in towards them both and putting their arms around them in one big group hug.

'I needed that,' Howard said, wiping his eyes with his sweatshirt sleeve. 'Claudia's asleep. We didn't tell her that you were coming, in case something happened to stop it at the last minute. I don't think she could have taken another disappointment.'

'Mom and Dad explained. You did the right thing. I came straight from the airport, but I can come back when Claudia wakes up, or if you need to get your head down?'

'I tried to sleep, but I couldn't switch off. But no worries, she'll be right.'

They followed him into the kitchen and Howard put the kettle on for a cuppa.

Annie held up a large bag, 'I've a few bits made for you both. Save you cooking for the next few days. I'll pop them in your fridge.'

As Annie loaded the fridge with goodies, Howard whispered to Rachel that he already had enough food to feed an army. His mother had had the same thought. They giggled quietly together, enjoying a moment of light relief.

'Do you mind if I pop up to see if she's awake?' Rachel asked.

'Course not.'

Rachel crept up the stairs and opened their bedroom door as quietly as she could. Claudia was fast asleep, curled up into a ball, with her two arms wrapped around a pillow. The image took Rachel back to their childhood. Claudia always slept like that, using a pillow as a teddy bear. On impulse, she climbed on to the bed beside her sister, spooning her as she'd done so many times when they were kids. Claudia didn't like storms and if there was the slightest chance of thunder or lightning, she always slept with Rachel.

Claudia's arms reached up to clasp hers and she felt her sister sob, unable to speak. Rachel couldn't find any words herself; all she could do was whisper endearments into her sister's ear and hold her gently.

'You came. I can't believe you came,' Claudia eventually said hoarsely.

'I'll always come when you need me. Always.'

And for a short time, as they lay there, they found peace.

They had to leave that room eventually, if only to eat, but Rachel was just glad to see her sister able to get out of bed. Together, they went downstairs and joined the others.

Howard jumped up immediately, tenderly helping Claudia walk to the couch.

'Can we not talk about . . . about what happened?' Claudia asked, looking around at her family. 'Not right now. I can't.'

'Whatever you want, love,' Annie said reassuringly. 'You just tell us what we can do to help and we'll do it.'

'You can start by making Rachel something to eat, her stomach is growling like a grizzly bear. And Howard, you must be hungry too.' Rachel wanted to laugh at the sheer joy of hearing her sister's usual up-front honesty.

Annie, too, almost skipped back to their kitchen, delighted to have something practical to do.

After a meal of lasagne and salad, Claudia began to nod off on the couch. She was still wiped from the surgery a few days earlier. So Rachel and her parents said their goodbyes, making plans to see the couple again the following day.

As it happened, Claudia was the one to arrive at Annie and Joe's the following day, before Rachel even had a chance to go to her.

'I needed a change of scenery,' she explained with a shrug. 'Come on, let's sit in the garden.'

Annie and Joe stayed inside, letting the two sisters chat on their own for a bit.

'You know, I've learned more about my insides over the

past few days than I ever did during sex education in school,' Claudia said with a laugh. 'I mean, I knew I had fallopian tubes – the name sounds vaguely familiar – but I never paid a huge amount of attention to what they might actually *do*.'

'Can't say I did either,' Rachel admitted. 'I always got a little queasy when they went into any detail.'

Claudia smiled, then winced. She was still tender from surgery, and the slightest movement could jar.

'Do you need a painkiller?' Rachel asked quickly, looking towards the house, where she knew her mother would have a stash of pills if they needed them.

'No, I'm good. I have these,' Claudia said, nodding towards her tablets sitting on the table beside her. 'But if you have a pill to take care of my broken heart . . .' her words trailed off.

'If there were such a thing, I'd get it for you in a heart-beat, Sis. But I think you have no choice but to work through this as best you can until you come to terms with it. At least, that's what I found when Lorcan died. I couldn't hide from the grief. Nor could the kids. We had to lean into it.'

A pair of plump fantail birds flew by, stopping to rest on the garden fence a few feet away. The two sisters watched them in silence for a moment, enjoying their double act as they looked around their surroundings, side by side.

'I'm not ready to lean anywhere yet,' Claudia said even-tually, 'but I'll try, I promise. You know this also means that there's a strong chance that I might have another ectopic pregnancy? Isn't that peachy? And that's only if I get pregnant again, now that my odds are slashed by fifty per cent.'

'It's so shitty, Sis.'

'The shittiest of the shitty,' Claudia agreed. 'Howard keeps telling me to focus on what the doctor said. That the majority of women who have only one tube left still get pregnant within eighteen months. And that we have options if we fail naturally.'

'He's right, but I don't think you are ready to hear all that yet,' Rachel admitted.

She thought about all the times well-meaning people had told her she should start dating again. That it was time to move on. Time for who? Because for Rachel, she didn't feel even remotely ready. Her heart and head were still firmly with Lorcan, and she wasn't sure that would ever change.

'I'd love a crystal ball, Sis. If I knew that one day I'd get to hold a baby in my arms, then maybe it wouldn't be so bad. It's the not knowing that scares me.'

Rachel understood that.

'And I was so looking forward to going from a blueberry to a jellybean.'

Rachel looked at her sister in confusion. 'Do I need to worry? Pack you off to the funny farm?'

'I keep forgetting that you haven't been pregnant. Your gorgeous children came ready-made. On all the pregnancy sites they have these days, they equate the size of your baby to fruit or something. And the fruit gets bigger week by week. I was so close to being a jellybean.'

'Is a jellybean technically a fruit?' Rachel asked dubiously.

'In my world it is. Get this, the fruits went all the way up to a cantaloupe.'

'Ouch,' Rachel said, crossing her legs.

She waited to see if Claudia would laugh at the intended joke and was relieved when she heard a soft chuckle.

Claudia rattled her pills in their orange jar, then sadly added, 'There were no jellybeans for me. Just a tub of painkillers.'

There wasn't anything to say to that, so Rachel put her arm around her sister again, and they rocked a little more on their porch swing.

'What if this is it for me?' Claudia asked.

'Don't ask me how I know this, but honestly, Claudia, I truly believe that this is not your story. I can see you and Howard with a houseful of children. All girls, I think, to drive poor Howard mad.'

'But he won't mind really because he will love us all so much,' Claudia added.

'Exactly. And you'll swap your convertible for a minivan. You will be the quintessential soccer mom. Because your girls will be fierce and will play sports and the piano, regular little superheroes.'

'Can my girls sing?'

'As well as you can . . . so not so much,' Rachel said, laughing and getting a shoulder nudge in return. 'But they look like you, which means they are so beautiful they make people stop and stare when they see them.'

'When will all of this happen?' Claudia asked in a voice so low, her words were almost lost in the early-morning air.

'Well, the thing is, you and I have this special skill. We know how to make life difficult for ourselves, don't we? We seem to have a knack at having to go a long way round to get to where we want to be. Unfortunately, this means you will have to be patient. But the wait will be worth it. Because you, Howard and your girls, well, you will be family goals for everyone lucky enough to know you.'

Claudia started to cry, and this time Rachel allowed herself to join in. She wished she had a wand that she could wave to make this dream a reality for her sister right now. But all she could do was be there for her, a safe place for her sister to fall. When they'd cried themselves a river, they wiped their eyes and noses.

'You are family goals too, you know,' Claudia said. 'After you and the kids left this summer, you know what Howard said?'

Rachel shook her head, so Claudia continued. 'He said that if he could be half the parent that you are, he'd be a happy man.'

Rachel exhaled deeply. She knew she probably shouldn't care what others thought about her as a mother, but somehow, being a stepmom had put her on the wrong foot with a lot of people. Validation, wherever it came from, was a welcome gift.

'That means a great deal. And the kids send their love, by the way. To be honest, everything looked good over there. Oscar even has a clipboard!'

'For the kids?'

'Not a bad idea, but no. For the business. He gave me a rundown on the orders received and dispatched. I swear, hearing him say, "four pairs of navy leatherette leggings dispatched" is a phrase I could never have predicted.'

'Too funny. But good for him. What about Belinda? How is she coping? She never struck me as the motherly type.'

'I would have thought the same myself – until recently, that is. Things were different for Lorcan in his childhood than they were for us, and I think that's why we've always seen her in a different way. He was in a boarding school for a start, so maybe they didn't have much of a relationship. But the way Belinda talks about him, it's obvious there was huge love. And there's no doubt that the kids have grown to adore Belinda, too. I think they get something from her that they don't get from Sheila, or indeed me. She speaks to them as if they are adults. And it seems to be working because I heard no complaints today, which is a good sign, because goodness knows my kids are not afraid to speak their minds. Olivia said that they are eating a lot of Marks and Spencer ready meals and they've been out to dinner a few times. They will go to Sheila and Adrian's on Wednesday as normal, which will give Belinda and Oscar a break.'

'You like Belinda, don't you?'

'Yes, I do,' Rachel answered assuredly, surprised that the answer was so easy to give nowadays. 'For one thing, I don't know how I would have got through the day I heard about you without her. When we got married, I was unsure about her. She seemed, I don't know, wary of me. She wasn't unfriendly but definitely stand-offish. And it was hard not to be swayed about her, seeing how difficult Lorcan's relationship with her was.'

'And you still don't know why?'

'Well, I think it has something to do with Niamh. When we visited Belinda and Oscar, their housekeeper told me that there had been a big row. I tried to get Belinda to open up, but she's saying nothing.'

'Juicy! You have to keep digging.'

'I have this feeling that there is a piece of the puzzle missing. If I can find it, see the whole picture, then I can start to make sense of things.'

'Maybe as Belinda gets to know you better, she'll feel more inclined to confide,' Claudia offered wisely.

'I hope so. For now, I'm just grateful to have them in all our lives. Most of all, it brings Lorcan back to us all a little. The kids love asking Belinda and Oscar about what he was like as a kid. They've heard all sorts of new stories about his childhood since we've been seeing them more. It's nice.'

Rachel pulled her jacket around herself, shivering in the early-morning breeze. 'It's getting chilly now, and Mom and Dad are getting a crick in their necks, straining to see what we're doing through the patio door window.'

Claudia smiled when she spotted the two of them hovering.

'I vote we take advantage of Dad being willing to do anything for us right now,' Rachel said. 'Let's send him on a mission to find the biggest tub of ice cream. And then, while he's gone, take control of the TV remote. Fancy a trip down memory lane? How about some *Beaches* or *Steel Magnolias*? Or perhaps some *Dirty Dancing*?'

'*Beaches*!' Claudia said. 'Howard won't let me watch those movies. He doesn't get why I want to watch something that is guaranteed to make me cry.'

'But that's the whole point! I remember one night Lorcan went out for a drink with his pals, and when he came home, he found me in bed sobbing. He was so worried that something awful had happened. I kept trying to tell him about Allie and Noah from *The Notebook* until *he* was nearly crying too. That was until he found that Allie and Noah were characters in a movie!'

Claudia started to laugh, 'Stop! He thought they were real people?'

'Yeah, the way I was talking, he was sure they were much-loved cousins from over here.'

'This is nice, Sis. I think the thing I miss most about having you around is the random chats we have about everything and nothing.'

Rachel grabbed Claudia's hand and kissed it. 'I miss this too. There's nobody in this world who I can do this with. One more thing before we go inside. I know things are shit right now – the shittiest of shit. But you will get through this. And, at the end of the shitty shit, you'll still have Howard. I wish . . .' She choked up as she tried to get the words out, but was determined to finish. This was about Claudia, not her. 'Just trust me when I say this. Life is easier with the right person by your side. You have that. You must always remember that.'

'He is a good man, isn't he?'

'The best of them.'

'Howard said to me yesterday that he didn't care if we never had children, as long as he had me.'

'There you go. He's a keeper,' Rachel said, thinking of her keeper that in the end was only on loan for a few short years.

'You'll meet someone else one day, Rae,' Claudia said sadly, knowing exactly what Rachel was saying.

Rachel shrugged non-committally. She wasn't so sure that there was anyone else for her. Her great love was Lorcan. And she knew she would rather have had him for only a few years than never at all.

THIRTY-ONE

Annie

Napier, Hawke's Bay

Annie and Joe watched their two daughters sitting on the wooden swing, heads bent low together, shoulder to shoulder, as they swung gently backwards and forwards.

No matter how old her children became, they would always be little ones to Annie. She worried about them now as much as she had when they were newborns and totally dependent on her. It was just a different set of worries, that's all.

'Remember the summer camp?' she said, turning to Joe. She didn't need to say any more. It was an occasion they both had etched in their heads and hearts forever. The girls had begged Annie and Joe to allow them to go to a summer camp – a week-long residential retreat in Hawke's Bay. The camp promised canoeing, hill climbs, barbecues and participation in challenges on land and water. Annie had been nervous about sending the girls off, but as Joe had pointed out, they were not kids any more. At thirteen and fifteen, they had good heads on their shoulders.

Midway through their time away, disaster struck. Annie received a call to say that a group of campers were missing, including both of their girls. The group had gone on a hike but hadn't returned at the designated time. After an hour more passed, the camp leaders had to raise the alarm. Joe drove them both to Hawke's Bay at breakneck speed. Deathly silence thickened the air between them as they fretted about their girls. When they arrived, they met four other sets of parents, and together, the group had three hours of worry as they waited for news from the search parties who were out scouring the trails. As it happened, the camp leader who was with the group had slipped and broken his ankle. The missing children were discovered by his side, completely unharmed.

'They were fine in the end is all I need to remember,' Joe said. 'Just a little shaken up, I think. And from my memory, very hungry! What made you think about the camp?'

Annie clutched her husband's arm. 'It struck me today that I've been worried many times about the girls over the years. But it's normally one or the other of them that I am concerned about. This is the first time since that camp that I've been worried about both of our girls simultaneously.'

As if knowing they were being talked about, Rachel and Claudia got up from the swing, so Annie and Joe moved away from the window and walked towards them.

'Need anything, love?' Joe asked Claudia.

Annie left Claudia and Joe to discuss treats and instead moved closer to Rachel. 'How does she seem to you?' she asked.

'Getting there. She's strong, Mom. She'll be okay,' Rachel assured her mother.

'So tell me about you, then. How were things with the Butlers before you left? Any change there?'

Rachel made a face. 'I haven't seen much of them, to be honest. Sheila and I still aren't really talking, but she tried to invite us over for Sunday roast recently. I couldn't go, because we were visiting Belinda and Oscar the same weekend, but I took it as a good sign that she was thawing a little towards me. The kids have had a few sleepovers with them, which they love, and we've stuck to the weekly visits after school. And it gives me a chance to catch up on work too.'

'And when was the last time you went out?' Annie inquired, concerned her daughter's lifestyle wasn't giving her much of a chance to let her hair down. 'You promised that you would do something fun, love,' Annie chastised Rachel when she got no answer. She knew exactly what that silence meant.

'With who, Mom?' Rachel snapped back, sharper than Annie was expecting. She'd clearly hit a nerve. 'I don't have any close friends in Dublin. And I don't have time to find any, either. Between the kids and work, I haven't got a moment. I meet myself coming backwards most days. And every time I put a waffle in the toaster for the kids, I can hear Sheila's voice in my ear telling me what a bad mother I am.'

'Rubbish. The kids that grow up fulfilled, happy and healthy are the ones that lived in a home with love. If

241

their school uniform isn't ironed, or they eat waffles from a toaster for dinner instead of organic hummus, none of it makes a difference. Doing everything perfectly doesn't make a good parent. That I know for sure.'

'Thanks, Mom,' Rachel said wearily.

'And here's one more word of wisdom for you,' Annie wasn't prepared to let this slide just yet, it was too important. 'You need to be kind to yourself too, Rachel. You look tired. Remember that if *you* feel good, the children will feel good too. Maybe there are some parents from the kids' school that would be interested in meeting up? Or a club you could join?'

Rachel shot her mom a warning look. Annie got the message and stopped this time. It was a delicate balance, finding the right thing to say. She didn't want to interfere, but also, how could she sit back and watch her vibrant, adventurous daughter live such a small life? Rachel had come out the other side of so much sadness; she had to find a way to move on.

She decided to risk saying one more thing.

'You are socially isolated over in Ireland, and it's not good for your mental health. I see you putting everyone else's needs first, but not much of you doing the same for yourself. Only you can decide what is best for your family, but *you* are part of that family too. It can't be only about what's best for Olivia and Dylan; it's about what's best for you also.'

'That's easier said than done,' Rachel replied, seemingly unprepared to even enter the conversation.

Annie hesitated. The question she had been wanting to ask had been preying on her mind for months, but she couldn't decide if it was the right time to bring it up.

Eventually, as Rachel's eyes searched her own, she stammered, 'Did you ever give any serious consideration to moving home? I'm worried that right now your life in Dublin is not working out for you. And it's difficult to witness.'

'There's nothing I'd love more. It hurts so much, the pain of missing you all. But if I take the children away from the Butlers and Bradleys, I'm transferring my pain to them. How can I do that?'

Annie had no answer for that. But at the same time, her job as a mother was to look after her daughter. She didn't want to hurt the Bradleys or Butlers, but this wasn't about any of them. It was about Rachel and the children. She decided to push it one bit further.

'If it's money, love, you can stay here with us. I know Claudia tried to tempt you with the villa, but you don't have to buy anywhere. You'll always have a home with us here.'

Rachel reached over to squeeze Annie's hand.

Annie never got tired of that. From the first time Rachel had held her finger with her tiny fist, to holding small hands as she jumped in muddy puddles, to now, gently squeezing each other's hands in love and support.

'It's not money that's stopping me, Mom. If I sold our house in Malahide, I'd have more than enough to buy the villa here if I wanted to. But I've also been thinking about buying somewhere else in Dublin, and that's what I'm closest to doing at the moment. I've been looking at Dalkey lately. It's on the coast, so I'll get to keep my sea views . . .'

Annie hadn't heard this mentioned before and felt a little hurt by the news. She began ticking off in her mind the reasons why Rachel should choose Hawke's Bay not Dublin Bay. But she swallowed all her reasons down. If Rachel wanted to stay in Dublin, and if moving to a new suburb made it easier to do so, Annie couldn't stand in her way.

'I better go in to Claudia. I don't want her on her own, getting maudlin,' Rachel said, perhaps sensing that Annie was finding the news hard. She leaned in and kissed her mother's cheek. 'I love that you worry about me, but please try not to. I'm fine, I promise.'

Annie didn't believe that for one moment. Whatever her daughters were right now, fine was not it.

THIRTY-TWO

Sheila

Malahide, Dublin

Since Rachel left, Sheila had gone for several walks every day, trying to catch a glimpse of the children and the Bradleys. But not once had luck been on her side. She hadn't seen sight nor sound of them. All she'd got from Rachel was a quick message via Jack to say that she was going overseas, and that there would be no change to the children's schedule. They'd see her as usual on Wednesday after school. The blasé way the girl had said that *Belinda and Oscar* were taking care of the children had taken her breath away.

Her grandchildren left in the care of those two? It didn't bear thinking about.

Adrian kept telling her to leave it be, that they would see the children as usual on Wednesday. But that was days away. Anything could happen to the children by then.

Were they even safe with the Bradleys? They hadn't reared Lorcan at all, the boarding school had done most of that. And they had a housekeeper at home in Belfast. What would they feed Olivia and Dylan? Did they even know how to turn an oven on? And Sheila didn't believe there was really an emergency in New Zealand. More likely, the girl was heading over there to put a deposit on that villa. Nothing would surprise Sheila less.

She put the finishing touches on a coffee sponge. It was one of her signature bakes, and anyone who had ever tasted it agreed that it was delicious. She looked up at the kitchen clock. It was six-thirty. By her reckoning, the children and the Bradleys should have finished their dinner now.

'Oh, a slice of that and a cup of tea. Just the ticket,' Adrian said, walking into the kitchen and interrupting Sheila's thoughts, licking his lips when he saw the cake.

'Exactly what I was thinking. But I think it's time to be neighbourly. Get your coat on, we're going visiting.' She placed the cake in a Tupperware container, snapping the lid shut with satisfaction.

Adrian groaned; this was not going to end well. He knew exactly where Sheila was planning on going. 'You can't go up to the house unannounced.'

'Just watch me.' Sheila would not stay away from her grandchildren. No way, no how.

THIRTY-THREE

Belinda

Malahide, Dublin

Vegetable art had been Olivia's suggestion, something they'd done in school and she fancied doing again, and Belinda couldn't think of a reason to say no. She cut potatoes in half and lined up broccoli spears and peppers, then opened up every tub of coloured paint the children owned.

Within moments, Belinda and Oscar had lost any semblance of control. The kids stamped paint on the pages in front of them, on each other, on Grandma's forehead and Grandpa's arms. The table didn't fare much better. Blobs of paint dripped from vegetables and landed on the chairs and the floor and Belinda hurried around the kitchen, wiping paint off every available surface. But no matter how fast she worked, the children were constantly one step ahead.

To her horror, before she could call the entire painting

activity to a halt, the doorbell rang. She looked at Oscar in panic. *Who could it be?* Just as she was about to tell everyone to hide, a face appeared at the window, peering in and waving.

It was Sheila.

Of course it was.

With as much dignity as she could muster, Belinda wiped her hands on a kitchen towel and let the two people she least wanted to see in the world into the house.

'I made you a cake,' Sheila said, handing a Tupperware container to her. Belinda watched as Sheila took in the scene before her, her eyes dancing with glee.

'That won't come out, you know, unless you clean it straight away,' Sheila said, pointing at the dining room table.

Can't resist telling me what to do already, Belinda thought to herself. *How does Rachel stand it?*

Before Belinda could actually respond, Sheila marched over to the dining room table where the artists were still at work.

'Look what I made, Nana Sheila!' Dylan shouted.

'That's wonderful, love. Aren't you clever? A fabulous piece of art.'

'And look what I made!' Olivia joined in. 'It's flowers made from vegetables.'

'Very imaginative,' Adrian said, joining them all at the table and kissing her head, then leaning in to do the same for Dylan.

'Why didn't you use the painting tablecloth?' Sheila asked, looking at Belinda.

The room was silent. Belinda and Oscar looked at her blankly.

'The children are only allowed to paint when the table is covered with an old oil tablecloth. It's a rule that my Niamh was most particular about,' Sheila said, a note of triumph more than clear in her voice. 'If you'd used the tablecloth, you wouldn't have a nightmare job ahead of you getting those paint stains out. It can get into the knots and grains of that wooden table, you see. You might have to sand it down and re-varnish,' she continued, taking a closer look.

'How very helpful. Well, we'll all know for the next time, won't we?' Belinda said coldly.

As if trying to temper his wife's rudeness somewhat, Adrian jumped in. 'Why don't you come down to the shop tomorrow and I can help get you sorted.'

Belinda was annoyed with herself for not thinking about preparing more before the children had begun their crafts. But more than that, she was annoyed that she had left herself and Oscar wide open to criticism from the Butlers. Who were once again convinced they had proven themselves to be the better grandparents, the grandparents who knew what to do in all circumstances.

'Don't worry, it's an easy mistake to make. Well, that is, when you aren't used to taking care of children,' Sheila said, a smile blatantly displayed on her smug face.

For a moment, Belinda allowed herself a most satisfactory daydream that resulted in the cake she held in her hand ending up smashed into the face of the woman in front of her.

THIRTY-FOUR

Rachel

Malahide, Dublin

As an emigrant, you learned to live with the heartache of goodbyes. It never got any easier, but at least you knew what to expect each time – along with jet lag, you dealt with emotional lag too. This time, however, when Rachel waved farewell to her family at the airport to begin her thirty-hour trip home, she felt a new depth of sorrow.

As she embraced her parents one by one, her pain grew heavier.

'It's been bloody good to have you home,' Joe said. 'Silver linings, and all that.'

Rachel leaned into her father, moulding into his embrace. Time flew away and she was a little kid again, back in her dad's arms, making her feel safe. When Lorcan died, the nagging feeling of homesickness had intensified triplefold. She'd had no choice but to live with it. But now, in her father's embrace, she felt the weight of her loneliness build up again.

'We'll video call you once you are over the jet lag,' Annie promised.

Rachel couldn't trust herself to speak, so she just nodded. Claudia had stayed at home with Howard. She'd claimed a headache, but Rachel knew she just couldn't bear to say goodbye any more than she could herself.

The only thing that made going home bearable was knowing that she would be reunited with the kids at the end of the long journey. She'd missed them so much. The first few days, in truth, she'd been fine. She'd been glad to have some time to herself, and not having two children to worry about meant she could focus all her attention on her sister, where it was needed. They'd sat up late several times over the week, watching movies together, crying and laughing, reminiscing. It didn't matter if she had crawled into bed at three a.m. (twice!) because she could lie in bed until midday the next day. And when she eventually stumbled downstairs, her mom would fuss over her and make her pancakes for breakfast. Nobody could make pancakes as her mom could.

But then a shift had come a few days ago. Rachel had become anxious, her waking moments dedicated to thinking about the kids.

Now, back on Irish soil, as she made her way back towards the Yellow Walls Road in a taxi, she imagined the forthcoming reunion. Her arms ached to hold the children again.

They were waiting for her when she pulled up in front of the house. As she took in the excited faces of the children, *her* children, her heart swelled.

'We got a puppy!' Dylan screamed as he launched himself into Rachel's arms. 'Did you buy me a present?'

'Ask Mom how Aunty Claudia is, first of all,' Olivia said, wise beyond her years as ever, and then launched herself at Rachel too.

Rachel hugged the children, breathing in their scent and feeling every anxious thought dissolve into their warm embrace. It had only been a day since she'd spoken to everyone, but evidently that was a long time. Had she heard Dylan correctly? A puppy?

'Oh, how I've missed you two,' she said, refusing to let them go yet.

And they were happy to snuggle in too. She looked over the kids' shoulders and said hello to Belinda and Oscar, who were watching their reunion with smiles on their faces. Belinda's hair, which Rachel had never seen in any style other than a low bun, now hung loosely around her face. And she was wearing one of the new loungewear sets that Rachel had started to stock at Rae's Closet – a jade-green two-piece with wide-legged trousers and an oversized long-sleeved top. She looked nearly ten years younger. Oscar, too, was sporting a relaxed look. His shirt sleeves were rolled up on either side as if he were about to do battle. And again, he looked younger somehow. At second glance, she realized they both also looked knackered. She felt uneasy, worried everything had been too much for the Bradleys. A week was a long time to take care of children when you weren't used to it.

Rachel finally disentangled herself from the kids' embrace and walked over to give her in-laws a warm hug, deciding that the era of air kisses was over for her. If

Belinda and Oscar had survived a week with her two kids, they deserved full-body hugs.

'Are you both okay? Did they break you?' Rachel asked.

'Mom!' Olivia exclaimed. 'We were perfect, weren't we, Grandma and Grandpa?'

'They were a delight. Angels,' Belinda.

'Their halos are held up by devil's horns,' Rachel joked, tickling the two kids, who roared with laughter. 'You know, it was the strangest thing; I could have sworn Dylan said you got a puppy.' She looked around, relieved not to see a creature bounding towards her.

A look passed between Belinda and Oscar. There was distinct uneasiness in that look.

'Please say you didn't buy the children a puppy,' Rachel said warily.

'We would never do that, not without your permission,' Oscar said quickly.

'Thank goodness for that. You gave me a fright for a minute.'

'But . . .' Belinda paused, clearly afraid to finish her sentence. 'I'm afraid that it appears not everyone is on the same page as us, on that matter.'

Rachel's heart dropped. She knew instantly who would be at the heart of all this. 'I'm not sure I am ready for this,' she said. She'd almost rather get back on another long flight than have to deal with a *puppy*. 'Go on . . .'

'Nana Sheila bought us a puppy!' Dylan screamed. 'And we got to name him whatever we wanted.'

'I wanted to call him Snowy,' Olivia said, ever practical, 'but Dylan vetoed that name. We had three vetoes each. And we picked Thor.'

They had discussed a puppy many times over the previous years. Rachel and Lorcan had said no to the suggestion, as well Sheila knew, and Rachel had continued to resist after Lorcan's death. It wasn't that Rachel didn't love dogs – she did – but she had enough on her hands without adding anything else to the equation.

'And where is Thor?' she asked, trying to keep her tone even, and reminding herself that this was not the kids' – nor Belinda and Oscar's – faults.

'Don't worry, Nana Sheila said she knew you don't like puppies and wouldn't allow Thor to live here. So she is keeping him at her house for us,' Olivia said. *That scheming woman*, Rachel thought as she gritted her teeth.

'Nana said we should go every day after school to feed him. He eats special food because his tummy is so small,' Dylan explained.

Rachel felt a little light-headed. This was how being blindsided felt.

'Let your mom come inside and have a hot drink,' Belinda said. 'Then we can fill her in on everything.'

'Oh, and Grandpa Oscar painted our table!' Dylan said. 'It's shiny.'

'Ah yes,' Oscar said, clearly hoping this wouldn't come up quite so soon, 'there was a little accident involving some fruit-related crafts. It was our fault; we let the children loose without the painting tablecloth. So I sanded it down and gave it a coat of varnish. Good as new.'

'You shouldn't have done that!' Rachel was mortified. 'Goodness knows that table has had plenty of paint marks over the years.'

'Oh, it wasn't any trouble at all,' Oscar replied, albeit not wholly convincingly.

As Belinda prepared coffees and hot chocolate for everyone, Rachel passed the children a bag full of presents to open. Both Claudia and her parents had bought them gifts, and Rachel had picked up some souvenirs too, not to mention the obligatory M&M chocolate from duty-free. While they were distracted with their new toys, Belinda updated Rachel with all the goings-on.

'School went by with no issues. We did our best with their homework, but I have to admit, I fear we might have confused Olivia with maths. It's changed a lot since I was in school,' Belinda explained apologetically.

'What's wrong with old maths? That's what I'd like to know,' Oscar said. 'From where I was sitting, it appeared they've overly complicated everything.'

'Hard agree!' Rachel said. 'I've had no choice but to get to grips with it all. Clumping. That's a thing, you know, in new math.'

Oscar shuddered. 'I felt like a dinosaur; I was so out of touch with it all.'

'You should see me doing Irish with them. Let's say that Google Translate and I have become very well acquainted.'

'The kids insisted that they are allowed a treat every day,' Belinda continued recounting the week's events. 'Now I would like it noted that I didn't believe them. But as their grandmother, I decided that I'd like to spoil them a little, so after dinner each night, we did let them have a cupcake or some ice cream.'

Rachel smiled, knowing that her children could be master manipulators when they wanted to.

'It sounds as though you've done an amazing job,' she said gratefully. 'Now talk to me about this puppy. Or do I not want to know?'

'Well, Sheila and Adrian called over a few times during the week. They weren't always expected,' Belinda said, as diplomatically as she could.

'Ouch. I know that feeling,' Rachel replied.

'I'm sure you'll hear all about it. Sheila seemed to have a knack of arriving at the most inopportune moment. But we had the easiest of weeks, honestly, with the odd chaotic moment.'

'I swear that woman is a witch,' Rachel said. 'She's the same with me. Last week I was shouting at the kids as she walked up the drive. And of course, she went on to tell me how damaging it is for children to live in a house where a parent has anger issues.'

'I don't know how you keep a civil tongue in your head with her,' Oscar said. 'She's most aggravating. Adrian's not too bad a fellow. Quite helpful. He has a bloody decent shop in the village.'

'The kids went to the Butlers on Wednesday after school and playschool as normal,' here Belinda paused, clearly struggling with how best to describe what happened next. 'Well, when we called over to collect them that evening as arranged, they refused to come with us.'

'Sheila had surprised them with their puppy after Olivia's return from school, and naturally, they didn't want to leave,' Oscar explained.

'That's horrible. I'm so sorry,' Rachel said, imagining how awkward that visit must have been.

'It was a tad difficult,' Belinda nodded. 'Sheila suggested rather unhelpfully in front of the children that they could stay the night with her. She said she had spare PJs for them and could bring them to school the next day. As soon as she made the suggestion, there was really no hope that we could get the children to come home with us. Not voluntarily, at least.'

'We didn't know what to do, Rachel,' Oscar's tone was apologetic now. 'But in the end, we felt it was better not to make a scene. So we left them there.'

Rachel was furious. She knew what the puppy was. It was a pre-emptive strike from the Butlers. The problem was, she already knew that no matter how she reacted, she would be on the losing side in this battle.

'Are you cross with us for not clearing it with you?' Belinda asked, looking worried. 'I'm afraid it was the middle of the night for you by then.'

'Oh goodness, no. I'm not cross with you both. You did the right thing.'

'Well, that wasn't the end of the story,' she continued grimly. 'On Thursday, it got a little complicated. We collected Dylan at two p.m., then did some grocery shopping with him before going back at three p.m. to collect Olivia. Sheila surprised us all by turning up at the school gates with Thor too.'

Somehow Rachel wasn't surprised by this in the least.

'Sheila said that she had promised the children she would do so. But it made things rather tricky for us,' Oscar said.

Belinda added, 'The kids insisted that they wanted to go back to Sheila's house again. And I must admit, I could understand the attraction. The little pup is rather cute.'

'That woman is incorrigible,' Rachel said, feeling her shoulders tense in frustration.

'She is rather. But don't worry, I've dealt with far trickier people in business, I can assure you,' Oscar said.

'I'm afraid to ask what happened next,' Rachel said.

'Well, I was aware that there were a lot of people

watching us,' Belinda continued. 'I wanted to get the kids into the car as quickly as possible, so I resorted to a little bribery myself.'

'Please don't tell me you bought them a puppy too.'

There was a moment of light relief as everyone laughed.

'You'll be relieved to know it was just ice-cream sundaes. Two scoops. With all the trimmings.'

'It worked like a charm,' Oscar said. 'No sooner had the word "sprinkles" come out of Belinda's lips than they had kissed that puppy goodbye and left Sheila behind.'

Rachel had to laugh, despite her annoyance. 'So did she turn up again yesterday?'

'I decided to head her off at the pass, so to speak,' Belinda replied. 'I gave her a quick call yesterday, and let's say that we had a frank conversation. She agreed to stay away. But she said that you would hear about it. Be warned. I'm sorry if I've made your situation with the Butlers any worse.'

'You haven't. By the sounds of it, you handled the situation beautifully.' Rachel slumped back into a chair, feeling exhausted. Even when she was nowhere near her, Sheila managed to cause trouble in her life. 'Dare I ask how things went with the business?'

Oscar picked up his clipboard. 'I thought you'd never ask.'

He ran through the status of orders pending and delivered. Looking at the numbers, Rachel realized that the business hadn't suffered in the least from her absence. If anything, there had been a slight increase in orders received.

'If you fancy coming to work for me full-time, Oscar, the job is yours. The pay isn't great, but my gratitude will be endless.'

Oscar beamed at the compliment. 'It's been a long time since I felt so useful. It was good to think about something other than tennis or bridge for a few days.'

'Well, anytime you feel like coming back, the door is open,' Rachel said, genuinely meaning it.

She suddenly had an idea as she watched her mother-in-law lean back in her chair in her gorgeous new lounge suit.

'Talking of Rae's Closet, Belinda?' she asked tentatively. 'Could I take a photograph of you wearing that? You look amazing.'

'Oh, you don't want that,' Belinda retorted, mortified by the suggestion.

But Rachel had her phone out and was insisting, showing Belinda how to stand and pose for the shot. 'That's it, one foot slightly forward, opposite hand on your hip. Look at you! You're a natural.'

And even Belinda had to admit that she looked good when Rachel showed her the shots. Rachel created a side-by-side image of Belinda and herself both wearing the same outfit.

'I love this! It shows that loungewear can look good on *every* body.'

And Rachel couldn't miss the bright smile on Belinda's face, who was obviously chuffed.

'Right, I think we should say our goodbyes and let you settle in,' Oscar interrupted.

'The fridge is full, and a few ready-made meals are waiting for you there. I didn't make them, of course, but they are nutritious and easy to prepare,' Belinda added.

Rachel wasn't sure she could adequately express how grateful she was. The Bradleys had surpassed every expectation she'd had. She walked over to the bookshelf in the

family room, pulling out an envelope she'd had the fore-
sight to leave there before she went to New Zealand. 'I
honestly would have been lost without you both this
week. This is a small thank-you. I figured that after a
week of the munchkins, you would both be tired, so I
arranged for you to have a full-body massage in the spa
you took me to in August.'

They looked genuinely grateful and surprised by the
gesture, both proclaiming that they needed no thanks.
And then, with another round of warm hugs and prom-
ises made to come and visit them soon, they were gone.

THIRTY-FIVE

Rachel

Malahide, Dublin

When Rachel was eleven years old, she received a juggling set from one of her friends for her birthday. For weeks, every day, she'd practised throwing balls in the air, moving from one hand to the other. She managed to get the hang of three balls quickly enough, but as soon as she added in the fourth or fifth, disaster always struck. Rachel wasn't a quitter. She was pretty stubborn and would dig her heels in when something didn't come naturally until she managed to work it out. But after weeks of frustrating attempts, her dad had suggested gently that perhaps she wasn't destined to be one of life's jugglers. Rachel had to agree, and so she passed the gift to the local charity shop. She hoped another child would have better luck than she had.

Now, as a young woman trying to juggle life as a single

mother and business owner, she realized that her skills with those balls had not improved with time. She picked up dirty laundry from Dylan's floor (he never seemed to grasp the concept of a laundry basket) and then went through the list of outstanding items she had to do this morning before collecting him from school. Only a few days home from New Zealand and already her trip was a distant memory. Her number one job was getting some clean clothes organized for the kids. And to solve the mystery of where all their socks had disappeared to. She'd bought them both seven new pairs at the beginning of the school term. Rachel had been smug when she'd opted to buy them both plain navy socks. Her thinking was that this way, the socks would be interchangeable when one went rogue. But the sock monster was having none of it and had somehow managed to gobble the lot up.

On top of this, the cupboards and fridge were in dire need of a big shop. Today was Tuesday. And that meant that Rachel felt particular pressure to prepare a healthy meal from scratch for the children. When they went to their grandparents, Sheila constantly quizzed them about what they ate at home. Olivia had told Rachel this, expressing bewilderment at why their eating habits fascinated Sheila so much. To Rachel, it felt like Sheila was gathering evidence.

She checked her watch to see how much time she had and discovered that, *damn it*, she was late again. She'd have to go shopping after she collected Dylan, not before. She quickly emptied the washer with a load of Olivia's clothes, threw them into the dryer, then placed Dylan's clothes into the washer. This time she wouldn't forget to dry them. Probably. Olivia's clothes had been through the wash twice for that reason.

She looked around her small utility room. It was a disaster area. Kicked-off wellies were at the back door and the countertop was adorned with bottles and glass jars, still waiting for their final destination in the bottle bank. Rachel picked up one of her bags for life and filled it with the recyclables. There was a bottle bank behind the supermarket on the main street. If she went there to do the shopping, she could kill two birds with one stone. She left the bottles at the front door along with a couple more bags, so as not to forget them when she left to pick up Dylan.

She needed more caffeine, so she made a quick cup and sat down briefly at her laptop. She clicked open her received orders and was delighted to see that her earlier live video, showing a range of maxi dresses for the summer, had gone down well. She'd sold out in all sizes in two of the styles and had only a few left in the last. She rang her supplier and placed another order, deciding to double the amount at the last minute. Then she updated her Facebook shop page with details of when she expected the new stock to arrive.

Rae's Closet was doing so well that she'd been thinking about expanding, perhaps hiring staff, and locating a warehouse to work from. Using the 'good' sitting room at home had served her well, but with the children getting older – and her business getting bigger – they all needed more space.

Rachel looked at an item that had been on her to-do list for days. *Call Sheila*. It was even underlined. She'd meant to do it on Saturday, Sunday and Monday too, but somehow she could always find something else to be doing.

Carmel Harrington

She had to talk to the woman about the puppy. Every day, the kids begged her to let them call over to see Thor, and so far she'd managed to stall them. But she couldn't put off the discussion any longer. For this puppy situation to work, she needed ground rules.

Sheila answered on the second ring, 'Are the children okay?'

Hello to you too, Rachel thought. Clearly they were past pleasantries now. 'Hello, Sheila. Yes, of course the children are fine,' she answered, holding back a sigh.

'You never call. So when I see your number, I can't help but worry.'

Always with the reprimanding.

'I need a quick word, that's all,' Rachel said, biting back a snappier retort. 'Is now a good time?'

'Well, as it happens, it is – because I need a quick word too.'

'Well, I wanted to check in about Thor. I was surprised to hear that you bought a dog.'

'I didn't know I had to ask your permission.'

'Not if the dog is yours, but you told the children the puppy is theirs,' she refused to be caught in Sheila's trap. 'You were clear about that to them, were you? Or do they have it wrong?'

Sheila sighed, 'Yes, we did say the puppy was theirs. Every child should have one. Niamh and Jack grew up with them. A man's best friend; it's such a true sentiment.'

'I love dogs, Sheila,' Rachel said cautiously, wary that every word held a potential trap. 'But as you know, when we discussed this many times in the past, Lorcan and I agreed that we didn't have the time to give to a puppy. And the children accepted that.'

'Well, as you don't have to take care of Thor, I'm not sure I understand why you are getting your knickers in a twist.' Sheila had lost all pretence at politeness now.

'My knickers are untwisted, Sheila, but I would like you to make it clear to the children tomorrow that the puppy is yours, not theirs. They can see Thor on Wednesdays as normal when they visit you. And I'll drop them down at the weekend too, to take him for a walk. But we need to make sure we are both on the same page.' Rachel thought she was doing a fantastic job at trying to keep her voice even. In reality, she wanted to scream at the woman.

'That's a little bit tricky, dear. The reason I wanted to talk to you was about the very same issue. The children are devoted to Thor. It's a joy watching them together. And they have asked Adrian and me if they can come here on a more regular basis. With that in mind, I would like to address the current visitation arrangement.'

Why was she using terms like visitation? There was something so official about it, it made Rachel uneasy.

'What do you have in mind?' she said through gritted teeth, already knowing she would regret asking. This woman would be the death of her.

'I think it would make sense if we collect the children on Friday afternoons after school and have them stay here until Saturday evening. I can wash their clothes for them. I noticed last Wednesday that Olivia's jumper had a yoghurt stain on it. She said it had been there for at least two days. And as for Dylan's trousers, both knees were muddy. It's not a good look for the children. We don't want the school to think the children are being neglected.'

At this Rachel could not keep her tone level. She said firmly, 'I do not appreciate that comment. Dylan dirties his trousers every day. That's what little boys and girls *do*, especially when they like to have rough and tumble in pre-school.'

'Well, think of it like this, if they come to me on Wednesdays *and* Fridays, that's two days I can do the washing for you. It's one less thing for you to worry about.'

Rachel could feel a scream begin to rush its way around her body, whipping her stomach, her head, her heart. It took every ounce of her self-control not to let it out. Instead, she forced herself to speak slowly and calmly. 'The children will be with me at weekends unless we arrange a sleepover,' she replied firmly, not even entertaining Sheila's suggestion, 'which I'm sure you'll agree, I am always happy to accommodate.'

Sheila couldn't disagree with that point. There was silence for a moment, but then she replied, 'Even so, I would like it to be a formal arrangement, with sleepovers every week. We also need to discuss school holidays, which I believe start next week. I'm happy to do week on, week off, or we can do split weeks, whichever works for you, dear.'

Rachel hit mute on the phone for a second so she could curse loudly into the empty room. Feeling marginally better, she unmuted herself and mimicked Sheila's patronizing formal tone. 'Sheila, what you are looking for is shared custody. You are not a parent. You are a grandparent. Your suggested increased visitation rights do not work for me. The answer is no.'

'We'll have to see about that, dear.'

The way she said 'dear' made Rachel want to throw a plate across the room. And then she realized the weight of Sheila's implication. 'What do you mean by that?' she asked, scared to hear the answer.

'It gives me no pleasure, but I think the time has come for me to push the green light with my solicitor, Maria Johnson.'

Rachel felt breathless with anger.

Sheila continued, 'I've had several concerns about you for some time. And I've voiced them with my legal team. You'll be hearing from them.'

With that, Sheila hung up, leaving Rachel holding her phone in shock. *Her legal team? Who the hell does the woman think she is?*

Rachel rang Ronan as she made her way to the car to collect Dylan, her heart still racing with adrenaline. It went to voicemail; it usually did during the day.

'I need you to call me ASAP.' Rachel could hear the panic in her voice, but she couldn't tone it down. 'Sheila has just told me her solicitor will be in touch. I'm going to need a lawyer, if not for this, then to keep me out of jail. Because I swear, I'm going to swing for her!'

Only when she was halfway to the school did she realize she'd left the damn bags for life and bottles behind her yet again.

THIRTY-SIX

Rachel

Malahide, Dublin

Once the kids were in bed, Rachel pulled a bottle of pinot noir from the wine rack in the kitchen. She was expecting Ronan any minute but couldn't wait for him to arrive. She'd never needed a drink more than she did right now.

Rachel thought about Lorcan at least once every day. She'd say to herself, *Oh, I must tell Lorc that.* Then she'd remember with a new, cruel jab that Lorcan wasn't there to tell any more. Yesterday, Dylan had almost tripped up coming out of school, but he'd recovered himself with such style it made her proud. And she couldn't wait to share her parental pride with Lorcan. Inane, silly, unimportant moments like that never relayed well when shared with anyone else. She'd tell them to Claudia or her parents, and they'd smile politely, but it wasn't the same. Lorc would have gotten how funny and also how cool it was too. Tonight, though, his absence cut particularly deep. She didn't just feel alone; she felt scared. She'd already lost too much; she couldn't lose the children too.

She was halfway through her first drink when Ronan arrived. There was something comforting about him being there. He didn't look like Lorcan, but they had similar mannerisms. The way they walked, the way they said certain words. He had taken his tie and suit jacket off and rolled his shirt sleeves up by the time he arrived; Ireland was enjoying a heat wave and his skin was tanned as a result, a smattering of freckles across his nose, in the exact same place that Lorcan used to get them.

Oh Lorc, where are you when I need you the most?

As Rachel recounted her conversation with Sheila, she moved on to her second drink. Ronan, though, declined to join her.

He took notes as she spoke, listening intently. 'I know Maria Johnson. She's got a strong track record of winning custody battles, unfortunately. And she's known for her ability to expose the opposing parent's weak spot.'

'Should I be worried?' Rachel tried to sound calm, but she was quite sure she didn't manage it.

'We need to take this threat seriously,' Lorcan responded, all professional. 'But don't worry, that's my job. We'll do everything possible to avoid court, which could be both lengthy and expensive. I'm thinking out loud here, but mediation might be a good route to go.'

'I have a vague memory of a distant cousin in New Zealand going through mediation during their messy divorce. I don't think it helped. They ended up in court anyhow.'

Ronan insisted that mediation had made great strides

over the years and that it was now a tool used with significant effect in custody battles. Rachel, though, remained to be convinced. Experience had taught her that Sheila Butler wasn't strong on compromise.

'Isn't it just dragging the inevitable out?' she asked, pushing the wine bottle away now. She'd had enough to feel feisty, but she knew she needed her wits about her. 'Should we just rip the plaster off and go straight to court?'

'We could do, but it will cost you the price of Olivia's college fees. Perhaps Dylan's too,' Ronan's face was grim. 'Trust me, Rachel. You might be surprised at how successful mediation could be for you all. In court, it's all about winning or losing. And from what I know about Sheila, she's a woman who likes to win.'

The wine began to sit uneasily in Rachel's stomach.

'The beauty of mediation used in the family law system is that it gives greater flexibility to all parties. People can meet in the middle,' Ronan insisted.

Rachel tried to imagine what the middle ground might look like. A vision of a dusty, arid desert popped into her mind.

'If we go for mediation, *hopefully* Sheila and Adrian will get the chance to see things from another perspective. And then change their demands. Trust me, this way we can keep the focus on the needs of the children.'

Rachel felt her chest constrict in pain at the thought that her children would ever find out about this. It would be horrific for them to feel like they were in the middle of any battle.

'The children will not be used as pawns. I won't have it.'

'And I won't let that happen either. You have my word.

And while Maria Johnson may be one of the best in her field, she's not *the* best,' Ronan winked.

Rachel appreciated that he was making an effort to lighten the mood. 'Well, maybe you can tell me whoever the best is, because I'd sure like to hire them.'

'Any more of that cheek, and I'll turn the clock on and start billing you for my time now,' Ronan laughed.

But instead of laughing, Rachel's heart began to hammer inside her chest at this.

'Speaking of billing, I'm afraid to ask . . . will I need to remortgage my house to pay for this?'

Ronan sat back in his chair and crossed his arms. It was a tricky question, especially between family. 'That question is a little like how long is a piece of string. The beauty of mediation is that you only pay for each meeting. But you'll get family rates for me, so don't worry about that. Let's just hope we can resolve this in a timely fashion.'

'And do I have to pay for the entire cost?' Rachel asked.

'No. You split the costs in half with the Butlers. But leave all of these details to Maria and me to sort out. For now, I think it's better you don't engage with the Butlers any more than you can help it, other than to discuss the usual things such as pick-ups and drop-offs for the kids.'

'If I never had to speak to any of them again, that's still too soon.'

From the beginning of her relationship with them, Rachel had felt like an outsider with the Butler family, but she'd known that her priority was to put the children first, so if that meant sucking up for their sakes, so be it. But now she would have to face the Butlers independently, whether in a mediator's office or a courtroom. It would be two against one.

She briefly wondered where Jack fit into all of this. She was so used to having him round, helping with the children, it felt strange that he might become one of the enemy ranks. She had always thought of him as her only ally in the Butler camp, but maybe he was part of the custody application too. She couldn't bear it if he'd known about it but not warned her. She sat silently, lost in her thoughts.

'I know it feels like a mess, Rachel,' Ronan's voice broke into her reverie. 'But you'd be surprised how many grandparents fight for more visitation rights or guardianship of children. The difference is that there is normally an issue with the parents' capabilities, which is most certainly not the case here.'

'How about grandparents trying to take children from the stepmother/adopted mother? I bet that's not so common,' Rachel said.

'Correct. But that's another good reason to try mediation. There isn't the same time in court for a judge to understand every nuance of a custody battle. In mediation, we can control the narrative. Every party gets to speak and be heard. And in theory, if we can reach an agreement, it will be far quicker.'

'Okay,' Rachel said finally. 'But remember, and this is a non-negotiable: I don't want the children to be involved. At all. They are not to be stuck in the middle between us all. They've lost too much already; I won't allow them to lose any more.'

'Spoken with a true mother's heart. Mediation will protect the children from conflict, I promise you. And hopefully, it will protect you too. It's less adversarial. I actually have a mediator in mind – Fergal Williams.

He is fair and reasoned. Give me twenty-four hours. I'll talk to Maria and we'll get moving on sorting this out.'

Ronan seemed so self-assured it helped to calm Rachel. Lorcan always said that if he ever needed anyone fighting in his corner, it would be Ronan.

'Thank you. Right, I'm going to check on the kids, then I plan on having another glass of wine,' Rachel said. 'Are you sure you won't join me? Even for one glass?'

'Not for me. I'm good with the water.'

Rachel left the room to go upstairs. Both kids were fast asleep, oblivious to the drama that surrounded them. She blew kisses to them both and, as she did so, she heard the doorbell go again. She closed the door to Dylan's room and made her way downstairs. By the time she got to the landing, Ronan had answered the door, and Jack stood awkwardly beside him in the hall. Rachel felt a shiver of unease seeing him there. This felt awkward already.

'Come on in,' she said and walked back to the kitchen.

Jack held up a bottle of wine. 'I thought you might need this?'

'Way ahead of you,' Rachel replied, pulling a glass from the cupboard for Jack and putting it next to her own on the table.

'You know what, I will have that glass of wine after all,' Ronan said, as he watched, his turnabout taking Rachel by surprise. She poured them each a glass, then held her own up in a small toast. 'To winning custody battles.'

As she clinked glasses with Jack, she couldn't help wondering which side he was toasting.

'So I heard the news. Are you okay?' Jack asked,

throwing Ronan a stinker of a look that, as far as Rachel could tell, was just in response to his very presence.

'I've had better days.'

He nodded.

'Tell me you are not part of it,' Rachel said faintly, unable to leave the question unanswered for one more moment.

'Of course not,' Jack said adamantly.

Ronan muttered something under his breath. It sounded a lot like 'horseshit'.

But Rachel didn't have it in her to referee whatever masculine rivalry these two had going on. She took another swig of wine and the alcohol began to do its job, finally shifting the uneasy, queasy feeling she'd had in her stomach all day.

'I'm a good mother. I don't deserve this,' she said, a little more forcefully than she'd intended.

'I know you are,' Jack replied.

Ronan, however, was more assertive. 'You should never have to defend your capacity as a mother!' he jumped in. 'It's outrageous that you've even been put in this position.' He looked pointedly at Jack as he spoke.

Rachel tried to ignore the antagonism between the two men. 'The thing is, I know it's difficult for your family, Jack. To see me as a mother to Olivia and Dylan when, to you all, it should be Niamh. I honestly understand that it must hurt like hell. But your family has to find a way to get past this. I am Olivia and Dylan's mother now, and I can't keep apologizing about it. I didn't plan to fall in love with Lorcan, but it happened, and I don't regret it.'

'Look, you really don't have to explain any of this to me. I get it,' Jack said.

Rachel couldn't help thinking that Jack was sitting on the fence a little too comfortably for her liking.

'But I feel like I do. I constantly have to justify every little thing I do to your mother.'

Ronan moved closer to Rachel as she spoke. 'Do you need a hug?' he asked, then, without waiting for an answer, he took her in his arms.

For a wonderful moment, Rachel leaned into the embrace, allowing herself to imagine it was Lorcan's arms around her.

There was a loud crash, and as Rachel looked up from Ronan's shoulder she noticed a glass of water on the island had gone flying, splashes landing on Ronan's arms. The noise pulled them apart in an instant.

'My bad. Sorry,' Jack said, looking sheepish.

'Don't worry.' Rachel stood up and moved away from Ronan, picking up a tea towel and beginning to mop up the spilt water. She watched Ronan wipe his arm and throw his own stinker of a look back at Jack. *What the hell is going on with these two?*

'Look, I'm not defending Mam. I can't agree with this custody application. But I do know that everything she does comes from a place of love for the children,' Jack said firmly.

'I don't doubt that. But Sheila constantly undermines me.' Rachel wasn't in the mood for appeasing Jack and being nice about his mother. Not after all Sheila had put her through. 'If there were an Olympic sport for giving backhanded compliments, your mam would be the world record holder.'

This broke the tension, and the three of them laughed together. Rachel emptied the last of the wine into their glasses and they clinked a toast. 'I miss having Claudia around to have the sibling bants with, but you two are a good substitute. My brothers from other mothers.'

Rachel giggled to herself. She felt a little light-headed; she was getting drunk. And since she planned to get so drunk that she passed out tonight, without any late-night tossing and turning with worry, she opened the second bottle.

'You could tell your mam to back off though, Jack,' Ronan said. 'If Sheila were my mother, I'd call her out on her behaviour.'

Jack ignored Ronan, turning to Rachel. 'I don't think Mam intentionally jabs you. It's just become a habit. I'm not sure she is aware of how hurtful you find the things she says.'

Rachel was pretty sure that Sheila knew precisely what she was doing. There was a look of satisfaction on her face as she dealt each blow. But she kept quiet.

'This puppy, that was definitely a sneaky move on her part,' Ronan said.

'Yesh, well played, Sheila,' Rachel said, her voice slurring a little now. She took another swig of wine, finishing her drink. She topped her glass up yet again, offering more to Ronan and Jack, who both said no.

'She likes to spoil the kids. That's all,' Jack said.

'I get that. But you cannot tell me that Sheila didn't decide to buy that puppy as a move to get the children to her house while the Bradleys were here. And as an enticement to increase the time they spend there.'

The guilt written all over Jack's face was all the answer Rachel needed.

'Yep, your mam isn't aware of what's she's doing. Not one bit,' Ronan said, sarcasm dripping from every word.

'Helpful as always,' Jack said.

'I do try,' Ronan replied with a wink.

Rachel looked between the two men, unsure what was going on but still understanding that these two had, as her father would put it, 'beef' with each other. She poured another drink, missing the glass and splashing some wine on the counter. She shrugged and raised the glass to her lips regardless. She liked this feeling more and more. Not caring. Going with the flow.

'Slow down a little, Rach,' Ronan said, watching her. Then he turned to Jack, 'Maybe it's time you went home, mate.'

'I'm good. But you feel free to leave any time you like.'

'You'd like that, wouldn't you?' Ronan said.

'Yeah. As it goes, I would.'

'What is goin' *on* here?' Rachel asked, waving her glass between the two of them.

Ronan took the glass from her hand and put it on the island. 'We're chatting. That's all.'

'You don't like Jack,' Rachel said, the wine helping her lose any social inhibitions. 'And Jack doesn't like you. Why is that?'

Both men made non-committal sounds.

Maybe it was the wine, or perhaps it was simply as a result of the day she'd had, but Rachel decided to push some more.

'And as I've got you both here, you can answer this. What did Niamh think of Belinda and Oscar?'

'She never really spoke to me about them,' Jack said tentatively, clearly unsure where Rachel was going.

She didn't believe that for a moment. Jack and Niamh had been close.

'Did she like them? You must know that,' she persisted.

'I don't think they had much in common,' Jack said.

'I know there was a big fight between Niamh and Belinda,' Rachel continued to push.

But Jack remained firm. 'I wasn't aware of one,' he responded.

Again, Rachel was sure he was lying; he couldn't look her in the eye. What *was* the big secret?

'Something happened that made Lorcan stay away from his parents. Are you sure you don't know?' she persisted.

A flash of colour appeared on Jack's face. 'You're looking for a drama that doesn't exist,' he warned.

'The thing is, there is drama . . . I'm surrounded by it! What about you, Ronan? Are you going to tell me that Lorcan never spoke about his fight with his parents? I know he had one.'

'I've told you, Rach. I hadn't seen Lorc for a few years before he met you. We drifted apart after he got married to Niamh. He was busy with the kids, I'm sure . . .'

Rachel searched Ronan's face but could only see sincerity there. But then again, it also looked like there were two of him. Rachel suddenly realized that she had gone from tipsy to downright drunk with her fourth glass of red.

'I don't feel very well,' she admitted.

'I think you should go to bed, Rach. It's been a big day, let's call it quits,' Ronan said soothingly.

And for the first time that night, Jack agreed with him. 'Go on up, Rach. We'll let ourselves out and lock up.'

Rachel looked at them both and felt tears fill her eyes. She felt drunk, yes, but more than that, she was over-whelmed with sadness and dread.

'I'm just so scared,' she whispered.

'It's going to be okay,' Jack said, moving to her side.

'I'm going to make sure of that,' Ronan replied, taking up a position on the other side.

'You won't let them take Olivia and Dylan from me?' Rachel asked, tears now streaming down her face.

'I give you my word; those children are going nowhere,' Ronan said.

'I won't let Mam and Dad do that, I promise,' Jack added.

She reached up and kissed Ronan on his cheek, then turned to do the same to Jack. Rachel had to believe them. Because after all, what was the alternative?

PART TWO

THIRTY-SEVEN

Rachel

Family Mediation Centre, Mount Street, Dublin

As Rachel sat in Dublin's city centre's mid-morning traffic, she replayed the events of the previous few months over and over in her head. Could she have done anything different to avoid the situation she now found herself and her children in? Truthfully, she wasn't sure she could. Despite her best efforts, it was apparent that Sheila and Adrian, and yes, she too, had reached an impasse. And they needed help to get through it.

Jack had come good for Rachel and had pleaded with his mother to think about the consequences of pressing the button on a custody battle. He had called Rachel a few days after her breakdown with him and Ronan, to say that Sheila had promised to at least think about it further, agreeing to delay things until after the summer holidays at the earliest.

And to show her appreciation for that stay of execution, Rachel tried to be flexible with visitation. She couldn't agree to the crazy demands of week on, week off visits during the school holidays, but she did allow the children to visit the Butlers whenever they wanted, including every Friday for the full day. They'd also had several impromptu sleepovers. Rachel had let herself believe that maybe their storm had passed.

The kids and Rachel also had a few more visits to Willow Lodge in Belfast over the summer holidays, and they all felt quite at home there now.

Then it was time to buy school supplies, books, uniforms and new school bags. Rachel invited all the grandparents to wave Dylan off to school on his first day, and they all turned up to have breakfast with them. There had been no snide comments; everyone had put on their best sunny side and together they'd taken Dylan and Olivia to school. Thankfully, they'd had no issues at the school gates with Dylan. He'd walked in, holding Rachel's hand, quite happily. Olivia said she was happy too, but Rachel didn't quite believe her.

But then, a few days later, Rachel had received a letter, via Ronan, from the Butlers' solicitor, Maria Johnson, outlining her clients' intent to apply for joint custody of their grandchildren. It took Rachel three re-reads of the letter to take in her situation fully. Even then, she'd felt like she was in an alternate reality.

Ronan had been brilliant. He'd dealt with Maria, who'd managed to get agreement from the Butlers that they would attend mediation with Fergal Williams at the Family Mediation Centre in Dublin. Rachel was given the option of attending alone or, if she wanted, with her solicitor,

Ronan, too. She opted to have him by her side because she wasn't sure she had the strength to deal with Sheila on her own. This in turn meant that Sheila wanted Maria Johnson in attendance too.

So here she was now, en route to the centre and ready to do battle.

Rachel scoured Mount Street for a parking spot. It was hit or miss mid-morning, but she had time, being early for their eleven a.m. meeting. The parking gods were in her favour; a Jeep pulled out a few doors from where she needed to be. The intention was that the opening meeting would take no longer than an hour, then another hour afterwards for post-match analysis. But as Ronan had pointed out, mediation wasn't a direct science, so she should be prepared to be a little flexible with that timing.

'Hey, you,' Ronan said, as she walked up to the centre. He was leaning on the black railings outside the red-brick building, looking sharp in a pale grey suit. 'Do you feel okay? You look a little pale.'

Rachel was glad to see him there. 'I feel nauseous, if I'm honest. I can't believe it's come to this. I feel like I'm letting Lorcan down.'

Ronan placed his hands on Rachel's shoulders, looking down a little so he was eye to eye. 'You get that thought out of your head straight away. Lorcan was bloody lucky he met you. And if he's watching, he's proud of you and the way you've conducted yourself throughout all of this.'

Rachel needed to hear that, and wanted to believe it too. But despite the kindness of Ronan's words, she couldn't stop the uneasy feeling. As they walked through the black glass door, it felt as if she was making her way towards the front line of battle. Sheila and Adrian were already inside, perched on the edge of their chairs outside the meeting room. They looked as nervous as Rachel felt. Their lawyer spoke on her phone as she paced up and down the hallway. She nodded at Ronan as she passed them.

In her head, Rachel had already imagined this woman to be a fierce dragon, breathing fire on all passers-by. Now that she'd seen her in the flesh, her imagination only magnified. Maria wore a trouser suit in a shade of red that shouldn't have worked, coupled as it was with her shock of red hair. But the result was both sexy and fierce. It suggested that the woman had a level of confidence that Rachel wished she herself possessed. She looked down at her own choice of clothes – a midi dress and blazer combo with white trainers. Ronan had told her to dress as she usually would. That she should not try to change who she was.

'You should have told me to wear heels,' she whispered angrily to Ronan.

'You're overthinking this,' he soothed. 'Relax. You look great.'

Rachel glanced at Sheila and Adrian. She wasn't sure what the done thing was when it came to greeting your dead husband's ex-in-laws when they were trying to take your children away from you. She stifled a giggle as she pictured how their faces would look if she ran over and tried to hug them. Her mom often said that the best form of attack was to kill someone with kindness, and she was sure she was right.

'You get more bees with honey than vinegar,' was one of Annie's favourite sayings.

Instead, though, she looked at Ronan for guidance,

feeling ill-equipped to deal with the situation. But he had his eyes locked on his phone. So Rachel decided she would have to be a big girl about this and make her own decisions. It wasn't like she could avoid the Butlers; in a few minutes, they would all be in the same room. She looked over at them again, this time with deliberation. Sheila's lips were pursed, a look she often had when she was in Rachel's company. Her eyes were fixated on a plant in the corner of the room that looked like it needed a good watering. To be fair to Adrian, he at least met Rachel's glance, giving a little shrug, as if to say he wasn't sure what to do either. She nodded back and, despite herself, gave him a half-smile, which he returned. That was as good as it could get for now.

At precisely eleven a.m., a man with greying hair stepped out of an office and approached them.

'Hello, I'm Andrew, Fergal William's assistant. I'm here to help this process go smoothly. Ask me any question that pops into your head. I've been here a long time and I've been asked absolutely everything before – nothing shocks me. Anyway, if you follow me, you can take a seat in the meeting room. Then I'll get Fergal. We don't stand on any ceremony here. So unless it jars, first names for us all, okay?'

'Told you, you didn't need heels,' Ronan whispered in Rachel's ear, placing his hand on the small of her back as he leaned in and nodding towards Andrew's jeans, open-necked shirt and white trainers. Rachel had never felt so relieved to see a pair of Adidas in her life. They followed him, one by one, down the corridor.

A large square table sat in the centre of the meeting room. Andrew waved towards the three vacant sides and told them that they could sit where they wished. 'I'll leave you to get settled. I'll be back shortly with Fergal.'

Rachel followed Ronan, who walked to the far side of the table. She was so glad she had him with her, taking charge of the situation. Sheila and Adrian followed Maria, the three of them sitting opposite them. And then silence fell over the room as they waited. Rachel thought about every TV courtroom drama she'd ever seen. She hoped Fergal favoured the kindly type rather than the cold officiator. The door opened and Rachel held her breath. This man was possibly the most critical person in her life right now.

'Hello everyone. Welcome. I'm Fergal.' His voice was deep and soothing.

He smiled at them all warmly and Rachel decided she liked him already. He didn't seem scary; in fact, he seemed quite approachable. She smiled back and went to join in the chorus of hellos, but her mouth was desert dry. Before she could stop herself, she was coughing loudly, her face flaming red as everyone turned to look at her.

'Please help yourself to water,' Fergal said, pouring himself a glass as he spoke.

There were an awkward few moments as they all passed the jug around, followed by a chorus of thank-yous. Funny how polite everyone became in situations like this, Rachel thought.

'I bet you are all a little nervous and unsure about what to expect today and further on in this process. So before we progress, I want to reassure you that my role here is to make sure that you feel heard. All of your feelings will be acknowledged by all parties. Today, I would like everyone to share their issues and concerns. At all times, we must listen respectfully and ensure that this space is one of dignity. Okay?'

Rachel felt like she was back in her principal's office again, about to receive a detention. They all nodded in assent.

'Once we've all stated our main concerns, then I'll put together the key issues that both parties need to address. Does that sound okay?'

They all nodded once more.

'And remember, I'm not here to force a solution or agreement on to any of you. The goal is to create a solution that's as close as possible to a win-win for each side. Yes, there will be a compromise needed for both parties, but if you come to this with an open mind and heart, we'll find a resolution without the need to go to court. Sound okay?'

'That sounds wonderful, Mr Williams,' Sheila said. 'Very well put.'

Rachel felt herself tense up. Trust Sheila to try to curry favour with the mediator. She'd be baking one of her apple pies for him next.

'Have you all signed the mediator agreement?' Fergal asked, unfazed.

Ronan and Maria both passed signed documents towards him. He gathered them up, picked up his reading glasses, then nodded in satisfaction. 'Everything is in order. So I suggest we begin. Maria, let's start with you. Can you outline exactly what Sheila and Adrian's requirements are?' He turned to Rachel and smiled, 'Don't worry, everyone will have a chance to speak.'

Maria spoke for the first time, her voice clear and cultured, exactly as Rachel imagined a lawyer would speak.

'Sheila and Adrian Butler are the grandparents of Olivia – eight years old – and Dylan – five years old, parents of their *birth* mother. Rachel Bradley is the children's stepmother. When my clients discovered Rachel's plans to take the children out of the country, they were distressed and outraged. Living close to the children, they have played an active role in their upbringing, but since the death of the children's father, the stepmother has pushed them away.'

'That's not true!' Rachel cried out involuntarily. She was so sick of hearing this same narrative over and over.

Fergal held his hand up, smiling warmly again at Rachel to take the sting out of his words. 'As I said earlier, we have to listen with respect. You will have your chance shortly, I promise you. Maria, please go on.'

'Sheila and Adrian are devoted grandparents; they have been a strong and continuous part of the children's life. In particular, when their daughter, the children's mother, Niamh Bradley, died, they stepped in and helped their son-in-law with both emotional and practical support in raising the children.'

'I'm sorry for your loss,' Fergal said, looking pointedly at Sheila and Adrian now. 'When did Niamh die?'

Maria looked at her notes, but before she could answer, Adrian spoke in a low, quiet voice, 'Almost five years ago – on the 10th December, at a little after three p.m. One moment she was standing in our kitchen, warming a bottle for Dylan. The next, she was on the ground.'

Sheila turned to look at Adrian and the room silenced as the impact of their pain reached them all. Rachel watched Sheila reach over to clasp her husband's hands as they both blinked back tears.

'Sorry,' Adrian continued, 'no matter how many times we have said that our daughter died or heard it said by someone else, it still hurts.'

'Please don't apologize. I can appreciate how painful this is. We can take a moment if you need,' Fergal said, but the Butlers both shook their heads, happy to go on.

'Very well. So Sheila and Adrian are looking for joint custody of the children?' Fergal asked.

Maria continued, 'The Butlers are reasonable people, and have come to today's mediation with an open mind. Yes, they could look for full custody of the children as is their right, conduit to the Guardianship of Infants Act 1964, and amended by the Children and Family Relationships Act 2015. But they are aware that the children and Rachel are close and therefore are applying for shared custody of the children. They have no choice but to do so, for a number of reasons. First and foremost of which is their belief that Rachel is a flight risk. They also require increased visitation rights – two nights during the week, alternate weekends and shared holidays.'

Fergal did not comment as Maria continued to speak; he just took notes, nodding now and then.

Rachel eyeballed her adversaries again. Hearing their demands like this infuriated her. She noted that Sheila was still unable to look her in the eye. Once Maria had finished speaking, Fergal turned to Ronan and asked him to outline Rachel's issues.

'First of all, an important clarification, if I may. And that is to make it clear that Rachel is the children's mother, not their stepmother, as Maria stated. I have copies of the adoption papers here for your records,' Ronan held up a copy of the adoption papers and, not for the first time and, she was sure, certainly not for the last, Rachel felt a quiet victory at having Ronan here to fight her corner. 'Secondly,' Ronan continued, 'Rachel has no plans to emigrate, and has made this clear to the Butlers on several occasions. However, if she decides that it's in the best interests of her family to relocate in the future, it is of course her right to do so. Thirdly, Rachel has never denied the Butlers visitation rights, recognizing their importance in the lives of the children. An informal arrangement has worked over the years, with the children visiting their grandparents after school every Wednesday. Weekend sleepovers are also a common occurrence, arranged informally between the Butlers and Rachel, with no issue up until now. Rachel commits to continuing to foster and encourage the children's relationship with their birth mother's family and the Bradleys, their father's family. She will not, however, agree to increased visitation.'

Fergal continued to take notes, then asked, 'May I see a copy of the adoption papers?'

Ronan passed a copy to Maria and Fergal.

'This has been a great start,' Fergal said when he had taken a long look at the papers. 'And listening to both Maria and Ronan, I think the first thing we need to do is address the issue of Rachel relocating to New Zealand. It appears that there are conflicting stories on this, so I'd like to start there. Rachel, let's start with you.'

Rachel took a deep breath and explained how her vacation to New Zealand led her sister to take her to the villa on Bluff Hill.

Sheila looked triumphant. 'You see, she even admits it,' she interrupted. 'Brazenly, I might add. You can't lie straight on the bed, the number of lies you tell, girl.'

Fergal held his hand up, 'Let's keep this cordial at all times, please.'

He turned to face Rachel, 'So from what you've shared, you have sometimes considered the benefits of moving home, to be closer to your family. And seeing this villa on Bluff Hill for sale prompted you to look at the option seriously?'

Rachel nodded. 'Yes,' she said, 'but although I looked into it, I never made any actions towards actually moving. I knew that I didn't want to in reality.'

She looked across the table at Sheila and Adrian, who were both obviously angry. Adrian had clenched his fists, and Sheila's face was an open book, so there was no hiding the fury she was directing towards Rachel. The atmosphere in the room swelled with their anger and Rachel felt her palms sweat in response.

She felt exposed, talking about her home life, her hopes and dreams. Over the course of thirty minutes or so, Rachel shared more with the Butlers than she had in the entire time she'd known them. But Ronan had stressed before they began the process that Rachel must be honest. Show everyone that she had nothing to hide.

She took a sip of the iced water, then placed the glass down on the table. Her hands were shaking too much to hold it safely. She looked to the empty seat on her right-hand side. For a moment, Lorcan appeared there and smiled at her. He might be gone, but she felt strength from his imagined smile and took a steadying breath, ready to continue her story.

'And have you lied about relocating to New Zealand?' Fergal asked now.

'No, I haven't lied. Dreams and reality are two different

things,' Rachel said firmly. 'I wasn't doing anything wrong by considering the best options for my family.'

Sheila sighed, as loudly as she possibly could, to make sure that everyone was in no doubt on where she stood with Rachel's statement.

'Why do you find it so difficult to believe me?' Rachel asked, breaking the formality to direct her question to Sheila.

'Because you made a mistake here, didn't you? You counted on the children to be able to keep your secret. But because they are so close to me, to us, the poor poppets needed to unburden themselves. I knew from the moment you arrived back from New Zealand something was going on. You were acting strange from the moment you walked in the front door. And of course, once you hosted that party, I realized I was right to be suspicious.'

'I was tired from the flight! And to be perfectly frank, Sheila, it can be difficult to deal with you. I need to be in tip-top form for that, and with jet lag, that wasn't the case,' Rachel replied.

Fergal held his hand up again, in a manner that Rachel suspected he had done hundreds of times before. 'I'd like to hear a little more about what happened when you returned home from New Zealand, Rachel. Let's see if we can get to the bottom of this.'

THIRTY-EIGHT

Sheila

Mount Street, Dublin

Sheila watched Fergal's face as Rachel told him about the things she had said at the adoption party. He glanced back at his sidekick, Andrew, and they shared a brief look of surprise.

Worried she was losing Fergal's support, Sheila jumped in. 'I will never forgive myself for upsetting the children that day,' she explained. 'But you have to understand that Rachel blindsided us with the adoption. Add that to the children telling me about Rachel's plans to move to New Zealand . . . well, it pushed me to my limits.'

'Sheila cried for hours after that row,' Adrian said, backing his wife up.

'As did the children and I,' Rachel countered.

Sheila bit her tongue. Why did Rachel feel the need to say that? She'd already told everyone about her tears, playing the sympathy card. But she wasn't the only one with feelings. Sheila took a peek at Fergal to gauge his reaction. She noted with satisfaction that he was once again nodding sympathetically in her own direction. A good sign, she hoped.

Maria had been clear from the start that they were unlikely to gain shared custody of the children unless they had some information about Rachel that showed she was an unfit mother, so Sheila had told Maria about the clothes and general chaos that their house always seemed to be in. A meaner person might have made a snide comment about the cobwebs that she'd found in every single corner of the house the last time she'd been there. But she wasn't a nitpicker, nor did she get any joy in pointing out anyone's faults. Still, she would sleep better at night now if she knew that there wasn't a nest of spiders about to fall into any of her grandchildren's mouths while they slept.

Maria hadn't seemed interested in Rachel's house-keeping skills, though. She'd insisted that they needed more substantial evidence of neglect than a messy house.

Swept away in her thoughts, she hadn't noticed Adrian nudging her, 'Sheila,' he was saying now.

She turned her attention back to Fergal and begged his pardon. He smiled and waved aside her apologies.

But he looked severe again as he asked Sheila to clarify, 'So the only information you have regarding a possible relocation to New Zealand is from that conversation at your daughter's graveside?'

Sheila shifted on her chair. She wasn't sure she cared for his tone. He didn't sound as sympathetic as she'd imagined he looked a few seconds ago.

'Well, yes,' she had no choice but to admit.

'And what is it that I've always said?' Fergal turned to ask Andrew, like a perfect double act.

'Just because you heard it, doesn't mean you know it,' Andrew replied loyally.

'That's it. It's one of my grandmother's sayings, that one, and it's never served me wrong. Rachel, can you clear up this misunderstanding?'

'With pleasure,' she answered, sickly sweet. She looked over at Sheila and Adrian and said, 'Do you think I'd ever make a decision as big as that without talking to you both first? Do you think that little of me?'

Sheila faltered a little. What if she *had* gotten it wrong about the move? But then she heard Dylan's voice in her head, talking excitedly about sharks and beaches and sunshine.

Adrian leaned across the table and said, 'We're very fond of you, Rachel. But we're scared too. We can't lose the children.'

Rachel paused for a second, then continued, 'I've already explained I showed the children the villa – from the outside, I might add – and how we had a "what if" daydreaming conversation. The kids were charmed by the idea of a swimming pool, which I think most children would be. I apologize that the children thought that daydream was a real possibility. I've spoken to them since. They know we have no plans to buy that villa.'

'Can we all agree that the children got the wrong end of the stick? I think that will be quite an achievement if we can move on from this,' Fergal asked the Butlers.

The Butlers answered at the same time.

'Yes,' Adrian said quietly.

'No!' Sheila cut across him. She leaned forward. 'If you have no plans to move, prove it and give us joint custody. That way, we are all reassured of your good intentions.'

'That's just ridiculous,' Rachel responded. 'I can never agree to such a thing. And it's unfair of you to suggest that I should.'

Ronan raised his hand, 'You want to terminate Rachel's right to live where she chooses with her own children? Out of interest, if you have joint custody, will you insist that she never leaves Dublin? Perhaps you'd like her to sign away her right to sell her house on Yellow Walls Road too?'

'There's no need to be flippant. You know that this relates to relocating to the other side of the world only,' Maria said coolly in response.

Sheila nodded in delight. She knew she'd chosen well with this one.

'I'm not sure it does,' Ronan countered. 'Rachel might wish to relocate to another county for work commitments. Or to move closer to the children's paternal grandparents in Belfast, for example. I'd be interested to know if Mr and Mrs Butler intend to take Rachel to court in any of those eventualities in the future?'

Sheila felt her heart plummet. She'd witnessed the Bradleys get closer to the children over the last couple of months and it had made her uneasy. But she had been so focused on her worries about New Zealand, it had never crossed her mind that there might be plans afoot to move to Belfast too. She had heard all about the fancy bedroom they'd redecorated for the children when they visited.

Then Ronan sighed, louder than necessary, Sheila noted. He was always with the theatrics, that man. She gave

Maria a pointed look. They were paying her enough; Sheila expected her to interject a bit more.

When Maria remained silent, Sheila took matters into her own hands. 'I object!' she said, feeling her face flush with frustration.

'To what?' Fergal asked.

'Mrs Butler is extremely distressed,' Maria jumped in. 'And Ronan, throwing around comments about relocating to Belfast is not helpful.'

Ronan made a face, 'Look, there's no doubt that this is distressing for *everyone*. But I think it's worth noting here the reason Rachel decided not to pursue relocating to her hometown.'

Sheila couldn't wait to hear whatever bull the girl was going to spout now.

Rachel looked at Fergal, avoiding eye contact with Sheila and Adrian. 'I know how close the children are to their Nana Sheila and Grandad Aidan – not to mention their Uncle Jack. I decided that I didn't want to take the children away from them. They've all lost so much already. And that's why I decided to stay . . .' her voice trailed off at the end.

Sheila felt her stomach flip at the girl's words. A shadow of doubt made its way into her mind. She heard Adrian emit a groan beside her, as if in pain.

Ronan took the reins. 'Look, we know the reason the Butlers have applied for joint custody is to ensure Rachel cannot relocate to New Zealand without their permission. We've shown, clearly, that their fears are unwarranted. Can we strike the joint custody application and work on the increased visitation issue?'

Maria leaned in for a whispered exchange with Sheila

and Adrian. 'Rachel seems genuine here. It doesn't look like she's moving to New Zealand. Let's move on from this and concentrate on increased visitation.'

Sheila felt Adrian's eyes boring into her. 'Please, Sheila,' he whispered. 'Let's go home and get back to living our lives, enjoy those kiddies while we can.'

She turned to look at her husband as he pleaded with her to give up. And for a moment Sheila almost said yes, because she was worn out from it all. She'd not slept a full night in months, tossing and turning as she worried about the children.

'Please,' Adrian tried one more time.

But then Sheila thought of Niamh, smiling as she cradled Olivia and Dylan on her lap, and she knew she had to keep fighting. For her daughter. She shook her head, looking directly at Maria.

Maria paused before turning back to Fergal. 'My clients remain firm that they want shared custody,' she confirmed.

The sound of a chair scraping back made Sheila jump. She looked across the table and watched Rachel stand up.

'I can't believe I ever put your feelings first, because you sure as hell never did the same for me.' Rachel's face was red now, her voice louder than usual.

Sheila crossed her arms. *Now we're seeing her true colours.*

Rachel continued, 'Or indeed those of the children. This should be about the children's welfare, first and foremost, and Sheila, your behaviour over the past few months has certainly not done that!'

'How dare you!' Sheila cried, outraged by the girl's accusations. 'I love those children; they are always my first and foremost concern.'

'Well, that wasn't the case at the adoption party, was it?' Rachel said, almost at screaming point.

'And we're right back to *that* again,' Sheila shouted back.

Fergal stood up, 'Everyone needs to calm down,' he said firmly, speaking over both women. 'Let's take a ten-minute break.'

Sheila and Adrian followed Maria outside the meeting room. They huddled together in a corner of the hallway.

Maria looked at Sheila and shook her head. 'You need to hold on to your temper. Let Rachel do all the shouting; you have to remain steady and calm.'

'The girl keeps playing the victim card,' Sheila said moodily.

'She seems genuine,' Adrian said in a small voice, moving a step away from Sheila.

She stared at him in shock. 'You would take her side, wouldn't you?'

He always took Rachel's side. It irritated Sheila no end. But that was his nature, he had always been a people pleaser. She loved him, but he could certainly be taken in by the wrong people sometimes.

'If we are going to win shared custody, you have to give me something else to work with,' Maria said sternly. 'Is there anything else questionable? Does she drink?'

'No more than any of us,' Adrian said.

And then Sheila remembered a conversation she'd had with Jack a few months ago. He'd been cross, telling Sheila that her actions had driven Rachel to drink so much that she'd passed out. She looked at Adrian, then back to Maria. Was this something they could use?

Ten minutes later, they were back in the meeting room. Rachel looked like she'd been crying, Sheila noted.

Adrian called over to her, 'Are you okay?'

Sheila threw her eyes up to the ceiling. But then the girl nodded tearfully. And for a moment, Sheila looked at her and saw a scared young woman. She felt a flash of guilt thinking back to the conversation she'd just had with Maria. *What had she done?*

'I can see how upsetting this incident has been for all concerned,' Fergal said, starting proceedings again. 'And I think it is a perfect example of how important honest communication is to create a nurturing and calm atmosphere for families.'

'I am always honest. I pride myself on that point. It's why we are here, I suppose,' Sheila said.

'That's good to hear, Sheila. But perhaps if you'd spoken to Rachel about the children's revelation about New Zealand quietly, you could have avoided the whole misunderstanding,' Fergal said.

'And the children's special day would not have been spoiled,' Rachel added.

'We do regret that bitterly,' Adrian said. 'We are genuinely sorry that the children were upset. I would rather cut my right arm off than cause those two kiddies any pain.'

Sheila couldn't disagree with that.

'I believe that you are genuinely sorry for upsetting the children. However, you've never once apologized to me or shown any remorse for how your actions made *me* feel,' Rachel said.

'I beg your pardon. I most certainly did!' Sheila replied incredulously.

'No, you didn't. You apologized to the kids, not to me.

You ruined what should have been an incredible day for our *family*. And one that was of the utmost importance to me.'

Sheila and Rachel locked eyes again. Sheila wanted to say sorry, she really did. Because she really was heartsick by her actions that day. But she couldn't back down. Any sign of weakness now might lose them the children. She had to keep that at the forefront of her mind.

Fergal wasn't going to let her off the hook, though. 'Can you acknowledge how upsetting this has been for Rachel?' he asked.

'It's upsetting for our entire family,' she replied. 'We are all walking around with scars. But may I ask Rachel one more question. Why didn't you tell Ronan to cancel the adoption proceedings after Lorcan died? You keep saying that you never felt any need to make things official, that it was all Lorcan's idea. Well, with him dead, why not cancel?'

Rachel blinked quickly.

'Do you need a moment, Rachel?' Fergal asked gently.

Ronan answered, 'I think that might be a good idea.'

'I'm okay, thank you,' Rachel jumped in, batting away the two men. 'I've had years of people questioning me; years of having the term stepmom thrown at me like it's a bad smell. I wore that badge proudly as it happens, always believing that love conquered all. I still believe that.'

She picked up the adoption papers from the folder in front of Ronan and held them in front of her.

'Now, though, I am glad that Lorcan pushed for this. Because I can see the importance of the paperwork I hold. I am the children's mother, in the eyes of the law. I get to decide who has visitation rights to my children. Not you, Sheila. *Me.* I am solely responsible for my children's wellbeing, and to be honest, I have concerns. Grave concerns about how confusing your behaviour is for Olivia and Dylan.'

'What are you saying?' Sheila said, her voice faltering for the first time.

'I'm saying, Sheila, that maybe you are right. Maybe we *do* need to go to court and see what a judge has to say about your rights as grandparents. This word "official" that you keep quoting is an interesting one. Are you "officially" grandparents now? Because I'm not sure that you are any more.'

Rachel held her head up high as she threw that grenade at Sheila.

Sheila looked at Adrian, his face a mirror to her confusion. Rachel had articulated their fear in one statement. Here, laid bare for everyone to see, was the real reason she was so upset about the adoption.

Because if Rachel was the children's mother, *where did that leave them*?

Sheila was left with no choice. It was time she threw a grenade back.

'Well, I am told that people who are reliant on alcohol often behave irrationally. Your eyes are red, dear. Have you been drinking again? Maybe you had a little nip of gin while we took a few minutes' break?'

'What are you going on about?' Rachel asked, alarm in her voice.

Sheila felt Adrian's eyes on her. But she was crystal clear on what to say and do next. 'I would like it noted that I am concerned about the welfare of the children. Rachel likes to drink. And has recently been so intoxicated that she passed out.'

Rachel gasped.

'Sheila,' Adrian said, his voice filled with disappointment, with dislike, even. He pushed back his chair and put a hand on Sheila's arm. 'That's enough.'

But Sheila had gone too far along this road now; there was no turning back.

'Sheila and Adrian have raised with me that they have grave concerns about Rachel Bradley's substance abuse. Binge drinking,' Maria confirmed.

'This is a joke, right?' Rachel asked, turning to Ronan, panic written all over her face. 'I don't binge drink.'

Ronan put his hand up, jumping in to back her up. 'This is preposterous,' he said. 'There is no evidence to back that allegation. Rachel is not dependent on alcohol, as well you know.'

'Many people are functioning addicts, with no external signs on display,' Maria pointed out.

'And many people are willing to completely lie to gain the upper hand in a custody matter,' Ronan spat.

Sheila felt dizzy. She had backed herself into a corner and her only choice now was to fight back.

'That's a serious claim, Sheila,' it was Fergal's turn now to speak. He looked at her gravely. 'Have you been witness to this binge drinking yourself?'

'My son Jack told me this himself. He's good friends with Rachel; I'm sure she'd agree. He watched Rachel drink several bottles of wine while the children slept upstairs. He had to lock up the house for her.'

Technically this was true, Sheila told herself. So why then did she feel so ashamed?

'How could you?' Rachel whispered across the table.

But really, what choice did Sheila have?

THIRTY-NINE

Rachel

Malahide, Dublin

They'd finished their first mediation session having achieved nothing. From Rachel's position, they were worse off than they'd been when they started. In addition to the custody issue, she had to prove she wasn't a raving alcoholic too.

When Fergal had suggested they end their session and regroup the following month, she was relieved. She'd taken several blows from the Butlers and didn't feel strong enough to take any more.

Fergal had sent them home, with a parting reminder.

'I'm mindful that all parties are grieving and that impacts these proceedings too. I want to continue joint sessions, but we can do individual sessions if things become too emotive. But there is something important that we can all agree on: all of you love the children. We have to remind ourselves that the children's rights must always be at the forefront of our minds. We don't want them to be lost in the competition for parental or grandparental rights.'

Ronan had said they were fighting dirty because they knew they didn't have a legitimate leg to stand on and that if they continued in this manner, they would have to stop mediation and go to court. He was confident that a judge would not entertain the Butlers' application for joint custody. But he wasn't as convinced that they couldn't get further visitation rights.

Her phone buzzed with a text message from Jack.

It's not how it seemed. Mam twisted my words. You have to let me call over to talk about this.

He'd sent her several messages since yesterday's mediation, but she'd ignored them all. As Rachel drove towards Sheila and Adrian's house now to collect the kids, she pondered if she could ever forgive him for his betrayal. Ronan had warned her about him, but she'd naively believed he was on her side.

Rachel hated driving in the dark, and on this dreary October evening, as she made her way towards Sheila and Adrian's to collect the kids from their Wednesday visit, it was drizzling too. She switched the radio off to maximize her concentration. This morning when she'd dropped them off at school, Olivia had once again been quiet and sullen, as she seemed to be all the time these days. It felt like not only were there ominous clouds in the night sky overhead; they were over their house in particular. In addition to Olivia being out of sorts, Dylan had wet the bed the night before. Despite Rachel trying her best to make it less of a big deal than he felt it was, he was mortified by it. When she spoke to her mom about it, Annie reassured her that it was probably just a reaction to starting school and would pass. She should try not to worry. But that was easier said than done.

Over the past few months, Rachel had done everything she could to make sure the kids weren't aware of the issues between her and the Butlers. But they were smart kids and had worked out that something was going on. She hoped Sheila and Adrian were clever enough to keep the kids out of it too, but as her dad often said: to assume was to make an ass out of you and me.

She arrived at the Butlers a little early and decided to wait in the car for ten minutes, as the thought of making small talk with Sheila didn't fill her with any joy. She parked a few doors up so that they wouldn't see her sitting there.

As she idly watched the street, Rachel noticed someone coming out of a house a couple of doors up from the Butlers. To her surprise, she realized that the slight figure, now running towards the Butlers' house on the other side of the road, was Olivia. Where the hell had she been? And who with? Olivia didn't notice Rachel's car in the darkness and continued running to her grandparents'. Sheila let her in as soon as she reached it, quickly looking towards Rachel's house in the other direction when she opened the door. Rachel turned the car around and moved so she was parked outside Sheila's house.

When she knocked, it was Adrian who opened the door, looking a little sheepish.

'Come on in, out of the rain.'

'I'm not stopping. I'll wait here,' Rachel replied tersely.

'They were good as gold, the best kids. Dylan is upstairs doing a jigsaw and Olivia is in the kitchen, but they're coming now.'

Olivia appeared first of all. 'Hey, Mom.'

'Hello, sweetheart,' Rachel replied, searching her daughter's face for any clues. 'Did you have a good day in school? Do anything fun this afternoon?' She was waiting to hear about where she had been.

'Not really,' Olivia said, too quickly, her face colouring.

And that's when Rachel spotted Olivia and Sheila share a look. It was only for the briefest moment, but it was definitely the look of one conspirator to another.

They were hiding something.

'I saw you leave someone's house down the road a few moments ago, Olivia,' Rachel said. She was addressing her daughter, but it was Sheila who answered.

'Oh, that. She has some new friends across the road she made during the summer holidays,' she said, as if it were no big deal.

'Who are they?' Rachel asked.

'The Middleton girls. Nice family,' Sheila answered.

'I don't know the name. Are they in your class, Olivia?' Rachel could hear the edge in her voice and cursed herself that she wasn't better at hiding how she felt.

'They, erm, don't go to my school,' Olivia replied, refusing to look at her mother.

Rachel could sense that she was missing something here, she just wasn't sure what. 'What school do they go to then, and how do you know them?'

'All these questions,' Sheila tutted. 'I don't see what the big deal is. Isn't it nice for Olivia to have friends on her street?'

Rachel ignored Sheila and kept her eyes focused on Olivia.

'Nana is right. It's no big deal, Mom.'

'I'm sure it's not. But I still need to know where you've been. You're eight years old, Olivia, and I'm afraid you've got many years ahead of you yet of listening to me demanding to know where you are. As far as I was concerned, you were here, with your grandparents, not in someone else's house.'

'I knew exactly where she was, though,' Sheila said. 'Honestly, you'd swear she was wandering around Dublin City on her own, not just a few doors away.'

'I won't apologize for wanting to know where my children are at all times, Sheila,' Rachel said firmly.

She realized that she wasn't going to get very far with this discussion with Sheila and Adrian listening in.

'Olivia, we'll talk about this at home. Go upstairs and hurry your brother along. Make sure you've gathered all your things up.'

As Olivia ran upstairs, Sheila decided the conversation wasn't over. 'Olivia needs friends. The girl is lonely. And she likes Anita and Carolyn. It did my heart good to see how happy she was when they got together today.'

'How old are these girls?' Rachel asked.

'I'm not sure,' Sheila answered honestly. 'Maybe twelve or thirteen. Fourteen at the very most.'

'Sheila! Olivia is eight years old. That's a big age gap. And what do teens want to be hanging around an eight-year-old for? How did she meet this Anita and Carolyn?'

Sheila didn't respond and threw another of her conspiratorial looks, this time in Adrian's direction, who, as per usual, was standing back and saying little.

Rachel decided to ask him directly, 'Adrian, how did Olivia meet the girls?'

He blushed, then said, 'I think she made friends with them on her phone.'

Suddenly every parental alarm was going off inside Rachel's head. 'Olivia doesn't have a phone,' she said, somehow already knowing what Sheila's response to this would be.

'It's an old phone of mine. I got an upgrade. It was going in the bin, so when she asked me for it, how could I refuse?' Sheila said.

'Olivia is not allowed a phone until she is twelve. She knows that. It's been discussed many times at home.' Rachel's voice could cut glass.

'Really?' Sheila's had now gone up several octaves.

'I told you to discuss this with Rachel to make sure it was okay with her,' Adrian said, turning to his wife.

'It's only used for games and stuff. There's no phone number attached to it. What harm can it be?' Sheila said.

'Does it have internet access?' Rachel asked.

'Only when she has wi-fi,' Sheila replied.

Give me strength! Rachel shook her head in disbelief at the woman. Was Sheila deliberately trying to wind her up? Olivia and Dylan ran down the stairs, bags and coats in their hands, Thor bounding behind them. Rachel turned to them, trying to bring a sense of lightness back to her tone. 'Say goodbye to your grandparents and Thor.'

Once the hugs and kisses were done, Rachel sent them out to the car. But before she left, she turned to Sheila, 'None of this is okay. Once I understand everything that's been going on, I'll be in touch.'

'Nothing is going on. Such unnecessary drama,' Sheila said.

'Sheila . . .' Adrian said, his voice full of reproach.

'Did you talk to Olivia about cyberbullying, cyber predators, phishing, scams, malware, *anything*?'

The startled look on Sheila's face was answer enough here. Rachel turned on her heel and marched out to her car, where the kids were waiting.

As the kids got ready for bed, Olivia kept watching Rachel, waiting for the inevitable axe to fall. She knew she'd been caught out, that she'd hidden something from Rachel. Rachel, on the other hand, needed time to process and calm down before she tackled Olivia. Sheila continuously undermined her parental authority and expected Rachel to let her get away with it. But it was one thing giving the kids extra chocolate when she'd said they'd had enough and another altogether giving a child a phone!

Once Dylan was settled in bed, she went into Olivia's room and sat down on the little girl's bed. Olivia's face was pale; her brown eyes looked like dark pools, glistening with unshed tears.

'Give me the phone.'

Olivia reached under her pillow and handed it to Rachel without a word.

'How long have you had it?'

'Since the end of the summer holidays.'

'What's the password?'

'Daddy's birthday,' Olivia said, and this time her bottom lip wobbled, cartoon-like, followed quickly by tears. 'I'm sorry, Mom,' she sobbed.

Rachel felt paralysed with indecision. Where was the

parent's handbook for moments like this? When you felt torn between hugging your child and screaming at them? She pulled a tissue from her pocket and wiped the tears from Olivia's face.

'The thing I'm most disappointed about is that you kept this from me, Olivia.'

'I wanted to tell you, but I was afraid you'd be cross.'

'If you are honest with me, Olivia, there's always a much stronger chance that I won't be cross with you. I don't like dishonesty; you know that. What do I always say?'

'That we must never have any secrets.'

'That's right. Now help me piece this all together.'

'When Nana got a new phone, I said to her that I wished I had one. So she said I could have her old one.'

'And did you tell her that you were not allowed a phone?'

Olivia nodded.

Bloody Sheila.

'Tell me about your new friends. How did you meet?'

'I follow them on TikTok. They make videos of themselves in OOTD.'

Rachel was surprised that Olivia knew the phrase – OOTD, Outfit Of The Day.

'I recognized our road, so I commented on their video. And then we chatted a little. I told them that you own Rae's Closet. They watch your Facebook Lives. They are so nice. And I've been to their house a few times.' At this admission, Olivia began to sob, her little body shaking.

Rachel pulled her daughter in towards her and held her until her tears subsided. 'There's no more phone, Olivia. Okay?'

Olivia nodded.

'And no more going to their house either. I can't protect you if I don't know where you are. Promise me. I need to hear you say you promise.'

'I promise, Mom.'

'Okay. Go to sleep. We can talk about this more tomorrow.'

Rachel sat downstairs and tried to work out her next step. Should she call Sheila and have it out with her on the phone? Should she go to see her tomorrow and work it out face to face? Or maybe she should wait until their next mediation session and do it the proper way. She contemplated calling Claudia but, as ever, the blasted time difference stopped her.

'Damn you, Lorcan!' she cried out to the kitchen cabinets. 'Why the hell did you have to die, leaving me to deal with all of this on my own?'

And then the doorbell went.

Rachel's first thought was that it was Sheila. Fired up, she felt ready to shout at the woman, so was almost disappointed when she opened the front door to find Ronan there.

'What are you doing here?' she asked, a little snappier than intended.

'I was in the area,' Ronan said apologetically. 'I can go if it's a bad time?'

She ushered him in. 'I'm just not in a very good mood, so be warned.'

'I figured that much from your sunny disposition when you opened the door. I've got chocolate biscuits if you fancy a cuppa? That's if you're not already lorrying into the vino.' He waved a box of Hobnobs at her and grinned. 'Too soon?'

'Watch out, Ronan, I'll shove those biscuits where the sun doesn't shine if you're not careful. Come in, sit down, I'll make us both some tea.'

As Rachel filled the kettle, she told Ronan about Olivia's phone and her new friends, the words spilling out in a torrent of emotion.

'Do you know these young wans up the road?' Ronan asked.

'Never clapped eyes on them before, or at least I don't think I have. They live at the other end of the Yellow Walls. I wouldn't have even known about Olivia being there had I not been early. Or if I'd walked up from home as I sometimes do. It was raining; that's why I drove up.'

'They are probably grand, and you are worrying about nothing.'

'The problem I have is all the secrecy, Ronan. I hate lies.'

'I know. But this isn't all terrible. I mean, if you think about it, the timing is great for you. How can Sheila be all sanctimonious when she's pulling stunts like this?'

'That thought had crossed my mind,' Rachel confessed. 'But for now, I'm too livid and not thinking about mediation. She encouraged my daughter to *lie* to me. How could she do that?'

Ronan sighed. 'Sheila has always been a puzzle to me. You better have a good look through that phone to make sure Olivia's not gotten herself into any trouble.'

'I'll swing for Sheila if she has.'

'Not before you win this mediation case. Might not look so good if we end up in court.' He ducked as Rachel swiped at him. 'When we go in next month,' he continued, all professional this time, 'we go in hard, and knock this drinking issue on the head.'

'How?'

'We'll demand evidence to back up Sheila's claims. I assume there isn't any?' He cocked an eyebrow, looking at Rachel in amusement.

'Of course not!'

'You have no DUI arrests, right? Good. And you've never had treatment for alcoholism or medical treatment for the same. We can get witness testimonies. Hell, I was there when you "passed out", I'll vouch for you. The Butlers are clearly willing to play dirty, but they won't beat us.'

Listening to Ronan speak, Rachel realized she no longer felt scared. She was angry; a fire was burning inside her. If she had to fight, then that's what she was going to do. And she was a woman prepared to do anything to protect her family.

FORTY

Rachel

Malahide, Dublin

Rachel put down the phone to Claudia feeling immeasurably stronger. Her sister had shared the best news: Claudia, Howard and her parents were all coming to Ireland for Christmas. Claudia said that they had originally planned to surprise her nearer to Christmas, but they didn't want to keep it from her with the mediation stress. For Rachel, just knowing they were going to be here within a few weeks made such a difference to her wellbeing. Hearing the strength in Claudia's voice also bolstered her. Claudia had come a long way in the months since her ectopic pregnancy and physically, at least, she was fully recovered.

Before Claudia hung up, she gave Rachel a piece of advice.

'You are playing into Sheila's hands by ignoring Jack.

It would be best if you had him on team Rachel. He's always been such a big supporter of yours; I'm not convinced that's changed. But if it has, you need to find out why. Call him.'

An hour later, Rachel drove down to the village and parked up on the marina. It was a bright, sunny winter's morning and perfect for a walk. Jack was waiting for her, two takeaway coffees in hand. They walked in silence for a few minutes along the Velvet Strand, watching the water ebb and flow. As the wind whipped her hair from her face, it felt as if some of Rachel's worries dashed off into the air too. She regretted that it had been weeks since she'd been down here. Between work and the kids, plus the stress of mediation, she'd forgotten to enjoy the beauty of a beach walk. They passed other walkers, some with dogs, and they all smiled their hellos to each other. Ireland of a thousand welcomes, Rachel thought. People were friendly here; she had to concede that. Another thing she'd forgotten recently.

Jack pointed to a bench a few feet away and they made their way over to it. They sat down and turned to face each other.

'I'm so sorry,' Jack said, not even bothering with any preamble.

Rachel searched his face and decided that he genuinely meant it. He looked stricken, in fact, close to tears.

'You threw me under the bus,' she said.

'I know. But not on purpose. I was trying to get her to stop her custody application. I told Mam and Dad how upset you were, so much so, you had drunk more than usual, that I'd never seen you so distraught. But I never even thought there was a possibility that she could use that against you. I swear!'

Rachel looked at Jack and decided to trust her instinct. 'I believe you,' she replied, still not back to her full warmth.

'You do? I've been so worried. I would honestly never intentionally hurt you.'

'I know.'

'And Mam knows that I'll never forgive her unless she amends her statement about the drinking. She's going to take that back at the mediation session next week.'

Rachel was shocked, but somewhat mollified by this news.

'You know the craziest thing about this? I think you and Mam could actually be friends. If she could get by her . . .' Jack searched for a word.

Rachel could think of a few, so decided to help him out. 'Stubbornness? Pettiness? Resentment? Contempt? Take your pick! Look, I know that I'll never be as good as Saint Niamh . . .'

'Niamh wasn't so perfect,' Jack interrupted.

Rachel looked at him in surprise, eyebrows raised.

'She had a secret cleaner,' Jack confessed.

Rachel nearly choked on her coffee. She was sure she must have misheard. 'Explain.'

'A woman who called in every Thursday morning to clean the house.'

Rachel started to laugh. Good for Niamh. 'And do you have that cleaner's number? Maybe I should take a leaf out of your sister's book and do the same.'

'Ha! Maybe you should. You work full-time, I just don't know how you do everything on your own.'

'I meet myself coming backwards most days. But why did Niamh have to keep that secret? Having a cleaner isn't that much of a big deal, is it?'

'Mam. You know what she's like. She holds people up to a high standard, and Niamh didn't want her to know that she wasn't the perfect housewife. Niamh used to buy ready-made dinners from the supermarket too. She'd hide the containers, reheat them in her dishes, then serve them up, pretending she'd whipped them up herself.'

Rachel's jaw nearly dropped theatrically. 'Why am I only hearing about this now?' she cried. 'And the stick your mother gave me at the adoption party about shop-bought cakes! Did Lorcan know about all of this?'

'Not about the food, that's for sure. She kept that quiet from everyone but me.'

'You were the keeper of her secrets,' Rachel said, laughing, then stopped when she saw a shadow pass over Jack's face. She had that same feeling again that she was missing an essential part of the Niamh story.

'Mam lashes out when she feels threatened. She didn't have a great childhood. My grandparents had a rocky marriage, so Mam lived in a war zone most of the time. I think that's why she works so hard to create the perfect family. She cannot bear to think that she'll lose it. She's also worried about how close you are getting to the Bradleys. You pointing out that she's no longer Olivia and Dylan's grandmother hurt. I know she's said bad things too, I'm not excusing them, but that was a low blow, Rachel. She's hurting too, remember.'

'I never knew that about her childhood,' Rachel admitted. 'That's rough. But your mam is a control freak, Jack, that's her problem. She has to stop dictating everything I do. Wait until she hears that I plan to invite Belinda and Oscar to Dublin for Christmas. My parents,

Claudia and Howard, are coming over from New Zealand too. I can picture her face when she hears that!'

'I know it must be frustrating for you, when Mam gets a notion. She can be controlling. But never mind that, I'm delighted to hear about your family. That's great news.'

Rachel took a satisfying sip of her coffee as she looked out over the horizon. She felt giddy, knowing that soon she would be able to share this beautiful view with her family.

Suddenly she turned to Jack. 'I'm so tired of talking about all of this custody stuff, Jack,' she exclaimed. 'Come on, take my mind off it all.'

Jack paused, then grinned. 'Well, here's a question for you. Will you still come to the annual Christmas fundraiser for the Irish Deaf Society? Please say yes.'

'Oh, I'd forgotten all about that! When is it on?' Rachel had been twice with Lorcan, but knew that it was family tradition to always support this event. Maybe this would be a way to close whatever gap had opened up between Jack and herself since all the chaos with his mother.

'The twenty-third. I can book tickets for your New Zealand crew too? Could be a fun night for everyone. Nice food, a few drinks, dancing . . .'

Rachel's heart sank as she pondered the reality of their blended family getting together again, the adoption afternoon tea in the front of her mind. 'It could also be a disaster, Jack, if things remain the same as they are now. Murder on the dance floor . . .' She shook her head.

'I'll tell my parents they have to behave?' Jack offered.

'It's not just that. After just one session in mediation we were all at loggerheads. I can't even begin to imagine where we might be by December. At that stage, we'll have done three. Or given up and be facing court,' she added gloomily.

'You could also have reached an agreement,' Jack remarked, ever one to find the positives, 'and be grateful for an excuse to celebrate that. Put all the horrible moments behind you.'

'I'm not sure I share your optimism,' Rachel responded grimly.

'Please at least think about it?' he suggested. 'This fundraiser is important for me. I've never missed hosting a table, it's my way of giving back. The Irish Deaf Society have helped me so much since I was a little kid, and I want you to be there. Bring the Bradleys too.'

Rachel knew he was desperate if he was suggesting that.

'I'll give it some thought, I promise,' she said. 'How about in the meantime, you tell me about this mystery girl you like, then I might agree! Or have you decided to give the gorgeous Lydia a chance?' Rachel laughed in delight when she spied Jack blushing. 'Spill the beans, Jack Butler!'

'Lydia is just a friend,' Jack said cautiously. 'I like her, but I don't want to date her.'

'Does Lydia know that, I wonder?'

He shrugged.

'So if you're not a smitten kitten with Lydia, who is the mystery woman?'

Rachel watched Jack's face as he blushed a second time. Whoever he was into, he had it bad.

'Ah, that would be telling.'

'Does the mystery woman know?' she pushed.

He shook his head. 'No, I'm nervous about telling her

how I feel. I nearly did a couple of times, but then I chickened out.'

'Are you worried she doesn't feel the same?' Rachel asked.

'I know she likes me, but I'm afraid it might be more platonic for her.'

'I hate that. When I was in my final year of Uni, I had the biggest crush on one of my lecturers. He was only a few years older than me and very handsome.'

'What happened?'

'Nothing!' Rachel said with a laugh. 'I just worshipped him from afar for about a year. And the more I decided I couldn't have him, the more he took up residence in my head. I swear it took a toll on my mental health there for a while.'

'I know that feeling,' Jack said. 'I feel torn all the time. When I'm not with her, she's all I think about. But when I'm with her, being close, without betraying my true feelings, is heart-wrenching.'

'Oh boy. That is a tough spot to be in.' Rachel thought for a moment. 'But what if it's not unrequited love? What if the person feels the same way?'

'I'm not sure I'm top of any most desirable bachelor list. Man with disability lives at home with his parents, works in a hardware store.'

'Nonsense, and quite frankly, that is an outrageous fish for compliments. But I'll bite. First of all, you are cute as hell. And you have proven time and time again that you have strength of character and resilience, so balls to that disability mention. You are kind. And funny too. Fantastic with kids, so will make a brilliant dad one day. And you don't just work at a hardware store, it's a family business that you have single-handedly dragged into the twenty-first century. As for living at home, well, that's an easy fix. Move out!'

'You make me sound half decent. If you're not careful, you'll give me a big head,' Jack laughed.

'That's because you *are* half decent, you idiot!'

Jack didn't have an answer for that, and just looked out over the boats in the marina, his face hard to read.

'Can you afford to pay rent somewhere? If the answer to that is yes, then I vote it's time for you to get some independence for yourself. And then, when you do get the nerve up to tell that woman you have feelings for her, you have somewhere to bring her home to. Nobody wants to go home to the future in-laws' house to do the nasty.'

'Rachel!'

'Don't tell me you haven't been thinking about that with your mystery woman?'

'Maybe. Once or twice. She's beautiful.'

'Well, I for one cannot wait to meet her. Right, let's take advantage of the sunny morning and go for a walk.'

And as they strolled along the sandy beach, the sun glistening over the green sea, Rachel felt a little more hopeful with every step. With Jack back on her side again, perhaps things would calm back down.

FORTY-ONE

Belinda

Malone Park, Belfast

Belinda sat in the study, thinking. Rachel had just called to invite them for Christmas dinner. She'd suggested that they come for a few nights to spend time with her New Zealand family and Belinda had happily accepted, assuring Rachel that she'd book the Grand Hotel for their stay. They spoke for a few minutes about the mediation case too. Belinda was shocked; it didn't sound like a promising start.

Now, she looked around the dark study. She rarely came in here. It was Oscar's space, she supposed, more than hers. She'd fallen out of love with it because it reminded her of an event that she'd rather forget.

One for which she had paid a heavy price.

Belinda had been playing a game of hide and seek with Olivia, who was then three. Lorcan and Oscar, then thick as thieves, had gone to the fishmongers. Niamh was upstairs in bed napping, feeling the effects of a tiring first trimester in her pregnancy with Dylan.

Belinda remembered standing behind the heavy drapes, feeling chuffed with her hiding spot. Olivia had been getting cross with her, demanding that she try harder to not be found, so this time she'd concealed herself really well.

When Belinda heard the door creak open, she held her hand over her mouth to stop herself laughing and giving herself away to the little girl. But then, to her surprise, she heard Niamh's voice. Belinda had been about to show herself, but there was something about Niamh's tone that made her pause.

'I told you not to call me on my mobile. What if Lorcan had been with me?'

Silence for a few seconds.

'No, you listen to me. I've told you before and I'm telling you again. It's over. It has been for months.'

Belinda felt her knees weaken, and she grabbed the windowsill behind her to steady herself. Who was Niamh talking to? And what was over?

'No . . . of course it isn't.'

Silence again as whoever was on the other end of the phone spoke.

'Do not call me again.'

Belinda heard Niamh's ragged breathing fill the room. Or was that her own breath she could hear?

She felt trapped behind the curtains, immobilized by the conversation she'd heard. Should she step out and confront her daughter-in-law? Or remain where she was?

Before she had a chance to ponder any further, Olivia burst into the room.

'Oh hello, Mammy,' she exclaimed. 'I'm playing hide and seek with Grandma. I've looked everywhere else, so she has to be here. Grandma, come out, come out, wherever you are!'

Belinda heard Olivia gleefully opening drawers and cupboards, giggling as she moved. And then the gig was up. The curtain was yanked back enthusiastically, and Belinda was revealed.

Olivia squealed in delight and jumped into Belinda's arms, but Belinda couldn't share her joy. She looked over Olivia's head and locked eyes with Niamh.

Mutual horror passed between the two women.

Niamh took Olivia from Belinda's arms, turned on her heels and walked out of the room, neither of the women saying a single word.

Replaying the memory, as she had done countless times before, Belinda asked herself what she could have done differently at that moment. With one grandchild in her arms and Niamh pregnant with another, she couldn't find the words to ask a question that she desperately did not want to know the answer to.

But ever since, she had tortured herself wondering – if she'd told Lorcan about that phone call right there and then, would fate have put him in a different place on the day of the crash? *And would he be alive now?*

FORTY-TWO

Rachel

Mount Street, Dublin

November arrived with a flurry of snowflakes and a bite to the air. As Rachel walked towards Mount Street, she reminded herself that each turning month brought her closer to seeing her parents, Claudia and Howard. Ronan had texted that morning, asking her to meet him for coffee thirty minutes ahead of the meeting at the mediation centre, and she was dubious about what was waiting for her on arrival, dreading more bad news.

She walked down the steps into a small cafe that sat in the basement of a red-bricked Victorian townhouse. And laughed out loud when she saw who was seated beside Ronan.

She ran towards Belinda and Oscar, emotions threatening to overcome her.

'Oh darling, come here to us,' Belinda said, pulling Rachel into her arms.

Oscar placed his arms around both Belinda and Rachel.

'I can't believe you're here!' Rachel said.

'We drove down especially. We wanted you to know that you are not on your own,' Oscar explained. 'We had a great run down the M1 actually; it only took us a little over an hour to get to Dublin. Now the traffic into the city, well, that was another thing!'

'You didn't need to do that. But I'm so happy you did,' Rachel said, meaning every word. Then she mock-slapped Ronan, who had a goofy grin plastered over his face. 'You never said a word!' She mouthed a thanks to him. She had a feeling that he was behind this, guessing she needed support.

'I ordered you a cappuccino,' Ronan said as the waitress arrived with their drinks.

'Do you want something to nibble?' Belinda asked. 'You look a little thin. Have you been eating?'

'I have that covered, I ordered some pastries too.' Ronan said, as the waitress also placed a large platter in the centre of the table. Croissants, chocolate brioche and raspberry Danish pastries were piled high, their sweet aroma making Rachel's stomach grumble.

They all picked one and had a happy few moments, munching and brushing flaky pastry from their mouths and fingers. And in those moments, Rachel could almost forget where they were heading next. *Almost.*

'How are you feeling about today?' Ronan asked, breaking the happy spell.

'I didn't sleep much last night. I kept imagining the things

Sheila might come up with next, to prove my inadequacies as a mother.'

'She's panicking because she knows she's wrong. Attack is always the best form of defence,' Oscar said.

'We stick to the plan, Rachel,' Ronan reassured her. 'We will not agree to any joint custody agreements. And if that means we go to court, so be it. I suspect Fergal will want to shelve that for now and focus on the visitation issues.'

'Okay,' Rachel replied, her heart sinking, even though she knew it might be essential.

'We might need to give a little in this area,' Ronan said gently and Rachel nodded.

'Their demands are unreasonable though, surely?' Belinda asked.

'They are looking for a lot, but they know they won't get all of that. Let's see how far they are willing to negotiate.'

Rachel put her Danish down on her plate, feeling so overwhelmed she wasn't sure she could hold herself up tall to face today. The words tumbled from her mouth before she even knew what she was saying.

'I wish I knew what Lorcan would want me to do,' she admitted. There was silence for a moment, then Oscar spoke.

'He would want the children to be with you. Of that, I am one hundred per cent sure.'

'I believe that too. But would he want me to agree to mid-week overnights? Or to go to court, to fight it out?' She looked at them all pleadingly, praying they could make the decision for her.

'It's an impossible situation. But sometimes, the only

person you can trust is yourself. We have faith in you, Rachel, so you must have faith in yourself too,' Belinda said reassuringly.

'I won't let you give away anything that I don't believe you'd have to in court,' Ronan said.

Rachel wished she had as much faith in herself as they appeared to, but she was second-guessing every single thing. She felt a mixture of regret and pride jumbled up inside of her. Pride that she'd finally stood up to Sheila at the end of the last mediation session, but regret that she'd had to play such a low card to do so.

'Right, we'd better go,' Ronan said, checking his watch.

'We'll walk with you,' Belinda said, linking arms with Rachel, the two men following behind them.

They arrived at the mediation centre just as Sheila and Adrian were crossing the street.

'What are you doing here?' Sheila asked pointedly to Belinda and Oscar. 'You can't go in there.'

'And good morning to you too, Sheila and Adrian,' Belinda said calmly.

'We're just here for moral support,' Oscar said, moving closer to Rachel and placing a hand on her shoulder.

Rachel turned around and hugged them both, fully aware that the Butlers were watching. But she was done caring about what they thought any more.

'I'm sorry you came all this way for only half an hour,' she said.

'Our pleasure. And there's no need to say goodbye. We'll be here waiting for you when you are finished,' Belinda said, making sure everyone heard.

Rachel followed Ronan into the meeting room. When

Fergal arrived, he addressed the room as he walked in, 'Can you believe it's November already? A month I love. It's a chance to tie up loose ends before the year ends, I always think. Will we all give that a go here today?'

A round of unenthusiastic affirmations was made.

Fergal continued, undeterred. 'It's natural to feel over-whelmed and stressed by this process. And when that happens, we often say things that we don't mean. We ended up our first session on a bad note, didn't we? Can we put that behind us?'

Adrian raised his hand, as a child might do in class.

'Yes, Adrian, what would you like to say?'

Adrian took a deep breath. 'Sheila and I would like to retract our comment about Rachel's drinking. She does not have and has never had an alcohol issue. We shouldn't have said that.'

Rachel was shocked. She could have climbed across the table and kissed him, she was so relieved. Maria didn't look as happy about this statement, though, and neither did Sheila, although she didn't say anything to object.

'Thank you. That's the spirit I hoped you would enter this process in. Sheila, is there anything you'd like to add?'

Sheila avoided eye contact but, graciously for her, said, 'I agree with everything that Adrian has said.'

'Thank you,' Rachel responded. And somehow, she knew that Jack had worked his magic here. 'I'd like to say something, too. It was wrong of me to say that you were no longer the children's grandparents. No adoption papers can ever change that you always will be Olivia and Dylan's nana and grandad.'

The room was silent for a moment as both sides let the apologies sit.

Fergal beamed at them all as if they were his best students. 'And here I thought I'd have to give you one of my pep talks to remind you why you entered this process. Now let's see if we can move forward today on the additional visitation rights. So, from what you've shared here before, am I right to understand that visitation rights have worked well previously with flexibility on both parts up to now? Why do you feel the need to formalize things?'

Sheila and Adrian shuffled on their seats. Both appeared unable to answer this question from Fergal, so Maria jumped in. 'Sheila and Adrian have been in the children's lives right from the start, but they fear the strained relationship they have with Rachel will harm their relationship with the children. And, in turn, their visitation rights. They would prefer to formalize additional access now to pre-empt any issues.'

'I have never kept the children from you both,' Rachel said calmly, hoping the positive mood from the start of the session would continue throughout.

'I'm afraid that's not quite true, is it, Rachel?' Maria said. 'Over the years, the Butlers have always been the main support to the children, stepping in to help Niamh and Lorcan. Then, more recently, Rachel too. But if I may give an example, when Rachel went back to New Zealand for another holiday, she broke their informal arrangement, leaving the children elsewhere. Incidentally, for someone who insists they have no interest in relocating to the other side of the world, Rachel seems to spend a lot of time over there.'

Rachel almost laughed at how ludicrous the statement was. 'Well, that's twisting the facts to a new level,' she said matter-of-factly.

Ronan spoke next, 'It appears Ms Johnson is confused about this matter. Or she was perhaps misinformed. Rachel did indeed return to New Zealand for one week in September, but, as the Butlers are well aware, it was due to a family emergency. I would suggest that Ms Johnson's attempt to suggest that it was anything else is outside the spirit of this mediation.'

Rachel didn't enjoy sharing her personal life, or indeed Claudia's, with the room. It felt wrong, and as she told the room about the heartbreaking reason for her short visit to New Zealand, she felt exposed and vulnerable again. 'My sister's life was in danger, as a result of an ectopic pregnancy.' She paused to collect herself for a moment. 'It's upsetting for me that I must continuously prove myself to the Butlers. Why is it that they always choose to discredit me?'

'We are sorry to hear about Claudia's loss,' Sheila said solemnly.

'Thank you,' Rachel replied. Sheila did look genuinely upset at the news.

'But why did you ask the Bradleys to watch the children, as opposed to us?' Adrian said. 'We were the obvious choice. That said a lot to us, Rachel. You would rather the children be with strangers than us, their loving grand-parents nearby.'

Rachel looked at Fergal and said, her voice coming out in a high-pitched strangle, 'The children *were* with their grandparents. My husband's parents.' She turned back to the Butlers and said, 'You both keep forgetting that you are not the only party in town.'

'We are fully aware that the children have other family members, but Belinda and Oscar are as good as strangers to them as far as we are concerned. The children have barely spent any time with them,' Sheila said.

'That might be correct in the past, but Belinda and Oscar have worked hard to re-establish a connection with the kids this year. We've visited them in Belfast several times. They've been to visit us, too. Not to mention that the children video-call them several times a week.'

'I didn't know anything about all that,' Sheila admitted.

Rachel smiled sweetly, replying, 'Well, maybe you don't know as much about everything as you'd like to think you do.' Seeing the look of shock on Sheila's face just spurred Rachel on to say more. 'And while we are discussing this, I did not ask them to take care of the children. They offered.'

'You could have said no. You know full well that we would have taken the children. We are only down the road. It would have made far more sense,' Sheila insisted.

'The Bradleys offered when I most needed the help. They wanted to spend time with the children, to strengthen their relationship. Why on earth would I say no to them? Just as I have never said no to you both when you've asked to see the kids. You can't have it every way. You keep talking about your rights. Well, all of the children's grandparents have rights too, in that case. Have you considered that? My parents love spending time with them too. And if you say once again that they are not real grandparents, I swear . . .' Rachel stopped, knowing that she had allowed her emotions to get the better of her, even without needing to hear Fergal sigh, or see Sheila smirk, or have Ronan give her a warning look.

Fergal, however, seemed to forgive her heightened emotions. 'It's understandable that at times we get upset.

I find a beneficial technique is to jot down something if it irritates you. Then you have time to think, digest, mull it over. And perhaps try to look at the issue from someone else's point of view.'

'Well, if that's the case, I'm going to need a bigger jotter,' Rachel said.

Ronan grinned, and Rachel was sure she saw the hint of a smile on Andrew's face too.

Sheila looked at Fergal and practically simpered as she said, 'Thank you, Fergal. I'll remember that tip. Adrian and I *are* closer to the children than the Bradleys and the Andersons. With good reason. The facts cannot be denied. The children's mother, our daughter Niamh, formally asked us to be Olivia and Dylan's childminder when she returned to work after her maternity leave. Niamh valued family above all else, and recognized the importance of us both playing a key role in the children's upbringing. We spent whole days every week with Olivia and were planning to do the same with Dylan. Then we stepped in when Lorcan fell to pieces after she . . . It was to be expected, of course, as Niamh was the love of his life.' Sheila looked at Rachel and locked eyes with deliberation. 'If I had a euro for every time that Lorcan said our Niamh was his soulmate . . .'

Rachel knew that comment was meant to cut and, job well done, it hurt. She didn't want to give Sheila the satisfaction of a response, though.

'I think what Sheila is trying to say is that nobody could blame us for believing that we would continue to play a key role in the children's lives,' Adrian said.

Rachel sighed and sat back in her chair. 'I truly give up. What's the point? I knew this process was going to be a waste of time. The Butlers have come in with a fixed idea and they will never see things from my perspective, no matter what I say.'

Fergal raised his hand and said, 'Sheila and Adrian, bear with me for a second. Let's dial this back to the adoption. Do you accept that it was Lorcan who suggested the adoption, not Rachel?'

'Yes, I can accept that,' Adrian said.

Sheila didn't object, so Fergal took that as a good sign.

'So was he part of Rachel's plan to take the children away from you both?' Fergal asked. 'I'm trying to understand if we would be in this same situation if Lorcan were still alive.'

Rachel looked at the Butlers with interest.

'Possibly,' Sheila said. 'There's no denying that after he married Rachel, Lorcan pulled away from us.'

'That's because he worked full-time. Throw in being a husband and father to two small children; he had little or no spare time,' Rachel said. 'But even so, I would like it noted that Lorcan *did* make time for the Butlers. Every Wednesday, he made it his business to be the one to collect the children so that he could spend time with you both.'

Fergal gently interjected, looking to the Butlers, 'It was natural that he would spend more time with you when he was with Niamh. But perhaps you can understand, too, that when he married Rachel, he now had new responsibilities and demands on his time.'

'I can only imagine the demands he had from Rachel. She never came with him to pick up the children. So he was always watching the clock, aware that he had to get back to her,' Sheila said.

Rachel exhaled with exasperation. 'Sheila, you decided

years ago that I was the wicked stepmother. I have been vilified at every move. No matter what I do or say, you twist it. I avoided Wednesday evenings at your house, aside from the fact that you never made me feel welcome, because I wanted to give you all a chance to talk about Niamh without me there. I wanted Lorcan and you all to have the freedom to remember Niamh, and their marriage, without feeling awkward about me.'

Fergal leaned in. 'Isn't it interesting how there are always three sides to every story? Yours,' he pointed to Rachel, 'theirs,' he pointed to the Butlers, 'and the truth.' At this, he pointed to everyone at once. 'The Butlers took offence that Rachel didn't go along on Wednesday evenings with Lorcan, without realizing that Rachel stayed away with only the best intentions. And Rachel had no idea that by staying away, rather than making things easier for everyone, it made the Butlers uneasy, believing there were ulterior motives at play. The thing is, in my experience, I've learned that when we are emotional, caught up in the moment, it's natural for us to only see things in black and white. It's the grey I'm interested in seeing here. I'd like you both to acknowledge, at least, that the grey exists. Can you do that?'

There was a silence while they all studied the table for a moment.

'I can,' Rachel said truthfully. 'I honestly never meant any disrespect. Whenever the subject of Niamh came up in my presence, Lorcan would get twitchy. And I felt there was tension.'

'Thank you, Rachel,' Fergal's eyes rested on her. 'It's never easy to admit that you might be wrong. To acknowledge that there may be another side to the story. Sheila,

Adrian, can you agree that you may have misconstrued things at times too?'

To Rachel's surprise, they both nodded. He placed his hands on the table.

'I think we've covered a lot today. We've managed to discuss many of the issues somehow, and I think all sides have had a chance to share how things look from their side. Let's take a short break and when we come back, I'd like to hear about this puppy.'

FORTY-THREE

Rachel

Mount Street, Dublin

Fergal looked around the room, as though he was trying to gauge the mood. Eventually, he spoke.

'I think,' he said slowly, 'that the children's puppy might be an answer to some of the issues.'

Rachel wasn't sure she liked the sound of this.

'Thor?' she asked suspiciously.

'Sheila and Adrian want to see more of the children and have asked for additional access. And I'm assuming you take . . . Thor – what a great name, by the way – for a walk every day?' he asked the Butlers.

'Every morning and evening.' Adrian nodded.

'And how far do you go for these walks?' Fergal asked.

'Oh, just to the end of the road and back, up to Malahide Castle or down to the estuary. But mainly, we go along the Yellow Walls Road.'

'Rachel, how would you feel about letting the children accompany their grandparents on Thor's walks?' Fergal said.

Rachel wasn't sure whether it was a good or bad suggestion.

'This could be a solution for everyone. Sheila and Adrian, you get to see more of the children. And Rachel, as it would be for a short walk, by the sounds of it no more than thirty minutes per day, it shouldn't intrude into family life too much,' Fergal continued.

'Mornings are chaotic as it is – getting the children ready for school – without throwing in an early-morning walk,' Rachel said.

'That's understandable,' Fergal agreed. 'Is there a time in the afternoon or evenings that would work, then?'

Rachel considered this for a second. 'Early evening could work, I suppose. After they've done their homework.'

'Excellent. What do you think, Sheila and Adrian?' Fergal asked.

'I love this idea,' Adrian said.

'Can we get it in writing that we get to see the children every evening for the dog walk?' Sheila asked.

'What if the children are tired or feeling off-colour?' Rachel objected. 'Or it's raining? Do they have to go for a walk because an agreement says so?'

'Let's park making it an official item to sign off on for now,' Fergal said. 'Rachel, in theory, are you happy to allow the children to walk Thor every evening with their grandparents?'

She took a moment to think about it. *Trust yourself.* That's what Belinda had advised. She knew the children would love adding this to their early evening routine. And it might bring some joy into Olivia's days too. Although they'd recovered from the phone incident, when she smiled, it still didn't fully reach her eyes.

'How do I know you won't turn a walk into you bringing the kids back to your house for dinner or treats every evening? We have a routine at home. I can't have that disrupted; it wouldn't be fair on everyone.'

'We could call to your house to pick them up and then drop them home on the way back. That way, it's understood it's for the walk and nothing more,' Adrian suggested.

Rachel smiled her thanks to him.

Ronan whispered to Rachel, 'If they do go to court for custody, it shows you've given reasonable access by agreeing to this. And don't worry, I'll make sure it's worded to protect you all for exceptions when a walk doesn't work.'

Agreeing to this felt akin to walking along the proverbial thin plank while hungry sharks circled below, waiting for their next victim. But with Ronan's encouragement, Rachel supposed it was time to make some concessions.

'Okay,' she said, nodding. 'I'll agree to daily dog walks after dinner each evening, assuming the kids have done their homework, are well, and weather is permitting.'

'That's wonderful,' Adrian said, beaming. 'Isn't it, love?' he asked Sheila, who couldn't but agree.

'Excellent. That's great progress, everyone,' Fergal stated, scribbling notes on the pad in front of him. Just when Rachel thought she might be able to take a deep breath, Sheila spoke again.

'We'd also like to have the children visit at weekends,' she said.

'They go down to see you and Thor every Saturday

and Sunday as it is, unless we have other plans,' Rachel pointed out.

'Yes, but we need regular weekend overnight access,' Sheila said.

'Why is it so important for you to have this included in the mediation agreement?' Fergal asked.

'Because I don't trust Rachel,' Sheila replied, not missing a beat.

Before Rachel could respond to that, Ronan said, 'I think we are finally getting to the heart of the issues here. If there is no trust, then it is difficult for us to reach any mediation agreement. Without it, we can't move forward.'

'What have I done to make you distrust me so much?' Rachel asked.

'Nothing at all,' Adrian replied quickly. He raised his hands as if trying to fill the air between his wife and Rachel.

'Weekends are important to us as a family, and I'm not willing to give them up,' Rachel said simply. 'During the week, we juggle a hundred different balls – school, home-work, work . . . it's fast-paced for all of us. We need time at the weekend to have quality family time together. Every Saturday morning after breakfast is board game time. The kids love it, and it's a time that I treasure too. And then on Saturday evenings, it's family movie night. Olivia is in charge of making snacks – she has a special tray she likes to use – then Dylan is in charge of making the sitting room cosy. Sunday mornings, we have breakfast in bed. The kids come into my room early, I make breakfast, and we eat sausage bagels while watching something silly on the TV. The children need that time with me and each other. It's unfair to make them give it up.'

'What about the importance of their time spent with us? We are not forcing them to come to us against their will; they love coming to see us,' Sheila pointed out.

'But the beauty of the current arrangement is the fluidity of it,' Rachel countered. 'Olivia and Dylan love that they can pop down to see you both at the weekends, and I would never want to come in the way of that. But it's equally important that we have time to be together, without always rushing to be somewhere else.'

Rachel slumped back into her chair, feeling exhausted from the constant back and forth. She wasn't sure she had the strength to continue this for much longer.

Ronan glanced her way, then said, 'I think it's worth reminding everyone that we're on unusual ground here. The Butlers are not parents. They are grandparents. As such, they do not have the same rights.'

'Our family are the last blood relatives that the children have of their *real* mother.' Sheila said.

'I am their real mother *too*,' Rachel said. 'I've lived in the shadow of Niamh for years. And it's bitterly cold.'

'I think you'll find that it's colder for Niamh in her grave,' Sheila said.

'Oh boy,' Andrew said, raising his eyebrows at Fergal.

Rachel looked towards Fergal, but he didn't intervene. Perhaps he thought it was time that they all aired how they really felt.

'What would you have me do, forget my daughter ever existed?' Sheila continued.

'Of course not,' Rachel said. 'But I don't think you realize how hard it is for me. I've had a third person in my marriage from the start.'

Fergal raised his hand at last. 'Let's take a beat and

remember that we need to be respectful here. I don't like the phrase "real mother". Niamh is the children's birth mother. But Rachel is the children's mother *now*. You cannot change either of those facts.'

'How is it disrespectful to call my daughter what she is?' Sheila shouted, tears in her eyes. 'It was Niamh who gave birth to those children, for goodness' sake, not Rachel.'

'But she's not here any more. And I am,' Rachel whispered back.

FORTY-FOUR

Rachel

Mount Street, Dublin

Rachel sighed, closing her eyes, a tension headache pounding between her temples. But she thought of Olivia and Dylan and knew she had to keep battling on. They needed her. They'd made her promise that she would never leave them, and she intended to uphold that.

She opened her eyes and looked at Sheila and Adrian, speaking softly.

'You always make it sound like I am less than Niamh. That somehow I'm not a real parent. But I am, and I love the children, as they love and need me too.'

'And you always make it sound as if you believe that the children are better off with you than they were with their mother,' Sheila said quietly.

Rachel felt a wave of sadness overcome her. She felt compassion cloud her anger at the Butlers. They had lost their child. That was a pain no parent should ever carry. She spoke as gently as could, trying to convey her sincerity to Sheila and Adrian, who looked as sad as she felt right now.

'If Niamh were alive, I wouldn't be here, I know that. But she died and I'm so sorry that happened. I cannot imagine the horror of that loss. But I also cannot keep apologizing that I fell in love with Lorcan and the children. Do you truly believe that the children would be better off without me?'

The question hurt every part of her, and she shrank back into her seat to try to put as much distance as she could between her and the answer that she knew was coming her way.

'Yes. I do,' Sheila said simply.

Fergal cleared his throat. 'That's a big statement to make, and one we need to address.'

He looked down at his notes, flicking through the pages, nodding every now and then.

'This is never going to go away. We are going to have to go to court,' Rachel whispered to Ronan.

He leaned in and whispered back, 'I think that's likely, yes. But Sheila's playing a dangerous game. She's stating that an adoptive parent does not have the same status as a birth parent. There isn't a court that will give credence to that, remember. I would be surprised if Maria isn't counselling her the same thing.'

He nodded in Maria's direction, who was whispering something to Sheila and Adrian.

Fergal cleared his throat and began again. 'I feel I need to remind the room that when a step-parent becomes the adoptive parent, they take on full parental rights and responsibilities regarding the child. If you cannot accept this, we will never reach an agreement.'

Rachel's eyes never left Sheila as Fergal spoke. Sheila paled and her shoulders slumped. She looked to Adrian and leaned in to him. He whispered and she nodded. *Has she finally cracked?* Rachel prayed that she had.

'None of this is personal, Rachel,' Sheila said, leaning forward towards her. 'I know you must think I'm the most horrible person, and I don't blame you. But I *have* to fight for the children. For Niamh. It's what she would want me to do.'

And with her words, it became clear to Rachel; Sheila was doing this for her daughter, not for herself. And she would never – could never – stop in her pursuit of what she thought Niamh would want. No matter the consequence. She felt so sad. Not just for herself, but for the Butlers too.

Fergal said, 'It's important for every child to know where they come from; I understand why you want Olivia and Dylan to remember Niamh.'

'I do encourage them to talk about Niamh all the time,' Rachel said, attempting to help.

'It strikes me,' Fergal said calmly, 'that both sides are really on the same side. With that in mind, I'd like to progress further on overnight access before we finish today. Rachel has explained how important weekends are for the family dynamic. I have a suggestion to make. The children visit their grandparents every Wednesday after school as it is. One possible solution is that the children stay overnight with the Butlers on that day. What do you all think?'

Fergal let the suggestion sit for a moment.

'What about weekends?' Maria asked.

'I would suggest that weekend visitation continues to happen as it does now, on a fluid basis,' Fergal replied.

Rachel leaned in to whisper to Ronan, 'I don't have a major problem with this. By the time the children get home to me as it is, it's eight p.m. and they are always cranky. I'd definitely prefer this as opposed to weekends. But I'm worried about making it official again, for the same reasons as the daily walks.'

'As with the dog walking, we'll make sure exceptions are listed in the agreement before we sign,' Ronan reassured her. 'Don't worry.'

'Okay,' Rachel agreed simply, 'in that case, I'm fine with it.' She hoped her gut was still pointing her in the right direction.

'If the Butlers take formal weekend visits off the table, then we are happy to agree to Wednesday overnights. But with the usual provisos,' Ronan said.

'Fantastic. So access would now be extended to daily walks of Thor with the grandparents and overnights every Wednesday. With weekend sleepovers to be agreed on an ad hoc basis. Maria?' Fergal said, looking towards the Butlers and their lawyer.

Maria and the Butlers whispered for a moment. Then Maria said, 'We can agree to that.'

Rachel couldn't help thinking that she was letting Lorcan down somehow. Had she agreed too readily? Should she have fought more? But she had to admit she felt relieved too. That at last they were making progress.

'One more thing,' Maria piped up, and Rachel groaned inwardly. 'We'd like to discuss Christmas,' Maria said defiantly, dashing any hopes of reaching the finish line in one fell swoop.

'That is not on the table for discussion,' Ronan replied swiftly.

'We've added it now,' Maria responded.

'I don't understand,' Rachel said, genuinely confused. 'Sheila and Adrian always call down on Christmas morning after mass to see the children and their Santa gifts. It's always been that way.'

Before Maria could start to respond, Ronan jumped in. 'Once again, I'd like to remind everyone that grandparents do not have any rights for access. We are right back to where we started again. To gain access in the courts, you need to prove that the parent is refusing visitation. And that's simply not the case here,' he said. Almost before he'd finished speaking, Sheila was shaking her head.

'Last year, we didn't get to spend more than a few minutes with the children,' she said, looking at Fergal pointedly.

Rachel thought they couldn't surprise her any further, but each time they came back with a new low. 'The children were distraught on Christmas Day last year. When you arrived it was at a particularly bad moment for them.'

'Which is why it was so important that we be there for them,' Sheila said.

'They didn't want *you*, Sheila,' her voice almost a snarl. 'They wanted *me*. If Olivia and Dylan had the choice, they would not have seen anyone on Christmas Day. I persuaded them to put a bright smile on their faces because I knew it was important to you both.'

'Rubbish. Why are we only hearing about this now?' Sheila said.

'Because I didn't want to hurt your feelings,' Rachel responded bluntly. She had no such qualms any more.

'Every now and then we have a moment where we are utterly floored by Lorcan's absence. That was one of them. In those moments, we – all of us – don't want to see anyone but each other.'

An uneasy silence descended upon them all again.

'Christmas is a tough time, especially when you've lost someone you've loved. Do you have plans for this year?' Fergal asked Rachel.

'My parents and sister are visiting from New Zealand. And I've asked my parents-in-law for Christmas lunch. I assumed the Butlers would visit on Christmas morning, as they have always have done.'

Adrian spoke, affirmatively, as though daring his wife to disagree with him. 'That sounds wonderful. And we do not need Christmas access written into any agreement. The children's place is with their mother.' He turned to Sheila and said with more force than Rachel had ever heard him use before, 'Let that be an end to it.'

Fergal clapped his hands once at that, as if he might burst into a round of applause.

'Well done, everyone. I think this is a good time to finish up for the day, but we'll meet again at some point to discuss the thorny guardianship issue.' He looked at each of them in turn. 'Take some time to think about what you all want to achieve here – it's a perfect time to reflect, over the coming weeks and Christmas holidays. Andrew will set up a date for early January. Until then, try to remember that giving up doesn't make you weak. It can mean that you are brave enough to let go.'

Fergal smiled at them all and walked out.

Rachel and Ronan walked outside together on to Mount Street, and Rachel looked upwards to the mottled grey sky. It was heavy with ominous dark clouds, low and full, ready to burst open.

She could only hope that behind the dark clouds lay the sun.

FORTY-FIVE

Belinda

Dublin

Belinda and Oscar found Rachel, as arranged, in Stephen's Green Park. She explained that Ronan had to dash back to the office, so she was on her own when she reached them.

'How was it?' Oscar asked.

Rachel made a face, and he said, 'That bad?'

'It's exhausting. I'm trying so hard to say the right thing, to respond in the right way, to be fair to the kids, to the Butlers . . .'

'You have to be fair to yourself too,' Belinda cut her off. 'Why don't we find a quiet restaurant to chat in?' she suggested.

'I'm not hungry,' she responded bleakly. 'You know, I'd prefer to walk around here, assuming the rain holds off. Would you mind?'

As they strolled through the leafy park, Rachel updated them both on the meeting. They listened quietly, letting her tell the story without interruption.

'So there you have it. Sheila and Adrian would rather the children have no mother than have me.'

'She's a silly woman,' Belinda said, genuinely flummoxed by Sheila's stubbornness. 'It's as if she's blinded by this idea that she's doing right by Niamh, so much so that she cannot see what's in front of her face.'

Belinda stopped by an empty bench. She couldn't put off what she knew would be a difficult conversation any longer. Closing her eyes for a moment, she prayed for strength, then said, 'Let's take a seat. There's something we have to tell you.'

Ever since Rachel had asked Belinda about a possible rift with Niamh, she'd fretted over what was the right thing to do. Oscar and she had kept Niamh's secret for so long, but now that they'd become close to Rachel, it felt wrong to keep this from her. While Rachel was in mediation, they'd finally made a decision to share what they knew with her.

'Niamh and Lorcan's marriage wasn't as perfect as Sheila remembers. Or perhaps knows. They were unhappy,' Belinda started tentatively.

Oscar jumped in, 'Lorcan used to visit us with Olivia on his own. Niamh always had an excuse as to why she couldn't join him, and to be honest, we were relieved, because when they were together they fought a lot.'

'I thought they were soulmates!' Rachel said incredulously. 'Or so I've been told repeatedly.'

'They got married too young, in my opinion,' Belinda said. 'And as can be the way, they outgrew each other. Lorcan was a homebody, and he liked a quiet life. Niamh liked to go out. I suppose, in hindsight, we can see now that they were fundamentally very different people. They clashed about politics, religion, how to rear the children, and even what to watch on TV. Diversity in a relationship is good, but you have to find some middle ground too.'

Belinda felt an ache as she shared these insights. She hated to think about him having even a moment of unhappiness in what had been too short a life.

'The reason we are sharing that with you is to give you an understanding of this next part to our story.' Oscar nodded encouragingly and Belinda was grateful for his support. If she faltered, she knew he'd be there to take over. 'We found out before Dylan was born that Niamh was having an affair.'

Rachel gasped out loud at this.

Belinda described the hide and seek game that had sent the house of cards crashing to the ground.

She pulled her woollen coat around her a little tighter, feeling shaky from finally sharing this revelation, one that she'd kept quiet for so many years.

'The missing piece of the puzzle – it's all starting to make sense. But I'm dumbfounded. I could never have predicted this,' Rachel said, looking from Belinda to Oscar and back again in total shock.

'Niamh begged me not to tell Lorcan. She said it had been over with this guy for several months when I found out, but that he had found it hard to let her go. Niamh wouldn't tell me who he was, other than to say she'd met him through work.'

'Someone in the bank, we suspect. It doesn't matter who, anyhow,' Oscar said.

'It was an awful time,' Belinda continued. 'Niamh was

pregnant. The weight of the secret weighed on my shoulders so heavily I began to feel depressed. I couldn't decide if I should tell Oscar, never mind Lorcan. What good would sharing the news do for anyone? I kept going through all the ramifications. And each time, all I could see was devastation if I spoke. Then Niamh claimed that the stress of my questions had caused her to bleed. She had an overnight in hospital and she said that if she lost the baby, it would be my fault.' Belinda pulled a handkerchief from her tote bag and dabbed her eyes. This was a difficult memory to share. With her own history of miscarriages, the burden of this accusation had caused Belinda to lose sleep for months.

'An incredibly cruel thing to put on Belinda's shoulders,' Oscar said. 'I could see that something was wrong, so I insisted that she tell me. And thank goodness she did. At least then I could share the burden.'

'I'm always much better with this man by my side,' Belinda said, smiling at Oscar. There were moments when the depth of her love for him overwhelmed her. And others, where she just felt grateful. This was one of those. 'We discussed it and, in the end, decided we would never tell Lorcan. He was excited about the baby and seemed happy. Plus, we couldn't risk causing Niamh any more stress.'

Rachel, however, looked as though she had more queries. She began tentatively. 'I'm sorry to have to ask this, but were you suspicious that this other guy could be Dylan's father?'

'Yes, it was our worst fear. But Niamh went through the timings with me, and there is no way it could have been anyone else's but Lorcan's. And it's true that when I overheard her on the phone, she said that they'd been over for months,' Belinda confirmed.

'Unfortunately, things were never the same with Niamh after that,' Oscar put in. 'She didn't trust us. Or maybe she felt guilty when she saw us; either way, she began to plant seeds in Lorcan's mind – telling him that we were always putting her down. That we found fault in all she did. That we didn't like her.'

'That's awful. It must have been such a hard time for you both.'

Belinda nodded. She thought about how she had been at that time. She had been so focused on keeping Niamh's secret that she'd missed out on too much with her son. She'd blamed herself, then hated Niamh.

'We called to Dublin to visit and it all came to a head,' Oscar said. 'I'd say Niamh was about six months pregnant at the time. It was a tense atmosphere. Niamh picked a fight with Belinda, then started to cry when Lorcan walked into the room. She clutched her tummy and Lorcan asked us to leave because we were apparently stressing her out too much. When Dylan was born we went to visit them at the hospital, but Niamh became hysterical when we walked in. It was as if she was convinced we were going to take her happiness away.'

Hearing Oscar's words brought Belinda back to that horrible day. It should have been one of the happiest of all their lives. A new grandson. But she never got the chance to properly meet him. 'We had to leave. Being there was doing no good. So we stayed away, sending gifts to the children. And then Niamh died.' Belinda's voice wobbled at the memory. She had been so angry with Niamh, for her cruelty to them all, but in a million years, she would never have wanted her to die.

'We went to see Lorcan immediately, but he was so

angry with us. He felt we were disingenuous, pretending to be upset about her death when we had made her so unhappy. And things just unravelled from there. We didn't manage to recover our relationship with him after that. And then . . .' Her voice trailed off.

'What a mess,' Rachel said, falling silent as she took in the shocking revelation.

'We never hated Niamh; that was the sad part. We didn't like what she had done to our son,' Oscar clarified. 'Nor what she did to us. I know we were painted in a bad light because we stayed away. But that wasn't our choice. Niamh forced our hand and we went along with it, because we wanted to protect their marriage.'

It was only then that Belinda acknowledged the full extent of how much that situation had impacted her life and Oscar's too. She looked at her husband and felt a rush of gratitude that he'd stuck with her through it all.

'After Lorcan died, I became frozen, somehow stuck in my regret,' she explained. 'I began to believe that if I had told Lorcan about Niamh's affair, maybe he'd be alive still. Maybe he wouldn't have been in that car on that day . . .'

Oscar sighed his disapproval. 'You know that's ridiculous. We made those decisions together.'

'You're right. You normally are.' She smiled and he half laughed at the comment. 'The problem was that back then I doubted myself all the time, no longer trusting my own judgement. It made me guarded with family and friends. With Oscar. And with you too for a while, Rachel.'

'I'm so sorry you went through all of this. But I'm so grateful you found a way out of it. I have grown rather fond of you both,' Rachel said, looking at them shyly. 'It's felt like I have surrogate parents here, with mine so far away.'

Belinda felt a wave of emotion overwhelm her. And holding back a sob, she told Rachel, 'I always wanted a daughter, and when Lorcan found you, he gave me one. We are always here for you.'

'Proud to be your surrogate father,' Oscar said, his voice gruff with emotion too.

They sat side by side on the bench for a moment, clutching hands gratefully for each other's support and love.

'So why have you told me all of this now?' Rachel asked.

Belinda took the girl's hands in her own. 'I've watched you doubt yourself. I did the same thing; it eats you away, self-doubt. And I can see that Niamh's secret is still rippling through this family, even now. I kept it secret from Lorcan, and it cost me precious time with him before he died. We want you to know everything because knowledge is power. It's up to you what you want to do with it.'

'I'd like to keep this between ourselves,' Rachel said immediately. 'But I'm glad I know, for myself. It helps knowing that Niamh was, like the rest of us, flawed.'

Belinda was proud of Rachel. It was the right thing to do; she could see that. While Belinda didn't like Sheila, she knew that finding out about this would only cause her pain. And as one mother to another, there was no joy in that.

She gave Rachel's hand one last squeeze, feeling protective of her. She loved this one, not because she was a mother to her grandchildren but because she felt like family to her too. And there was nobody and nothing that could keep her away from her family this time.

FORTY-SIX

Rachel

Dublin Bay, Dublin

Rachel had taken a day off. Not just from Rae's Closet, but from the stress and strain of the past few months and in particular the last mediation session, two weeks previously. Christmas had officially begun and her diary brimmed with Christmas shows and carol concerts.

Today, she had Dylan's nativity play, followed by a visit to see Santa Claus, and tomorrow, her family would be arriving from New Zealand. She got to the hall a full thirty minutes early, but even so had to settle for a seat in the third row. She reckoned some of the parents must have camped out in the hall since the school opened at nine a.m.

Yesterday she was in this same school hall to watch Olivia take part in a Christmas sketch. Olivia had opted for a non-speaking role and looked awkward throughout the entire show. She hated being on stage. Nevertheless, Rachel had been so proud of her, knowing she was totally out of her comfort zone. She looked over to the side aisle, where Olivia sat cross-legged with her classmates to watch Dylan's play. Olivia was smiling and laughing as she watched her brother ham it up as he walked on to the stage. This was the Olivia that Rachel missed.

Dylan himself was so excited about his performance, you couldn't help but get swept along with him. And it was a truth known to all parents that magic happens when a group of five-year-olds earnestly perform the nativity. Whether they are Mary or Joseph, or the fourth shepherd from the right (as played splendidly by Dylan), they would throw themselves into the role. And no matter how much practice the kids put in, something was always sure to go wrong.

As the play ended, Dylan took a deep bow, a huge toothy smile on his face. Then his tea-towel head-dress fell to the ground, making the audience giggle. Rachel held her breath, hoping the costume malfunction wouldn't upset him. But in true Dylan style, he casually picked up the blue and white checked tea towel and placed it back on his head without missing a beat. She could learn a lot from her son. He took life and all the curveballs it threw at him in his stride. Rachel joined in with the rest of the parents as they whooped and cheered their own little Junior Infants and their nativity play to its conclusion. Dylan looked for Rachel from the stage, waving enthusi-astically when he spotted her.

'Wonderful, just wonderful!' Rachel shouted out, not caring in the least when a couple of mothers nearby looked over to her in surprise. And her heart constricted to almost bursting point when she saw Olivia proudly cheering her little brother on too. His eyes flicked between them both and he beamed so brightly, so delighted with himself, that it made Rachel well up. She was a sucker for this time of year. Every Christmas carol and sparkling light was a nostalgic note, a warm embrace. Rachel wiped tears away that insisted on falling. She found it impossible to watch her children perform in any show without feeling emotional. It was the innocence imprinted on their faces and their earnestness as they threw themselves into their roles that got her.

Lorcan used to tease her for being such a softie. She would place her sunglasses on to hide the emotion when she'd well up, then he'd pull her in close to him, wiping her tears with his thumb, never caring who was watching them. Rachel felt a shiver run over her and, for a moment, she felt Lorcan's presence beside her again. She wasn't religious, she didn't know what she believed about the ever after, but sometimes, like now, she knew without a doubt that it wasn't the end when you breathed your last.

She whispered to Lorcan now, *Are you watching the kids, my love? Wasn't he amazing, our little boy?* From wherever he was, his answer to her was to brush a stray tear from her cheek.

As they reunited with their families, the sound of children's chatter brought her back to the hall. Dylan's teacher made a little speech and thanked the children and the school; it was as good as the Academy Awards for everyone in that hall. Then he announced that the children were free to go. Olivia ran over to Dylan and Rachel for a big group hug.

They made their way home, where Rachel had left a

change of clothes for the children on their beds. She'd bought matching Christmas jumpers for each of them for their annual Santa Claus visit, a favourite family tradition Lorcan and Niamh had started, that continued now every year. They never missed visiting Arnotts department store on Henry Street, Dublin.

'Mom, these are so cool!' Dylan exclaimed when he saw Rachel and Olivia. They all had 'Merry Christmas Ya Filthy Animal' emblazoned across their bright green jumpers, a nod to *Home Alone*, which they'd recently watched together and loved. The kids had been shouting the phrase out to each other for weeks, feeling a little naughty, but with full permission from their mom. They walked to the train station wrapped up in winter woollies, Olivia and Dylan on either side of Rachel and holding her hands. The mood was jubilant, and Rachel clasped it tight, painfully aware that happiness can be a fleeting thing.

The train arrived on time and they watched Dublin Bay whizz past them, the windows of their carriage becoming a frame for the spectacular Irish coastline. The afternoon sun was already beginning to set and the skies darkened; dusky pinks and inky blues danced side by side as they said hello to each other.

'We're lucky to live in such a beautiful part of the world,' Rachel said. 'I love looking at the ocean. It makes me feel so happy. What do you think, kids?'

'Me too,' Dylan said.

'You always agree with everything Mom says,' Olivia said, throwing her eyes upwards.

'But that's because I *do* agree,' Dylan insisted.

'I'm delighted you agree with me,' Rachel said calmly.

'And I'm going to let you both into a secret. It's comforting for me to think that the water that flows from Dublin Bay is part of the same water that flows into Hawke's Bay.'

'For real?' Dylan asked.

'I never knew that,' Olivia admitted.

'I only know because your daddy told me. One day, when we were walking along the Velvet Strand in Portmarnock, I was having a moment, I suppose, missing home and our beach there. Remember Cape Kidnappers beach near Nanny and Gramps's?' The kids nodded. 'Well, your daddy told me that all rivers, while they come in different shapes and sizes, all eventually run into the four oceans, and they in turn flow into the world's biggest ocean. So you see, we're all connected, no matter how far apart we are.'

Rachel watched the Velvet Strand change to the sandy promenade in Clontarf, thinking about the wonder of nature and the world they lived in. And then the windows hinted at a new world, saying goodbye to the ocean and hello to the city. They arrived with great excitement at Pearse railway station. The kids ran on, dragging Rachel by the arms to speed her up, past Trinity College, over O'Connell Bridge and on to Henry Street, with its Christmas garlands lighting up the cobbled thoroughfare. They arrived at Arnotts department store, where the real Santa hung out every festive season, absolutely giddy with anticipation. Despite queueing for a long time, there were plenty of activities to keep adults and kids alike entertained, and by the time they met Santa, posed for photographs and posted their letters to the North Pole, their excitement was at fever pitch.

They called into Dunne & Crescenzi on South Frederick Street for some tapas then, sleepy and satisfied, Rachel led the two tired children back to the train to return home to Malahide. They snuggled into either side of Rachel as the train rocked them both to sleep.

It had been a perfect day, Rachel thought as she held them both.

Over the past few months, she had become so caught up in the custody battle that she'd forgotten to enjoy the pleasures of simply being the children's mom. She made a vow to herself to make sure she always savoured moments like this one.

Rachel gently nudged the children awake a few minutes before reaching Malahide Station. They passed the Velvet Strand once more, but this time the horizon line where the sea and the sky met was blurred into one inky-blue, starlit vista.

'Look how pretty it is,' Rachel whispered to them both.

'Groups of stars are called conversations. We learned about it in school,' Olivia said sleepily.

Rachel hid a smile. 'That's right, sweetheart. Groups of stars in the sky are called *constellations*. If you look closely enough, you can see shapes in them.'

The three of them peeked out the window, searching.

'Why are some stars brighter than others?' Dylan asked.

'I know that! The stars that are closest to us, shine the brightest,' Olivia answered.

'You are a clever girl,' Rachel said, genuinely impressed with Olivia's knowledge. 'But I think there's another reason. Do you know that lots of people, including me, believe that when you die you become a star?'

She let the children think about that for a moment.

They looked at her and then at the sky again, unsure whether this was true.

'Your mammy and daddy in heaven are stars up in the sky, watching over us, shining their light upon us whenever we need it,' Rachel said, pointing upwards.

A sigh of wonder escaped both Olivia and Dylan.

'How do we know which of the stars are theirs?' Dylan asked, his nose almost touching the pane of glass, as he peered out the window.

'That's simple. You need to look for the stars above us that are the most twinkliest. Because when we miss someone in heaven, their star will always shine the brightest of all, so that we can find them when we need to.'

They looked up to scan the sky for the stars above Dublin Bay, and then Olivia called out, pointing northwards, 'Look, Dylan.'

Rachel followed her finger and sure enough, side by side, two stars illuminated the sky, brighter than the other clusters around them.

'That's Mammy and Daddy,' Olivia whispered, then she reached out and placed her hand on the window. Dylan clambered over Rachel's knees and did the same.

The train trundled into Malahide Station, and they jumped off on to the platform.

'Carry me, Mom,' Dylan asked, and Rachel scooped him up into her arms. He was long, tall for his age, but light, so she could still manage him. Olivia moved in close beside the two of them, and together, they looked upwards to the stars above the bay.

FORTY-SEVEN

Rachel

Malahide, Dublin

It felt like Christmas morning had arrived early, waking up knowing that in a few hours, Rachel would see her family. She'd never needed her parents more. Knowing that they would still be here for her last mediation session in early January gave her strength too. Rachel suspected that court was inevitable, but she didn't regret trying to avoid it. And if nothing else, both sides would have a better understanding of each other when they sat in front of a judge.

Rachel looked around the house now with a critical eye, pleased with what she saw. The house gleamed; she'd polished and cleaned it to perfection. And, to top it off, it was now decked and bedazzled with Christmas decorations. A tree sat in the corner of the family room, covered in twinkling fairy lights. Rachel defied anyone not to get excited about the festive season with two children in the house.

367

'Is it time yet?' Olivia asked, walking into the family room. Both she and Dylan had been ready to leave for the airport for hours, as impatient as Rachel was for everyone to arrive.

'Not long now,' Rachel promised.

'It's going to be the best Christmas ever, isn't it?' Dylan asked, joining them and jumping up and down.

'Yes, it is,' Rachel promised.

She thought Olivia looked a little pale.

'If anything is bothering you, anything at all, you can tell me, okay?' Rachel said to her, trying to read her face.

'I know,' Olivia replied, then walked out.

'Some girls were mean to her last night when we were on our walk with Thor,' Dylan said, matter-of-factly.

'Which girls?' Rachel asked.

'They live near Nana and Grandad. They stopped Olivia when we walked by them and whispered something to her. Olivia said it was nothing, but I think she was crying,' Dylan said.

'Thank you for telling me that,' Rachel said, ruffling his hair. Those bloody girls again. It appeared Rachel's instinct about them was correct. She was annoyed with herself that she'd allowed the mediation drama to distract her from this issue. She picked up her phone and immediately texted Sheila.

Hey Sheila. I have a feeling that something is going on with those Middleton sisters and Olivia. Can you make sure she stays away from them when she's at your house, please?

They are nice girls, Sheila responded.

Good to know. Humour me, please. I have an uneasy feeling. I'd rather keep them apart.

A minute or so passed, then Sheila came back to her.

Okay. We can walk along the estuary with Thor, so we're not passing their house.

An hour later, Rachel and the kids stood in the arrivals hall at Dublin Airport, which was aglow with festive cheer. A giant Santa Claus made Dylan literally whoop with excitement. Families walked through the double glass arrivals doors to be reunited with their loved ones, and Olivia and Dylan held up a large homemade banner every time the door opened. On their fourth attempt, Annie and Joe walked out, wearing matching Santa Claus hats and pushing their trolley in front of them. Rachel wasn't sure who squealed the most, but she suspected it might have been her. They all ran towards each other, and for a few moments it was a blur of hugs and tears as they all embraced.

Rachel felt someone tap her on the shoulder.

'Have you got one of those hugs for me, Sis?' Claudia said, pulling Rachel into her arms. Then the children moved in too, with Howard, Joe and Annie placing their arms around them all.

A woman who was also clutching a banner offered to take a photo. She snapped a shot of them all, arms entwined, tear-filled eyes, the kids in their grandparents' arms, Rachel in Claudia and Howard's. As Joe said afterwards, if you needed a visual explanation of what happiness was, you just needed to look at that photo.

Back at home, Rachel watched her family as they sat in her dining room and drank cups of strong tea and coffee, and couldn't quite believe that they were here.

'The house looks wonderful,' Annie said. 'I love your Christmas tree.' She walked over to admire the baubles, smiling as she took in the many handmade ones that the children had obviously crafted.

'We decorated it together. I put the star on top of the tree,' Olivia said.

'I had to get a chair for her. Last year, I lifted her, but she's getting too big for me!' Rachel said, pulling Olivia in for a hug.

'They've both grown inches since the summer. I can't keep up with them,' Annie said, laughing as Dylan measured himself against his grandad. 'I hope the bits we brought over fit them.'

'We're going to get another tree for the family room,' Dylan said. 'I'm going to choose it.'

'Two trees. Well, that's something,' Joe said.

'Let me know if you need a lie-down. I know the flight is long. Olivia's room is ready for Mom and Dad. Claudia and Howard, you have Dylan's room. He has bunk beds, but I've put a double blow-up mattress in there.'

'I can sleep on the sofa,' Howard offered.

'Yeah, that's about right,' Claudia said under her breath, moving away from him, in what looked like a pointed way.

Rachel hoped she was joking but couldn't miss the hurt look that Howard gave her.

She quickly said, 'The kids are forever coming into my room for sleepovers. They are delighted with the excuse to be in my bed for a few weeks.'

'Why don't we bring the bags up, Sis? We can leave

the kids to keep Mom, Dad and Howard entertained,' Claudia said.

They hauled up the bags between the two of them and placed them in each of the kids' bedrooms, then sat on the edge of Dylan's bed to take a breather.

'How are you? You look better, less pale than when I last saw you,' Rachel said.

'Getting there. I'm glad to be here, in a way. I've been a little melancholy back home, thinking I should be five months pregnant now. Being here will stop me over-thinking things.'

'And are you trying again?'

'Supposed to be. But . . . well, it's difficult.'

Rachel watched Claudia's face clouded with sadness and her heart ached for her.

'Are things okay with you and Howard?'

'As good as they can be, I suppose. We are trying to keep our sanity by not getting our hopes up. We've reduced our odds by fifty per cent, so . . .' She let the sentence hang.

'It's going to happen for you. I know it is.' But even as she spoke, Rachel knew her words sounded trite.

Claudia picked up a Buzz Lightyear cushion from Dylan's bed and hugged it close to her. 'I was sure last month that I was pregnant. I felt all the same symptoms I'd had when we were pregnant the first time – sore boobs, tired, nauseous. But then I got my period. I'm refusing to go down the testing route until I'm fairly sure it will be positive. I can't bear the thought of peeing and seeing a big fat negative. It might push me over the edge.' She threw the cushion back on to the bed. 'You know what, let's forget about all of that for now. It's too depressing, and I'm determined to have a great Christmas.'

Rachel zipped her mouth.

'Any further developments with the out-laws?' Claudia asked.

'We're all ever so polite when we see each other every evening for the dog walk. But other than those few moments of enforced chit-chat, we studiously avoid each other and all conversations about custody. I see Jack a good bit, though. He comes up a few times every week to see the kids.'

'Good man, Jack. And what about Christmas?'

'They know that I'm making a big dinner for all of us and the Bradleys. I don't intend to invite them, but they'll come down on Christmas morning, as normal.'

'If that old cow Sheila gives you any guff, send her my way.'

'Ah, she's not that bad,' Rachel said, surprising herself that she was defending the woman.

'Not that bad? She's made your life a living hell for years. Don't go all soft on her, Rae.'

'I'm not going soft . . . but today, I want to enjoy having you all here, so let's just not talk about it.'

Rachel threw a pillow towards Claudia, who picked up a fluffy cushion and threw it back. It was like old times back at home as teenagers – chatting, joking, keeping each other in line.

'Will Howard be okay on that?' Rachel frowned, looking down at the blow-up bed. It looked small. She couldn't imagine Howard's long frame sleeping on it.

'He'd sleep on a bed of nails. I promise you, five seconds after his head hits the pillow, he'll be out. But don't be surprised if you have a third guest for a sleepover in your room. If he starts snoring, I'm out of here.'

'I don't miss Lorcan's snoring. It's the only part of him that I didn't like.'

'I love the sound of my husband snoring, is something that no woman ever said. Last week, I woke up swearing I could hear the lawnmower going in the garden. Nope, just my beloved.'

When they went back downstairs, they found the kids snuggled between Joe and Annie on the couch, watching one of the Harry Potter movies. Howard was snoring on the chair beside them.

'Told you,' Claudia said as he put-put-putted in his sleep, and they were off again, laughing, giddy at their shared joke.

'Swap places with me,' Annie said to Claudia. 'I want to catch up with Rachel.'

'You can watch me prepare dinner,' Rachel said, pulling a chair up for Annie. 'You look good, Mom. I like your hair like that.' Annie normally wore her long brown hair, peppered with grey strands, in a messy low bun. But now it was loose, in soft waves around her face. She looked so like Claudia, whereas Rachel was more like Joe.

'I missed those kids. They give the best cuddles,' Annie said. 'When do they finish up school for the holidays?'

'One more week to go. Although if Olivia had her way, she'd never go back.'

'Things no better there?'

Rachel took in a deep breath, wishing she had more positive news to share. 'It's as if Olivia lost her lane since Lorcan died. She can't quite find her way back into a new one now.'

'It's an awkward age,' Annie said. 'I can do some positive affirmations with her this afternoon if you'd like?'

Rachel smiled, thinking about her childhood, which was filled with her mother's chants, all supposedly to make her feel better about life.

'I believe in me. I will always be on my side. Those are the two I remember the most. You made me say them every night before I went to sleep.'

'Well, it worked, didn't it?'

'I guess so,' Rachel replied.

'You don't sound so sure, love.'

'I had a nightmare a few days ago. I dreamt Fergal said that the children were better off with Sheila and Adrian. I saw them together, happily living their lives without me. Oh, Mom, it nearly finished me off.' Rachel shivered at the memory.

'That's your subconscious playing your worst fears. That's all. If there was any question about you being the kids' mother, then yes, maybe a question should be asked. But you were not Lorcan's girlfriend, a flash in the pan. You were his wife, the children's mother, for some time before he died. The Butlers are grieving, if you ask me – Sheila in particular. Her actions are not those of a sane woman. She's a woman in pain if ever I've seen one.'

Rachel couldn't disagree with that. 'Maybe you can try some of your affirmations out on her too.'

'Might not be a bad idea, you know,' Annie replied.

'What would you get her to say?' Rachel asked.

'I am not afraid,' Annie said, her voice soft as a caress. 'That's what's driving Sheila, I would imagine. Grief feels like fear to most people.'

'It feels like that to me too,' Rachel said.

From the moment she had opened the door to the two

Gardaí bringing the news of Lorcan's death, fear had been a predominant emotion in Rachel's headspace.

'So what's on the agenda for tomorrow?' Claudia asked, walking in to join them and disrupting their sombre mood. Rachel was grateful. She didn't want her entire time with her family to be spent talking about the Butlers.

'Well, tomorrow Belinda and Oscar are due to arrive from Belfast. Once they've checked into their hotel, they are coming up here for a light lunch. And then . . .' Rachel paused, 'we're going to a dinner dance for a charity that Jack works with. I got us all tickets as a fun surprise. I thought we could do with a bit of light relief.' Annie and Claudia grinned at the idea, and Claudia began dancing round the kitchen table, pulling Rachel into a waltz with her.

Then she stopped suddenly, saying, 'What will I wear?'

'I've thought of that,' Rachel replied. 'I have a couple of dresses you can borrow, samples from Rae's Closet. And I've arranged for Dad and Howard to rent tuxedos in a local hire shop tomorrow. They just need to go down and get measured.'

'I must have a sixth sense; I packed a dress in case we ended up anywhere fancy!' Annie said.

Seeing their reaction, Rachel was pleased she had eventually given in to Jack's sales pitch. He was always so helpful to her and she knew how much it mattered to him that she went, so she thought she owed him that much. As she watched Claudia twirl her mother around the kitchen now, she thought about how, no matter how much she didn't want to see the Butlers, she couldn't wait to have a night out with her family. And at least no one could say she wasn't trying.

FORTY-EIGHT

Rachel

The Grand Hotel, Malahide

The children sat cross-legged on Rachel's bed, watching her apply one last slick of lip gloss. She took two steps back to take a look at herself from head to toe. She couldn't remember the last time she'd gotten this dressed up. Her style was normally relatively informal, so putting on a full-length silver gown in itself was a big deal, never mind the chance to go to a black-tie event. She began to feel bubbles of excitement fizz their way up inside her, a feeling she'd not had for a long time.

Claudia had been right all those months ago in New Zealand: it was time that she began to start living again. Lorcan may be gone, but Rachel was alive, and right now, with her whole family around her, that felt damn good. She turned to face the children and did an elaborate twirl for them, while they both clapped loudly.

'You look like the fairy from the Christmas tree,' Dylan declared.

'I think you look perfect, Mom,' Olivia sighed. 'I wish I had a dress like that.'

'Well, one day, when you are a big girl, you can borrow this any time you like.'

'Promise me.'

'I pinky promise you.' Rachel held out her little finger to make the vow unbreakable.

'Can I wear it one day too, Mom?' Dylan asked.

'You can't wear that. It's for a girl,' Olivia said, giggling.

'Ah, but lots of boys wear skirts and dresses, the same way we gals wear trousers,' Rachel patiently explained.

'In Scotland, men wear kilts all the time. Uncle Jack told me that,' Dylan said. 'I would like a kilt one day. The triplets in *Brave* all had them, remember? Can I ask Santa for one?' He jumped up and began swinging an imaginary sword.

'You've already sent your letter to Santa. I think it's too late to change that now,' Rachel said, panicking slightly at the thought. 'And now I need to get a move on. Danielle will be here in a minute to look after you. Remember what we agreed: you can watch one hour of TV, then it's straight to bed.'

'I can't wait to see what Aunty Claudia is wearing. I bet it's even more sparkly than your dress,' Olivia said, running out of the room with Dylan hot on her heels.

Rachel grabbed her jacket and clutch bag, then followed the kids downstairs. Olivia wasn't far wrong about her aunty's dress. Claudia was wearing a pink and gold sequinned fitted dress that cast light beams all over the kitchen ceiling as she moved. Annie wore an emerald-green

Fifties party dress, complete with a black netting under-skirt, and Howard and Joe both looked great in traditional black tuxedo suits.

'I'm telling you, we're a good-looking family. Just look at us,' Joe said. He was beaming with pride. 'And your mom is wearing a dress she wore in 1985. Imagine that. She's got the same figure today that she had back then.'

'You're making me blush,' Annie said, clearly delighted with the compliment, swirling her underskirt for them all.

'I swear, if I can just fit into my dress once I've eaten anything tonight, I'll be gobsmacked!' Claudia said with a laugh. 'There's not much room in this, I can tell you.'

Everyone laughed along with Claudia, but Rachel noticed Howard didn't join in, instead frowning as he watched his partner twirl.

Danielle arrived then, gathering the kids on the sofa, asking them all about their week in school and promising bedtime stories. She was such a pro; she always knew to distract the kids so Rachel could leave with minimal fuss. She had babysat for them for years, as a teenager herself and now for extra cash while she was in university.

As they drove through Malahide village, Rachel felt a swell of pride for her hometown, which looked Christmas-card pretty. Every shop front twinkled with fairy lights while overhead hanging lights in bright reds, greens and golds lit up the street with festive cheer. Her favourite part was the rows of trees that lined the road, standing to attention, each with their own set of sparkling fairy lights.

'All we are missing is snowflakes, then I'd start to believe we'd fallen into a Hallmark movie set,' Annie said, gazing up at the lights around her.

'I can see why you love it here, Rachel, it's a gorgeous village,' Joe said.

'It's not Napier, but I'll give Malahide this: it's not a bad substitute,' Claudia agreed reluctantly.

A full moon hung low over the Irish Sea in the bay to their left as they drove through the gated entrance of the Grand Hotel, and the stars shone brightly over Dublin Bay.

'Well, that hotel certainly earns its name. It *is* grand,' Joe said, taking in the stately hotel, with black pillars flanking the ornate entranceway.

'Oh gosh, you should see the sunset from here as well. On date nights, Lorcan and I often came here for a drink. It's spectacular watching the sun go down over the water,' Rachel said, her mind a blur of happy memories of sitting at the water's edge with Lorc.

The car fell silent, and Rachel had a familiar, sinking feeling. Would she ever be able to remember Lorcan out loud without making everyone uncomfortable? She liked to talk about him and their life together, but when she did, her family – and most people, in fact – weren't sure how to respond, afraid that she might burst into tears at the mere mention of his name. She changed the subject quickly, determined that nothing would mar the evening's lovely atmosphere.

'Here are some pieces of useless information for you all about the Grand Hotel,' she said instead. 'In the First World War, this hotel was taken over by the British Army so that they were ready for a German invasion. Oh, and it was once painted completely in pink, in honour of the old owner's favourite drink – pink champagne!'

'Well, I suppose we should be grateful his favourite

drink wasn't absinthe! I'm not sure bright green would have been quite as inviting,' Joe said, making them all laugh.

Rachel parked up and they all made their way into the large lobby. The concierge directed them to the Tara Suite, where the event was taking place. A large table planner showed them where to sit and, as they walked over, Rachel made a small wish to herself that everyone would get on tonight.

Sheila, Adrian and Jack were already at the table, and no sooner had Rachel and her gang said their hellos and sat down, than Belinda and Oscar walked in. Annie and Joe waved at them enthusiastically. They'd had a warm and happy catch-up earlier today at lunch, cementing the budding friendship they'd started at Rachel and Lorcan's wedding.

Claudia elbowed Rachel as Sheila and Belinda eyed each other up from across the room. As the new pair reached the table, Rachel and Claudia watched while the two women leaned in for a theatrical air kiss.

'That colour suits you, Sheila. What a beautiful dress,' Belinda said coolly.

Rachel couldn't help but agree. Sheila was wearing a mulberry fitted sheath dress with pearls, and admittedly looked lovely.

Sheila responded in turn, examining Belinda's mid-length, dusky pink chiffon dress, before declaring, 'And that shade of pink is one I would usually associate with a much younger person, but you can just about pull it off.'

'Thank *you*,' Belinda said.

They all retook their seats and Jack offered them wine. As the room filled up, sounds of laughter and merriment buzzed around them, but their table remained awkward and ill at ease with each other. Rachel felt as if they were two distinct groups who happened to be sitting together by mistake. It reminded her of her honeymoon cruise with Lorcan; each night they'd sit with strangers at dinner, politely making conversation, while wishing they could be at a table for two instead.

When the waitress came over to their table to take their food orders, the mood warmed slightly, everyone discussing which options were best.

As everyone chatted around them, Jack looked at the empty seat beside Belinda and leaned over Rachel to ask whether Ronan was still coming.

Secretly, Rachel wanted to know the answer to this question too. Belinda had asked for a third ticket for him when Rachel had invited them to the dance, and Rachel had been looking forward to spending time with him, away from the mediation meeting room.

'He was in court today and is running late, but he assures me he'll be here. I wonder should we order for him?' Oscar turned to Belinda, directing this question at her.

'Did someone mention my name?' Ronan said. Everyone glanced up, most of the group looking delighted.

'You always knew how to make an entrance,' Belinda said, accepting a kiss on her cheek.

'Don't you look pretty in pink? I'll have the soup, then the turkey and ham,' Ronan said.

'You didn't even look at the menu!' Rachel said.

'No need. A dinner dance at Christmas, it has to be turkey and soup. It's a by-law in Ireland.'

The waitress giggled, clearly charmed by Ronan.

'He brushes up well,' Claudia whispered to Rachel, who had to agree with her.

'Now, what have I missed? Who's flirting with who, is anyone drunk on bubbles yet, and if not, why not?'

'He's fun, too,' Claudia whispered again. She was right; Ronan's addition to the table had changed the atmosphere already. His cheeky charm made everyone loosen up a little and, coupled with the wine and the Christmas songs belting out of the speakers, it began to feel like a party. While they waited for their food to arrive, the MC announced that envelopes would be passed around to each table so that everyone could make their bids for the items in the silent auction. Prizes ranged from holidays in Spain to a smart TV, as well as the obligatory whiskey bottles and chocolates. Every item was displayed on a continuous loop on a large white screen in front of the stage.

'I've got my eye on that TV, so hands off everyone!' Rachel said, waving her pen in the air. She scribbled €200 down on the auction slip, the most she could justify.

'I fancy that holiday in Spain,' Sheila said. 'Put an offer on that one too,' she instructed Adrian.

'Way ahead of you. I could do with some sunshine on my old bones.'

Rachel felt herself relaxing with every sip. So far, people were behaving themselves. Claudia, however, was perhaps a little too relaxed. She had drunk an entire bottle of white on her own and it was showing. Rachel noticed Howard watching Claudia with concern. Grief made you crazy – proper losing your mind, nut-job crazy – and Rachel recognized the look in her sister's eyes, having been there herself in the not-too-distant past. She made a mental note to take Claudia out for a walk tomorrow, just the two of them, so that they could talk. Then she filled her sister's water glass up again.

'What do I want water for, silly? We're having a party!' Claudia said, her words now slurring a little.

'I've got this,' Howard mouthed to Rachel, which reassured her a little. Between the both of them, they'd make sure that Claudia was okay.

FORTY-NINE

Rachel

The Grand Hotel, Malahide

After dinner, the MC announced the silent auction winners, the running total updating on a big screen behind him. When it came to the TV, Rachel sat up and crossed her fingers. 'Come on, universe.'

The MC shouted, 'Well, this item proved to be popular. We had bids ranging from fifty euros – come on – to the thousands!'

'Well, that's me out then!' Rachel said to the table, then laughed. 'I bid two hundred.'

'The winning bid was for two thousand euros!' the MC shouted. 'Our winner has asked to remain anonymous but has said they are donating the prize to a Rachel Bradley on table nine.'

Everyone started to whoop, and Rachel felt her cheeks flush with shock.

'Oh my goodness, who would do that?' she asked. She turned to her parents, her brow creasing. 'Mom, Dad?'

'Sorry, love, that's too rich for us! I put all our money on the iPad.'

Rachel saw Oscar whisper something to Belinda and immediately guessed it was them. They were so generous; she should have known they'd do that.

'Thank you,' she said warmly.

'No idea what you're talking about,' Belinda said, with a big grin.

'It's too much, but oh my goodness, I cannot wait to set that up!' Rachel said.

'It's the very least you deserve. And for an amazing charity, so we are happy to support. Now enjoy the evening,' Oscar said.

A few months ago she would have found the gesture too extravagant, but now, knowing them as she did, she recognized it for what it was – a genuine and loving gift, from two people who cared about her.

Rachel and Claudia squealed with delight when an Abba tribute band came on to the stage wearing Seventies white jumpsuits. As they began belting out 'Waterloo', the atmosphere in the room became charged. And by the time they started their second song, 'Dancing Queen', the dance floor was packed.

Claudia pulled Rachel to her feet. 'You and me, shaking our booty, now!'

They ran to the dance floor, holding hands and giggling like their younger selves. As Rachel began to lose herself in the beat of the music, she felt more alive than she had for the longest time. Her heart rate accelerated and she felt happiness rush over her as she and Claudia both threw their bodies about, queens of the dance floor. Then Ronan arrived on the dance floor, with Annie close behind.

'You look like you're having fun,' Ronan shouted.

She responded by grabbing his hand and letting him twirl her around. Then she turned to her mom and threw her arms around her too, hugging her close.

'I'm so happy you're here.'

'Me too, my love, me too!'

By the time the song ended, most of their party had joined them, and everyone had matching smiles on their faces. Sheila and Adrian were even doing a decent jive. Belinda and Oscar had moves too, Rachel realized, watching them twirl around the dance floor. A few songs later, she noticed Jack was sitting on his own at the table. She went over to ask him to join in.

'I can't dance,' he said plainly.

'I'll help you.' Rachel grabbed his hand and led him to the dance floor. Holding his hands, she half waltzed, half jived him about, the two of them laughing hysterically at their crazy made-up dance.

If the night had ended at that moment, it would have been perfect. Rachel would have gone home, smiling, happy with a bundle of new memories made.

But life was too messy for that.

Suddenly, Howard stopped dancing. He looked at Claudia, who was shimmying and twerking in front of Ronan, possibly a little too suggestively with her hips.

'She's letting her hair down, that's all,' Rachel shouted into Howard's ear, desperate to smooth things over.

'She's been doing that a lot lately,' he said, his face stony.

'Come on, let's grab a drink,' Rachel thought it was better to remove him from the scene of the crime. She felt uneasy. Back at their table, she filled up their glasses with pinot noir.

He raised his glass to her, but his eyes never left the dance floor, where Claudia was now laughing hysterically at something Ronan had said to her.

'What's going on with you two?' Rachel asked.

'You tell me. Because you have a better chance at getting her to open up than I ever do.'

'You've been through a lot this year. That takes a toll.'

'For sure. I'm worried about her, though. She's been drinking a lot. Most nights she goes to bed wasted.'

'That's not like Claudia,' Rachel said, frowning. They both enjoyed their nights out, always had, but they weren't big drinkers. But then she thought about last night, when she'd noticed Claudia drinking several large gins.

'I know why she's doing it. I get it. But the problem is that when she wakes up every day, she doesn't just have a hangover; she also has her grief to grapple with,' Howard said.

'I knew she was struggling, but I didn't realize it was that bad. I'm so sorry.' Rachel eased her feet out of their heels and leaned back in her chair. 'But I know my sis, she's strong. She'll find her way through this. Just don't give up on her.'

'I love her. I'm not going anywhere. But she's going to have to let me in at some point. I think she's forgotten that she's not the only one grieving,' Howard said bitterly.

'And what about you, then? How are you doing?' Rachel asked gently.

'I'm lonely. I thought that was an emotion reserved for people who lived on their own. Who knew?' He studied his nails, a flush on his face at his admission.

Rachel reached over and clasped his hand for a moment. 'I understand that one. You'll get through this. I know you will. You two are amazing together, and you'll find a way back together, I know it.'

The tempo slowed down, and the rest of their gang returned to the table, sweat glistening on everyone's face from the dancing. Everyone except Belinda, who looked as impeccable as she'd done when she'd first arrived in the room.

'How do you do that?' Rachel asked her. 'You always look so good.'

'Botox,' Belinda whispered back. 'It blocks the nerve signals that make you sweat. Trust me, dear, diamonds used to be a girl's best friend, but then came Botox and fillers. Next time you visit, I'll bring you to my guy. My treat.'

'You are a wonder – you do know that?' Rachel said truthfully, bowing to her.

'I do try,' Belinda said with a wink. 'It's good to see you having fun.'

'I love to dance. Always have done.'

'Who's up for a shot?' Claudia interrupted them by shouting, leaning on the back of the chair.

'I think you've had enough,' Howard said.

'Don't be such a bore,' Claudia answered, making a face. 'Isn't he a bore, everyone?'

'I tell you what; I'll stop being such a bore if you start acting like my partner again,' Howard said. The table fell silent.

'She didn't mean that,' Annie said, horror written all over her face.

'I can talk for myself,' Claudia replied, but she didn't

look so sure any more. She looked like she might burst into tears.

Rachel grabbed her hand and whispered, 'Come to the bathroom with me. Now!'

Once they were in the quiet of the ladies, Claudia turned to look at Rachel intently. 'I was having some fun. Is that so bad?' she asked.

Rachel checked to make sure they were on their own, before replying, 'Fun is always good. You seemed to be hitting the drinks a little too hard. And you were a bit full-on there with Howard. Calling him a bore in front of everyone wasn't fair.'

Claudia's eyes met Rachel's in the mirror. 'He was pretty angry, wasn't he?' She put her face in her hands, sobering up as she thought about her actions.

'Yep, and I don't blame him. I think you and he need to have an honest conversation. He's hurting too, Claudia. And if you don't open up with each other, you'll not survive this.'

'Maybe I don't want to survive this.' Claudia's eyes filled with tears and she dropped her head so her hair fell over her face.

'Yes, you do. You just don't love the situation you're in right now, but it will change.'

'Everywhere I look, I see pregnant women. Cradling their bumps tenderly. And I feel so jealous. It takes over everything. Today, when we went for a walk in Malahide Castle with the kids, I swear, we met twelve pregnant women. *Twelve*. I counted.'

Rachel thought about the times she'd watched couples holding hands and how it made her feel. 'You know, one day I was in Tesco, doing the weekly grocery shop, when

I saw a couple arguing playfully about which melon they should buy. I felt a fit of rage and I swear I picked up a cantaloupe and very nearly threw it at them. I mean, well for them, that they had each other to argue with.' As soon as she said it, Rachel realized how ludicrous the story was.

The look of shock on Claudia's face made Rachel giggle, before quickly reassuring her, 'I didn't throw it!'

Claudia began to laugh, joining in with Rachel, and the two of them clung to each other as the laughter took hold.

'I'll never look at a melon again without thinking about you,' Claudia said.

Rachel stopped laughing and returned to the matter at hand. 'You'll get through this,' she told Claudia firmly. 'I know I keep saying it, but that's because it's true. I would know.'

'You are so annoying when you are right,' Claudia said, hitting Rachel on her arm.

'And maybe ease off on the sexy dancing with Ronan too.'

'Oh God, I'm mortified. I was all over him, wasn't I?'

'Let's just say I've not seen twerking like that in a long time.'

'Did Howard see that too?'

'He did.'

'No wonder he called me out about my behaviour.'

'He'll get over it. He loves you. But like I said, maybe slow down on the drink.'

'I wanted to forget for a while. That's all.' Claudia closed her eyes for a moment.

'I get it. And so does Howard. All I'm suggesting is that

you party *with* Howard, as opposed to without him. I think he might need a night off too.'

'Did everyone hear our row?' Claudia asked.

'I'm afraid so.'

'I'll look forward to a little lecture from Mom and Dad tomorrow about the evils of binge drinking,' Claudia said.

'Nip it in the bud. Tell them you know you were wrong before they decide to rant at you,' Rachel advised. She'd been there too many times before.

The door opened, and Rachel recognized Jack's friend, Lydia. She smiled and said hello. Lydia acknowledged the greeting with a slight inclination of her head, but she didn't return the smile and threw a look at Rachel that was anything but warm. Claudia gave her another dig on her arm. She'd have a bruise soon if Claudia didn't find a new spot to hit her. Lydia walked into one of the toilet cubicles, clearly not interested in chatting.

'What's up with her?' Claudia whispered.

'No idea. She's a friend of Jack's. Maybe she didn't recognize me.'

'In fairness, you are quite forgettable,' Claudia teased as she reapplied make-up.

'Cheek. Once met, you never forget. Ha! I'm a poet. Now give me some of that lippy and re-do that smudged mascara,' Rachel said.

After repairing the damage of the warm dance floor, they both washed their hands, ready to leave. At the same time, Lydia walked out of her cubicle and washed her hands beside them.

Rachel decided to try one more time. She made sure she was facing Lydia, so she could read her lips, and said, 'I'm Rachel. I met you with Jack a couple of times.'

Lydia grabbed a towel and dried her hands, 'I know who you are.'

'Ouch!' Claudia said under her breath. Rachel shot her a look that said, 'Not now!'

'Lydia, are you okay? Have I upset you in any way?' Rachel asked.

'It's not fair to lead someone on,' Lydia said, standing still by the sinks.

'Hey, I was dancing. Lighten up,' Claudia said, her voice defensive.

'I think she means me,' Rachel said carefully, unsure what Lydia could be referring to. 'But I'm not sure I understand why.'

'If you are not interested in Jack, the least you could do is tell him.'

'What on earth are you talking about?' Claudia was confused too. 'Is there something going on with you and Jack?'

'No! He's like my brother, for goodness' sake,' Rachel replied hurriedly, keen to squash all potential rumours.

'Are you sure he knows that?' Lydia asked. Before even waiting for an answer, she turned on her heel and walked out.

'Woah, that girl does *not* like you,' Claudia said. 'And what the hell is she banging on about Jack for?'

'I swear I have no clue. She's barking up the wrong tree anyhow. He already told me he's into some other girl.'

'She needs to lighten up. Jeez. Some attitude on that. Come on, I better go out and eat some humble pie with my man.'

They made their way back to the table, passing Adrian and Sheila, who were back jiving on the dance floor. Annie and Joe were chatting with Oscar, who had his arm around Belinda's back, gently caressing her shoulder. It was such a tender gesture, it brought a lump to Rachel's throat.

All three older couples had shared a lifetime and still so obviously loved each other. That was something.

Rachel pushed aside an imaginary version of Lorcan and her, in their sixties, also dancing in each other's arms. But she couldn't let herself go down that route, not here.

She sank back into her seat, ready to relax and enjoy the rest of the night. But on the other side of the table, a heated discussion between Howard, Ronan and Jack, who were all standing up, was gaining volume. Hadn't they had enough drama for one night?

'What's going on?' Claudia asked, hurrying up behind them, with Rachel close behind her.

'Ask your boyfriend,' Ronan said, holding his hands up.

'I'm not going to sit back and watch someone flirt with you, Claudia. I might be boring, but I'm not a fool.' Howard crossed his arms.

'Oh baby, you are not boring. And I'm so sorry I made you feel like you had to do this. I wanted to let off steam, that's all,' Claudia said, trying to rest a hand on his arm.

Howard shrugged it off and pointed to Ronan, 'Just keep away.'

'I didn't do anything, mate. I've no interest in anyone else's woman.'

'Bullshit,' Jack interrupted. Then, to everyone's shock, he shoved Ronan hard in the chest, enough to make him stumble backwards. While Jack was several inches shorter than Ronan's six-foot frame, he enjoyed the gym and could pack a punch. His blond hair seemed to stand up on end.

'What has gotten into everyone tonight?' Ronan shouted, grabbing a chair to stop himself falling.

People began to stare, aware that something was going on. Jack's face had turned scarlet. Rachel grabbed his arm, telling him to calm down.

'We're going for a walk, Jack,' she said, leading him away from the table. 'Ronan, you sit down and have a drink with Belinda and Oscar.'

Rachel led Jack to the lobby and found a free table in the corner. They sat down, and she gave him a moment to calm down. His breathing was ragged; he was clearly upset.

'What was all that about?'

He shrugged and made a face.

'You look just like Dylan does when he throws his toys out of the pram,' she said, trying to lighten the mood.

'Ronan winds me up.'

'That's obvious. But what I'd like to know is, why?' She kicked off her heels again and tucked her legs up under her on the soft chaise. She felt like she'd had to do a bit too much counselling tonight, especially for what was supposed to be her first proper big night out.

'I just don't like him,' Jack said, but that didn't tell her anything she didn't already know.

'You need to give me a little more here.'

'It's a feeling. He struts around the place like a cockerel,' Jack said, puffing his chest out.

'Ronan is lovely when you get to know him,' Rachel said. 'You might like him if you just gave him a chance.'

'That's not happening any time soon.'

'If this is about Claudia, it was her who was flirting with Ronan, not the other way around.'

'Maybe. But he didn't have to take it. A real man would've walked away.'

Rachel sighed, clearly fighting a losing battle. These Butlers weren't great at backing down. That was something she knew all too well already.

'There must be something in the wine tonight,' she said, instead. 'Your friend Lydia had a go at me earlier too.'

Jack's face blanched. 'What did she say?'

'She accused me of leading you on! Said I should put you right.' Rachel laughed at the absurdity of it, waving to signal to a waiter for some water, or possibly a strong coffee. 'I told you she had the hots for you, Jack. But you need to let her know how you feel. Tell her about this woman you are into, so she's not wasting her time.'

Jack closed his eyes for a moment and took a deep breath, then muttered, 'Fuck it.'

Then he leaned forwards and kissed Rachel on the mouth.

FIFTY

Rachel

The Grand Hotel, Malahide

The last person to kiss Rachel was her husband. And she was ill-prepared for anyone else to kiss her, least of all Jack. She was so shocked at first she didn't move. She neither reciprocated nor moved away, simply sat in a stunned, statue-like silence until he pulled away.

'So now you know,' Jack said.

What did she know? Had she fallen into an Alice-type rabbit hole? Her mind began to run through all the conversations she'd had with Jack about his mystery girl.

And then she got it.

'Oh God, Jack, I'm such an idiot.'

'My mystery woman.'

Rachel tried to find words to say, anything at all to make this moment less awful than it was.

Jack looked at her, and then he whispered, 'It's always been you, Rachel. I love you.'

She felt dizzy. How had she not seen this coming? His admission hung in the air between them as the ballroom doors burst open and a group of party-goers danced the conga out into the lobby while the band played 'Take A Chance on Me'. The universe had a pretty mean sense of humour.

Rachel looked at this man in front of her – a man whose company she liked more than most in this world. His curly hair, damp from dancing and the heat of the ballroom, made soft tendrils around his face. And his eyes, chocolate-brown pools, were kind and trustworthy. She saw all of that. And she saw his soul too, the very essence of a good man. And she wished with all her heart that she could find a part of her, any part, that fancied him.

'I think I fell in love with you the moment Lorcan brought you home. I didn't realize it at the time, or at least didn't want to admit it to myself. But since he died, I've not been able to deny how I feel. Spending time with you is my favourite time of any day.'

'Oh, Jack.'

Could she learn to love him in the same way he loved her?

'Choosing between confessing my feelings for you or staying in the friend zone has been all I've thought about for months. But I can't hide how I feel any more. Even if it means losing you as a friend, at least I'll know that I've been truthful and tried.'

And that's when Rachel realized she could never fake anything with this man. Jack had been so brave, telling her how he felt. He deserved the same honesty from her.

'You'll never lose me, Jack. And telling someone you love them is always a good thing. Thank you so much for trusting me with that.' She took a steadying breath and reached over to clasp Jack's hands between her own. Her answer was clear in her mind. 'I love you too, Jack . . . but not in the way you want me to.'

The hardest part of her admission was the look of resigned acceptance on Jack's face. He'd expected her to say as much.

'I'm so sorry,' she whispered, and she meant it with every part of her.

'I know you are. But you don't have anything to be sorry about,' he said gruffly. 'We can't help who we love.'

'No, we can't.'

'I have to ask, though. If you didn't love Lorcan, would I have had a chance?'

Rachel cared too much for Jack to use her dead husband as an excuse, tempting as it was.

'The truth is I am still in love with Lorcan, and I'm not ready to move on from our marriage yet. But I know that whenever that time comes, I'll still see you as my brother. Nothing more.'

'I kinda knew that too. I saw how you looked at Lorcan, and you've never looked at me that way.'

Jack crossed his arms across his chest and they sat in awkward silence. Rachel didn't know if she should remove herself, but she couldn't leave things like this.

'Are we okay?' she asked. 'I don't want to lose you.'

'Loving someone who doesn't love you back sucks. But I don't regret telling you. Maybe saying it out loud will help me get over you. I might need a little time, but you'll never lose me. Can you promise me one thing, though?'

'Of course.'

'Don't end up with that asshole Ronan. Please.'

'He's not interested in me.' *Was he?*

'You'll see,' Jack said. His tone was stern, but he didn't seem to want to expand. 'We'd better go back in to make sure Howard has calmed down. I feel bad, actually. I kind of egged him on.'

They walked back to the ballroom and Rachel was relieved to see peace reigned. Claudia and Howard were kissing like teenagers at their first school disco. Ronan was telling a story to Oscar and Belinda that had the pair of them in stitches. But both sets of parents were watching for them, clearly worried about the row. Jack sat down beside Sheila and Adrian to reassure them he was okay. Rachel joined Annie and Joe.

'Never a dull moment,' she said.

'Is he okay again?' Joe asked. 'I've never seen him so agitated; he's usually such a pleasant fella.'

'Ah, love can make you do strange things,' Annie said, laughing when she saw the shocked expression on Rachel's face. 'Don't look so surprised! I saw the way he's been looking at you.'

'Well, I wish you'd given me a warning, Mom!'

'Did you at least let him down gently?' Annie asked.

Rachel hoped she had. She wouldn't ever want to hurt Jack; he was too important for her. The music changed as the band slowed things down. As they began to sing 'Fernando', couples began to make their way to the dance floor. Sheila and Adrian, Belinda and Oscar, Claudia and Howard, until it was just Rachel, Jack and Ronan left. Rachel thought about excusing herself and heading to the bathroom, but she was half afraid the lads would start fighting again if she left them on their own. She grabbed her mobile from her purse instead and decided to bury her head looking at photos to avoid talking to either of them.

Ronan called over to her, 'Take pity on this single dude and dance with me, Rachel!'

She glanced at Jack and he looked at her as if to say, I told you so.

And then all other thoughts left her mind. Her mobile phone vibrated in her hand with a new text message, from Danielle:

Call me Rachel. Dylan's been in an accident.

FIFTY-ONE

Rachel

The Grand Hotel, Malahide

Rachel called Danielle as she ran out of the noisy ball-room, dread sobering her up instantly.

'I'm so sorry, I'm so sorry,' Danielle was babbling already when she picked up the phone.

'Calm down and tell me what's going on,' Rachel replied in a voice that belied the panic that she felt inside. She leaned against a pillar in the lobby for support, straining to hear what Danielle was saying.

'Dylan fell out of your office window and banged his head I didn't know what to do so I called an ambulance and we're on our way to Beaumont Hospital.' This was delivered in one fast sentence.

The hysteria in Danielle's voice helped to calm Rachel down. One of them needed to take control. She went into super mom mode, ready to move boulders to keep her children safe.

'It's okay, Danielle. You did the right thing. Is he . . . conscious?' Rachel's nails cut into her palm as she waited for an answer.

'He's a little sleepy, but the paramedics are talking to him, keeping him awake.'

'That's good. Now, where's Olivia?'

Please God let the girl have had the sense not to have left Olivia on her own.

'With Mrs McSweeney next door.'

'Good. You've done all the right things. Now, Danielle, I need you to be strong.' She forced her voice to sound authoritative. 'Stop crying and tell Dylan that Mom is coming, that she's on her way to meet him at the hospital. Make sure he knows I'll be there very soon. I'll meet you in Beaumont . . .' she looked at her watch, 'by eleven p.m. Call me if anything changes.'

Rachel hung up, then turned to Ronan and Jack who had followed her outside, their faces both mirrors of worry. She filled them in on the little she knew.

'What can we do?' Ronan asked, ever practical. He rolled the sleeves up on his shirt, as if he was getting ready to fight.

Fight, Dylan, fight for your mom and your family. We need you to be okay.

Jack handed Rachel a tissue for the tears she wasn't even aware she was crying. 'Once a boy scout,' he said, then pulled her into him for a hug.

She only allowed herself to stay there for the briefest of moments before she pulled away. 'Can you both let everyone know what's happened? Send Claudia and

Howard home in a taxi ASAP to collect Olivia from the neighbour's. She's going to be very distressed. I'll let you know how Dylan is as soon as I can.' Rachel picked up her purse and ran for the exit.

'Wait! I'm going with you,' Jack called out. 'Can you take care of the family?' he asked Ronan. And for once, the men were in agreement, Ronan nodding and running back to the ballroom.

They were in luck; a taxi sat directly outside the lobby entrance. The journey itself felt endless though, despite the taxi driver breaking every law possible to get them to the hospital in record time. All the while, Rachel kept saying a mantra over and over in her head.

Dylan will be fine. Dylan will be fine. Dylan will be fine.

When they arrived at the hospital, they scanned the information board for directions to A&E. Jack found the sign first and grabbed Rachel's hand, pulling her in the right direction. Together they raced down the corridor, dodging the stretchers and wheelchairs that lined the edge of the tiled floor. They found Danielle pacing the A&E reception area, waiting for them. Her face was white as a sheet, her brow furrowed in deep anxiety.

'He's in there with a nurse. They said you should go in when you arrive.' Danielle pointed straight away to a triage room. Leaving Jack with Danielle, Rachel found a nurse who led her towards a blue curtained cubicle. With no idea what would meet her on the other side she took a deep breath, vowing to hold it together for her boy, no matter what.

'Dylan, sweetheart, Mom is here,' Rachel said, running towards him. He started to weep as soon as he saw her and, for a moment, they clung to each other as sobs racked his body. He felt so thin and small in her arms, as if the fall had somehow diminished him. She was so relieved to see him awake and conscious, for a moment she barely noticed the bloodied gash on his head.

'What did you do, sweetheart?'

'I fell out of the window of your clothes room,' Dylan said, his voice weak and thin.

Rachel could not begin to understand how that had happened. What was he doing in her Rae's Closet room?

The curtain moved back and the nurse returned with a doctor.

'I hear we have a brave little boy here. I'm Doctor Javapour. You can call me Javvy,' he said to Dylan.

'There's no braver boy than my Dylan. How is he?' Rachel asked, stroking Dylan's arm gently in the way that he loved.

'That's what I'm here to find out. Now, Dylan, tell me, were you trying to be superman?'

This made Dylan giggle. The doctor began a series of neurological exams, checking his vision, reflexes, balance.

'Do you know how high the fall was from?' the doctor directed this question at Rachel.

'Maybe four feet? He said he was in our sitting room, which is downstairs. I use that room as my office.'

'That's good. You gave your head quite a bang when you fell.' He'd turned back to Dylan now.

'It hurts,' Dylan said.

'I bet it does, buddy. But we'll get that all sorted soon, don't you worry.' He turned to Rachel and said, 'He's lost a lot of blood and has a possible concussion. We'll send him for an MRI scan shortly, then we'll see what's what. But early signs look good; try not to worry.'

Rachel's face must have shown that she was doing the exact opposite as the word 'scan' sent her into a panic. She moved closer to Dylan, putting her arms around him.

Doctor Javapour said reassuringly, 'Childhood head trauma is rarely more serious than a concussion, and let's all be grateful that Dylan didn't jump from a second floor. We might have some broken bones to contend with then.' He turned to the nurse and gave her some instructions as he wrote on Dylan's chart.

'I'm tired, Mom,' Dylan said.

Rachel scooped him into her arms and held him close. So many questions ran around her head, but they would have to wait for now. Once Dylan was okay, there would be time enough to work out why he hadn't been in bed. She grabbed her phone and quickly sent a text to Claudia.

Is Olivia okay? Can't call yet.

Claudia responded straight away:

Fine. Concentrate on our boy. Sending you both so much love. Call me when you can. x

That was one less thing to worry about. Rachel knew that Olivia was in good hands with Claudia and Howard. Time seemed to move at half beats as they waited for the scan. And with every passing minute, Rachel's fears for Dylan intensified. He was so sleepy, but she was terrified that if he went to sleep he wouldn't wake up again. To keep him awake, she told him stories about when he was a baby. The children were always fascinated by tales like these, and one of Dylan's favourites was a story of him peeing on her, so she began with that.

By the time an orderly with a bright smile arrived to take them for the scan an hour later, Rachel's nerves were raw. But she could not have been more proud of her little boy; he did everything he was asked, without complaint. He did look scarily pale, though, which only emphasized the red blood that mingled in his blonde curls. Once the scan was complete, they returned to the same triage cubicle, the orderly once more wheeling Dylan's bed back, with Rachel holding his hand as they went.

When they got back to their cubicle, Caroline, their nurse, settled him in and checked his stats again.

'Is he allowed to sleep?' Rachel asked. 'It's way past his bedtime and he's exhausted.'

'Of course he's tired, the little poppet. You let him nap and I'll be in regularly to check on him. Try not to worry. Press the call button if you need me in the meantime.'

Dylan dozed on and off, while Rachel sat by his side, her eyes never leaving his face. She listened to the rhythmic sound of the machines beeping as they took Dylan's stats while he slept. Outside, she could hear the bustle of medical staff moving in and out of cubicles. A baby cried in the distance and there were shouts from a woman who sounded quite drunk. Rachel couldn't fathom that a short few hours ago she was on a dance floor, throwing moves to Abba.

She heard her phone buzz again. She checked it quickly and scanned through a dozen messages from the family, each offering support and love. Rachel knew that they must all be out of their minds with worry. She messaged

Jack to say that she'd be out to talk to him as soon as possible. She knew that if she updated him, he'd take the initiative to pass on the information to everyone else. For now, though, her complete attention was focused on Dylan. He responded with a love heart emoji within seconds. He must have been watching the phone for updates.

Caroline came back with a tray in hand, containing a small silver teapot and cup and saucer. She smiled warmly at Rachel, nodding towards her gown, 'It looks like you were on a night out when all the shenanigans happened. Nice dress. I grabbed a cuppa for you. Thought you could do with it.' Rachel felt a rush of gratitude.

'Caroline, you are too kind. Tea is exactly what I need now. You know, I'd forgotten I was wearing this. I must look a right state. We were at a charity ball when I got the call Dylan had been in an accident.'

'You must have gotten quite a shock, you poor thing. Never a dull moment, eh?' Caroline picked up the chart at the end of Dylan's bed. 'By the way, as Dylan's blood type is quite rare, AB negative, can I check if you or Dylan's dad have the same blood type?'

'Does he need a transfusion?' Rachel's voice rose an octave in panic.

'Not at all. I'm just being overly cautious. Only asking in case we need to call on you,' Caroline said, smiling.

Rachel looked at the blood on Dylan's head and felt a shiver run through her at the idea Dylan might need more blood. She whispered, 'Dylan's dad died last year. I'm Dylan's adoptive mother. And my blood type is O positive, so I'm no use to him.'

Caroline put the chart back and turned so she could look Rachel dead in the eye, 'On the contrary, you are the most use to him. He needs his mama, there's no doubt about that, whatever blood type you have,' she said, with great kindness in her voice.

Rachel kicked herself back into mom gear. 'His birth grandparents on both sides are still alive. I'll check with them about blood types.'

'We probably won't need anyone to step in. Hopefully his scan result will come back in the clear. And we should hear news on that soon,' Caroline assured her.

Rachel looked down to Dylan, who was deep in sleep by now. 'I need to update Dylan's uncle; he's out in the lobby. Can you stay here for a moment while I run out and do that? I don't want to leave him on his own.'

'Course. I need to write up his sheet anyhow. Don't forget to drink this tea, though. You look as white as a ghost.'

Rachel kissed Dylan on his forehead, promising she would be right back, then made her way to reception.

And that's where she found everyone, sitting or standing in the lobby, waiting for news. But seeing them – Sheila and Adrian, Belinda and Oscar, her own parents, Ronan and Jack, side by side united, everyone with nothing but love for her boy – made her tremble with emotion.

This crazy ensemble was Dylan's family. And when the chips were down, they were here. For Dylan. For her too.

Then, with perfect timing, Claudia burst through the revolving doors, wearing trainers and a sweatshirt over her sparkly dress.

'Howard is with Olivia, don't worry. She's asleep on the couch in his arms, so I had to come here. I couldn't stay away, but I'll go right back if you prefer.' She scanned Rachel's face for signs that she should be with Olivia instead.

'I'm grateful that you are all here. Thank you. But I can't tell you much yet. He's had an MRI scan and we're just waiting to hear the results of that,' Rachel said.

'Oh, sweet Jesus,' Sheila said, blessing herself.

Rachel sympathized; she knew how scary those words sounded.

'Is he awake?' Belinda asked.

'Dozing on and off. Scared and confused. As am I. I cannot work out what happened,' Rachel said.

'We put Danielle in a taxi home when we got there,' Annie said. 'She told us that she put the kids to bed, read them their story, and thought everything was perfect. But about an hour later she heard weird sounds coming from your office. When she went in, she found Olivia and Dylan at the window. She said Dylan was trying to stop Olivia throwing a black sack out. He lunged forward to grab it, and that's when he fell. Danielle just kept saying she ran as fast as she could but couldn't reach him in time.'

Rachel's head spun. What on earth had Olivia been throwing out the window? 'This doesn't make any sense. What am I missing?' She looked frantically from her mom to her dad, hoping they might have the answer. Her head began to pound and she felt a little nauseous.

'We'll get to the bottom of it, love. The priority right now is to take care of Dylan,' Joe said, putting his arm round her. She leaned into his familiar embrace.

'Can I borrow your jacket, Dad? I'm feeling a bit exposed here, in my dress.'

It was Claudia who answered. 'I've got you covered, Sis,' she said, handing a small tote bag to Rachel. 'I threw a few bits in that I thought you'd need.'

Rachel pulled out a sweatshirt and put it on. 'Thanks, Sis. I'm going to head back, but I need to check something with you all before I go. Dylan's blood type is quite rare. I actually didn't realize that.' Rachel paused, waiting for Sheila to make a predictably barbed comment, but she remained silent for once. 'Anyhow, the nurse asked me which family members share the same blood as him, in case there's any need for a transfusion. Which is unlikely, she assures me.'

'We're both O positive,' Belinda said. 'I only remember because we just had our annual check-up. So the rare blood type must be from Niamh's side.'

'I can't remember what blood type Niamh had,' Sheila said, shaking her head. 'I'm so sorry, Rachel, I know I probably should, but I've no clue. She was shockingly healthy as a child. But I would have thought if it was rare, we'd have known.'

'We'll get tested, and if they need any part of me, they can have it,' Adrian said.

Jack moved closer to Rachel. 'I'm O positive.'

He ran his hands through his hair, then looked across the lobby. He was looking increasingly distressed.

'Fuck it,' he said eventually, for the second time that evening. 'You might need to ask Ronan what blood type he is.'

The look that passed between Ronan and Jack was filled with so much loathing, it coated the air between them.

'I'm not sure about the relevance of cousins' blood types,' Rachel said impatiently. She turned to her mother-in-law to say something else, but Belinda was staring at Ronan and Jack.

'Not this,' Belinda said, grasping for Oscar's hand. He stood by her side with a matching shocked face.

'Can I have a word in private, Rachel?' Ronan asked, grabbing her arm. But Rachel tugged herself free. What was up with everyone? She needed to get back to Dylan. The boys' petty arguments could wait.

'I have no idea what's going on, but whatever it is, it will have to wait,' she replied impatiently, making a move towards Dylan's room.

But as she went, she caught Jack's eye and he looked so stricken, it made her stop in her tracks.

'Rachel, wait. Please,' Ronan begged.

She turned towards him slowly, a sixth sense telling her that whatever Ronan needed to say was going to change everything.

'I have a rare blood type too – I'm AB positive,' Ronan said in a low voice.

A deathly silence fell over the small group.

And that's when the last catastrophic event of the night crashed down around them.

Rachel's legs felt weak. The wine from earlier rose like acid in her throat. Her mind reeled with questions. If Ronan had the same blood type, what did that mean?

Belinda brushed past her and grabbed Ronan's arm. 'It was *you*?'

'Please. Don't,' Ronan said. He looked like he was about to throw up; his face had turned grey.

Oscar moved closer too, his face flushed with anger. 'You and Niamh?' he croaked. 'How could you?'

'What's going on? What did you and Niamh do? Will

411

someone tell me what they're talking about?' Sheila asked in a rush, confusion overtaking her.

Jack turned to his parents, taking a deep breath before he opened the lid on the final secret. 'I'm sorry you had to find out this way. But Niamh and Ronan were having an affair.'

Rachel reached out for Claudia, who caught her, literally holding her up.

'And he thinks he's Dylan's father, doesn't he?' Adrian said, also finally getting it.

Rachel felt sorry for him, feeling the same shock that lined Adrian's face. She watched the fallout from Jack's words as if they were in slow motion. She looked around the group of people standing in a semi-circle around her. Sheila crumpled in front of her eyes. To Rachel's surprise, it was Belinda who got to her side first and held her up.

Ronan placed his face in his hands, then said weakly, 'It's not how it seems, I promise. I'm so sorry.'

Oscar grabbed Ronan's tuxedo jacket by the lapels and hissed, 'If we weren't in a hospital lobby, I'd knock you right out. Lorcan was your *cousin*. Your friend!'

Adrian turned to Jack. 'You should have told us!' he shouted angrily.

Belinda took a shaking Sheila to the plastic seats behind them and they sat down together, leaning into each other for support.

Then Rachel heard her name called out. Caroline was beckoning her, 'Doctor Javapour is on his way. We have the results of the scan.'

Rachel turned to Claudia. 'Do not let Ronan leave. If he is . . . if we need . . .'

'He's going nowhere,' Claudia said firmly. And the look

of determination on her face left Rachel in no doubt that if Claudia needed to, she would rugby tackle Ronan to the floor to make sure he didn't move.

With one last look of horror at Ronan, Rachel ran back to Dylan's cubicle, praying for good news.

FIFTY-TWO

Jack

Beaumont Hospital, Dublin

As a kid, Jack had told himself that while he might be partially deaf, he had superpowers to make up for it. And it was true; while he'd partially lost one of his five senses, the other four had become enhanced, stronger.

As he watched Rachel walk towards the nurse, he might not have been able to hear everything clearly, but he understood all that was going on around him. He looked at the room before him as though watching a movie in slow motion, observing rather than participating.

His eyes rested first on his parents, who looked like they had taken a bullet. His heart splintered for them. They had always believed Niamh to be a perfect daughter, wife, mother. The news that she'd had an affair before Dylan was born would have sent them reeling.

Meanwhile, Ronan was pacing the floor, but Jack

couldn't help feeling only satisfaction that the son of a bitch had been found out. He'd watched Ronan for months now as he moved in on Rachel and the kids with not a care in the world. The charming good guy that everyone liked. Jack had wanted to tell Rachel about Ronan's affair with Niamh so many times, but he just couldn't find the words. He'd made a promise to Niamh that he'd never break her secret.

And Jack knew that he would have kept that promise, would never have breathed a word about the affair to anyone, if not for the secret potentially costing Dylan his life.

As Jack continued to observe, he watched Oscar take his jacket off and place it around Belinda's shoulders. She was shaking, Jack noticed. That would be the shock, he supposed. He read Oscar's lips as he told Belinda that 'everything is going to be okay', reaching up to wipe a tear with his thumb.

But Belinda obviously didn't believe him: her mouth formed the words 'How can they take away Dylan's father for a second time?' and her eyes flipped from Oscar to Ronan, her face flushed with anger.

Jack moved a little closer, angling himself so he could see what she said to him next.

'You can *never* tell Dylan, do you hear me?' she was saying now to Ronan, whose head was bowed. 'He's lost his father once; you will not take Lorcan away from him again, or so help me, I'll put a knife into you!' Feeling her rage, Jack believed her entirely.

Next, Jack watched Rachel's mom Annie make her way over to his own mam and put her arms around her. Annie was lovely; she had a calming way about her. He hated

Carmel Harrington

seeing his mam so upset and he wished there was something he could do to help. It felt like she had cried her way solidly through the last five years. Too many tears, too much pain and grief. It had changed her. Some days he didn't even recognize her; she wasn't the kind, warm mother of his childhood any more. There was a sharpness to her now.

'It's okay. It will all be okay. Rachel won't let anyone say anything to Dylan. She'll protect him,' Annie was saying to Sheila now, comforting her.

Jack watched all their lips, reading their torment, back and forth as they tried to make sense of everything.

'I was so angry with Lorcan when he met Rachel. I thought he'd moved on too fast; I kept saying to Adrian and Jack that I couldn't believe he fell in love again so quickly,' Sheila said.

'And all along, it was Niamh who'd already moved on,' Adrian finished for her.

His mam started to cry and, to his horror, he saw his dad join in. Watching them so vulnerable made him want to weep too. He felt guilt hit him in his chest, full force, that he had played a part in their distress. Should he have spoken to Ronan privately? But the secrets and lies of the past five years had already eaten him up. He was sick of it all, and before he'd had a chance to really think about what he was about to reveal, it was out, bare, in all its ugliness.

'I'm glad Lorcan had Rachel for those few years before he died,' Belinda said. She had moved over to sit with Sheila and Annie, now. The three women leaned in towards each other.

'Do you think he knew about the affair?' Sheila asked. 'Is that why he moved on so quickly to someone new?'

'I don't think he knew, but I can't be sure of that,' Belinda said.

'But grief has no time limit,' Annie said. 'None of us can put a timer on when someone should or could move on. For some, they never will. Others, like Lorcan, are ready in what some might perceive to be too short a time.'

Jack looked back towards the triage room where Rachel was right now, and wondered if she was one of those that never moved on from their grief. That saddened him. What a waste. He turned back to the waiting room again.

'It felt like Lorcan erased every part of Niamh when he took up with Rachel,' Sheila said. 'It hurt so much, and so I took it out on her. I blamed her for things she had no part in.'

Claudia walked over towards the three grandmothers. 'We all do things we regret when we are in pain. Trust me.'

Jack moved in closer to his family and the Bradleys and finally broke his silence.

'I think Niamh sent Rachel to Lorcan,' he said. 'She knew that the children needed a parent, that Lorcan was going to die too. And every one of us here should be so grateful that Rachel came along when she did. Imagine for one moment what life would be like for Olivia and Dylan if she weren't here? Right now, there is only one person that Dylan wants next to that hospital bed, and that's his mom.'

'Well said,' Oscar said, clapping Jack on the shoulder.

Jack noted he spoke at exactly the right volume this time. Why had he got so upset with him before? It mattered not, when you really thought about it. He reached over and patted Oscar's shoulder, smiling his thanks.

'Rachel's coming over,' Adrian said suddenly, and they all moved to meet her.

She was in tears, but Jack knew the moment he saw Rachel that the tears were of relief, not sorrow. That's the way it was when you loved someone. You knew every part of them.

'Dylan's going to be fine,' Rachel exhaled, in a rush of emotion. 'There's no damage from the fall. We have to stay overnight, in case of concussion, and he needs a couple of stitches in his cut, but we can go home in the morning.'

The group rallied around Rachel, and everyone hugged her and then each other. There were no sides now, just one united family celebrating a dodged bullet.

'Can I . . . Do you . . .' Ronan stuttered and stammered, unable to finish his sentence. He stood on his own, a few feet back from everyone else. Jack almost felt sorry for him. Almost.

'Go home,' Rachel said coldly. 'I'll talk to you later.'

'I'm so sorry, Rachel. I feel horrendous,' Ronan tried again, almost pleading.

'You know what, Ronan, I don't care how you feel right now.' Rachel turned to face Jack. He noted that even now, amid the drama, she was careful to make sure he could see her lips as she spoke. And he felt his heart constrict in love once more. Would this ever get easier?

'You all need to go home. There's no point staying here any longer. I know there's a lot to talk about, but it can wait,' Rachel said.

'I can stay with you,' Jack offered.

'Go home. We'll both need you tomorrow.' She moved towards him, looking at him with such warmth it made him want to cry, in a way he'd not done since he was a kid. Yes, he'd sobbed when Niamh died, but this was a different sadness.

A bittersweet loss.

Jack pulled Rachel into his arms and hugged her goodbye.

FIFTY-THREE

Sheila

Malahide, Dublin

Sheila had thought that she was done being shocked by anyone or anything in her life. She'd seen it all in her sixty-odd years. But tonight had just about finished her off.

'You okay?' Adrian asked, walking into their bedroom in his blue checked Marks and Spencer's PJs. He'd worn a variation of these his entire married life. The shade of blue might change slightly, or the size of the check, but other than that, they stayed the same. And Sheila found comfort in that.

She noted that Adrian looked his age for the first time in his life; the lines on his face were more pronounced when he frowned and the weight of the night's revelations lay heavy on his shoulders.

'I don't know how I am, love,' Sheila answered truthfully.

She looked at the bedside alarm clock and saw that it was one minute to three a.m.

Adrian followed her gaze and said, 'Hard to believe that it was only six hours ago that we walked into the hotel for the dinner dance. We should be climbing into a taxi to come home. Instead it feels like days ago, doesn't it?'

'True for you. And it was such a lovely night.' They both sank into the pillows on their bed. Sheila's bones ached in a way they hadn't ever done before. Every part of her was exhausted.

'We have to talk about this mess,' Adrian said.

'I don't think I can. Not yet.'

Adrian climbed into bed beside Sheila and pulled her into his arms.

'We didn't know Niamh at all, did we?' Sheila whispered.

'We didn't know that part of her,' Adrian said. 'But we knew our daughter.'

'How could she have done that to Lorcan?' Sheila was aghast at the thought of it. When Sheila had made her wedding vows, she'd meant every word of them. And she could never fathom infidelity. She knew it happened, that it was part and parcel of life, but it had always baffled her. Adrian and she had had their moments over the years, where the fizz drained out of their marriage and everything felt a little flat, but neither of them went running off after anyone else. They'd stuck with each other and found a way to add some more pop to their lives.

'I can't get Lorcan out of my head. Did he know?'

'I hope not,' Sheila said, feeling guilty for every lousy thought she'd ever had about him. 'I gave him such a hard time for moving on with Rachel. I equated that to him cheating on Niamh when all along . . .' She couldn't finish the sentence.

'I know. We both have some serious thinking to do about how we've behaved over the past couple of years. But for now, we both need to close our eyes.' A yawn escaped him and he wiped his eyes, as tears of tiredness leaked down his face. 'We've got a big day tomorrow. There's a lot to be sorted.'

Adrian kissed Sheila on her forehead, reassuring her that everything would be okay. They'd make sure of it.

Sheila set the alarm, not that she thought they'd need it. Something told her that she wouldn't sleep much tonight.

FIFTY-FOUR

Belinda

Malahide, Dublin

In the end, Dylan was discharged the following afternoon. Rachel had texted everyone, saying they were both going to bed to recuperate, but invited them over the next morning, which just happened to be Christmas Eve, for a late breakfast.

'This wasn't quite the Christmas Eve we expected,' Belinda said, as Oscar pulled into Rachel's drive at ten a.m. They sat in the car for a few moments, as though readying themselves to go in.

'I don't think we've had as eventful a few days in years,' Oscar said, shaking his head.

'Even with all the upset, though, strangely I've not felt this alive in a long time,' Belinda admitted.

'Seems foolish now, that we stayed away for so long. I'm not really sure why,' Oscar said.

'I'll regret it to the day I die,' Belinda said. 'And the fault lies with me. I was the one who kept saying "no" every time Rachel invited us. I stupidly thought that if I stayed away, it wouldn't hurt as much.'

'It's the opposite, though, isn't it? Seeing the children makes me feel closer to Lorcan,' Oscar said.

Belinda grabbed her compact powder from her handbag and dabbed her nose delicately, making sure everything was as it should be. Satisfied, she snapped it shut. 'I cannot wait to give them both a cuddle.' She paused and whispered, 'What do we do if it turns out that Lorcan isn't Dylan's father?'

'We do nothing,' Oscar said resolutely. 'That boy is our grandson, no matter what. That's how I see it.'

'I couldn't agree more.' Belinda was relieved to hear Oscar was on the same page as her. But before they could chat any further, they saw Sheila, Adrian and Jack walking towards them, all with the same anxious look on their faces. Belinda understood why. They all needed to see Dylan with their own eyes, to make sure he was okay.

'Did you sleep?' Sheila asked them warmly when they stepped out of the car.

'Not a wink for us,' Belinda said. 'What an absolute mess.' She reached up to smooth a stray hair that whipped across her face.

They stood in awkward silence for a moment. Belinda was worried about how Sheila might react to the fact that they'd known about the affair all along. Would they blame her and Oscar somehow? She didn't want any more arguments to happen in front of Rachel. She'd had enough to deal with. And truthfully, Belinda wasn't sure she could take much more herself either. She took a deep breath.

Before they went inside, it was time to clear the air. There was no point keeping any more secrets.

'I need to tell you something before we go inside,' she began, looking for Oscar's hand for support. 'When Niamh was pregnant with Dylan, I overheard her talking to someone on the phone. She was telling the person that they were over. I didn't know who was on the end of the phone, but it was obvious they'd been having an affair.'

'You weren't the only one keeping a secret, Jack. But in a million years, we never suspected it could be *Ronan*,' Oscar added.

Belinda watched shock register on both Sheila and Adrian's faces. She felt sorry for them. They'd had a lot to take in over the past forty-eight hours.

'Did Niamh know you'd overheard her?' Adrian asked.

Belinda nodded, feeling heartbroken at the thought of explaining what happened next. Oscar gallantly took that job on.

'Look, I don't want to say anything bad about your girl. But it needs to be said. Niamh drove a wedge between Lorcan and us before she died. Belinda promised not to tell Lorcan, but even so, Niamh pushed us away, fabricating stories about us being mean to her. I need you both to know this, so you don't think any less of us. We never did anything to intentionally hurt Niamh, no matter what she said to you all. We knew her secret and she couldn't trust us. I suppose fear made her push us away.'

Sheila made a strangled sound.

'I'm sorry,' Belinda said softly.

'How can you be nice to us after what Niamh did?' Sheila whispered.

'None of us are responsible for our children's actions,'

Belinda replied with certainty. 'And anyway, you were grieving. That was all that was important. Not our feelings, or whether we'd had our egos bruised.'

'Thank you. I can't imagine it's been easy for you, keeping this secret, or indeed telling us now,' Adrian said.

Belinda felt relief that she had finally let the secret go, a burden lifted from her.

'Come on, let's go in and see Dylan,' Jack said. He rang the bell, and Howard opened the door to let them in.

Dylan was on the couch with Rachel and Olivia when they got inside, the three of them snuggled under a velvet throw.

Dylan's little face broke into a huge grin when he saw them all. 'I've got a *huge* cut on my head. Look!' he told them. A square bandage covered the stitches and he pointed at it excitedly as Rachel explained that he would need to go back in three weeks to have them removed.

'Come over and give the kids a cuddle,' she said, jumping up from the couch to make room for them.

Olivia followed her mom, though, clutching her like a lynchpin. Belinda's heart constricted in love for the little girl, who looked pale and scared. She must have had such a shock seeing her brother fall, not to mention the horror of the paramedics and ambulance arriving.

The Bradleys and Butlers didn't move. They looked at Dylan, then at each other, feeling awkward about who should go first.

Belinda gestured to the Butlers, 'You go first.'

Sheila replied, 'No, not at all; you go first.'

Jack shook his head dramatically at their nonsense and walked over to Dylan. 'Hey, dude. I keep telling you, don't jump without a parachute. Rookie error.'

Dylan started to giggle. Sheila and Adrian joined them on the couch, and both took a moment to hold Dylan close.

Belinda watched sympathetically as Sheila struggled not to cry. She felt the same way. She'd cried what felt like an ocean since last night. But today was not the day for more tears.

Jack kissed Dylan on his head, then called over Belinda and Oscar, who also held the boy close. That hug, as he reached up and wrapped his small arms around her neck, felt like the most precious thing in the world. Her love for him overwhelmed her. She felt someone's eyes on her and looked up to see Sheila watching her, nodding in understanding.

Eventually, the two sets of grandparents were sitting on either side of their grandson.

'I hope you're hungry. Annie and Claudia have made enough food to feed the street,' Joe said, coming into the family room. 'Does my favourite grandson want one or two sausages?'

'I'm your only grandson, Gramps!' Dylan said, laughing, as he walked hand in hand between Sheila and Belinda into the kitchen.

'Shout your orders for tea, coffee or juice to Howard and Joe. I wasn't sure what everyone liked, so I've made a little of everything,' Annie said as everyone walked in.

Belinda looked at the table, which had platters of pancake stacks, sausages, bacon and eggs, toast and pastries. Her stomach began to grumble as the beautiful salty and sweet aromas hit her. They all ate their meal, chatting about Santa Claus and his imminent arrival. Dylan's appetite wasn't diminished in any way, Belinda noted, as he gobbled his way through several pancakes and the two sausages he'd ordered from his gramps. But she also noticed that Olivia ate very little, just sat with her seat close to her mom. Whatever was going on with her, she was not herself.

After breakfast, Howard suggested a Lego competition with Dylan and Olivia in the family room. Rachel had to coax Olivia to join them, promising she would join them herself in a few moments.

Once the kids were distracted by Howard, Rachel turned to the remaining group in the room and said, 'Right, let's keep our voices low, okay? I don't want the children to hear anything, so no loud and dramatic statements from anyone.'

They all murmured their agreement.

'Before we get to last night's dramas, let's get to the whole baby daddy issue,' Rachel said. 'Jack, can you tell me why you thought Ronan was Dylan's dad? Did Niamh tell you that he was?'

'No, she always denied it,' Jack explained. 'She confided in me about the affair a few months before she was pregnant with Dylan. Niamh said she'd finished things with Ronan because she loved Lorcan and wanted to make a go of it. But I guess I knew there had to be a possibility that he was Dylan's dad. The timelines were too close.'

'We didn't know anything about this, Rachel. I swear that to you,' Sheila said. 'I feel foolish now.'

'It's nothing you need to apologize for,' Rachel said briskly, 'and anyway, there's no point dwelling on that now. What's done is done. But what I can tell you all is that, despite what Ronan *thinks* he knows, we can all relax. Ronan is *not* Dylan's father. Caroline, the nurse, said it's impossible that he could be, with his blood type.'

Rachel's face broke into a huge grin and everyone gasped with relief at the news.

'Oh, thank God,' Sheila exclaimed, then quickly apologized for speaking too loudly.

Even though Belinda had said she'd believed Niamh, that Lorcan was Dylan's father, deep down, a niggle of doubt had refused to go away. Now, years of worry dropped in an instant from her shoulders. Had Ronan been the father, she couldn't even begin to work out how complicated things would get for Rachel and the children.

Rachel continued, 'I called Ronan last night. We didn't talk for long; I wasn't in the mood to chat. I suppose at some point I'll have to have a conversation with him. But right now I'm too cross. He knows that he's not Dylan's father, though, at least. And to be honest, I'd rather drop the subject now. Christmas has been miserable for everyone since Lorcan died. I think it's time we all tried to move on from that and make tomorrow special for the kids, if not for ourselves. Niamh's actions are in the past, and I'd like to leave them there. I will not allow this to cloud tomorrow for them. I want them to have a special day, filled with new happy memories.'

There were murmurs of agreement from everyone.

'We'll make it special for them,' Annie promised.

'We will, and you have an army of people here to support you,' Belinda added, looking around the table at the group of people, who somehow were beginning to look more like a family and less like a warring tribe. 'Talking of which, what can we do to help?' she asked.

'Well, the fridge and larder are already heaving with food, but there's a trifle to be made if you fancy helping me in the kitchen?' Annie said, taking charge. 'And we could get a head start on prepping the vegetables for tomorrow.'

'I'm not a natural in the kitchen, but I do take instruction very well. So you're on!' Belinda said, feeling quite excited at the prospect of rolling up her sleeves and helping.

'I had planned on being the perfect hostess and not letting any of you do a thing but sit down and be waited on,' Rachel said sighing.

'Nonsense. You've had practically no sleep for two days! You need to rest today so that you are ready to give the children that special day they deserve,' Sheila said. 'And I'd like to help too, Rachel. If you need me, of course. We won't impose, I promise you. I could start by taking charge of that trifle. I've been known to make a good one. Only if it's all right with you.'

'That would be really great, Sheila. Honestly, I appreciate all of your help. Thank you, everyone. But before you all head to the kitchen, there is just one more thing to discuss. I need to fill you all in on how the accident happened,' Rachel said.

'Wait till you hear this,' Claudia said, whistling softly. 'Mom had to hold me back. I wanted to go up there and tell them what's what.'

Rachel continued, waving at Claudia to stop interrupting. 'The black sack that Olivia was throwing out of the window was stock from Rae's Closet. Mostly loungewear and my Christmas bobble hat and scarf sets. It turns out that the two Middleton girls from up the road have been blackmailing Olivia.'

Everyone gasped, then clamped their hands over their mouths when Rachel shushed them.

'I'll fecking kill them, so help me God,' Sheila hissed.

Belinda nodded emphatically. She would be right beside Sheila on this!

'I know that feeling,' Rachel said. 'A month or so ago, Olivia was in their house.'

Belinda knew this must have been when she was with Sheila and Adrian. And the guilt on their faces showed that they knew this too.

'The girls gave Olivia a makeover, which of course she was excited about. But she didn't realize that they made a video of her while she was changing her clothes. They threatened to put the video of her in her underwear on to TikTok. Unless she stole from Rae's Closet, that is.'

'The little bitches,' Jack said.

'You were right. You said you thought they were up to something,' Sheila whispered to Rachel. Her face was sunburn-red and her voice shook.

Belinda was proud of Rachel. She could have put the knife in here, making Sheila feel worse than she obviously did. Instead, she let it go, with a small shrug.

'I knew that something was up with Olivia, but she wouldn't say what. She's been carrying this on her own for weeks. No wonder she's been so withdrawn and quiet. So anyway, the other night, Dylan heard her going downstairs and followed her. When he saw her filling a black sack with clothes, he knew that Olivia was doing something wrong. He tried to stop her throwing the bag out the window and somehow in the tussle, he fell out. Thankfully the bag of clothes broke his fall.'

'It's all my fault, Rachel. I'm so sorry. You called this,' Sheila said.

Belinda knew that Rachel would be well within her rights to have a go at Sheila, tell her that *yes*, it was all her fault. But Rachel, of course, continued to respond with true grace.

'You misjudged a situation,' she said grimly. 'But the fault lies with the Middleton girls. And they are not going to get away with it. I'm going to go up there now to get the video footage and make sure their parents know what their girls have been up to. But I could do with some support. Do you fancy being my wing woman?'

'Try and stop me,' Sheila said, standing up tall.

'I'm coming too. This is a job for all of us,' Belinda said. There was no way she wasn't going to join in.

Rachel turned to Annie, 'You better come too, Mom. Let's show those girls what happens when you mess with *three* grandmothers.'

Then Sheila cleared her throat and they all turned to look at her. *Please don't say something silly.*

But Sheila added, 'You mean, three grandmothers *and* a mom. I think that's a pretty powerful combination.'

FIFTY-FIVE

Rachel

Malahide, Dublin

Although Dylan sported the bloody scars of his fall, Rachel knew that it was Olivia who was the most damaged by the accident. When she returned from the Middleton house, she took Olivia aside for a private chat in her bedroom.

'I don't want you to worry about that video any more.'

Olivia's eyes opened wide at this. 'What happened?'

'Well, let's just say the women in your family are not to be messed with! The four of us went up to the girls' house together. Anita answered the door. She nearly passed out when she saw us all standing on her doorstep. I asked to speak to her parents, who are decent people, I might add. They were horrified to hear about the video and blackmail.'

'Did they believe you?' Olivia asked.

'Anita and Carolyn caved in pretty fast and started to

433

cry when your Grandma Belinda started to talk about legal action.'

Rachel smiled to herself as she remembered Belinda's long speech about extortion and then her mom throwing in the intense psychological trauma both the children and family had suffered.

'And then your Nana Sheila threatened them with her rolling pin, and that finished them off. They confessed to it all.'

Rachel had to suppress a giggle at this memory.

'Did they give you the video?' Olivia asked. 'How do we know that they won't go ahead and share it anyhow?'

'It's deleted. We made them get rid of it in front of us all. Their parents were furious and confiscated all the girls' devices there and then. It's over, sweetheart.'

Olivia shook her head and began to cry. 'I'm so sorry, Mom.'

'I know you are. Do you know the thing that's upset me most of all?'

'That I lied?'

'That you didn't come to me when you got yourself into this mess. Olivia, you have to know that no matter what you do, no matter what scrapes you get into, I will always be your safe place to fall. That's my job as your mother. I might not agree or like what you've done, but I will always help you, support you, guide you to solve your problems.'

'I wanted to tell you, but I was too scared,' Olivia said.

Rachel looked at her little girl, and her heart broke that she had already learned this harsh lesson in life. She was too young to deal with this, but somehow she would have to find a way.

'I hate it here,' Olivia said.

'Right now you do, but that will pass. You'll get through this, sweetheart, we all will. And you'll become stronger too. With me right by your side, no matter what.'

'I'll never keep a secret from you again,' Olivia said.

Rachel thought to herself, *Oh yes, you will, because that's what we women do. We keep secrets from loved ones, to protect them and to protect ourselves.*

But she kept all of that to herself.

'Is everyone cross with me?' Olivia asked.

'Not one bit. They all love you and are only upset that you are too. And I have a surprise for you. Nana Sheila and I were talking – there's no point in us both making a big turkey. So they will come to us for lunch tomorrow, and then on Stephen's Day, she's invited all of us to hers. Won't that be nice?'

'And you don't mind?' Olivia asked, suspicion on her face.

Rachel surprised herself by replying in honesty that she didn't.

At that moment, Rachel's phone buzzed. It was Ronan. 'I have to take this call,' she apologized to Olivia. 'Go on downstairs. Close the door on your way out, I'll be down in a minute.'

She took a steadying breath and answered the call.

'Hey,' Ronan said, as soon as the call clicked on.

'Hey.'

'How's Dylan?'

'Back to himself. He had a lucky escape.'

Rachel then filled Ronan in about Olivia's video and the blackmail.

'I'll get a letter written and delivered immediately to the parents,' Ronan said.

435

'No, you won't. It's all taken care of,' Rachel replied.

She felt irritated by his assumption that she needed his help in sorting this out. But there again, a few days ago, she would have gratefully accepted it. Now, her skin crawled a little, just talking to him. He'd betrayed Lorcan. And he'd betrayed her too, befriending her. Would he have ever told her about Niamh and his suspicions about being Dylan's father? She doubted it.

'Are you okay?' Ronan asked. 'You know, after last night and . . .?' his voice trailed off.

'I'm fine,' Rachel snapped.

'Good. I suppose I'm on everyone's hit list?' Ronan asked, with a small laugh.

'Don't expect season's greetings from the Butlers or Bradleys, I think is a fair assessment.'

'And what about you, Rach?'

'I'm sad for you and Niamh, but most of all for Lorcan. I'm trying to keep perspective, because after all you didn't murder anyone; you both made a mistake. But it was a cruel mistake with consequences that changed lives. And truthfully, I wish it were one of those secrets that had gone to the grave with Niamh.'

'If it's any consolation, I hate myself more than you ever could. And our friendship, I need you to know that it was genuine for me. I've loved spending time with you this past year. I find myself thinking about you all the time. One of my colleagues in work joked that I must have a crush on you, the amount of time I spend talking about you.'

He paused and Rachel's heart skipped a beat.

'And in the spirit of honesty, I think I might have feelings for you, Rach.'

Rachel's skin prickled at this admission. Because a

couple of days ago, had he said it, she would have been flattered. Now she only felt disgust. Jack had been right about everything.

'Are you freaking kidding me?' she said. This man was delusional if he thought she'd ever look at him with anything other than distrust.

'I suppose I should have expected that,' Ronan said quietly. 'I knew that it was a bit of a long shot that you might feel the same way before all of this, never mind now.'

He sighed and Rachel felt a twinge of sympathy for him.

'Look, I just want you to know that I'll always be here for you and the kids if you ever need my help,' Ronan continued.

Rachel thought he did sound genuine about that, but she planned to put some distance between him and her family, for everyone's sake.

'I'm going to get a new solicitor, Ronan. Don't try to persuade me otherwise.'

The phone went silent for a moment as he considered this. 'Okay. That's your right. But do me a favour; let me finish up the last session of mediation with Fergal in January. And then if we need to go to court, I'll find you someone to take over.'

Rachel pondered it for a second. It was true that Ronan had been incredible in the mediation sessions, had kept her on an even keel while still being sharp and fiery when he needed to be. And she didn't want to have to start afresh with someone new.

'Fine,' she agreed eventually. 'I've got to go now, though. I'll talk to you in January.'

Rachel hung up before giving him a chance to respond, throwing the phone to the bed. Then she lay down, closing her eyes for a moment. She had to trust her instincts that it was the right thing to do, to cut Ronan out of their lives. For the children and for Lorcan too.

She took ten minutes to just lie there in stillness, a chance to take a beat. It helped, that moment of quietness. When she went downstairs, it was as if she were walking into a different house. Christmas songs were playing in the background. Claudia, Howard and the kids were placing wrapped gifts around the tree. Joe, Adrian and Oscar were carrying in bags full of last-minute grocery shop buys. And Sheila, Belinda and Annie were laughing together in the kitchen as they debated whether a trifle should have custard or not.

'Don't you dare make a trifle in my house without custard,' Rachel said, in a mock stern voice, coming up behind them.

Annie walked over and put her arm around Rachel's shoulders. 'At last! A voice of reason! Thank goodness you came in at this moment. These two are in cahoots and outvoting me.'

Sheila turned to Belinda. 'I know when I'm beaten. Rachel's the boss. Time to layer up that trifle with custard so. It won't kill us, I daresay.'

Rachel felt a bit shaky. Had Sheila just said that she was the boss? And the world didn't stop spinning? Everyone carried on, chopping and whisking? It was a Christmas miracle.

'Is it too early for a sausage roll? I am partial to one on Christmas Eve,' Belinda said.

'I've got you,' Sheila answered, pulling a tray from the oven.

'They look so good,' Belinda said. 'Reminds me of

Christmases when I was a kid, back on the farm. We always had a full kitchen then, too, everyone pitching in together.'

'I never knew you grew up on a farm,' Sheila said in surprise.

'I'll warrant there's a lot we don't know about each other,' Belinda replied, then squealed when she burnt her finger. 'That's what I get for being impatient.'

'Butter, the only cure for a burn,' Sheila advised. Then she said, 'Okay, Belinda, I have to ask. Is that tan real or from a bottle?'

Belinda looked at her for a moment, as though deciding what to reveal. 'Fake,' she replied with a smile. 'I'll write down the brand name for you. No streaks, dries in seconds and doesn't stain the bed linen.'

Sheila looked at her in wonder.

'And I want to know what face cream you use. You don't have a single line. Since I had my operation this year, I've found new lines popping up left, right and centre,' Annie joined in.

'Botox,' Belinda replied, this time not missing a beat, and they all began to laugh heartily.

It was as though Rachel had fallen into a parallel universe. Sheila copped her looking at them, open-mouthed. 'Rachel, why don't you go in to your children and have one of those snuggles they always rave about?' She shooed Rachel towards the sofa.

'I should be helping,' Rachel protested.

'You look like you are about to pass out from exhaustion. Let us take care of this, just this once,' Sheila said, quickly squeezing her hand. Then she added, almost shyly, 'Your mammies have got this.'

And Rachel couldn't think of one reason to say no.

FIFTY-SIX

Fergal

Family Mediation Centre, Mount Street, Dublin

The stepmom versus the grandparents. *Final battle*, Fergal Williams thought to himself, as the door to his office clicked open.

Andrew walked in. He looked tired, Fergal noted. He understood that feeling himself. Lately, Fergal had found it harder to swing his legs out of bed each morning. Andrew had worked by Fergal's side for almost thirty years. They'd been through a lot together, and, somewhere along the way, they had become friends as well as colleagues.

'Your next family are waiting in the meeting room for you,' Andrew said. He picked up Fergal's blazer jacket that hung on the back of the door and held it out to him.

'You don't need to do that any more, old friend.'

'Old habits die hard,' Andrew replied.

'We've seen hundreds of families battle it out in our meeting rooms, haven't we, Andrew? But this case is unlike anything I've ever mediated before. Grandparents versus a step-parent fighting for custody. It's been such an unusual case.'

'It's the kids I feel for. They must have been through so much, the poor mites. Five and eight years old. That's the same age as my own grandchildren. Too young to have lost both their parents.'

'Ah, but there lies the rub, Andrew. They still have a mother – Rachel, who loves them. And there's no doubt that the grandparents are devoted too.'

Andrew brushed off some unseen lint from Fergal's shoulder. 'And today is last-chance saloon for them all?'

'Yes, it is. We have gone as far as we can in mediation. If they fail to come to an understanding today, then I'm afraid it's the courtroom for this family. There's no other choice.'

'How do you think it will go?'

'I've no idea. I'm hoping that Christmas might have provided a last-minute miracle for them all. There are no baddies in this case. But they cannot seem to meet on middle ground. The children are lucky in that they have an abundance of love – that's something for us all to hold on to at least.'

Together they made their way towards the meeting room.

'Anything I should know before I go in?' Fergal asked.

'Remember we gave permission for a few extras to join us for this session. The maternal grandparents, Sheila and Adrian Butler, have brought their son Jack. He's partially deaf, so perhaps make an effort to face him as you talk.'

'Noted.'

'Our stepmom Rachel Bradley has quite a contingent with her too,' Andrew continued to read. 'Her parents Annie and Joe Anderson are here as well as her deceased husband's parents, Belinda and Oscar Bradley.'

'I almost feel like I know them all already,' Fergal chuckled, 'we've heard so much about them over the last few months. But I think it's good that all three sets of grandparents are here.'

Andrew raised his eyebrows and said, 'You think that's *good*?' which made the two colleagues chuckle. Because based on the stories shared over the previous mediation sessions, things never went well when everyone in this big, blended family got together in one room.

Fergal and Andrew walked into a silent meeting room. Not a single word was being spoken between the groups. Fergal took his seat on the raised platform at the top of the boardroom table and acknowledged the chorus of 'good mornings' with a nod. He took a moment to consult his notes once more, to settle the prominent participants in his mind. There was no jury in a mediation room. The burden to negotiate an agreement for these fine people lay solely on his shoulders. And as with every case, he carried that burden heavily.

On his left were the Butler family. Sheila and Adrian sat apart, a little more than was normal for them. Was that telling? And the young buck beside Adrian must be Jack. At first glance, he looked calm and collected. But years doing this job helped Fergal pick up on a nervous tic or two from the many clients who sat in front of him. Jack was clicking the top of his pen on and off, and there was a slight shake to his hand. Fergal nodded in satisfaction.

He never liked the cocky ones who thought they knew everything.

Fergal then turned his gaze to the right-hand side of the table. Rachel Bradley looked less scared than usual. On one side were her parents, Joe and Annie Anderson. He guessed this because Rachel was the living image of her father. He noted that Annie held her daughter's hand under the table, and Joe's arm was stretched behind his wife's back, reaching his daughter's shoulder. They were united, this three. Fergal's heart broke a little for Rachel. He knew how impossible her situation was.

On the far side of Rachel sat her in-laws, Belinda and Oscar Bradley. Fergal saw all walks of life in this mediation room. You could always discover financial differences on the people's faces in front of him. It wasn't an absolute, but it was a decent generalization to make. Those without financial issues typically had fewer lines in their brows. Perhaps helped with Botox, but money also bought better teeth, straightened and whitened. Looking at them now, there was no doubt in Fergal's mind that Oscar and Belinda had money. It was written on every part of them.

Fergal heard Andrew shuffle some papers behind him and knew that was his subtle way of bringing Fergal's attention back to the matter at hand. It was time to start and see how the cards were going to fall for this family.

FIFTY-SEVEN

Rachel

Family Mediation Centre, Mount Street, Dublin

Rachel shifted in her chair, trying to make herself comfortable. The warmth of her parents and the Bradleys on the other side of her bolstered her. There seemed to be nerves on the other side of the table too. She noticed Adrian reach over to stop Jack fiddling with his pen.

Fergal cleared his throat and they all turned to him. Rachel hoped that anything he had to say could help them reach a decision today.

'Let's begin, shall we? First of all, I see we have some extra guests today. A little unusual for mediation, but that's okay. I like to shake things up anyhow. No Maria or Ronan, I note?'

Rachel looked over at Sheila and they smiled, nodding once, in agreement.

'We decided we didn't need them for today,' Sheila said.

Rachel had been surprised and more than a little relieved when the Butlers suggested a few days previously that they all leave their solicitors at home for their final mediation session.

As Sheila had said about Ronan, in her typically forthright manner, 'I can't be looking at that man. It would turn my stomach.'

Rachel couldn't agree more. They'd decided not to discuss mediation during the Christmas holidays, and that rule had worked well for them all. Rachel had relaxed in the Butlers' company for the first time since she'd met them. Maybe it was having her own family by her side, or perhaps they'd all mellowed a little since the night of the party. Either way, they were all on firmer ground.

On New Year's Eve, Rachel decided to have one last celebration with everyone. The Bradleys joked that the Grand Hotel should give them a rewards card they spent so much time there, as it was there that they returned. And as the three families mingled with ease together, Rachel couldn't help but marvel how far they'd come since the charity ball, only a week previously, when everyone had been awkward and strained in each other's company.

While Rachel was relieved at Sheila's suggestion that they leave Ronan and Maria out of today's session, she couldn't help also feeling apprehensive. Could she do this on her own? Annie had picked up on her daughter's fear and said she'd like to go with Rachel if nobody objected. Her offer had snowballed an avalanche of offers from the others who all said they'd like to be there too.

In the end, Jack had said, 'We're all involved in this, aren't we? Why don't we all go?'

Claudia and Howard had stayed at home with the children. So here they were, the rest of them, ready for the last battle. Rachel introduced her parents and the Bradleys to Fergal, then Sheila did the honours for Jack.

'How's Thor working out?' Fergal asked, smiling warmly at them all.

Rachel exhaled. Thor was a good place to start. They'd all grown to love that puppy.

'A cheeky monkey,' Sheila replied. 'A little too fond of my slippers. Every pair ruined.'

'I think he means, how's the walking with the kids going,' Adrian said with a smile.

'Oh, of course, you do. Sorry,' Sheila laughed. 'That's my favourite part of every day.'

'And the children's too. It's been a welcome addition to our routines,' Rachel said. And she was being honest. It had been working beautifully. Even the couple of occasions when the kids didn't want to go because they were doing something else hadn't resulted in a world war either.

'Well, I'm glad to hear it,' Fergal continued to smile. 'So we've one item left on the table. The issue of joint guardianship. Sheila and Adrian, have you had any further thoughts on this?' Rachel watched him glance back to Andrew.

Rachel held Annie's hand under the table. This was it. Despite the difference the past week had made, if the Butlers refused to let joint custody go, Rachel had no choice but to go to court.

She was surprised when it was Adrian who spoke for them. He usually let Sheila take the lead.

'We've talked about this for months and could come to no resolution. And in the past few days, as it got closer to today's meeting, it's been all Sheila, Jack and I have discussed at home.'

Sheila continued, 'I had to get out of the house yesterday, we'd been around so many circles, I was dizzy. So I went to Niamh and Lorcan's grave. I stood there, hoping my child would give me a sign because I honestly felt so conflicted. I don't want to hurt you, Rachel; none of us does. But we have to do what we feel is right. Inside of here.' Sheila pointed to her chest. Then she looked at Jack. 'In the end, my prayer was answered. We got clarification from our child. But not from Niamh. From Jack.'

Rachel turned to look at Jack, who she noted was blushing a little. He never liked the attention focused on him. She held her breath as he spoke.

'I asked Mam and Dad if they were going to take me to court one day,' Jack explained. 'If I get married and have a family of my own, I might decide to emigrate. And if so, what happens then?'

Rachel exhaled and marvelled at the power of that question Jack had posed.

'I won't lie, Jack's words shook us,' Sheila admitted. 'As I thought about it, I realized how unfair we've been to Rachel.'

The room was so quiet you could have heard a pin drop. This admission was more than Rachel had ever dared to hope for.

'Christmas was an eye-opener for us and we've come to understand something that you all knew a long time ago.' Sheila pulled her shoulders back and spoke with strength and quiet grace, 'Rachel is the children's mother. And she must decide for her family, without any influence or interference from us, where she wants to live. We only ask that she lets us remain in the children's life forever, wherever that is.'

Rachel heard a sharp intake of breath from either side of her. And she felt her heart beat so fast, she thought it would leap from her chest on to the table in front of her. She hadn't realized how much she needed this acknowledgement from Sheila, until it was offered. And then this was followed quickly by another thought, *Is this over?*

'You understand that if you withdraw your application for joint custody, if Rachel does decide to relocate to New Zealand, you cannot stop her?' Fergal clarified.

'We understand,' Adrian said firmly, turning to look at Sheila, whose eyes were locked on Rachel opposite her.

'Can you forgive us? Can you forgive *me*?' Sheila whispered to Rachel.

Rachel answered in the only way she knew how – she jumped up and ran around the table towards Sheila, who leapt to her feet too, meeting her halfway.

'You were thinking of Niamh. You were being a mother, that's all,' Rachel whispered to her as they embraced. The room erupted into applause.

'This is a first, Andrew,' Rachel heard Fergal mutter as the group all stood up to embrace each other, one by one.

'Most unusual. But you know what, I think I like it,' Andrew replied, and the two men joined in with the applause.

FIFTY-EIGHT

Rachel

One year later

Napier, Hawke's Bay

Rachel looked up to the darkened evening sky. A meteor shower was promised tonight and everyone had gathered in the back yard, excited to catch glimpses of the shooting stars. Rachel watched the kids play, kicking a ball back and forth to each other while they waited for the explosion in the sky to happen. They'd changed over the previous twelve months. Both were leaner and longer, their hair bleached from the New Zealand sun and their faces freckled and brown. But more than their physical changes, they'd become happier with each passing day too.

Time.

They say it is a great healer. Well, looking at the kids now, Rachel figured they were testament to that.

'It's a beautiful night,' Claudia said, joining Rachel.

'It's so still. I love this view at all times of the day, but late at night, when the sky is full of stars, that's my favourite. How are the ankles?' Rachel asked, looking down to inspect her sister's legs.

Eight months pregnant, Claudia's legs had begun to swell up if she didn't take it easy enough.

'I'm good. But honestly, the heartburn is a bloody mare,' Claudia moaned.

'You just ate two bags of smoky bacon chips. That'll do it every time, even if you're not pregnant,' Rachel teased.

'Well, the baby wants what the baby wants, what can I say?' Claudia said, cradling her tummy.

'Come sit down and have a cold drink,' Howard shouted over to the two sisters.

Rachel linked arms with Claudia as they walked back towards the outdoor dining room and the rest of the family.

'I think I'll need an early night. All that fresh air today has tired me right out,' Sheila said, resting her head on Adrian's shoulder.

'The sun suits you, Sheila. You look beautiful,' Rachel said, taking in her tanned face, with freckles across her nose.

'Have a glass of this, it will wake you up,' Belinda said, filling Sheila's glass with pink Prosecco. They clinked glasses. Somewhere over the previous few months, once they'd stopped disliking each other, they'd become friends. Annie had started a WhatsApp group, Three Glam Grans, and from what Rachel could gather, they rarely went a day without messaging each other. Rachel still felt a little

450

disconcerted, though, when she saw them giggling together over a glass of wine. She half expected them to fling it at each other instead of sipping it.

'What I love about it here is that, no matter how many places we visit, each landscape is more spectacular than the last. We've been here almost a month now and every day has revealed a new natural wonder. I'll be back,' Oscar said, taking a swig of his beer.

'Has it been a month? This has been the fastest holiday I've ever had. We'll be back too, won't we, love?' Sheila asked Adrian, who happily agreed.

'Let's not talk about going home. Not yet. We've got a few more days, and I intend to enjoy every moment,' Belinda said.

Annie and Joe came out through the double glass doors at that moment, carrying two large platters.

'We have a cheese board and a few other snacks. In case anyone is peckish,' Annie said. They placed the food on the table, then sat beside their daughters. Howard, the unofficial barman of the night, handed them both a cold beer.

'Being pregnant sucks,' Claudia grumbled, holding up her bottled water.

'You are my hero, taking such good care of our precious cargo,' Howard said, putting down his beer and kissing Claudia.

'You look happy,' Annie said, turning to Rachel, who couldn't keep a big smile off her face. She loved moments like this, all of them together, chatting, laughing, *living*.

'That's because I am. It's so good to be here, to see this,' Rachel said, quietly nodding towards the lovebirds as everyone else started chatting amongst themselves. 'And it's been so much fun showing my hometown to everyone too, over the past few weeks.'

'They've had a great time. We all have, having everyone together again,' Annie said.

'The skies are so clear; I don't think I've seen the stars shine so bright as they are right now,' Rachel whispered, looking upwards.

Ever since that Christmas night with the kids, when they'd looked out over Dublin Bay at the stars overhead, they had become amateur stargazers. They adored looking for unique celestial features in the skies, and it had become a magical part of their family life. One that they all treasured. And somehow, whenever any of them needed to see Niamh or Lorcan, a star would appear, twinkling from heaven, brightest of them all.

'No regrets?' Annie asked.

Rachel's answer was to kiss her mom's cheek.

After their final mediation last January, when Sheila and Adrian had dropped their joint custody application, life had gone on pretty much as it had before. Belinda and Oscar had returned to Belfast once more, but they knew that no invitation was needed to visit Rachel and the kids, the door was always open to them. Sheila, Adrian and Jack had got busy with the store and its New Year sale. The kids had gone back to school, and thankfully there had been no more issues with the Middleton sisters. And Rachel had thrown herself into Rae's Closet to stop herself from thinking about how much she missed her family now that they were gone.

Rachel had gone to see a house in Dalkey that had incredible views of Dublin Bay and almost put an offer in for it. But something had held her back, and she couldn't put her finger on what it was.

Then that summer, Claudia had called to tell Rachel about her pregnancy. Rachel had been so excited for her, but that excitement had dwindled almost immediately when she'd realized how much she was going to miss. She'd begun planning her vacation, hoping to be able to spend as much time as possible with Claudia and her new niece or nephew.

One evening, while the kids went for their daily walk with Thor, Sheila had asked Rachel if she fancied some company. Adrian had taken the kids and the dog to Malahide Castle, while Sheila had stayed behind with Rachel for a cup of tea.

'You've lost your sparkle again,' Sheila remarked as she spooned sugar into her drink.

Rachel was confused by the comment, reaching up to smooth her hair back into its ponytail self-consciously.

Sheila went on, 'You got your sparkle back when your parents and Claudia were here at Christmas. But it's gone again. You miss them.' It wasn't a question, but a statement of fact.

Rachel felt tears prick her eyes: she couldn't deny it. The ache she felt inside her overwhelmed her at times.

'I watched you and your parents throughout Christmas. You and your mom in particular,' Sheila continued. 'You are very close, aren't you?'

'She's one in a million.' Rachel nodded, looking at Sheila warmly, pleased that she had noticed.

'Your relationship reminded me of how Niamh and I used to be,' Sheila said. 'We had that ease too, we both knew each other so well. She was my best friend. And for a long time, I was hers. I know experts tell you that's

wrong, but I've always thought that was a load of malarkey. If a parent can't be a friend to their kids, I give up.'

'I think you have something there,' Rachel agreed and they clinked their mugs together.

'I went up to the grave yesterday for a chat with Niamh. You know how I like to do that. And I wished, silly really, I wished for the hundredth time that I could see her one more time.'

Rachel moved her chair closer to Sheila at this point and rested her hand on her arm. 'If I could make that wish come true for you, I would.'

'I know you would. You have a big heart. It took me a while to cop that on,' Sheila confessed, 'but better late than never, I suppose.'

'All water under the bridge now,' Rachel said, and she meant it. She held no grudges. Neither of them did.

Sheila looked at Rachel for another moment, and then she said, 'I keep thinking that if someone tried to keep Niamh or Jack away from me, I'd be so cross. That's what I'm doing to you and your parents. I'm keeping you from each other. Because you want to go back home, don't you?'

Rachel was unable to breathe. The question had winded her. She was afraid to answer it, because if she spoke her heart's desire out loud, there would be no going back from it.

'If you weren't worried about hurting us and the Bradleys, you would go. You'd buy that villa or one like it, and the kids would grow up in Hawke's Bay, not Dublin Bay.'

'I'm not going,' Rachel was firm on this. 'I promised

you I wouldn't take the children from you and I won't break it.'

'But you should, if that's what you and the children want,' Sheila said calmly. She no longer seemed panicked at the idea. Instead she was reassuring. 'I won't lie, we don't want to lose you, of course we don't. But I also need you to know that we won't stand in your way. Not if it's what you all truly want.'

After that conversation, Rachel had been unable to think of anything else. She had spoken to the kids at length, offering them the possibility of a new beginning for their family in Hawke's Bay. Rachel told them that only if all three of them wanted to go would they do so. All for one, and one for all. And together, they had agreed that it was the right thing for them – they needed a do-over.

It felt right, in their hearts.

Everything had happened quickly after that. Jack had surprised Rachel by saying he'd like to buy her house, something that Sheila and Adrian had been delighted with as they still had him close by. And Jack had found some much-needed independence. Despite the villa being on the market for some time, Rachel had been shocked to discover that it was still for sale. So Howard made an offer on the villa on Rachel's behalf and they all held their breaths waiting to hear if it would be accepted.

When Claudia had rung with the good news, she'd said, 'Of course your offer was accepted, the universe would not dare keep you from that villa. You were always meant to live there.'

Saying goodbye had been heart-wrenching for everyone. As they walked through the departure gates, Rachel had turned for one last look at the family they were leaving behind. Sheila and Adrian, with Jack standing in between them both, strong as always for his parents, and Belinda in Oscar's arms. Waiting on the other side of the world, at the arrivals gate, would be Annie, Joe, Claudia and Howard.

Rachel's heart filled with love for them all – her big, messy, complicated and utterly wonderful blended family. And as the grandparents and Jack waved her and the children goodbye, she felt their love too.

And so, plans were made for this holiday, the first of many Christmases they would all spend together in New Zealand. The villa had enough room for everyone, and Rachel meant it when she told them that they were welcome to visit as often as they liked. Oscar had even told Rachel earlier today that he was thinking about buying a vacation home in Napier, which she'd actively encouraged.

The kids were also going back to Ireland next week with their grandparents for a two-week holiday – one week in Belfast, then one week in Dublin. Jack, who was at home, taking care of the family business, would bring Olivia and Dylan back to New Zealand for his own vacation here afterwards. And his girlfriend Lydia was also joining them. He'd spent Christmas with her and her family; reports back were that they'd all gotten on famously. They'd only been dating two months; he took his time to see what Lydia already knew – that they were perfect for each other. But once they'd had one date, he'd realized how blind he'd been and was all in.

Now, as Rachel sat under the stars with her family, she looked at her beautiful whitewashed villa, with the portico fretwork and stained-glass windows. She still pinched herself that her childhood dream had come true. From the moment they moved in, she'd felt at home here. Claudia was right all along: this *was* where she was meant to be.

Since she'd left New Zealand for Ireland five years previously, Rachel had been through incredible highs and devastating lows. But each of these had a purpose.

They all led her to the children.

She looked down, now, at Olivia, who was sitting on a patch of grass, her arm loosely slung over Dylan's shoulders as they looked out over the bay, at the starlit sky.

She could not remember a life that didn't have them in it. They were her heart, her life, her everything. Rachel walked down to join them, dropping down to sit behind the two of them.

'That's Mammy's star over there,' Olivia said, pointing upwards to the north.

'And that one near it, over there, is Daddy's!' Dylan added.

Rachel followed their gaze and sure enough, there were two stars, a little apart from the others, shining brightly just for them.

She closed her eyes and spoke to Lorcan in her mind, in the way she still did and maybe would never stop.

Hello, darling. Can you believe it? All of us here, together, one big, happy family. And not one single row!

She looked at Dylan, their gorgeous boy. Healthy and happy, loved by them all.

Did I do the right thing, Lorcan?

She looked up to the stars and thought about that

fateful night, one year ago. On the night of Dylan's accident, Rachel *did* speak to Caroline, the nurse, about blood types and paternal genetics. But Caroline had been unable to rule out the fact that Ronan was Dylan's father. The only way to do that was through a DNA test, she'd explained. In the darkness of night, with her child sleeping beside her in the hospital cubicle, Rachel had picked up her mobile and called Ronan.

They'd talked for over an hour about his affair with Niamh, his regret, and what the consequences of a DNA test might be, if it revealed that he was indeed the father.

But Ronan hadn't been ready to be a father, even if that's what the test showed.

It was Rachel who'd first said out loud what they both were thinking.

'I can tell everyone that it's impossible you are the father. That the blood types don't correlate,' she whispered to him, hearing his sharp intake of breath. 'They won't check. They'll just accept it, they'll want it to be true.'

'And there's a good chance I'm not anyhow, so it's not even a proper lie,' Ronan had added, without missing a single beat. He'd clung to Rachel's suggestion like a drowning man to a life raft. And his readiness to do this only confirmed to her that it was the right thing to do.

'It *is* a lie, Ronan. Let's not dress it up any other way,' she'd admonished.

But, Rachel told herself, it was a white lie, and one that she'd had no choice but to tell.

'Should we do a test, just for ourselves, to know the truth?' Ronan had asked.

Rachel had taken a deep breath, trusting her gut once again. She spoke firmly, 'No. You are not Dylan's father,

Lorcan is. And we will never say another word about it. There's no going back from this. Swear it now and we will never speak of this again.'

'I swear it,' Ronan had promised.

Rachel carried that secret burden with her, but she did so willingly for the children. She locked it deep in her mother's heart and would keep it there forever.

'Mom, look!' Olivia shouted now, followed by a loud 'Wow!' from Dylan.

A flash of white light flew across the dark sky, appearing like a ball of fire. As it got closer, it burned out and faded, leaving a greenish glow behind it. A beautiful shooting star.

'Daddy gave us a firework display, didn't he?' Olivia said.

'He was the *bestest* daddy in all the world!' Dylan replied.

Rachel crouched down and pulled her children into her arms, her eyes not leaving the sky where the star had been. Lorcan had found a way to answer her question. She *had* done the right thing.

She would have moments where she doubted herself for the rest of her life. But then Rachel reminded herself that she'd made that decision instinctively, from an unconditional love for both Dylan and Olivia.

She would devote her entire life to them.

She would protect and guide them, give them shelter and a safe place to fall.

Rachel was their mother, and as such, her love had no end.

'You know what I know for sure?' she said to them both.

They smiled because they knew what was coming. Rachel told them this every day, at least once.

'I love you!' she cried out, to her children and to the stars above the bay.

ACKNOWLEDGEMENTS

Writing a book is hard, but it would be impossible without the many people who tirelessly turn a first draft into a finished novel! Many make up my book village, supporting me either behind the scenes or right by my side.

Thank you for your generous support:

Rowan Lawton (whom the book is dedicated to), and her team at The Soho Literary Agency, plus Abigail Koons and Rich Green, in the USA.

Lynne Drew and Lucy Stewart, whose insightful edits helped polish *A Mother's Heart* into the book it is today. Thanks also to Kimberley Young, Charlie Redmayne, Kate Elton, Emma Pickard, Susanna Peden, Sarah Bance, Francisca Fabriczki, Anne O'Brien, Holly MacDonald, Conor Nagle, Patricia McVeigh, Tony Purdue, Jacq Murphy, Ciara Swift and many more at my publisher, HarperCollins.

Caroline Grace Cassidy, Alex Brown, Claudia Carroll, Vanessa O'Loughlin, Debbie Johnson, Marian Keyes, Cathy

Kelly, Sheila O'Flanagan, Susan Lewis, Cathy Bramley, Milly Johnson, Katie Fforde, all such talented writers, who inspire and support me so generously. Thank you for being in my corner.

Jayne Maguire, Julie Garland, Jenny Wilton and Stephanie Cross, who helped with elements of my research as I wrote *A Mother's Heart*.

The book retailers, media, bloggers, reviewers, libraries, book clubs and festivals whose passion to put books into readers' laps helps me, and all authors, every day.

The members of the Curl Up with Carmel Book Club (come find us on Facebook if you'd like to join), with special thanks to the admin team – Valerie Whitford, Genevieve Stratton, Rachel Mahon. It's a lot of fun talking books with you all.

Ann (over thirty years my person) & John, Margaret & Lisa, Sarah & John, Liz, Siobhan, Maria, Caroline & Shay, Fiona & Philip, Davnet & Kevin, Gillian & Ken – all of you, the very best of friends. Thank you for the giggles and long chats over coffee, lunches and drinks, help with the kids when deadlines took over, and for never failing to turn my books face side out when you spot them in a bookshop!

Hazel Gaynor and Catherine Ryan Howard – we never leave anything unsaid, do we? One of these days we'll break WhatsApp audio. You know how much you mean to me, but in case there is any doubt, I love you both.

Tina & Mike, Fiona, Michael, Amy & Louis, Michelle, Anthony, Sheryl & Damien, Fiona, Matilda & John, Ann & Nigel, Evelyn (original Mrs H!), Adrienne & George, Ev, Seamus & Paddy, Leah – all part of my lovely, big family of O'Gradys and Harringtons. I love you all. Special thanks to my mum, Tina, who is my first reader and biggest cheerleader.

As always, my final thanks goes to my H's, who put the Happy into this HappyMrsH! My husband Roger, my children Amelia and Nate, my stepdaughter Eva, and George Bailey, our cockerpoo (who never leaves my side) – the love we share as a family is my everything.

A Q&A with

Carmel Harrington

A Mother's Heart is a novel that deals with some difficult issues, including step-parenting, adoption, conflict and forgiveness. What inspired you to tackle this story?

When I start a new story, I decide what issues I'd like my characters to face. And I want those issues to reflect those we all experience in modern-day life. In *A Mother's Heart*, I wanted to write about a complicated blended family. This led me to a whole new set of issues as the story evolved! It's a subject I have a personal connection to because, like Rachel in the story, I am a stepmother too. But I'm happy to report that my family have not been through the same drama that Rachel and her family endured!

My stepdaughter Eva is nineteen – beautiful, intelligent, and with a dry wit like her daddy's. She was three years old when we met, hair in two pigtails and cute as a button. We fell in love with each other pretty quickly. She loved all things Disney back then, but we used to lament that all stepmothers in the fairytales were wicked. This, of course, isn't the case at all. I wanted to readdress the balance a bit in creating Rachel's character. Rachel is a tribute to all those step-parents who choose to love their stepchildren.

Were there any subjects within the book's pages that you found particularly hard to write about?
Exploring each of the mothers' grief was complex and, at times, emotional for me. It was impossible to write about Rachel, Belinda and Sheila's losses without for a moment putting myself in their shoes. Losing a child – at any age – is the ultimate tragedy. My heart broke for every parent that has had to face the utter devastation of saying a final goodbye to their child.

You bring the locations in the book to life so well. How important is place in your writing?
Thank you! I always think of locations as supporting characters, really. It's just as important that they are brought to life as it is to ensure my characters are authentic. I've always had wanderlust and have travelled all over the world. Sharing that love through my novels is great fun. Also, fun fact, my godparents, Ann and Nigel Payne, lived in Hawke's Bay many years ago, which is why I chose that particular spot in New Zealand.

Did everything pan out the way you expected it to as you wrote the book, or were there some surprises along the way even for you?
I will be careful how I answer this because I know that some readers like to flick to the end matter before they've

read the book! Yes, I'm looking at you! No spoilers, I promise. The final reveal in the last chapter only came to me as I reached that part of the story. By that stage, the characters were chattering away to me, whispering all sorts of truths. I love it when they become 'real' people to me, with strong opinions on how their story should be told!

Which character was your favourite to create, and why? Do you relate to any of the characters more than others?
Hands down, the most fun character to write was Sheila! Her behaviour was deplorable, but I adored writing those big dramatic scenes where she was at her worst. Rachel's afternoon tea, in particular, when Sheila's shenanigans caused havoc, is one of my favourite scenes in the book. And while it's hard to forgive some of the things Sheila says, I understand why she said them. Her actions and words came from a place of fear and grief.

Tell us a bit about how you write and what your typical writing day looks like.
Once the kids go to school at 9 a.m., I do a quick tidy up of the house. Then I'll have my breakfast while having a catch up on my social media accounts. I'm at my desk by 10 a.m. though, and ready to start my day. I check my lists on Reminders, an app I love. The satisfaction of ticking off items is so gratifying! I do love a good list. I begin writing or editing by 11 a.m. at the latest. I'm working on 2023's novel now, and my aim is to write at least 3,000 new words each day. I like to write on my iMac desktop, which has a large screen. I have a writing room that has views of our gardens. It's a lovely space to work. I take a break at 3 p.m. when the kids come

home from school. Once homework, dinner and the usual after school activities are complete, I'll go back to my desk for a few hours in the evening. When working towards a looming deadline, it's not unusual for me to continue working until midnight! I get so involved in the story I find it hard to step away. I try not to work at the weekends or during the school holidays to keep that work/life balance in check.

The characters in the book come together to create a unique family. Do you think it's important to represent alternative family situations in your books?

I know from personal experience that families come in all shapes and sizes. Aside from being a step-parent myself, there are several blended families within my immediate family and friend circle. We live in a diverse world made up of blended, remarried, single parent and cohabiting families, and it's of enormous importance that this is reflected in my stories.

What would you most like readers to take away from the book? What do you consider to be its standout message?

While you may not get the 'happy ever after' that you initially dreamed of, that doesn't mean that you can't find a new way to be happy. And always remember that families are created by love, not blood.

Do you have any thoughts on what might happen to the characters beyond the final page?

I like to think that there is romantic love in Rachel's future. She wasn't ready for that in this part of her life story. But she's a young woman with such a beautiful heart. I think she deserves to find another great love at some point in the future. Now, what Sheila has to say about that . . .

What have you been reading recently?
I recently discovered Kristin Hannah, and I adore her emotional, transportive novels. I've just finished *Winter Garden*, and it sent me to the ugly cry. There's a scene about 90% in that broke me. She's now one of my go-to authors, and I'm making my way through her backlist. I'm also halfway through Lucinda Riley's *Seven Sisters* series – beautiful historical romances with a mystery at their heart.

Reading Group Questions

1. *A Mother's Heart* is a book dealing in tricky decisions. Could you understand the basis for all the different characters' views?
2. Rachel didn't want to be a mother before she met Lorcan and his kids. How do you think you would have reacted in a similar situation?
3. All the characters make up a unique kind of alternative family. Do you like reading about these different kinds of representations?
4. Were there any particular moments in the book that made you suddenly see things differently?
5. What about any moments that you found particularly shocking? Did you see the plot twists coming?
6. Both the Bradleys and the Butlers have lost children, but they react differently in the circumstances. What did you think of the contrast?
7. How did you feel by the end? Do you think all the characters deserved redemption, or was there anyone you weren't ready to forgive?
8. Which part of the novel has really stayed with you? What would be the one thing you'd say about it if recommending it to a friend?

And if you enjoyed *A Mother's Heart*,
why not pre-order Carmel's latest
moving and heartwarming book

The Girl from Donegal

Coming 2023